Rhetor Zacharias

The Syriac Chronicle Known as that of Zachariah of Mitylene

Rhetor Zacharias

The Syriac Chronicle Known as that of Zachariah of Mitylene

ISBN/EAN: 9783337218652

Printed in Europe, USA, Canada, Australia, Japan

Cover: Foto ©Andreas Hilbeck / pixelio.de

More available books at **www.hansebooks.com**

THE
SYRIAC CHRONICLE

KNOWN AS THAT OF

ZACHARIAH OF MITYLENE

TRANSLATED INTO ENGLISH
BY
F. J. HAMILTON, D.D.
AND
E. W. BROOKS, M.A.

METHUEN & CO.
36 ESSEX STREET, W.C.
LONDON
1899

CORRIGENDA

P. 3, note 5.   Omit the second sentence.

P. 20, note 3.   *For* fol. iii. *read* fol. 111.

P. 23.   *For* Moris *read* Mori, and again on p. 42.

P. 27, note 2.   The latter part of this note refers to the word "voices" higher up on the same page.

P. 40.   *For* Silentarius *read* Silentiarius.

P. 47, note 9.   *For* [Syriac] and [Syriac] *read* [Syriac] and [Syriac].

P. 66, note 2.   *For* [Syriac] *read* [Syriac].

P. 71, note 2.   *For* vi. *read* lxxxvi.

P. 100, note 1.   *For* [Syriac] *read* [Syriac].

P. 116, note 3.   *For* [Syriac] *read* [Syriac].

P. 159, note 1.   *For* [Syriac] *read* [Syriac].

P. 167, note 6.   *For* [Syriac] *read* [Syriac].

P. 168.   Transpose notes 2 and 3.

P. 169, note 5.   *For* "Magisterian" *read* "Magistrian."

P. 172, note 2.   *For* [Syriac] *read* [Syriac].

P. 178, note 6.   *For* [Syriac] *read* [Syriac].

P. 208, note 4.   *For* βερεδάριοι *read* βερηδάριοι.

P. 318, note 12.   *For* 56 *read* "56."

IN THE INDEX

P. 343.   *For* ἀποθήκη (!) *read* ἀποθήκη (?).

P. 344.   *For* ταμδεῖον *read* ταμεῖον.

INTRODUCTION

IN Brit. Mus. Add. MS. 17,202 there is a historical work in Syriac, which has been published by Dr. Land[1] under the title of *Zachariæ Ep. Mitylenes aliorumque scripta historica Græce plerumque deperdita.* In the MS. the Chronicle bears no author's name, but is simply entitled, *A volume of records of events which have happened in the world.* Extracts from the same work are contained (also anonymously) in *Cod. Syr. Vat.* 146[2] (formerly 24), fol. 78 ff. An account of these extracts, with quotations, was given by Assemani,[3] and the whole was published with a Latin translation by Mai in 1838.[4] A passage found among these Vatican fragments is quoted by Dionysius Bar Tsalibi as from "Zachariah the Rhetor and bishop of Melitene,"[5] whence Assemani entitled the author "Zachariah of Melitene." The name of Zachariah is confirmed by the fact that Brit. Mus. Add. MS. 12,154 contains two extracts from our Chronicle, which it cites as from the "Ecclesiastical History of Zachariah."[6] Further, Evagrius, in bks. 2 and 3 of his History, frequently cites a Monophysite writer whom he calls Zachariah the Rhetor, and these citations agree closely with our text. "Zachariah the Rhetor" is also cited by Michael the Syrian[7] (who is copied by Gregory Abu'l

---

[1] *Anecdota Syriaca*, vol. iii., Leyden, 1870.

[2] On the cover it is numbered 145.   [3] *Bibl. Or.* vol. ii. p. 54 ff.

[4] *Scriptorum Veterum Nova Collectio*, tom. x.

[5] Assem., *B. O.* vol. ii. p. 53.

[6] Fols. 151, 158. See Land, Introd. p. xiii. Another extract with Zachariah's name is found in Add. 14,620, fol. 28 (*ibid.* p. xiv).

[7] In the Arabic translation in Brit. Mus. MS. Or. 4402, which is far superior to the Armenian epitome (translated into French by Langlois). As the original Syriac is as yet inaccessible, I frequently for brevity's sake write "Michael," where I mean the Arabic translator. [The Syriac text is now being published by M. Chabot.]

I

Farag) for the first Synod of Ephesus, the story of the Seven
Sleepers, events of the reign of Marcian, and the plague in that
of Justinian.

On turning, however, to the work as preserved in the London
MS. we find that in the appendix to bk. 2 the author states that
bk. 3 is drawn "for the most part from the Chronicle of Zachariah,
a rhetor, which he wrote in Greek to a man named Eupraxius,
who lived at the Court, and was devoted to the service of the
king and queen"; and the first chapter of bk. 3 opens with the
preface of Zachariah addressed to Eupraxius. Again, in the
appendix to bk. 6 it is stated that that book is derived "from
the Greek Chronicle of Zachariah the Rhetor, who wrote down
to this point at great length, according to the Greek practice of
diffuseness." From this it is clear that the work of Zachariah
ended in 491, and that he was only one of the authorities used
by the compiler of the work before us, who followed him in
bks. 3–6 only, and to whom the name of Zachariah was
wrongly attached by later writers. This is confirmed by the
facts that each of the bks. 4–6, and no others, is stated in
the preface to be taken from Zachariah, that the words
" Ecclesiastical History of Zachariah " are found at the top of
the page (with two exceptions in bk. 1) in bks. 3–6 only, and
that the citations in Evagrius are confined to these same
books. (See Land, Introd. pp. x–xiii.)[1]

As to the identity of Zachariah, the Life of Isaiah the monk,
published by Dr. Land[2] from Brit. Mus. Add. MS. 12,174,
fol. 142, is in the MS. ascribed to " Zachariah the Scholastic,
who wrote the Ecclesiastical History," and a Life of Severus
by the same author has been published by Dr. Spanuth[3]
from a MS. at Berlin (Sachau Collection, 321).[4] From the

---

[1] In spite of these facts Land ascribes bk. 7 to Zachariah. The different
character of that book is enough to show that it is derived from another source. It
does not, however, follow that it was not taken from another author, distinct from
the compiler. The list of bishops in 7. 15 must be drawn from an author who wrote
in 518, 519. See Land, Introd. pp. xi, xii. On the other hand, the end of 7. 6
was written after 540.

[2] *Anecd. Syr.* iii. p. 346.   [3] *Progr. des Gymn. zu Kiel*, Göttingen, 1893.

[4] Zachariah tells us in this Life that he also wrote a Life of Peter the Iberian ; but
the Life contained in this MS. and in Brit. Mus. Add. MS. 12,174, and edited by Dr.

latter we learn that Zachariah was a native of Gaza, that he studied law in company with Severus at Alexandria and Berytus in the reign of Zeno, and that he practised as an advocate at Constantinople, where he was living at the time of writing the Life. There can therefore be little hesitation in identifying him with the " Zachariah of Gaza " to whom an ode of John of Gaza is addressed, with the " Zachariah " to whom several letters of Procopius of Gaza are addressed,[1] and with the author of the Dialogue, *De Mundi Opificio*,[2] inscribed "Ζαχαρίου Σχολαστικοῦ Χριστιανοῦ τοῦ γενομένου μετὰ ταῦτα ἐπισκόπου Μιτυλήνης," who in his preface states that he had studied at Alexandria. The " Melitene " of Dionysius Bar Tsalibi is therefore an error for " Mitylene."

Now Zachariah of Mitylene was present at the Synod of 536, but in 553 the see was occupied by Palladius. Hence we may infer that Zachariah, a rhetor or scholastic of Gaza, residing in Constantinople, between 491 and 518 wrote an Ecclesiastical History of the years 450–491, and also between 511 and 518 wrote a Life of Severus,[3] at a later time, conforming perhaps to the Chalcedonian faith,[4] was made bishop of Mitylene, and died or was deposed between 536 and 553.[5] The courtier Eupraxius, to whom the History is dedicated, is mentioned also in the Life of Severus in terms which imply that he was dead,[6] from which it seems to follow that the History was written before the Life. He is no doubt the same as Eupraxius the chamberlain, to whom a letter of Severus is addressed.[7]

Raabe (Leipzig, 1895), is not his (see Raabe's Introduction). The Life of Theodosius, published by Land (*Anecd. Syr.* iii. p. 341) from Add. 12,174, is ascribed by him to Zachariah ; but the discrepancies with the account in our 3. 9 make this ascription very doubtful. All these lives exist in Syriac only.

[1] Mai, *op. cit. præf.* p. xiv.   [2] Migne, *Patrol. Græc.* vol. lxxxv. p. 1012.

[3] The Life of Isaiah is mentioned in that of Severus, and is therefore earlier. Similarly that of Peter.

[4] His name is not among the signatures to the decree of the Synod of 536, and he may possibly have been a nominee of Anthimus.

[5] There are some notices of Zachariah in the Plerophoriæ of John of Majuma, lately published in a translation by M. Nau, chs. 70, 73. From ch. 70 it appears that he gave up his secular career before 519. (*Revue de l'Orient Chrétien*, 1898, *Suppl. trim.* pp. 375, 377.)

[6] *Vit. Sev.* p. 28, l. 1, 2, " Eupraxius of illustrious memory."

[7] Wright, *Cat. Syr. MSS. Brit. Mus.* p. 944.

Zachariah's work then forms the basis of our Syriac author's bks. 3–6.   The author did not, however, incorporate Zachariah in full, but epitomated him, as is clear from the fact that Evagrius quotes as from Zachariah a statement which is not found in our text.[1]   On the other hand, the main narrative in these books is so homogeneous that in general we may assume that no other source was used.   In 3. 1, however, occur three passages which are found in almost identical words in John of Ephesus,[2] and must therefore have been interpolated either from John or from a common source, since the identity of language forbids us to postulate a common use of the Greek Zachariah.   To another source also may be ascribed the list of Emperors and short secular chronicle with which bk. 3 concludes, the chronological summary at the end of the preface to bk. 4, for which the authority of a certain $\chi\rho o\nu\iota\kappa\acute{o}\nu$ is cited,[3] and the notice of Zeno's death and the secular events of his reign in 6. 6.

The compilation opens with an introductory chapter containing a general plan of the work, from which it is clear that the whole work, heterogeneous as it is, is the deliberate composition of one man, not a mere collection of extracts.   As to the personality of the writer, there are two possible indications, one in 7. 5 (p. 161), where, in speaking of a certain Gadono who took part in the campaign at Amida in 503, he says, " I know him "; and another in 9. 18 (p. 264), where the same expression is used of an Italian named Dominic or Demonicus, who fled to Constantinople during the Gothic rule; but in neither case can we feel certain that the author is not copying the expression of some other writer,—a supposition which is supported in the former instance by the early date of the events related, in the latter by the fact that John of Ephesus, whom

---

[1] Evagr. iii. 18; cf. also ii. 10.

[2] *Anecd. Syr.* iii. p. 120, l. 6–9 = *Anecd. Syr.* ii. p. 363, l. 6–9; *Anecd. Syr.* iii. p. 123, l. 11–13 = *Anecd. Syr.* ii. p. 363, l. 1–5; *Anecd. Syr.* iii. p. 119, l. 11–16 = a passage quoted by M. Nau in his analysis of the second part of Jo. Eph. ap. "Dion." (*Revue de l'Orient Chrétien*, 1897, *Suppl. trim.* p. 457.)

[3] Cited also in ii. 1 (p. 93, l. 9, Land) for the death of Decius and accession of Gallus, and in the appendix to bk. 2 for the length of the life and reign of Theodosius II.

our author appears to have used (see below), resided at Constantinople, while our author's interests lay entirely in the East.[1]   As to the place of writing, in 12. 5 the author speaks of an event which happened at Amida as happening "here," from which it may be inferred that he was living at Amida, or at any rate in Mesopotamia;[2] and a connexion with Amida is also rendered probable by his acquaintance with Eustace, the architect of Amida, which may be gathered from 9. 19 (p. 267), the special mention of the Amidene who was appointed to command the guard at Alexandria in 10. 1, and the author's intercourse with the Amidene captives mentioned in 12. 7 (p. 329).[3]   If 7. 3–5 is original, the intimate acquaintance with the history of Amida there shown must further be added.

The date of writing is given in 1. 1 and 1. 3 as A.S. 880 = A.D. 569.   This must have been the date of the completion of the work, of which different parts were written at different times; thus 12. 4 was written in 561, and 12. 7 in 555; 10. 12, which I have restored from Michael (see below), would appear, on the *prima facie* interpretation of the words to have been written in 545; but, since the style of the narrative makes it incredible that it was written within a year of the events recorded, "this year 8" must be understood to mean "this year 8, with which we are now dealing."[4]   Throughout the history of Justinian's reign the author speaks of the Emperor in terms which imply that he was still living.

In respect of the date a difficulty arises from the use of John of Ephesus, which use seems to be proved by the facts

[1] No passage corresponding to this occurs in the analysis of Jo. Eph. given by M. Nau from "Dionysius," but I can hardly believe that the whole of Jo. Eph. is preserved by "Dion.," since the analysis contains no record of the Synod of 536 or of the death of Theodora.

[2] In 12. 6 "the cities here" = the cities of Mesopotamia; but, on the other hand, the fact that this somewhat obscure event is recorded makes it probable that the author was a native of Amida. Jo. Eph. was also an Amidene, but the late date of this event makes it unlikely that the narrative was derived from his work (see below). Moreover, at that time he seems to have been living in Constantinople or Asia Minor.

[3] On the other hand, Dodo the anchorite, whom he quotes as an informant in 8. 5, seems to have been a native of Emesa.

[4] Similarly "this year 4" at the end of 12. 5.

concerning the letter of Simeon of Beth Arsham in 8. 3.　Of this letter our author and John (preserved in the Chronicle attributed to Dionysius[1]) have practically the same version, and this version is an abbreviation of the original letter, which is preserved in Brit. Mus. Add. MS. 14,650 and in a MS. in the Museum Borgianum and has been edited by Prof. Guidi.[2] Now two men cannot have made the same epitome of the same document; hence one must have copied the other; and that the copyist was our author appears from the fact that in his work the letter stands alone, while in John it is embedded in a narrative of Homerite affairs.　Again, our author's account of the bishops of Amida in 8. 5 is so similar to that in Assem., *B. O.* vol. ii. pp. 48, 49, that, though the divergences show that it is not slavishly copied from it, it is scarcely credible that it is wholly independent.[3]　The second part of John's History was, however, not completed before 571,[4] while our author, as we have seen, finished his work in 569.　It is not, however, necessary to suppose that the whole of John's second part was published at one time; indeed we know from his own statement[5] that a narrative of the persecution which began in 518, which, if not a portion of the Ecclesiastical History, must have been afterwards in great measure incorporated with it, and may well have included an account of the persecution of the Homerites, was published by him thirty years before 567.　If, indeed, this date is to be taken literally, it is too early for our purpose, since the headings of the lost chs. 2, 3 of our bk. 10,

[1] Assem., *B. O.* vol. i. p. 364.　It has been shown by M. Nau, in *Bulletin Critique*, ser. 2, tom. ii. p. 321 ff., and by Prof. Nöldeke, in *Vienna Oriental Journal*, tom. x. p. 160 ff., that the attribution of this Chronicle to Dionysius is a mere blunder of Assemani; but, as the name is too well established to abandon, I refer to it as "Dionysius."　I may here add that from Mich. (fol. 223) it appears that the work of Dionysius, whose preface is there given in full, began at 582, and was a continuation of Cyrus of Batnæ.

[2] *Atti dell' Accademia de' Lincei*, ser. 3, tom. vii.

[3] See also Hallier, *Untersuchungen über die Edessenische Chronik*, p. 67.　His argument from the list of banished bishops, which Mich. (fol. 161 v.) quotes as from Jo. Eph., is, however, not quite conclusive, since our author's account in 8. 5 is somewhat different, and the correspondence as to Akhs'noyo may be explained if both drew from the letter to which our author refers.

[4] Jo. Eph. pt. iii. 1. 3.

[5] *De Beat. Orient.* 35 (*Anecd. Syr.* ii. pp. 203, 212 ; transl. pp. 130, 135).

dealing with the persecution of Abraham Bar Khili at Amida in 537–539, correspond with chapters in " Dionysius," [1] who wrote out John, and must therefore be assumed to be derived from the latter's work.[2] In one of the fragments of the History,[3] however, John mentions an account of this persecution written by him, from which it follows either that the history of the persecution was not written before 539, or that a later work dealing with this second persecution was afterwards added. In either case we have a sufficient explanation of our author's use of John. Our author did not, however, merely copy John of Ephesus, even for events preceding 540. For instance, John's account of the earthquake of Antioch in 526 is preserved,[4] and is quite different from our author's, and his account of the persecution at Edessa under Asclepius [5] is very hard to combine with the narrative in our text (8. 4). But the true relation between the two can only be solved when the full text of " Dionysius " has been published.

This complication often makes it impossible to determine whether a particular passage of Michael is derived from our author or from John; and therefore, though the references should give only sources and parallels, not derivatives, I have thought it best to give the references to Michael throughout rather than venture on arbitrary decisions,[6] which might be misleading. As Michael is not published, I have added references to his copyist Gregory.[7] There is, however, one test by which it is sometimes possible to discriminate, and that is the method of dating; for John dates by Seleucid years only, while our author uses also the indictional reckoning, and generally writes the numeral in Greek, a practice found also

---

[1] *Cod. Syr. Vat.* 162, fol. 96. I made a cursory examination of this MS. in 1894, but I owe most of my knowledge of " Dionysius " (apart from Assemani's extracts) to M. Nau's analysis (see p. 4, note).

[2] It does not follow that the narrative itself was copied, since our author may have taken his subjects from John, and given his own account of the events.

[3] *Anecd. Syr.* ii. p. 294 ; transl. p. 221.

[4] *Anecd. Syr.* ii. p. 299 ff. ; transl. p. 224 ff.

[5] *Anecd. Syr.* ii. p. 291 ff. ; transl. p. 219 ff. .

[6] This does not apply to the Zachariah books, in which there can be no doubt that he copies our author.

[7] The references to the *Chronicon Syriacum* are to the edition of Bedjan.

in the Edessene Chronicle.[1]   The use of this method in certain passages in Michael has enabled me to restore some lost chapters in bk. 10.

The first book, after the introductory chapter and a discussion of the chronology of Genesis, contains the History of Joseph and Asnath,[2] the Acts of Silvester,[3] and the narrative of the discovery of the relics of Stephen, Gamaliel, and Nicodemus by the presbyter Lucian,[4] concluding with a short account of two early Syriac writers.   Bk. 2, ch. 1, contains the Acts of the Seven Sleepers,[5] while in ch. 2 the continuous historical narrative opens with the Synod of Constantinople in 448, and at the end of bk. 9 it is brought down to the capture of Rome in 536. Bks. 2–6 are almost wholly ecclesiastical, but bks. 7–9 contain much valuable information on secular matters, particularly on the relations between Rome and Persia.   So far the work is practically complete,[6] but the

---

[1] See Hallier, *op. cit.* p. 41.

[2] The translation from the Greek is ascribed to Moses of Ingila.   This chapter has been translated into Latin by Oppenheim (Berlin, 1886).   Part of the Greek version of this legend and a Latin epitome were published by Fabricius (*Cod. Pseudepigr. V. T.* vols. i. and ii.), and a complete text in Greek and Latin has now been published from several MSS. by the Abbé Batiffol (Paris, 1889–1890).   The Greek text has been again edited by V. M. Istrin (Moscow, 1898).

[3] The Greek Acts are published in Combefis, *Christi martyrum lecti triumphi.* Portions are also given by Cedrenus, and in a shorter form by Geo. Mon. and Zonaras.   A Latin version with large additions exists in a book entered in Brit. Mus. Catalogue under " Eusebius," and supposed to have been published at Strassburg in 1470.   Another with slight variations is in Mombritius, *Sanctuarium*, vol. ii., and the Jewish dispute was published by Wicelius (Maintz, 1544).   An epitome is in Surius, *Act. Sanct.*, Dec. 31.   The Syriac Acts are also in Add. MS. 12,174, but without the Jewish dispute.   See article of A. L. Frothingham in *Memorie dell' Accademia de' Lincei*, 1882.

[4] Lucian's letter exists in two Latin versions in Migne, *Patr. Lat.* vol. xli. p. 807 ff. The Greek original is mentioned by Fabricius (*Bibl. Grœc.* vol. x. p. 327), but is not published.   An epitome is given in Photius, *Bibl. Cod.* 171, which contains a passage found in our author but not in either of the Latin texts.   Another Latin version, with slight variations from the first of the two in Migne, is published in Mombritius, *Sanctuarium*, vol. ii.

[5] For the various versions of this legend see *Act. Sanct.*, Jul. vol. vi. p. 375 ff., and Guidi, *Testi Orientali Inediti sopra i Sette Dormienti di Efeso* (*Atti dell' Accademia de' Lincei*, ser. 3, tom. xii.).   The Greek Acts are in Migne, *Patr. Grœc.* vol. cxv. p. 428.   A Syriac version similar to our author's is in Add. MS. 14,641, fol. 150.   El. Nis. quotes the legend from "John the Jacobite," *i.e.* John of Ephesus.

[6] Setting aside small tears and obliterations, the only losses are a part of i. 6,

remaining books are unfortunately fragmentary. Of bk. 10, in which the history is continued to 548, we have the headings of the chapters complete and portions of the chapters themselves;[1] the lost chapters I have been able in part to restore from Michael, Gregory, and the fragments of James of Edessa.[2] Bk. 11 is wholly lost: of bk. 12 we have a fragment extending from the middle of ch. 4 to the middle of ch. 7, and dealing with the years 553–556. The original work was, as we are told in the introductory chapter, brought down to 569.

The legendary matter at the beginning, though of great value for comparison with other versions of the same legends, stands quite apart from the rest of the work ; and, as it does not contain anything which does not exist in Greek or Latin, it does not appear worth the space that would be required for translating it, and is therefore omitted. Of the remainder the translation of 1. 9, bk. 2 (omitting ch. 1), and bks. 3–7 is the work of Dr. Hamilton,[3] while for the introductory chapter, bks. 8 and 9, and the fragments of bks. 10 and 12[4] I am responsible.

Since Dr. Land, as he states in his preface,[5] thought it better to spend his time in copying fresh documents than in revising his transcripts, his text is naturally far from accurate, and an examination of the MS. has enabled us in many instances to correct it. The MS. itself, however, is considerably corrupted, and supplies a text inferior to that of the Roman MS., which is later in date. All departures from Land's text on the authority of the MS., or of Cod. Rom. (which I have examined), or by conjecture, are noted, except in the case of (1) punctuation, including plural marks ; (2)

where a leaf has been lost, and the end of 1. 5, which is also missing. The beginning of 1. 6, also contained on this latter leaf or leaves, is supplied by Dr. Land from Add. MS. 7190.

[1] 10. 16 and a part of 10. 15, missing in Cod. Brit., are found in Cod. Rom.

[2] Brit. Mus. Add. MS. 14,685.

[3] A translation of bks. 3–6 was privately printed by Dr. Hamilton in 1892. No other continuous translation, except of the Vatican fragments, has as yet appeared.

[4] The epitome of Ptolemy's Geography in 12. 7 is omitted.

[5] P. xiv.

division of words ; (3) final ‿ or ○ ; (4) foreign proper
names and technical terms, where there is no doubt what is
meant. In many places assistance has been derived from
the work of other writers, of whom mention is made in the
notes.

E. W. BROOKS.

A VOLUME OF RECORDS OF EVENTS WHICH HAVE HAPPENED IN THE WORLD

BOOK I

THE first chapter, an apology for undertaking the work.

The second chapter, an epistle containing a request with regard to the table of generations in the book of Genesis.

The third chapter, a defence of the table of generations in the matter of the chronological canons, which are set down below.

The fourth chapter, an epistle containing a request with regard to the translation of the Greek book of Asyath, which was found in the library of the house of Beruya, the bishops from the city of Rhesaina.[1]

The fifth chapter, an answer to the epistle.

The sixth chapter, a translation of the book of Asyath.

The seventh chapter, a translation of "Silvester, Patriarch of Rome," relating the conversion and baptism of Constantine, the believing king, and the disputations of the Jewish doctors.

The eighth chapter, the revelation of the repository of the bones of Stephen and Nicodemus and Gamaliel and Habib his son.

The ninth chapter, about Isaac and Dodo, the Syriac doctors.

---

[1] Cf. ch. 4 (p. 15, l. 24, L.), "in the library of the memorable bishops who were called the family of the house of Beruya from the city of Rhesaina, in the possession of a lad of their kin named Mor'abdo . . ., I found a little book . . . called the book of Asyath."

THE FIRST CHAPTER

MEN who were moved like irrational beasts (and they were merely animal[1]) by foul habits and wicked customs and brutal instincts and earthly[2] life[3] and evil tradition[4] handed down from one to another, in the eager pursuit of passions, in the corruption of the flesh, and in the impure desires of the body, men whom the Scripture named flesh, saying, " My spirit shall not dwell with men for ever, for that they are flesh " ;[5] whom Solomon also calls ungodly, saying, " Ungodly men with their words and with their works called upon death and thought it their friend ; and they melted away and sware and made a covenant with it, because they are worthy to be part of it. For they said in themselves (and they did not reason aright), ' Our life is short and in sorrow,[6] and there is no further remedy at the death of a man, and no man hath appeared who hath been released from Hades. For we were suddenly born, and hereafter we shall return to be as though we had never been : for the breath in our nostrils is as smoke,[7] and reason as a spark stirred in our heart; which being extinguished,[8] our body shall be as ashes, and the breath shall be scattered abroad as thin air, and our name shall be forgotten after a time, and no man shall remember our works, and our life shall pass away as the trace of clouds, and as a mist that

---

[1] The MS. has ܩܘܡܝܢ, not ܩܘܡܝ, as L. prints.

[2] The MS. has ܐܪܥܢܝܐ, not ܐܪܥܢܝܐ, as L. prints.

[3] πολιτεία.   [4] Read ܡܫܠܡܢܘܬܐ for ܡܫܠܡܢܘܬܐ.

[5] Gen. vi. 3.   [6] The MS. has ܒܟܡܝܢܐ, not ܒܟܐܒܐ, as L. prints.

[7] The MS. has ܬܢܢܐ, not ܬܢܢ, as L. prints.

[8] Before (ܝ)ܕܥܟܬ the MS. has ܘ, which L. does not print.

is driven away before the beams of the sun, and its heat is heavy upon it.   For our life is a shadow that passeth away, and there is no remedy at our death: for it is sealed, and there is none that returneth.   Come on therefore, let us enjoy these good things: and let us speedily use the creatures in our youth.   Let us fill ourselves with choice wine and ointments: and let no blossom[1] of the air pass by us: let us crown ourselves with the flowers of the rose-tree before it be withered: and let none of us be without voluptuousness until our old age; and in every place let us leave a token[2] of our voluptuousness: for this is our portion and this is our inheritance'";[3] these did as[4] Moses bears witness: "The whole earth was of one language, and of one speech.   And it came to pass, when they removed from the east, that they found a plain in the land of Sin‘ar; and they dwelt there.   And they said, each man to his fellow, 'Go to, let us cast bricks and burn them with fire.'   And they had brick for stone, and slime had they for mortar.   And they said, 'Go to, let us build us a town and a tower whose top may reach unto heaven; and let us make us a name, lest we be scattered abroad upon the earth.'"[5]   And they toiled and built zealously,[6] and laboured in vain at the tower.

And[7] yet again the tribes of Reuben and Gad and the half tribe of Manasseh, when they turned back from the rest of the tribes of their brethren, who had taken possession of the land of promise, and came to Gilgal by the side of Jordan in the land of Kh'na‘an, built there with stones which they

---

[1] The MS. reading is ܣܘܒܝܚ, not ܣܘܒܩܚ, as L. prints.

[2] σύμβολον.   [3] Wisd. i. 16–ii. 9.

[4] Omit ܕ before ܐܝܟ.   [5] Gen. xi. 1–4.

[6] ܣܟܝܗܘܬ. This word occurs again in bk. 7, ch. 9 (p. 224, l. 13, L.), where Payne Smith proposes to read ܣܟܝܗܘܬ. The word, however, is found in both MSS. at that place, and occurs again here, where ܣܟܝܗܘܬ, "frequently," does not suit the context. In both places the most suitable meaning is as above. The corresponding adjective occurs in ch. 7 (p. 73, l. 5, L.), and in bk. 12, ch. 5 (p. 325, l. 23, L.), where the meaning seems to be "violent" or "stormy"; see note on 12. 5.   The adverb also occurs in 7. 6 (p. 215, l. 2, L.).

[7] Josh. xxii. 9–27.

collected a great altar to see to by the side of Jordan. And, when the rest of the tribes heard of it, Phineas the son of Eli'azar the priest and the chiefs of the congregation, the captains of the hosts[1] of Israel, came to them and inquired at their hands concerning this; and they returned them answer, "It is that it may be a witness between us and you, that your children may not say to our children in time to come, 'What have ye to do with the Lord God of Israel, ye children of Reuben and children of Gad? For behold! the Lord God hath set a border between us and you, even this Jordan.' And we said, 'Let us take us occasion and build us an altar, not for sacrifice, nor for offering, but for a witness between us and you, and between our generations after us.'"

And[2] again Gideon, after he had overthrown the Midianites, spread a garment and asked each man for the earrings of the prey which the men with him had gathered; and the weight of the earrings that he asked was a thousand and seven hundred[3] measures of weight: and Gideon took them and made thereof a *lufro*,[4] and put it in his village, even in 'Ofrah: and the children of Israel went astray after it, and it became a snare to Gideon and to his house.

And[5] again the mother of Micah of Mount Ephraim, she also received eleven hundred measures of silver from her son, and made a graven image and a molten image.

And again Absalom the son of David " in his lifetime reared up for himself an image in the dale of the kings: for he said, ' I have no one to keep my name in remembrance ': and he called the image after his name : and it was called ' Absalom's hand,' unto this day."[6] And Methodius also, bishop of Olympus and martyr, in the work which he addressed to Aglaophon concerning the resurrection of the

---

[1] Read ܙ for ܘ before ‪ܬܫܒ̈ܘܠܐ‬.
[2] Judg. viii. 24–27.
[3] Read ‪ܩܫܒ̈ܬܐ‬ for ‪ܟܘܒ̈ܟܐ‬.
[4] The Syriac corruption of the Heb. אֵפוֹד (*efod*) with the preposition ܠ prefixed.
[5] Judg. xvii. 1–4.   [6] 2 Sam. xviii. 18.

dead, tells a story about Phidias,[1] a craftsman and sculptor, who wrought an ivory[2] statue, beautiful to behold, and, in order that it might last a long time and not be destroyed or spoilt, poured oil under its feet and anointed the rest of the sculpture.

And we see images of divers persons in divers places, and we find records[3] written on papyrus concerning divers events which have happened in the world, and statues set up to preserve the memory and extol the merits of those who are dead.

How just and right is it therefore for the discreet and earnest to see that the rest of the events which have occurred from time to time after those chronicled in the three Ecclesiastical Histories of Eusebius, Socrates, and Theodoret, which are scattered about and not collected in one book, are, as far as is possible, collected together from epistles or manuscripts or trustworthy reports and set down for the benefit of the believers and of those who care for right instruction and mental excellence! May the recording of them have the help of Christ our God, to whom we pray that He will give us wisdom and eloquence, that without confusion we may write the true account of the things which have happened!

Now, since in the Syriac manuscripts of the table of generations in Genesis there is a certain variation and divergence[4] from the Greek,[5] and no small deficiency in the number of years, it is right for us and in harmony with our work and reasonable[6] that it should begin with the book of Genesis, and after this should continue with the book of Asyath,[7] and after that with that of Silvester and the conversion[8] of Constantine the king and his baptism, with regard to which Eusebius has failed to give an accurate account and Socrates has missed the truth (for the king was not baptized

---

[1] Method. *ap.* Epiph. *Hær.* lxiv. 18, Phot. *Bibl. Cod.* 234.

[2] Read ܩܘܠܣܐ ܡܪܝܪ for ܩܘܠܣܝܪ with Sachau (*Academy*, June 1871).

[3] ὑπομνήματα.　　　　[4] The MS has ܗܘܝܐ, not ܗܘܐ, as L. prints.

[5] Read ܕ for ܠ before ܩܘܠܝܐ.

[6] Insert ܘ before ܡܫܠܬܐ.

[7] The Syriac form of the Hebrew אסנת, "Asnath."

[8] κατήχησις.

at the end of his life, as he [1] wrote, since the story of his conversion by Silvester is also preserved in writing and in pictures at Rome in several places, as those who have been there [2] and come to us have seen and tell), and further concerning the revelation of the repository of the bones of Stephen and his companions, and concerning Isaac and Dodo, the Syriac [3] doctors.

And here we will end the first book; and afterwards, from such sources as we can find, we will write about the succeeding events in books and in the chapters contained in them severally, as written below, from the thirty-second year of Theodosius the son of Arcadius to the year 880 of the Greeks. [4]

Now [5] we beg [6] that the readers or hearers will not blame us, if we do not call the kings victorious and mighty, and the generals [7] valiant and astute, [8] and the bishops pious and blessed, and the monks chaste and of honourable character, because it is our object to relate [9] facts, following in the footsteps of the Holy Scriptures, and it is not our intention on our own account to praise and extol rulers with flattering words, [10] or to revile and insult with rebuke those who believe differently, provided only we do not find something of the kind in the manuscripts and epistles which we are about to translate.

---

[1] *I.e.* Eusebius; but perhaps we should read ܐܘܟܬܒ, "they wrote."

[2] ܬܡܢ either is out of place or should be again inserted after ܘܗܘ.

[3] Read ܣܘܪ̈ܝܝܐ for ܣܘܪ̈ܝܐ.

[4] 569. The same date is given in ch. 3 *ad fin.*

[5] Cf. Socr. bk. 6, *præf.*

[6] Read ܒܥܝܢܢ for ܒܥܝܢ.   [7] στρατηγός.

[8] ܥܪ̈ܝܡܐ. The dictionaries give only a bad sense to this word; but here and in bk. 9, ch. 17 (p. 286, l. 3, L.) a good sense is imperatively required. It occurs again in bk. 3, ch. 11 (p. 131, l. 26), where either meaning would suit, and in 7. 13 (p. 230, l. 15), where the good sense is much the more probable.

[9] Insert ܕ before ܣܘܥܪ̈ܢܐ.

[10] The MS. has ܫܘܦܪ̈ܩܐ, not ܫܘܦܪ̈ܩܐ, as L. prints.

BOOK I

CHAPTER IX

ISAAC the teacher, a native of Syria, issued forth from one of
the monastic dwellings of the West; and he in his diligence
went up to Rome, and he also travelled to other cities. And
he had books which were full of profitable teaching, containing
all kinds of comments upon the Sacred Scriptures, following
Ephraim and his disciples.

And Dodo also was a worthy monk of Samkè, a town
belonging to the district of Amida. And on account of the
captivity and famine which occurred in his days in that
country, he was sent by the chiefs of the people to the king;
and he proved himself very acceptable. And this man also
had, as it appears to us, about three hundred works, more or
less, upon every matter taken from the Divine Scriptures, and
concerning holy men, and hymns.

2

BOOK II

THE BEGINNING OF THE SECOND BOOK

AFTER the *Ecclesiastical History* of Eusebius of Cæsarea, both Socrates and Theodoret, in the treatises which they successively composed, reaching down to the thirty-second year of the reign of Theodosius the Less, wrote for the memory and profit of the prudent, as best they were able, accounts of the transactions and matters that occurred in various places, which they were diligent in learning from the volumes, and letters, and records,[1] and words of living speakers, that they examined.

And accordingly I also, insignificant though I be, am beginning to write, as you asked me, for the instruction of the brethren, and for the gratification of the lovers of doctrine, and for the confirmation of believers, Christ our Lord and God consenting and aiding and giving the word of power—by your great advice, diligent brother, and while you pray that I may write the truth with eloquence without confusion or cause for blame.

For when, making a commencement of this treatise of the second Book, I am relating, as concisely as possible, without prolonging the discourse or being wearisome to the reader or tedious to the hearer, what I was able[2] to discover from records and Acts[3] or from letters,—truth that was carefully examined,—I shall set down here the truth of the resurrection, which took place in the days of Theodosius the king, of the bodies of the seven youths who were in a cave in the district

---

[1] ܗܘܦܘܡܢܝܘܬܐ, *i.e.* ὑπομνήματα.

[2] ܐܫܟܚܬ, MS., not ܐܬܐܫܟܚܬ, as L. prints.

[3] ܦܪܝܣܘܬܐ, *i.e.* πεπραγμένα.

of Ephesus, and the Syriac records ; both to keep them in the memory of the saints and for the glory of God, Who is able to do all things.

And then I shall set down briefly in the form of chapters, so that the account may not be enlarged of the events of one period which we write in detail in the Acts that are found in every place, what happened during the ten remaining years of the life of Theodosius, but in this Book I am writing them so to speak—what happened in Constantinople respecting Eutyches the archimandrite and Flavian the chief priest, and the Synod of thirty-one bishops and twenty-two archimandrites who met together and who brought about the deprivation of Eutyches ; and also respecting the second Synod which was held in Ephesus concerning Flavian in the days of Dioscorus and Juvenalis [1] and Domnus, and the one hundred and twenty-eight bishops who were with them.

And then I begin with the third Book.

CHAPTER II

THE SECOND CHAPTER TELLS ABOUT THE HERESY OF EUTYCHES THE PRESBYTER, AND HIS DEPRIVATION

There was, in the days of king Theodosius, one Eutyches, a presbyter and archimandrite, a recluse belonging to those who dwell in Constantinople. This man was visited by many (who resorted to him ostensibly on account of his chastity and piety) who happened to be in the city, and especially by the soldiers of the palace, who were lovers of doctrine. For at that time Nestorius, who was ejected, was being justly reviled because of his filthy doctrine. This Nestorius it was who held and taught base opinions respecting the Incarnation of God the Word ; and he imagined that the two Natures existed separately in Christ our God after the union ; and he held the precedence of the infant who was conceived and formed in the Virgin, whom he also called

----

[1] ܩܘܒܠܝܘܣ, MS., an evident mistake for ܩܘܒܠܝܘܣ.

Jesus and Christ; and he thought that God the Word at length descended upon Him, views scarcely differing from those of Paul of Samosata, and much the same as the teaching of the school of Diodorus, which he studied, accepted, and loved; but he lightly and without compunction refused to call the ever-virgin, holy Mary, by the title "Theotokos,"[1] even though the true doctors who were before him, Athanasius and Gregory and Basil and Julius, and the others, had so called her; and, moreover, he also censured them, as the letter testifies which he wrote from Oasis to the clergy and citizens. Whereupon, many being disturbed by his doctrine, a Synod, consisting of one hundred and ninety-three bishops, was assembled at Ephesus; and it carefully examined his teaching; and it called upon him three times, according to the canonical rule of the Church, to apologise and to censure his own interpretations, and at length to confess Jesus to be God the Word Who became incarnate, one Person and one Nature, as the doctors of the holy Church teach. But he would not consent, as also Socrates relates in the short account which he wrote of him, and which is fully told in the original Acts.[2] Consequently his deprivation took place in the days of Celestine, Cyril, and Juvenalis, before the arrival of John of Antioch and his attendant bishops, who were delayed.

It[3] was somewhere about this time that Eutyches, wishing to affirm the one Nature in Christ, rejected the truth of the body derived from the Virgin, which God the Word took in her and from her. And in the conversation which he held with those who came together to him, this same Eutyches affirmed an inaccurate dogma,[4] not having been well instructed.

But he taught many that (the Word became flesh)[5] as

---

[1] It is impossible to give in English the exact equivalent of this theological term; neither "God-bearer" nor "mother of God" quite meet the case.

[2] [Syriac], *i.e.* πεπραγμένα.

[3] Mich. fol. iii. *v*; Greg. *H. E.* i. p. 159 ff.

[4] The text [Syriac] [Syriac] [Syriac] is corrupt. Possibly for [Syriac] we should read [Syriac], and for [Syriac], [Syriac].

[5] Some such words must have dropped out of the text; both Michael and Barheb^r· supply the omission as above.

the atmosphere assumes bodily form and becomes rain or snow under the influence of the wind, or as water by reason of the cold air becomes ice.

And[1] when the report of his vile teaching was published abroad it was investigated by Eusebius of Dorylæum, who happened to be in the city; and he informed Flavian, the chief priest, concerning it, and he gave him an indictment.

And he was called upon three times by thirty-one bishops who were there and twenty-two archimandrites, to come forward and apologise for his opinions, and abjure them, and make a written statement of the true confession. And at first, indeed, he would not do so, at one time saying that it was[2] his fixed determination[3] to remain in perpetual seclusion, and again, that he was sick, and had a cough, and was old; (and he made these excuses) relying upon the aid of the soldiers of the palace, who were his friends. Now the king heard of these matters. But at last, when his deprivation was decreed to take place, he was compelled to appear before the council of bishops ; however, he did not recant his doctrine with whole-hearted sincerity, but kept on saying, " Just as you teach two Natures in Christ, so do I say."

And, behold! all these things are written expressly, one after another, in lengthened discourse in the Acts of that Council. However, that we may not make our narrative too long, but may compress much into small compass, as the wise man says,[4] we refrain from relating them again in detail and writing them down here. Then his deprivation took place. Now in the accusations against him and in the interlocutions,[5] and more especially in what was said by Eusebius of Dorylæum when contending with him, the two Natures after the union were expressly taught in conformity with the doctrine of Nestorius.[6] And the interlocution of Flavian set forth[7] the same views. And[8] Eutyches, rejecting the party of Flavian

---

[1] Liberat. 11.

[2] Liberat. 11.

[3] ܐܣܘܟܝܐ?, MS., ܐܣܘܟܝܐ, L.

[4] Sir. xxxii. (LXX. xxxv.) 8.

[5] ܡܠܠܘܣ?, i.e. διαλαλιαῖς.

[6] This seems to be the sense of the passage, but the text is evidently corrupt.

[7] Reading ܡܠܬܗܝܢ for ܡܠܬܗ.

[8] Liberat. 11.

and Eusebius, who deposed him, sent a libel[1] to Rome to Leo, who was the chief priest there, begging that these matters should be investigated in another Synod ; with regard to which libel he received a reply. And when the party of Flavian heard it they also wrote,[2] and sent the Acts of the Council concerning Eutyches to Leo. And the latter wrote to Flavian the letter called the Tome, in which there are many heads that have been condemned by the dogmatic[3] doctors ; which also were censured at that time by Dioscorus and his followers, and again by Timothy the Great, who was with him, and by many treatises of others, which we omit to mention again here and to write down.

CHAPTER III

THE[4] THIRD CHAPTER GIVES AN ACCOUNT IN CONCISE TERMS OF THE SECOND SYNOD WHICH WAS HELD IN EPHESUS, ABOUT THE MATTER OF FLAVIAN THE CHIEF PRIEST AND EUTYCHES THE MONK

Accordingly a Synod was convened, the second in Ephesus, about the matter of Flavian and Eutyches ; and it was held in the presence of the legates of Leo, who were sent with his letter. And the bishops came together there to the number of one hundred and eighty-eight, the chief rulers among them being Dioscorus of Alexandria, and Juvenalis of Jerusalem, and Domnus of Antioch. And the contents of the Acts of the Constantinopolitan Council concerning Eutyches were examined ;[5] and Flavian and Eusebius were ejected. And an outcry was raised by the bishops who were there ; and they anathematised every one who would say, "There are two

---

[1] Or petitions ܠܝܒܠܐ, *i.e.* λίβελλοι. For this letter see Leo, Ep. 21 (Migne, *Patr. Lat.* vol. liv.).

[2] Leo, Ep. 22, 26.

[3] ܕܘܓܡܛܝܩܘ(?), *i.e.* δογματικοί.   [4] Liberat. 12.

[5] An exact translation of the text as it stands is impossible. Perhaps for ܘܐܬܒܚܫ we should read ܘܒܚܫܘ, and render it, "And they searched in the Acts for what was done in Constantinople concerning Eutyches."

Natures in Christ after the union." But a question [1] was also raised again there about what Theodoret of Cyrrhus wrote censuring the twelve Heads which Cyril drew up against Nestorius, who was previously banished ; and about the letter of Hibo of Edessa which he wrote to Moris of Nisibis in opposition to Cyril and in favour of Nestorius ; and about what he said in his interpretations concerning Jesus Christ and Mary, as his own deacons, who were his accusers, testified. And besides these the partisans of John of Gaios [2] and others were deposed. But Eutyches the archimandrite was received, because he presented a libel of recantation [3] to the Synod, which was held there in Ephesus, and confessed the true faith. But the Synod appointed Anatolius as bishop of Constantinople in the room of Flavian, and then dispersed.

CHAPTER IV

THE FOURTH CHAPTER DESCRIBES THE REGULAR SUCCESSION [4] OF THE CHIEF PRIESTS WHO HELD OFFICE FROM THE FIRST SYNOD OF EPHESUS TO THE DEATH OF KING THEODOSIUS, IN THE DAYS OF VALENTINUS,[5] WHO WAS SUCCEEDED BY MARCIAN, THE CONVENER OF THE SYNOD OF CHALCEDON IN BITHYNIA, WHICH MET IN THE YEAR SEVEN HUNDRED AND SIXTY-FOUR OF THE GREEK ERA OF ALEXANDER

With respect to the regular succession of the chief priests from the first Synod of Ephesus to the death of Theodosius, it is pertinent to our subject to relate who they were. In

---

[1] For ܩܠܐ, "question," it would perhaps be better to substitute ܩܠܐ, " outcry."

[2] ܝܘܚܢܢ. No doubt John of Ægæ is meant (Brooks).

[3] ܡܬܛܦܝܣܢܘܬܐ. It may stand either for ܡܬܛܦܝܣܢܘܬܐ, " consent," "agreement," etc. ; or for ܡܬܛܦܝܣܢܘܬܐ, " recantation." This libel is given in Mansi, vol. vi. p. 629. As there is no recantation in it, perhaps the former meaning may be the one intended by our author.

[4] ܩܬܣܛܣܣ = καταστασις.   [5] *I.e.* Valentinian.

Rome, after Celestine, Leo was bishop for twenty-one years and forty-three days; and in Alexandria, after Cyril, Dioscorus was bishop for eight years and three months. And in Constantinople, Maximus[1] for two years and two months; and after him, Proclus for two years and two months; and after him, Flavian for six years; and after him, Anatolius for eight years. In Antioch, Domnus was bishop after John; and after him Maximus. And in Jerusalem, Juvenalis was bishop for thirty-six years, who, holding the same position, was present at the three Synods, because the time of his years was protracted.

CHAPTER V

THE FIFTH CHAPTER CONTAINS THE LETTER OF PROCLUS, CHIEF PRIEST OF CONSTANTINOPLE, TO THE ARMENIANS. IT IS A VERY EXCELLENT LETTER, SHOWING THE FAITH OF THE MAN; AND TO PRESERVE IT IN MEMORY WE HAVE TRANSCRIBED IT[2] HERE FOR THE BENEFIT OF THE BELIEVING BROTHERS

THE LETTER OF PROCLUS.[3]

" Beloved, the mystery of the true faith is true love, and the pure undoubting confession of the Trinity equal, undivided, and susceptible of no addition; and a mind not varying in its state, but steadfast in its faith towards God. That is the faith which we do not possess on tables of stone, as in the type, but receive on the tables of our hearts, as in a mystery; tables (I say) which are nailed to the cross, and are inscribed with the sprinkling of the blood of God. And it is right for us not only to believe, but also to follow earnestly after virtues and morals worthy of the faith.[4] For virtue is to be chosen by everyone, especially by those whose beauty of soul has not been corrupted by a hateful life of lusts. There are indeed

---

[1] *I.e.* Maximian.　　[2] ܦܘܠܣܗ, MS., not ܦܘܠܣܗ, as L. prints.

[3] Migne, *Patr. Græc.* vol. lxv. p. 856, and *Patr. Lat.* vol. lxvii. p. 409.

[4] Down to this point the Syriac text is quite different from the Greek.

many kinds of virtue. For even the heathen, drowned in
error and lost in mind, wrote memorable things [1] concerning
this virtue.   But as for this nature which is visible and flows
on without cessation, they only felt [2] after it in their written
teaching.   But either their sight was dim from length of time,
or they were blinded by error, so as to hinder them from the
perception of the truth and from real virtue.   For they say in
their teaching that there are four kinds of virtue, namely, justice,
self-restraint, wisdom, and fortitude ; which things, though they
are to be highly accounted, yet are exercised here below and
have their sphere upon the earth.   They say, indeed, that
fortitude is the contest with fierce nature, and self-restraint
the triumph over the passions, and wisdom the distinguished
government of cities,[3] and justice right division.   And thus they
ordered and arranged the world, according to that which is in
the law,[4] and they defined wickedness on both sides.   However, anything superior to and transcending this visible scene
they did not understand, nor were they able to describe it in
writing.   But with the blindness of their mind they have contracted virtue itself, and have shut [5] it up within what is visible
alone.   The Christians, however, by whose own faith the eyes
of their heart have been enlightened, whose master and teacher
is the blessed Paul, have declared that to be [6] virtue which lifts
us up to God, and which governs in orderly fashion the things
that are on earth.   This most illustrious Paul, then, considered
that there were many kinds of virtue ; but he especially
preached about these three, namely, faith, hope, and love.
For faith gives to men something which transcends human
nature, and causes that fleshly nature, as yet encompassed
by many passions, to hold converse with spiritual beings.

---

[1] ܡܟܣܪ̈ܢܝܐ, L. ; ܡܟܪ̈ܢܝܐ, MS.   I suggest ܡܬܟ̈ܪܢܝܐ, and translate accordingly.
The Greek is διαφόρως.

[2] ܡܟܘܠ, MS. ; it should be ܡܟܘܩ ; the Greek is ψηλαφῶντες.

[3] ܢܝܚܐ ܐܘܪܚܐ ܕܡܕܝܢܬܐ ; the original is τὴν ἐν ταῖς πόλεσιν ἀριστοκρατείαν.

[4] Or, as by law.

[5] By reading ܢܚܒܫ for ܢܚܒܩ we obtain the sense of the original
περιέκλεισαν.

[6] ܐܬܝܗܒܘ, MS., ܐܬܝܗܒ, L.

For the knowledge of that which angels and spiritual hosts did not know on account of its sublimity, faith imparts to men, who walk upon the earth and wallow in the dust, and it brings them near to the Throne of the Kingdom, and it tells them of that Nature which is without beginning and without end ; and by the rays of light which it diffuses, it drives away darkness of thought[1] from the soul; and when it has cleared off all gloom and denseness from the heart, then it causes that to be clearly seen which is comprehended in its invisibility, and also is seen in its incomprehensibility. But hope shows things to come in the present, not as in a dream, one can say, but forcibly ; and, without a doubt, confirms in the mind that which is future as if it were actually seen ; and it forms before a man's eyes, so to speak, what he is still expecting. For this hope is superior to every restraint, and brings near, without delay, the thing expected to him who is expecting it.

" But love is the chief of all our mysteries, for it persuaded God the Word, though He is always on the earth, near to all and with all (heaven and earth being filled by Him), to become incarnate and come by means of the flesh. And, being God, He became also man ; He retained that which properly belonged to Himself on His own part, and He became like us on our part. These two then agree together, for faith is the mirror of love, and love is the completion of faith. We believe, therefore, that God the Word became incarnate without undergoing any change ; and we rightly so believe, for this is the foundation of our salvation. For His nature receives no change, nor does it cause any addition to the Trinity. Thus indeed do we also ourselves believe.

" Every Christian, therefore, who is not rich in faith, hope, and love, is not what he is named ; but even though he seem to have subdued his flesh and to have delivered himself from the passions of his soul, he is not meet for the crown of victory, inasmuch as he maintains the outward appearance[2] of virtue, but he is not united to Him who crowns the conquerors that have resolutely contended on behalf of virtue in faith and

---

[1] I venture to read ‫ܢܘܗܪܐ‬ for ‫ܢܘܗܐ‬ ; the Greek is τὴν ἀχλὺν τῶν αἰσθησέων.

[2] ‫ܐܣܟܡܘܬܐ‬, MS. (i.e. σχῆμα), not ‫ܐܣܟܡܘܬܐ‬, as L. prints.

hope and love. Faith, then, according to what we have said,[1]
is the chief of all blessings; let it therefore be kept without
guile, and let us not tarnish it by the falsehood of human
thoughts, neither let us toss it about in the midst of confusing
voices, nor by the explanations of those who are reputed to be
wise: for faith is not to be explained; faith is a mystery.
Let it then remain within the limits of the Gospel of the
apostles; and let no man dare to contend in his explanation
with this faith by which he is saved, and which he confessed
in baptism by the signature of his tongue. For this lofty
height of faith has repelled every attack and all vaunting and
rashness, not of man only, but also of every spiritual nature.
And the blessed Paul testifies, crying out, ' If we or an angel
from heaven should preach anything beside what ye have
received, let him be accursed.'[2]   For the angel has been
appointed to minister and not to preach doctrine, and he
brings punishment[3] upon any who does not remain[4] in his
allotted station, but seeks after what is too high for his
nature; but even though[5] he displays the exaltation of his
nature, let not the novelty of his preaching be received. Let
us then guard what we have received with sleepless care; and
by the bright shining of our faith let the eye of our soul be
always open.   But what have we received[6] from the Divine
Scriptures except this, that God by His word created the world
out of nothing and brought the creation, which had no previous
existence, into being; and made man in His own image and
likeness, and honoured him by the law of nature; and gave
him the commandment when he was in a state of freedom;
and showed him how to help himself,[7] that by the choice of
the good he should flee from the evil; and the propensity of
man being biassed towards the evil expelled disobedience

---

[1] ܐܝܟܢܐ, MS., not ܐܝܟܢܐ, as L. prints it.

[2] Gal. i. 9. ܟܣܐ, MS., ܟܣܐ, L.   [3] Or, and punishment comes.

[4] ܟܡܘܩܐ, MS., not ܟܡܘܩܐ, as L. prints it.

[5] Mr. Brooks suggests that this is the correct reading ܐܦ, Gk. εἰ καὶ, not ܐܦ, as in the text.

[6] ܩܒܠܢ, MS., not ܩܒܠܢ, as L. prints.

[7] ܠܥܘܕܪܢܗ, his own help or profit.

from Paradise? And again, by the fathers and patriarchs, and by the Law, the judges, and the prophets, our Creator instructed our nature, that we should keep far away from sin, and should concern ourselves about the good and do it. And at last when sin established its kingdom over us by our own will, because the law of nature had been corrupted on its part,[1] and the written law had been despised, and the prophets, after the manner of men, brought deeds to remembrance but did not raise up our fleshly humanity from the depth of the evils, God the Word Himself, even He who is without beginning and without end, incomprehensible, invisible, and almighty, God the Word (I say) came and became incarnate; for He could be whatsoever He willed. God the Word then, Who is one of the Trinity, became incarnate; but He became incarnate because He so willed. And wishing to show[2] everywhere that He was really man, He was born from the Virgin. For the evangelist did not say that He entered into a perfect man, but that He 'became flesh,' meaning thereby His natural beginning and referring to the origin of His birth. For just as a man who is naturally born does not come forth complete in the perfection of active power all at once, but the seed of the nature at first becomes a body, and afterwards, little by little, at length attains the strength of the passions and of the whole active power; so God the Word went to meet the origin and root of the birth. God the Word then became perfect man, and He did not take away anything from His own unchangeable nature by the miracle which He wrought—a miracle which did not enter into the heart of man to conceive, but which we learn by faith and have not comprehended by investigation. And having become man, He saved by His flesh the whole human race, and He paid the debt of sin, in that He died as man for all men; but as God the hater of evil, He destroyed him that had the evil power of death, that is, Satan. But He showed the capability of the Law by fulfilling all righteousness. And He gave to our nature its pristine beauty; and by becoming man He honoured the nature

---

[1] Or, had become obsolete.

[2] By reading ‏ܢܚܘܐ‎ for ‏ܗܘܐ‎ we get the sense of the original δεῖξαι.

which was derived from the earth, and showed Himself to be its
Creator.   There is therefore one Son, for we worship the Trinity
in unity, and we do not introduce a fourth into this number; but
there is one Son, begotten from the Father, without beginning
and without end, through whom we believe that the worlds
were made, He Who was from that root, He Who without flux
sprang from the Father; that same God the Word Who,
without change of place, issues from the Father, yet remaining
as He is.   For although[1] He became man and appeared on
the earth, yet He did not depart from Him who begat Him.

"God the Word therefore wished to save the being whom
He created; and He dwelt in the womb which is the gate of
the universal nature of all, and He revived and blessed the
womb, and by issuing forth from it He sealed[2] it.   And by
His supernatural birth He showed that He became incarnate
in a manner transcending reason; for there are none among
the beings above and beneath who know how He became
incarnate.   There is not, then, one who is Christ and another
who is God the Word (away with such a thought!), for the
divine nature does not know two sons; He therefore was
begotten the only One from One; for where there is not
copulation of parents, there duality of the offspring is not
possible.   'In the name of Jesus Christ,' indeed, 'every knee
shall bow, of things in heaven and on earth, and of things under
the earth.'[3]   For if Christ is another and not God the Word,
then of necessity Christ must be mere man; and how can the
exalted nature of heavenly beings bow the knee and worship His
Name, if He be not God of God? or how shall we receive the
voices of prophets, crying, 'God appeared upon earth and held
converse with men'?[4]   For concerning His Incarnation it is
said, 'He appeared,' and the expression, 'He held converse,'
is used concerning His converse which He displayed with men
in the end of the ages.   For thus He that is exalted in greatness showed His almighty power; and as the universal Ruler
to Whom everything is easy, He remained what He was on
His own part, and became what He willed for us.

[1] Read ــܩ| for ܩ| ; the Greek is εἰ καὶ.
[2] ܘܗܒܡܬ, MS., not ܗܬܡܝ, as L.   [3] Phil. ii. 10.   [4] Bar. iii. 37.

"But if the swaddling clothes, and the lying in the manger, and the growth of the body, and the sleeping[1] in the ship, and the weariness on the journey, and the occasional hunger, and all those things which happened to Him Who was truly man, be a cause of stumbling to some persons, let them know that if they be in doubt concerning His sufferings, they deny the dispensation; but when they deny the dispensation they do not believe in the Incarnation, but when they do not believe in the Incarnation they lose their own lives. For if from the foundation of the world a man was not born who trod a way of birth like this,[2] let these new Jewish wranglers[3] show it, and then indeed their troublesome contention[4] will be disclosed. But if this is the universal beginning of nature, and God the Word truly became man, how then, while confessing with us the dispensation, do they deny the sufferings? Let them therefore choose for themselves one of two things: either let them by denying the sufferings deny also the dispensation and be reckoned among the ungodly; or, if they accept the benefit which is derived from the dispensation, let them not be ashamed of the sufferings. I am amazed indeed at the blindness of their heart, who by a newly invented way have trodden the path that leads to error. For I myself know and have rightly learned from the Holy Scriptures only one Son; and I believe in one nature[5] of God the Word Who became man, and the same endured the sufferings and wrought the miracles, Who was begotten from His Father before all things, and became incarnate in the end of the ages, and was born from Mary, the *Theotokos*. And we confess that He is God over all, and we introduce no foreign element into the nature of the Deity, for no addition is possible to the Trinity in Unity; but the same Lord Jesus Christ, by Whom were all things, also endured our sufferings and carried our infirmities,

---

[1] ܡܪܒܥܐ, MS., ܡܪܒܥ, L.

[2] By transposition of the word ܠܐ the Syriac would give the same sense as the Greek, *i.e.* "a man was born who trod a way of birth unlike this."

[3] Read ܡܬܚܪܝܢܐ for ܡܬܚܪܢܐ.   [4] Read ܩܪܒܐ for ܩܪܒܐ.

[5] ܟܝܢܐ, so (tempted by theological bias) the Monophysite translator rendered the ὑπόστασις of the original.

as the prophet[1] says; and He, being the same, wrought the miracles and suffered in our stead.

"But perhaps in their contention these new Jews will strive with us, inventing thoughts weaker than a spider's web, and say that if indeed the Trinity be one essence then the Trinity is without suffering; and our Lord Jesus Christ is reckoned in the Trinity, and He is God the Word, therefore He is without suffering; consequently He Who was crucified must be another, and not God the Word Who is without suffering. Truly they who speak in this fashion are weaving the texture of a spider's web, and they who excogitate these new definitions are writing upon water; and 'thinking themselves to be wise they have become foolish, and their silly heart is darkened.'[2] For the eye, which has been dazzled by the brilliant light of the sun, cannot see clearly; and the mind that is sick cannot receive the sublimity of the faith.

"What then do we say? That, so far as the Godhead is concerned, the Trinity is one essence, and is exalted above all sufferings. And when we say that the Son suffered, we do not mean that He suffered according to Nature, for His Nature is above sufferings. But in confessing that God the Word, one of the Trinity, became incarnate, we give a reason for the understanding of those who in faith ask us why He became incarnate. Because man who was formed[3] in the image of God, and to whom imperial freedom was given, erred in this freedom, and was led by the counsel of the deceiver; and he gave himself up to error, and he became the slave of lustful passions—passions all of which exercise dominion over a composite being—passions whose end is death—passions which none among the created beings is able to destroy. God the Word willed to destroy those passions whose end is death. He willed, indeed, to become incarnate and to be a composite being; that is, a perfect man in all points like us, sin only excepted; because it was not possible for that Nature, which is incorruptible, intangible, and invisible, to receive passions, for all passions are struggles of all composite

---

[1] Isa. liii. 4. [2] Rom. i. 21, 22.

[3] ܐܬܬܨܝܒ, MS., not ܐܬܬܨܝܒ, as L. prints it.

beings.   For with that exalted Nature of the Godhead, which alone is uplifted high above all things, there is no composition ; passion therefore was unable to enter where composition could not be.   God the Word then willed to destroy the passions which reign over nature subject to passions (as we said before) whose citadel was death ; and He became flesh from the Virgin, in a manner that He, God the Word, knew ; and He became man perfectly, being at the same time God over all. For He did not abandon what properly belonged to Him when He became like us ; but being God, He became man, for such was His will.   He emptied Himself, therefore, by His own will by taking the likeness of a slave, and He became man, and suffered in our stead, by His own will, though His Godhead was not in any respect limited ; and thus He saved the whole human race.   Wherefore Gabriel also, when announcing the might and dominion of Him that should be born, said to Mary, ' He shall save His people from their sins.'[1]

" But the people are not the people of a man but of God, and a man cannot deliver the world from sins, because he also entered into the world in a state of corruption.   But necessarily He is the same ; He is not divided into two (away with such a thought !) ; but being one, by being born from a woman, He shows that He is[2] truly man ; but by becoming man without copulation, and preserving His mother's virginity, He declared Himself to be God.   The Lord Jesus Christ, therefore, Who came into the world and held converse with men, as the Holy Scriptures testify, saved the world. Now, if Christ be man, and not God the Word, how did He create everything in the beginning, when He Himself had no existence ?   For if man was later than the (other) created things, it is evident that this Christ also did not bring into being what had existence before Him.   How then does Paul cry, saying, ' There is one Lord Christ, through Whom were all things ' ?[3]   For if all things were through Christ, it is evident that Christ is God the Word.   The evangelist also testifies, saying, ' In the beginning was the Word, and

---

[1] There seems to be a confusion between Matt. i. 21 and Luke i. 31–33.

[2] I venture to read ܗܘܐ for ܟܝܢܐ.   [3] 1 Cor. viii. 6.

the Word was with God, and the Word was God. He was in the beginning with God, and all things were by Him.'[1] If, therefore, the evangelist cries that all things were by the Word, and Paul, interpreting this expression, says, There is one Lord Jesus Christ, by Whom were all things, it is evident that Christ is God over all. But if the objectors bring forward to us the voices of the Scriptures, in which He is called man, namely, that of Peter, who says, 'Jesus of Nazareth, a man ';[2] and of Paul, who says, ' By that man in Whom God has ordained that we should believe ';[3] and of our Lord Himself, Who says respecting Himself, ' Why do ye seek to kill Me, a man ? '[4] let them know that either through their dulness they have been hindered from the understanding of Scripture, or through their wickedness they are perverting what is well written,[5] according to their own deceitfulness. For also Christ is truly man ; but He became man, not having been so before, but only God ; for just as He is uncreated God, so also He, the same, is man, truly, personally,[6] and certainly, without change and without any kind[7] of phantasy. And we do not confess that the body of our Lord is from heaven ; indeed we excommunicate everyone who says so ; but we confess that it is by the Holy Ghost and the power of the Highest which overshadowed the holy Virgin Mary, the *Theotokos*. But if the Virgin did not bear God, then she who remained undefiled is not deserving of admiration. But if the voices of the prophets foretelling the incomprehensible nature of our mystery, cried out, ' Behold a virgin shall conceive, and bear a son, and they shall call His name Immanuel, which is, God with us,'[8] why

[1] John i. 1-3. [2] Acts ii. 22.

[3] Acts xvii. 31. It is interesting to notice that the Syriac version (‏ܟܝܼܡ ܕܝܼܢܐ‎ ‏ܐܢܫ ܕܩܝܼܡ ܘܐܦܢܝ ܠܟܠ ܐܢܫ ܠܗܝܡܢܘܬܗ‎, "through the man whom He has ordained, and has converted everyone to the faith of Him ") forms a connecting link between the Greek original and the rendering given above.

[4] John viii. 40. [5] Reading ‏ܐܬܠܒܟ‎ for ‏ܐܬܠܒ‎.

[6] ‏ܩܢܘܡܐܝܬ‎, MS., ‏ܩܢܘܡܐܝܬ‎, L.

[7] Read ‏ܣܟܐ‎ for ‏ܣܟܝ‎ ; the latter would convey a positively wrong meaning. Of course ‏ܘܕܠܐ‎ must also be omitted. " Nullam suspicionem phantasiæ," Lat. (Brooks).

[8] Isa. vii. 14 ; Matt. i. 23.

do they take away from the glory of His mother, seeing that He Who was born in lowly fashion is God over all?[1]   But perhaps the objectors will raise this objection, that truly every one who is born is of the same nature as the mother who bore him; if, then, she who bore him was human, it necessarily follows that he who was born was human also.   Ye say well, O vain babblers! but then the child is of the same nature as she whom the birth-pangs smite when he who is born comes according to the natural course; however, the naturally-born child is corrupt from the beginning, because copulation precedes corruption.   But where this reproach did not even enter the mind, but there was an ineffable miracle, the birth having been supernatural, there He that was born was God.   We confess Him to be the same who created the world, and gave the Law, and put the Spirit in the prophets, and in the end of the times for the sake of the life and salvation of men became incarnate and was made man; and He inspired the apostles, and sent them forth for the salvation of people and nations. Let us flee, then, my brothers, from these troubled streams of error; I mean the doctrines that fight against God—namely, from the mad folly of Arius, who was dividing the indivisible Trinity; and from the rashness of Eunomius, who limited beneath his science the incomprehensible nature; and from the frenzy of Macedonius, who would sever from the Godhead the Spirit proceeding not departing;[2] along with all the other heretics lost in their error; but especially from this new doctrine and blasphemy formulated by Nestorius, who far surpasses the Jews in his blasphemy.   For those former heretics were despising the everlasting Son, Who is from all eternity with the Father, and depriving the root of its fruit; but these teachers of our day by their doctrine are bringing in another in addition to Him Who is from all eternity, Who became man for our salvation, so that they make a plurality of sons in that one and incorruptible Nature which is from one essence.

---

[1] This is a troublesome passage for the translator.   Mr. Brooks supposes that the word ‮ܐܠܐ‬ has dropped out of the text through homoioteleuton, and he renders "because He that was born was born through condescension, Who is God over all."

[2] Or, proceeding immutably.

Let us say, then, with Paul, that Christ is He Who 'made both one'; [1] for of Jews and heathen through baptism, He has created one new man, and by His power He made that one, which, through the exercise of its freedom was divided. Let these impious teachers, then, dread the sentence of judgment if what was divided has been brought into unity, but that one Person Who made both one is, after their manner of reasoning, divided.

"But now we shall leave the multitude of words and come to the concise statement of true doctrine. Whoever desires to know that the alone and only-begotten Son, Who was before the life of Abraham—that the same became incarnate in the end of the times, let him ask Paul, who thunders with his voice, declaring rightly that He Who was born from the Jews in the flesh is the everlasting God; for, while telling and declaring the contempt of the Jews and the contention of the people with God, and the root which is the Father,[2] and the seed which is Christ our Lord, he says thus, 'Whose is the adoption'[3]—for God cried through His prophets, 'Israel is My son, My firstborn and My glory';[4] and indeed they reaped immeasurable glories from the constant miracles and the covenants with Abraham, which told of the multitude of the people and the blessings—'and the giving of the law,'—that of Mount Sinai, which was written by the finger of God,— 'and the promises,'—both the land of Palestine and that in the seed of Abraham the nations should be blessed,—'whose are the fathers,'—for in the night of error they arose and as stars of the faith—'from whom Jesus Christ appeared in the flesh, Who is God over all.' And he does not say this only and deem it sufficient; for also indeed the beginning of God the Word, Who is without beginning and without end, is not from the time of His birth by Mary. Who then is this Christ? He Who was begotten of the Father before the worlds in a manner which the mind of created beings cannot comprehend, and in the end of the times took flesh and became

---

[1] Eph. ii. 14.

[2] The Greek is Ἀβραάμ; it may be that we should read ܣܘܗܝܒܐ for ܐܒܐ.

[3] Rom. ix. 4.   [4] Ex. iv. 22 and Isa. xlvi. 13.

man from the Virgin Mary, the *Theotokos*; He Who was shut up in the womb and in the cave, in a manner which He Himself knows; He Who was laid in the manger; He Who grew in the flesh; He Who came down to the lower parts of the earth, and by His own will endured all the sufferings of men, that He might be believed to be man, and to be no other than the One Who came down; but He Who came down and He Who went up is the same; however, He did not go up first, but came down. For He did not become God by addition (away with such a thought!), but He became man by the dispensation, for the race of men was in need of this. And you shall not hear this from me or from any other, but from Peter and from Paul—Peter when he says, 'Thou art Christ, the Son of the living God';[1] and Paul also, who learned by revelation from the Father concerning the Son, and says, 'When God Who separated me from my mother's womb and called me by His grace, was pleased to reveal His Son by my means.'[2] This Paul has truly taught you who Jesus Christ is when he cries and says, 'Of whom is Christ in the flesh, Who is God over all, blessed for ever.'[3] What occasion of calumny does not the word of Peter and Paul drive away from those who love calumny! for he called Him 'Christ' to show that He truly became man; he said of Him, 'Who is of the Jews in the flesh,' to show that His existence does not date only from the time when He became incarnate;[4] he said of Him, 'He is,' to tell us by his mode of expression that He is without beginning; he said of Him, 'Who is over all,' to proclaim Him Lord of created things; he said of Him, 'Who is God,' that we should not be drawn aside by the outward appearance and sufferings so as to deny his incorruptible Nature; he said of Him, 'blessed,' that we should worship Him as the Ruler[5] of all, and not regard Him as a fellow-

---

[1] Matt. xvi. 16.   [2] Gal. i. 15, 16.   [3] Rom. ix. 5.

[4] In the translation above I adopt Mr. Brooks' suggestion, that we should read ܡܢ instead of ܠܟܠܗܘܢ. The rendering of the text as it stands would be, "that He did not become incarnate from the Gentiles, but was from thence alone." This change brings the text into harmony with the Greek and Latin.

[5] ܡܫܒܚ, MS., not ܡܒܪܟ, as in L.'s text.

slave; he said of Him, 'Who is for ever,' to show that it is He Who by His word created all things, visible and invisible, whereby His Godhead is glorified. We have, then, Christ Who is God over all, Whom we shall worship, and we shall say to the heretics, 'In whomsoever the Spirit of Christ is not, he is none of His.' For we have the mind of Christ, and therefore we look for the revelation of God our Saviour, the Lord Jesus Christ, Who Himself shall reward the well-doers with the crown of victory, but the despisers with the recompense[1] of their rashness. See, then, my brothers, that no man rob you by impious words, or turn you aside by false science from the simplicity and unadorned modesty of the pure beauty of the faith. But again, I repeat to you the word of Paul, 'Beware lest any man rob you by the vain philosophy of the traditions of men'[2]—men who are inventors of vain things, who have not taught us as the prophets and apostles teach, but have gone astray by their own wisdom and followed the interpretation of their own mind; wherefore their teaching is a stumbling-block to the Church of God, which He purchased with His precious blood. For other foundation of the true faith can no man lay except that which is laid, that there is one God, the Father, Ruler of all, and one Lord Jesus Christ, by Whom were all things, Who is from all eternity with the Father, from Him and of the same Nature with Him; and one[3] Holy Spirit, the Lord and Life-giver, Who proceeds from the Father, and together with the Father and the Son is worshipped and glorified. Stand, then, in one spirit and one mind, and fight for the faith, and be not in anything troubled by the adversaries, but keep the tradition which you have received from the blessed Fathers, who,[4] out of the whole creation, met together by the operation of the Holy Spirit, and preached to us the true and undefiled faith, which we have from one end of the earth to the other."

The end of the letter which the blessed Proclus, bishop of

---

[1] ܩܘܪܝܟܢܐ, MS., not ܩܘܪܝܢܐ, as L. prints.   [2] Col. ii. 8.

[3] ܟܝܡ, MS., an evident mistake for ܚܕ.

[4] From this point the Greek and Latin are different from our text.

Constantinople, wrote to Great Armenia of the Persians, concerning the true faith.

But [1] Theodosius lived, as the Chronicle informs us, fifty years; of these he reigned forty-two years, for he was eight years old when he began to reign. And the acts of thirty-two years of his reign are related in the ecclesiastical history of Socrates, and those of the other ten years more are written concisely above in this second Book. He died then in the three hundred and eighth Olympiad; and Marcian succeeded him in the kingdom. And in the year seven hundred and sixty-four by the reckoning of the Greek era of Alexander, he gathered to Chalcedon a Synod of five hundred and sixty-seven bishops, whose acts we shall describe as concisely as possible in this third Book which is written below, and in its chapters, which have been taken for the most part from the history of Zachariah the Rhetorician, which he wrote in Greek to a man called Eupraxius, who lived in the royal palace and was engaged in the service of kings. But the body of the holy John the bishop, who is called Chrysostom, had been brought back from the place of his banishment, and it was honoured with a procession in Constantinople. And Eudocia the queen, the wife of Theodosius, went to Jerusalem for prayer, and returned, and then died. But Geiseric [2] subdued Carthage of Africa and reigned over it. And John the general [3] was killed by the servants of Arbindus, [4] and there were earthquakes in various places. And then Theodosius died.

---

[1] Mich. fol. 115 v.

[2] ܐܙܝܣܪܝܟܘܣ, Ζιντήριχος.

[3] ܐܣܛܪܛܝܠܛܘܩ, i.e. στρατηλάτης.

[4] ܐܪܒܝܢ, i.e. Areobindus (Brooks).

BOOK III

THE beginning of the third Book, which (inasmuch as it is from the history of Zachariah the believer, who wrote in Greek to one Eupraxius by name, a minister of the king, and engaged in his service) records the events that took place in the Synod, which met at Chalcedon, after the death of Theodosius, in the days of Marcian, in the year seven hundred and sixty-four by the reckoning of the Greeks. And the number of the bishops was five hundred and sixty-seven, who were brought together in consequence of the exertion of Leo of Rome, and the letter that he wrote to the king and his wife Pulcheria. And the Synod sent Dioscorus of Alexandria away to Gangra of Thrace, and appointed Proterius bishop in his stead, and received the letter of Leo, which is called the Tome. And the other matters, which occurred in Jerusalem, or in Alexandria, or in other places during the life of Marcian, that is, a space of six years and a half; behold they are written down here distinctly in these twelve Books below and the chapters contained in them.

The first chapter relates the events which occurred in the Synod of Chalcedon, until the public address of Marcian the king to the bishops assembled there.

The second chapter tells about the banishment of Dioscorus to Gangra, and the consecration of Proterius in his stead ; and the events which occurred in Alexandria upon his entry there.

The third chapter relates the events which occurred in Palestine, concerning Juvenalis of Jerusalem, who broke his promises, and separated from Dioscorus, and agreed to the Synod. And when the citizens of Jerusalem and the

Palestinian monks learned this, they appointed, as bishop in his stead, one Theodosius, a monk; who, in his zeal, had attended and watched the Synod closely, and then went back to Palestine and told what had occurred at Chalcedon.

The fourth chapter tells of Peter the hostage, the son of the king of the Iberians, a wonderful man, who was taken by the people of Gaza; and they brought him to Theodosius of Jerusalem, by whom he was consecrated as their bishop.

The fifth chapter tells about the flight of Theodosius of Jerusalem, in consequence of the king's threats; and also about the return of Juvenalis, by force, to Jerusalem, and the great slaughter that ensued upon his entry there.

The sixth chapter gives an account of a certain blind Samaritan, who smeared his eyes with the blood of the slain, and they were opened.

The seventh chapter tells how Christ appeared in vision to Peter the Iberian, bishop of Gaza, and told him to depart from thence, and also himself to suffer banishment of his own accord.

The eighth chapter tells about a certain monk, named Solomon, who acted cunningly, and went in to Juvenalis of Jerusalem, and threw a basketful of dust upon his head, and reproached him.

The ninth chapter tells how Theodosius of Jerusalem was taken, and was imprisoned in a house containing lime, and there he ended his life.

The tenth chapter tells about the heresy of John the Rhetorican, and how this heresy was anathematised by Timothy, the bishop of Alexandria, after him.[1]

The eleventh chapter tells about the mission of John the Silentarius, from the king to Alexandria.

The twelfth chapter tells about Anthemius, and Severus, and Olybrius, and Leo the Less, and what happened in the seven years of their reign.[2]

---

[1] Probably ܩܒܪܘܛܪܝܣ has fallen out, and the translation should be "after Proterius."

[2] Here the text adds, "The thirteenth Book tells about the accession of Marcian, and about the council of bishops which came to Chalcedon, and what took place in the council until the public address of the king to the bishops."

CHAPTER I

THE[1] FIRST CHAPTER OF THIS BOOK TELLS ABOUT THE
EVENTS WHICH OCCURRED IN THE SYNOD, BEING
TAKEN FROM THE HISTORY OF ONE ZACHARIAH
BY NAME, WHO BEGINS TO WRITE IN GREEK TO
EUPRAXIUS AS FOLLOWS

Since it is acceptable unto you, and desired by you,
Christ-loving Eupraxius,[2] who are dwelling in the royal palace,
and are occupied in the service of kings, to learn what
happened, in the reign of Marcian, to the holy Church of
God ; and who they were who, in regular succession, were the
chief priests in Alexandria, and Rome, and Constantinople,
and Antioch, and Jerusalem, from the time of the Council of
Chalcedon—that Council which, ostensibly convened about the
matter of Eutyches, introduced and increased the heresy of
Nestorius ; and shook all the world ; and added evil upon
evil ; and set the two heresies, one against the other ; and
filled the world with divisions ; and confounded[3] the faith
delivered by the apostles, and the good order[4] of the Church ;
and tore into ten thousand rents the perfect Robe of Christ,
woven from the top throughout : therefore we, anathematising
those two heresies, and every wicked teacher of doctrine
corrupt and contrary to the Church of God, and to the
orthodox faith of the three holy Synods, which skilfully maintained the true doctrine ; shall, to that end, employ this
history which you urged us to undertake.

After the death of the holy Cyril of Alexandria, who
carried on the conflict against many corrupt doctrines, and
exposed them, Dioscorus received the throne as his successor ;

---

[1] Evag. ii. 4, 18 ; Liberat. 13.

[2] ܐܘܦܪܟܣܝܘܣ ܗܘ ܕܕܘܟܪܢܗ ܢܨܝܚ ܘܪܚܡ ܡܫܝܚܐ
ܕܐܝܬܘܗܝ ܗܘܐ ܚܕ ܡܢ ܡܗܝܡܢܐ ܕܩܘܝܛܘܢܐ ܡܠܟܝܐ.
" Eupraxius of illustrious and Christ-loving memory, who was one of the eunuchs
of the royal bedchambers," *das Leben des Severus* (ed. Spanuth), p. 28.

[3] ܒܠܒܟ, MS., ܒܠܟ, L.   [4] ܐܘܛܟܣܝܐ, *i.e.* εὐταξία.

and he was a peaceable man, and also a champion;[1] although he had not the same promptitude and boldness as Cyril.

At that time Theodoret and Hibo, who, along with Flavian of Constantinople and Eusebius, were deposed by the second Synod of Ephesus, which met there in the days of Theodosius, about the matter of Eutyches and Flavian—Theodoret of Cyrrhus, because he wrote twelve censures upon Cyril's Heads against Nestorius; and Hibo of Edessa, because he wrote a letter to Moris of Nisibis, reviling Cyril—were, both of them, upholding the doctrine of Theodore and Diodorus. And Theodoret[2] went up to Leo of Rome, and informed him about all these matters; and, with the gift which blinds the eyes of the soul, he got the better of him. Whereupon Leo composed[3] that letter which is called the Tome, and which was ostensibly written to Flavian against Eutychianism. But Leo also wrote to Marcian the king, and his wife Pulcheria, and warmly commended Theodoret to them.

This[4] Marcian favoured the doctrine of Nestorius, and was well disposed towards him; and so he sent by John the Tribune, to recall Nestorius from his place of banishment in Oasis; and to recall also Dorotheus, the bishop who was with him. And it happened while he was returning, that he set at naught[5] the holy Virgin, the *Theotokos*, and said, " What is Mary? Why should she indeed be called the *Theotokos*? " And the righteous judgment of God speedily overtook him (as had been the case formerly with Arius, who blasphemed against the Son of God). Accordingly he fell from his mule, and the tongue[6] of this Nestorius was cut off, and his mouth was eaten by worms, and he died on the roadway. And his companion Dorotheus died also. And the king, hearing of it, was greatly grieved; and he was thinking upon

---

[1] ‎ܐܓܘܢܣܛܐ‎, *i.e.* ἀγωνιστής.

[2] Jo. Eph. ap. " Dion." See Introd. p. 4, note.

[3] Here an extract in Cod. Rom. begins.　　　　[4] Evag. ii. 2.

[5] ‎ܡܛܠܩ‎. This word occurs again in this chapter (p. 47, note 3), and probably in bk. 7, ch. 7 (p. 117, note 4); the Lexicons do not give any other reference.

[6] Evag. i. 7.

what had occurred, and he was in doubt as to what he should do.

However, written directions from Marcian the king[1] were delivered by John the Tribune to Dioscorus and Juvenalis, calling upon them to meet in Council, and John also informed them of what had happened to Nestorius and to Dorotheus.

And when the bishops of every place, who were summoned, were preparing to meet at Nicea, Providence[2] did not allow them; for the king[3] issued a new order that the assembly should be convened to Chalcedon, so that Nicea might not be the meeting-place of rebels.

Then[4] the Nestorian party earnestly urged and besought the king that Theodoret should be appointed the president of the Synod, and that, according to his word, every matter should be decided there.[5]   And when they met at Chalcedon, Theodoret entered in and lived there boldly, like an honoured bishop; he who a little time before had been ejected[6] from the priesthood by their means.   And Dioscorus and the chief bishops were vexed and troubled on account of the haughty insolence which the man displayed; but they could not put a stop to it, because of the royal authority, though they saw that the canons were despised by him, and by Hibo also, with the help of the Roman legates of Leo, who were aiding and abetting them.

And when Dioscorus was proclaiming the doctrine of the faith in the Synod, and with him Juvenalis, and Thalassius of Cappadocia, and Anatolius, and Amphilochius of Side, and Eusebius of Ancyra, and Eustace of Berytus; then, as by a miracle, Eusebius of Dorylæum also agreed with them; for they saw that the Nestorian doctrine of the two natures was confirmed, and established there, by the co-operation of John of Germanicia, who fiercely contended, in the course of the dispute there, with the side which said, " It is right for

---

[1] ܕܡܠܟܐ, Cod. Rom.   [2] ܩܝܡܘ, i.e. πρόνοια.

[3] Evag. ii. 2 ; Liberat. 13.

[4] Jo. Eph. (*Anecd. Syr.* ii. p. 363).   See Introd. *l.c.*

[5] Here extract in Cod. Rom. ends.

[6] ܐܦܩ, MS., not ܢܦܩ, as L. prints.

us to confess Christ after His incarnation as one Nature from two, according to the belief of the rest of the Fathers, and not to introduce any innovation or add any novelty to the faith."

Wherefore, John of Germanicia, and the rest of the Nestorian party, with Theodoret at their head, brought about the deprivation of Dioscorus ; because he said, " It is right for us to believe that Christ became incarnate *from* two natures ; and we should not confess two natures after the union, like Nestorius.

And [1] then Anatolius, the bishop of the royal city, cried out in words to this effect, " Not for the faith is Dioscorus deposed ; but he is set at nought [2] for refusing to hold communion with the chief priest, my lord Leo."

And after the outcry of many, and after the things had been spoken which have been written in the Acts [3] of that Council, at last those bishops being forced to do so, defined our Lord Jesus Christ to be *in* two natures. And they praised the Tome of Leo, and they called that an orthodox definition which said, " There are two Persons, and two Natures, with their properties and their operations." And this being so, they were required to subscribe under compulsion ; those very priests who, a little time before in the days of the blessed Theodosius, being assembled at the second Council of Ephesus, cried out many times, " If anyone shall say ' Two natures to two,' let the Silentiarius come up ! " [4]

And when they repeated this over to Dioscorus, by means of John the chief of the Silentiarii, and asked him to agree to it, and to subscribe, and get back his throne ; he said, courageously, " Sooner would Dioscorus see his own hand cut off, and the blood falling on the paper, than do such a thing as that." Whereupon he was sent into banishment to Gangra,

---

[1] Mansi, vol. vii. p. 104.

[2] I do not know what ܠܥܟܐ means. Probably it is a copyist's error.

[3] ܩܘܪ̈ܝܩܣ, *i.e.* πεπραγμένα.

[4] The words are written over an erasure in the MS. The Synodal Acts give εἰς δύο τέμνε. Probably ܢܩܡܘ is a mistake for ܩܡܘ, and ܣܠܛܝܪ̈ܝܐ has crept in from below. Transl. "Cut in two the man who speaks of two natures" (Brooks).

because the Nestorian party published the report about him, that his opinions were the same as those of Eutyches.

And I think it well, omitting many of his sayings, both what he spoke and wrote to Domnus of Antioch, and in the Synod of Chalcedon itself, which testify concerning the faith of the man, that his faith was like that of Athanasius, and Cyril, and the other doctors, I think it well (I say) to make a written extract out of what he wrote from his place of banishment to Secundinus, in the following words :—

" Omitting many urgent matters, this I declare, that no man shall say that the holy flesh, which our Lord took from the Virgin Mary, by the operation of the Holy Spirit, in a manner which He Himself knows, was different to and foreign from our body. And, indeed, since this is so, they who affirm that Christ did not become incarnate for us, give the lie[1] to Paul. For he has said, ' Not from angels did He take (the nature), but from the seed of the House of Abraham '; to which seed Mary was no stranger, as the Scriptures teach us. And again, ' It was right that in everything He should be made like unto His brethren,' and that word ' in everything ' does not suffer the subtraction of any part of our nature : since in nerves, and hair, and bones, and veins,[2] and belly, and heart, and kidneys, and liver, and lungs, and, in short, in all those things that belong to our nature, the flesh which was born from Mary was compacted with the soul of our Redeemer, that reasonable and intelligent soul, without the seed of man, and the gratification and cohabitation of sleep.

" For if, as the heretics think, this was not so, how is He named ' our brother,' supposing that He used a body different from ours ? And how, again, is that true which He said to His Father, ' I will declare Thy name to My brethren ? '[3] Let us not reject, neither let us despise, those who think in this way. For He was like us, for us, and with us, not in phantasy, nor in mere semblance, according to the heresy

---

[1] ܡܟܕܒܝܢ, MS., not ܡܟܕܒܝܢ, as L. prints.

[2] Read ܙܪܘܬܐ for ܙܪܘܡܐ.   [3] Ps. xxii. 22.

of the Manichæans, but rather in actual reality from Mary, the *Theotokos.*   To comfort the desolate[1] and to repair the vessel that had been broken, He came to us new.   And as Immanuel, indeed, He is confessed ; for He became poor for us, according to the saying of Paul, 'that we, by His humiliation, might be made rich.'[2]   He became, by the dispensation, like us ; that we, by His tender mercy, might be like Him.   He became man, and yet He did not destroy that which is His nature, that He is Son of God ; that we, by grace, might become the sons of God.   This I think and believe ; and, if any man does not think thus, he is a stranger to the faith of the apostles."

And although[3] this apostolic man had been well versed in this confession of faith from the beginning of his life, yet he was deposed and sent into banishment, because he would not worship the image, with its two faces, which was set up by Leo and by the Council of Chalcedon ; and because he refused to hold communion with Theodoret and Hibo, who had been deprived on account of their blasphemies.

But the story goes that when, on one occasion, he saw Theodoret sitting upon the throne in the Council, and speaking from it, and not standing and making his defence, as one should who had been canonically deposed from the priesthood ; then he himself arose and descended from the throne and sat upon the pavement, saying, " I will not sit with the wicked, nor with vain persons will I enter in."

Whereupon the partisans of Theodoret cried out, " He has deposed himself."   But the other bishops cried out, " Our faith[4] is perishing.   If Theodoret, who holds the opinions of Nestorius, be accepted, we reject Cyril."   And then Basil, the bishop of Tripolis, stood up and said, " We ourselves have deposed Theodoret."

But they say that Amphilochius was beaten on his head by Aetius the deacon, to make him sign.   It was this Aetius who went to Theodoret by night, and made a complete copy

---

[1] ܐܪ̈ܝ, MS., ܐܒܝ̈ܪ, L., and for ܢܣܝܟ read ܢܣܝܠܐ.

[2] 2 Cor. viii. 9.   [3] Here an extract in Cod. Rom. begins.

[4] The faith (Cod. Rom.).

for him of the Symbol of the two Natures ; and when [1] it was accepted by the bishops, and they agreed to it, then Theodoret insolently [2] derided [3] them, saying, " See how I have made them taste the leaven of the doctrine of Nestorius, and they are delighted with it ! " [4]

" But Eustace of Berytus, when he signed the document, wrote in short hand,[5] " This have I written under compulsion, not agreeing with it."   And he wept very much, as did also others who proclaimed the compulsion and exposed the hypocritical profession of faith which was made, because the chief senators were present time after time at the discussions, and closely watched the proceedings of the Synod. But, at last, the king came there, with his wife Pulcheria, and he delivered a public address [6] in the Martyr Church of Euphemia in the following terms :—

" From [7] the first time that we were chosen and accounted worthy of the kingdom by God, amidst all the care of public business, no concern whatever in which we might be involved [8] was allowed to hinder us, but we made it our choice to honour the true faith of the Christians, and to accustom [9] the minds of men to it, with purity ; all novelty of false doctrines and preachings that do not agree with the well proved doctrine of the Fathers, being taken out of our midst.   Therefore we summoned this holy Synod that it might cleanse away all darkness, and put away filth of thoughts : that so, in pure mind, the doctrine of the faith which is in our Lord Jesus Christ might be established," and so on, to the same effect.

When the king had finished his public address, the bishops praised him and the Senate, and also the letter of Leo, affirming with respect to it that it agreed with the faith of the Apostle Peter.

---

[1] Jo. Eph. Fr. (*Anecd. Syr.* ii. p. 363).   See Introd. *l.c.*

[2] ܡܟܪܝܩ, p. 199, note 4.   [3] ܡܟܠܣܐ, see p. 42, note 5.

[4] Here an extract in Cod. Rom. ends.

[5] In signs ܒܣܡܝܘܢܐ, *i.e.* ἐν σημείοις.

[6] ܦܪܘܣܘܩܝܐ, *i.e.* προσφώνησις.   [7] Mansi, vol. vii. p. 132.

[8] ܢܬܥܪܝܠ, MS., ܢܬܥܪܝܠ, L.   [9] ܢܠܟܡ, MS., ܢܠܟܡ, L.

CHAPTER II

THE SECOND CHAPTER TELLS ABOUT THE BANISHMENT OF
DIOSCORUS, AND THE CONSECRATION OF PROTERIUS
IN HIS STEAD; AND ABOUT THE SLAUGHTER WHICH
ENSUED UPON HIS COMING IN; AND THE CHURCH
FUNDS, WHICH HE EXPENDED UPON HIS ALLIES THE
ROMANS, BUT WHICH, BY RIGHT, BELONGED TO THE POOR

The Synod having received such an end as this, Dioscorus [1]
was decreed to be a confessor, and was sent away to live in
Gangra; and Proterius was appointed bishop in Alexandria,
in his stead. This Proterius [2] had been a presbyter on his
side, and had contended earnestly against the Synod at first,
but afterwards, with the object of snatching the see for himself, he became like Judas, a betrayer of his master, and like
Absalom, of his father; and he showed himself a rapacious
wolf in the midst of the flock. And many who were unwilling he afflicted and ill-treated, to force them into agreement with himself. And he sent them into banishment, and
he seized their property by means of the governors [3] who
obeyed him in consequence of the king's command.

Whereupon, indeed, the priests, and the monks, and many
of the people, perceiving that the faith had been polluted,
both by the unjust deposition of Dioscorus and the oppressive
conduct of Proterius and his wickedness, assembled by themselves in the monasteries, and severed themselves from his
communion. And they proclaimed Dioscorus, and wrote his
name in the book of life as a chosen and faithful priest of God.

And Proterius was very indignant, and he gave gifts into
the hand of the Romans, and he armed them against the
people, and he filled their hands with the blood of believers,
who were slain; for they also strengthened themselves, [4] and
made war. And many died at the very Altar, and in the
Baptistery, who had fled and taken refuge there.

---

[1] Evag. ii. 5; Liberat. 14.

[2] Here begins an extract in Cod. Rom. which continues to end of chap. viii.

[3] ܩܨܝܐ, MS., ܩܨܐ?, L.   [4] Or, " became exasperated."

CHAPTER III

THE THIRD CHAPTER NARRATES THE EVENTS WHICH OCCURRED IN PALESTINE RESPECTING JUVENALIS OF JERUSALEM, WHO BROKE HIS PROMISES, AND SEPARATED HIMSELF FROM DIOSCORUS. AND THE MONKS AND THE CITIZENS OF JERUSALEM HEARD OF THE MATTER FROM THEODOSIUS, A MONK, WHO, THROUGH ZEAL, WAS PRESENT AT CHALCEDON, AND WHO, AFTER HAVING CAREFULLY WATCHED THE PROCEEDINGS THERE, CAME TO JERUSALEM AND GAVE INFORMATION ABOUT THEM; AND THEY MADE HIM BISHOP BY FORCE, INSTEAD OF JUVENALIS

And in Palestine, indeed, there were evils like these, and worse. But from what cause I shall now tell. When Juvenalis was summoned to Chalcedon, and he learned from John the Tribune the will of the king; and also that Nestorius, who had been recalled, died on his return from banishment; then he (inasmuch as he was persuaded that the doctrine of the Tome, which favoured the opinion of Nestorius, was corrupt) summoned the clergy, and gathered the monks and the people together; and he exposed this false doctrine, and anathematised it. And he confirmed the souls of many in the true faith. And he charged them all, that if he should be perverted in the Synod, they should hold communion with him no more.

And at first when he went there, he made a great struggle, along with Dioscorus, on behalf of the faith. But because the royal pressure[1] was brought to bear; and because of the flattery and compliments of the king, who himself waited personally upon the bishops at the banquet, and showed great condescension to them; and because the king also promised that he would give the three provinces of Palestine to the honour of the see of Jerusalem; then the eyes of his mind were darkened, and he left Dioscorus the champion[2] alone, and

---

[1] ‎ܐܢܢܩܝ‎, *i.e.* ἀνάγκη.   [2] ‎ܐܓܘܢܣܛܐ‎, ἀγωνιστής.

4

he went over to the opposite side. And he treated with contempt the oaths which he had made in the name of God. And both he and the bishops who were with him agreed and subscribed.

And [1] when Theodosius the monk, and his companions who were in close fellowship with him, and who zealously watched what was taking place in the Synod, heard about this they returned quickly to Palestine; and they came to Jerusalem, and told about the betrayal of the faith. And they called all the monks together, and gave full information to them.

And the monks assembled, and prepared themselves, and went to meet Juvenalis as he was coming. And they reminded him of his promises, and that he had failed to keep them. And they made this one request of him, that he would censure the proceedings which had taken place, and anathematise them. But he showed himself like Pilate, saying, " What I have written, I have written." And the monks said to him, " We will not receive you then, for you have broken [2] your oaths and your promises." So he returned to the king.

But the assembly of monks and clergy went back to Jerusalem. And the people, and the bishops who were with them, were distressed,[3] and they consulted together as to what they should do. And they decided to appoint another bishop instead of Juvenalis. When they were speaking of the chaste monks, Romanus and Marcian, and of other men of wonderful excellence ; at length [4] it was agreed that they should appoint Theodosius, who had been found zealous, and who also had contended for years on behalf of the faith. And they took him by force, while he persisted in refusing, and conjuring them not to do so, and begging them to allow him to be the helper of the person whom they appointed from amongst themselves. However, they would not yield to his entreaties ; but blessed him and placed him on the throne. And when

---

[1] Evag. ii. 5.   [2] ܠܟܣܪ̈ܝ, MS., not ܠܟܣܪ, as L. prints.

[3] For ܢܟܘ̈ Cod. Rom. has ܟܢܩܘ. Transl. " and they gathered the people and the bishops who were with them."

[4] Evag. ii. 5.

the other cities of Palestine heard it ; inasmuch as they knew
him to be a man of surpassing virtue, and zealous for the
truth ; they severally [1] brought persons to receive his blessing
and be admitted to the priesthood.

CHAPTER IV

THE FOURTH CHAPTER TELLS ABOUT PETER THE IBERIAN ;
AND HOW HE ALSO WAS TAKEN, AND WAS BROUGHT
TO THEODOSIUS BY THE PEOPLE OF GAZA ; AND HE
BECAME THEIR BISHOP

Among these also was Peter the Iberian, a man wonderfully celebrated throughout the world, a king's son, who had
been given as a hostage to Theodosius ; and who was beloved
by him and by his wife Eudocia, on account of his excellent
parts. And he was brought up in the king's palace ; and he
was placed in charge of the royal horses. But he resigned
this appointment, and gave himself up to the discipline of
Christ along with John the Eunuch also, who was his
sponsor, and his father by water and the Spirit. And they
prospered, and God wrought signs by their means in Constantinople. And they fled from thence, and betook themselves next to the wilderness of Palestine, and there they
loved and cultivated the monastic life. And although after
this manner they desired to be hidden, yet they became
greatly celebrated ; and they wrought signs like the apostles.

And as they were changing from place to place, they
arrived opposite to Gaza and Majuma. And the men and
the women and the people of all ranks and ages went out and
seized Peter, and brought him to Jerusalem to Theodosius,
whom they besought to make him their bishop.

And he laid many charges against himself, and refused
ordination. And against his will Theodosius laid his hand
upon his head and consecrated him, for he knew the man.

[1] For ‌ Cod. Rom. has ‌. Trans. " brought persons to him."

And when he became violently agitated, and called himself a heretic ; then Theodosius hesitated [1] a little, and said to him, "My cause and thine are before the Judgment Seat of Christ." And he changed his words, saying, "A heretic indeed I am not, but a sinner." And Theodosius, being well acquainted with the man, blessed him as priest for the people of Gaza.

But there were other excellent deeds done by this man, which, however, I omit, lest I should make my narrative too long.

CHAPTER V

THE FIFTH CHAPTER TELLS ABOUT THE FLIGHT OF THEO-DOSIUS OF JERUSALEM, IN CONSEQUENCE OF THE KING'S THREATS ; ALSO ABOUT JUVENALIS, WHO RETURNED WITH AN ARMY OF ROMANS ; AND THE GREAT SLAUGHTER THAT ENSUED UPON HIS ENTRY THERE

And when Theodosius was prospering in this manner, the report [2] of all that he was doing reached Marcian the king. And Juvenalis returned, having with him Count Dorotheus and an army ; for the purpose of taking Theodosius, and making him a prisoner, and deposing all the bishops whom he had made in his district, and punishing [3] the monks and the people, and expelling them in consequence of their insolence and rashness in setting up Theodosius as bishop in Jerusalem. But, by the desire of the queen, Peter the Iberian alone was to be spared ; even though he should not consent to hold communion with the other bishops.

And when Juvenalis arrived at Neapolis, he found a large number of monks there ; and at first he tried to seduce them, simple men as they were, and single-minded, whose arms and helmet were the true faith and works of righteous-

---

[1] For ܠܗ Cod. Rom. has ܠܗ.

[2] Evag. ii. 5.   [3] ܢܣܝܘܡ, MS., not ܢܣܝܡ, as L. prints.

ness.   These he endeavoured to persuade to hold communion with himself.   And when they turned away from this proposal with disgust, unless he would anathematise the violent transactions of Chalcedon; he then said, " It is the king's will." And they still refused.   Whereupon he gave orders to the Romans and the Samaritans, who smote and killed these monks, while they were singing psalms and saying, " O God, the heathen are come into Thine inheritance, and they have defiled Thy holy temple; and behold they are making Jerusalem a waste place!"[1]

And some of the Romans were overcome with pity, and wept.   But some of them, along with the Samaritans, killed many of the monks, whose blood also was poured out upon the ground.

CHAPTER VI

THE SIXTH CHAPTER TELLS ABOUT A CERTAIN BLIND SAMARITAN WHO DREW NEAR WITH FAITH, AND SMEARED HIS EYES WITH THE BLOOD OF THOSE THAT WERE SLAIN ; AND HIS SIGHT WAS RESTORED[2]

There was a certain blind Samaritan who deceived his own guide, and said, " Since mine eyes cannot see the blood of the slaughter of these Christians, so that I may delight myself in it; bring me near and I shall feel it."   And when the guide brought him near and caused him to feel it, he dipped his hands in the blood.   And he prostrated himself upon the ground ; and he wept, with prayer and supplication, that he might be a sharer in their martyrdom.   Then he arose, and smeared his eyes, and lifted up his hands to heaven ; and his eyes were opened, and he received his sight.

And all who were witnesses of this miracle, were astonished and believed in God.   And the blind man also believed, and was baptized.

But the party who administered the king's orders, laid

[1] Ps. lxxix. I.   [2] ܐܬܦܩܚܝ, MS., not ܐܦܩܘܚܝ, as L. prints.

hold upon the surviving believers, and expelled [1] them from the whole district.

CHAPTER VII

THE SEVENTH CHAPTER RELATES HOW OUR LORD APPEARED TO PETER THE IBERIAN, OF GAZA; AND TOLD HIM THAT HE MUST DEPART ALONG WITH THOSE WHO WERE EXPELLED

But they say that Peter the Illustrious was at rest, being left undisturbed by all, both on account of the king's orders, and the loving care of the queen for him.

But he saw the Lord in a vision, saying to him indignantly, "How now, Peter! Am I being expelled in My believing servants, and art thou remaining quiet and at rest?" Then Peter repented and obeyed, and he arose and left Gaza; and he joined those who were expelled, and departed with them.

CHAPTER VIII

THE EIGHTH CHAPTER TELLS ABOUT A CERTAIN ZEALOUS MONK, NAMED SOLOMON; WHO ACTED CUNNINGLY, AND WENT IN TO JUVENALIS, AS IF HE DESIRED TO BE BLESSED BY HIM, AND THREW A BASKETFUL [2] OF DUST UPON HIS HEAD, AND REPROACHED HIM

And Juvenalis, having by means of the armed force [3] of the Romans expelled the believers and the monks who were in the country district, arrived at Jerusalem and sat upon the throne. And he paid no regard [4] at all to his promises, nor to the slaughter which had occurred upon his entry there, nor to the falsehood of his oaths.

[1] For ܘܐܣܝ Cod. Rom. has ܐܣܝܘ, and for ܩܘܪܒ, ܘܩܘܪܒ.

[2] ܐܣܩܝܕ, *i.e.* σπυρίς. [3] ܩܒܘܣܝܣܘ, παράταξις.

[4] ܩܠܗ, MS., not ܩܠܗ, as L. prints.

Then a certain monk, Solomon by name, was stirred in his spirit; and in this honourable garb of chastity, and as if desiring to be blessed by the chief priest himself, acted cunningly, and filled a basket with dust and ashes, and placed it under his armpit, and drew near to Juvenalis. And the latter was glad when the monk came in to him. And Solomon, being received by him, said to him, "Let my lord bless me." And, as the Roman guard permitted him to draw near and come close to Juvenalis, he took out the basket of dust and emptied it on his head, saying, "Shame upon thee, shame upon thee, liar and persecutor!" And when the Roman guard were about to strike him, Juvenalis would not allow it. And he was not enraged, but was rather moved to penitence by this, and shook the dust from his head. So they only put out the monk from his presence. And he ordered that money for his expenses [1] should be given to him, and that he should leave his country. The monk, however, refused the money, but left the country.

CHAPTER IX

THE NINTH CHAPTER TELLS HOW THEODOSIUS, BEING SOUGHT FOR BY THE ROMAN ARMY, WAS TAKEN AND IMPRISONED IN A HOUSE CONTAINING LIME; WHERE AT LENGTH HE DIED

But Theodosius, when he was sought for by the king's orders [2] through the whole province,[3] assumed the garb of a Roman, having on his head hair and a helmet; and he went about confirming and encouraging the believers. At length, however, when he arrived at the parts about Sidon, he was taken and delivered up to the Romans by one of his own friends.

And the Nestorian party were so enraged against him, because he had been going about through the whole world, and

---

[1] ܐܢܠܘܣܐ, *i.e.* ἀνάλωμα.   [2] ܕܛܝܩܘܡܛܐ, *i.e.* διατάγματα.

[3] ܗܘܦܪܟܝܐ, *i.e.* ὑπαρχία for ἐπαρχία. ܕܡܠܟܐ has probably crept into the text by mistake from the line above (Brooks).

exposing and anathematising the false doctrine of Nestorius, that they went up to the king, and persuaded him to grant that the man should be given into their charge and keeping. And they took him and imprisoned him in a small house, belonging to the monks, in which there was quicklime.

And these followers of Nestorius used to go to him in troops, and dispute with him, hoping that under pressure of great affliction he would change his mind, and agree to their will. And he prevailed over them all and repulsed them; and as they departed [1] from him ashamed and confounded, he said, " Even though I am imprisoned and thereby prevented from going about in the different places, according to my former custom; yet as long as the breath is in my nostrils, the word of God shall not be imprisoned in me; but it shall preach that which is true and right in the ears of the hearers."

But the Eutychian party also imagined that he would agree with them; and they came together to him, and entered into discusssion with him. And in like manner, contrary to their expectation, he showed them to be in agreement with Valentinus, and Manes, and Marcion; and that their heresy was a wicked one, worse even than that of Paul of Samosata, and Apollinaris, and Nestorius. And so they, in their turn, departed from him, being condemned by him.

And because they laid one affliction after another upon him, his soul also continued steadfast in the good fight.

While there he met with some writings of John the Rhetorician from Alexandria, which were full of false doctrine and very defective, and it is a heresy; and he exposed the man and anathematised him. And having finished his course, and contended in the fight, and kept his faith, at length he died. And departing from the prison, he went to be with Christ our Lord. And he left the example of courage to the believers.

[1] ܩܠܒܝܢ, MS., not ܩܠܟܝܢ, as L. prints.

CHAPTER X

THE TENTH CHAPTER GIVES A RECORD OF THE HERESY OF
JOHN THE RHETORICIAN OF ALEXANDRIA; AND HOW
IT WAS REJECTED AND ANATHEMATISED

John was an adherent of Palladius the Alexandrian
sophist, and was second to him; and for that reason he was
called the Rhetorician; because that next to sophistry
comes rhetoric, and therefore by that name the philosopher
is surnamed.[1]

This man, in the days of Proterius who succeeded Dioscorus,
saw that the whole city of Alexandria hated Proterius, some
in consequence of their zeal for the faith, and others because
they had been plundered and persecuted by him, with the
object of making them agree to the Synod and accept the
Tome.   He then sought to ingratiate himself with the people,
and to present a fine appearance, and to collect money for
himself, and to be celebrated with this empty glory.   And
not having read the Holy Scriptures, and not understanding
the meaning of their mysteries, and not having exercised
himself in the writings of the ancient doctors of the holy
Church, and not knowing what he was saying, or that about
which he was contending, he was puffed up[2] to write a sort of
proof that, after the manner of a seed, God the Word was
wrapped up in the body; and that He suffered in His own
Nature, if indeed He suffered at all.   But he denied that
the Word was united to a human body; and he would not
confess the natures from which One Christ appeared.   But he
prepared and collected words, saying, " It can by no means
be called a nature, as indeed without the seed of a man in
the Virgin the Incarnation took place."   And he said, " Therefore Christ was neither by her nor from her."   And he did
not agree with the doctors of the Church, who declare that the

---

[1] An exact translation of this passage is impossible. I have tried to give what
appears to be the sense of it.

[2] ‎اِزدهي‎. See note 4, p. 199.

human nature was united to God the Word, and that He became man.

And with vain words such as these he used to chatter; and he also wrote books. And in these he was self-contradictory; sometimes agreeing with Apollinaris, sometimes with Eutyches; and again, stating what was quite new. And because he was in doubt about the subject of his writings, lest they should be reviled,[1] he did not subscribe his books with his own name. But at one time he wrote the name of Theodosius, the bishop of Jerusalem, upon one; and again, the name of Peter the Iberian upon another; that even the believers might be deceived by them and accept them.

But they say, that on one occasion, Peter the Iberian met with one of them, which had been written in his own name, in a certain monastery; and when he took it and read it he was full of indignation, and he anathematised the man who wrote it. And not there alone, but also in Alexandria, and in Palestine, and in Syria, both he and Theodosius anathematised the writings of this man.

CHAPTER XI

THE ELEVENTH CHAPTER TELLS HOW JOHN THE SILENTI-ARIUS WAS SENT BY THE KING, AFTER THE DEATH OF DIOSCORUS AT GANGRA, TO EXHORT THE ALEX-ANDRIANS TO BE UNITED TO PROTERIUS

But when the report of the death of Dioscorus reached the Alexandrians, there was great trouble and sorrow. And after his death, on account of the love that they had for him, they proclaimed him as a living man,[2] and his name was set in the Diptych. But let no man even of those, whose endeavour it is to revile what is not done in exact order, find fault.

But the believing party were desirous of appointing a bishop instead of Dioscorus. However, they were afraid of

---

[1] Or, remain unknown.

[2] ܠܚܝܐ܂, MS., not ܠܚܝܐ܂, as L. prints.

the threats of Marcian the king; for he was sending letters in every direction, and fulminations against all who would not agree to the Synod and receive the Tome. For so it was, that when he heard of the men of Alexandria, and of their intention to appoint a bishop for themselves after the death of Dioscorus, he sent John, the chief of the Silentiarii, with a letter from himself exhorting the Alexandrians to be united to Proterius.

And this John was of the same mind as the king, and he was an astute[1] man. And when he came and saw the crowd, the numbers of monks arrayed in chastity, and possessing readiness of speech in defence of the faith, and also the strong body of the common people who were believers, with whom he had to deal, he was astounded, and said, "I am ready, if the Lord will, to inform the king and to plead with him on your behalf." And he received from them a petition—which gave information concerning their faith; and concerning all that happened to them at the hands of Proterius; and concerning the impious conduct of the man, and his wickedness, and the Church property which he expended upon vanity—written at length in words which I omit to reproduce here, lest I should be tedious to the reader.

And when John returned to the king and told him about these matters, he said to him, "We sent you, indeed, to persuade and exhort the Egyptians to obey our will: but you have returned to us, not according as we wished, since we find you an Egyptian." However, when he perceived the things that were written about Proterius, in the petition which the monks sent, he blamed the pride and the craftiness[2] of the man. And while he was occupied with this matter, he died, having reigned six years and a half.

But Morian[3] also, who reigned four years along with him, died.

And after him, Anthemius, and Severus, and Olybrius received the kingdom. And one year after, Leo the First was associated with them. So that the lives of these four made up seven years.

---

[1] ‎. See note, p. 16.

[2] ‎, MS., not ‎, as L.   [3] *I.e.* Majorian.

CHAPTER XII

THE TWELFTH CHAPTER TELLS ABOUT ANTHEMIUS, AND
SEVERUS, AND OLYBRIUS, AND LEO; WHO REIGNED
TOGETHER AND IN SUCCESSION, SEVEN YEARS

When Anthemius had reigned five years he was killed by
Ricimer. And Severus, having reigned one year with him,
died. And Olybrius, who reigned after Severus along with
Anthemius for one year, died. And Leo the First also died,
having reigned with Anthemius for three years, and two years
after.

In the first year of Leo indeed, Antioch was overturned
by the earthquakes which occurred; and there was also a
great fire. And in the second year of his reign, Sulifos, the
Gothic tyrant, was killed. And in the third year of his reign,
Aspar the general[1] and his sons were killed.

But there is in this third Book and in its chapters, which
are written above, a period of thirteen and a half years. And
it is made up in the following manner:—Of Marcian and
Morian six years and a half; and of Anthemius, and Severus,
and Olybrius, and Leo the First, who reigned in succession and
together, seven years.

And this period begins from the third[2] year of the three
hundred and fifth Olympiad, and it ends in the three hundred
and eighth Olympiad.

---

[1] ܐܣܛܪܛܝܠܛܣ, *i.e.* στρατηλάτης.

[2] ܬܠܬ, MS., not ܬܠܬ, as L. prints.

BOOK IV

THIS fourth Book also, inasmuch as it is from [1] the History of Zachariah the Rhetorican, relates (in its twelve chapters that are written down distinctly below) and makes known the events occurring after the death of Marcian, and Morian, and Anthemius, and Severus, and Olybrius, who reigned in all twelve years, as the Chronicle testifies—these events (I say) it makes known which took place in Alexandria, and in Ephesus, in the days of Leo, and Leo, during a period of twenty years. It tells about the consecration of Timothy the Great, surnamed the "Weasel." And how Proterius, who was appointed as the successor of Dioscorus by the Synod of Chalcedon, was killed; and how, after his death, his clergy presented a libel to Timothy, and sought to come to the Church; but the zealous priests, on the side of Timothy, and the people would not allow them. Whereupon they went to Rome, and informed Leo about the matter; who wrote a letter to Leo the king censuring the consecration of Timothy.

But this Book, further, tells about the letter of Timothy to Leo censuring the additions which had been made in the Synod, and the Tome.

And, moreover, it tells about John, who was the bishop in Ephesus after the resignation of Bassianus; and about the encyclical letter of Leo the king, which he wrote to the bishops, with the object of eliciting from them their written opinions respecting the definitions that were made in the Synod. And they all, with the exception of Amphilochius of Side, wrote in praise of these definitions.

---

[1] Or, "being, so far as it goes, drawn from," etc. This may be an intimation that our Syriac text is a compilation of extracts from the original Greek.

This Book, further, tells how Timothy was banished to Gangra, and from Gangra to Cherson; and that his successor was one of the Proterian party, another Timothy surnamed Salophaciolus.[1]

And it, moreover, tells about Isaiah the bishop, and Theophilus the presbyter, who showed themselves to be Eutychians; and about the letter which Timothy wrote respecting them, and by which he exposed them.

The first chapter tells about the consecration of Timothy the Great, surnamed the " Weasel "; and the events which then occurred.

The second chapter shows how Proterius was killed, and dragged away; and his body was burned with fire.

The third chapter explains how after Timothy appeared as the sole bishop, the other clergy also, who were adherents of Proterius, presented a libel by which they showed themselves desirous of coming to the Church; but[2] the zealous priests, on the side of Timothy, would not allow them.

The fourth chapter tells how these men, because they were not received by Timothy, got ready and went up to Rome and gave information to the chief priest Leo (respecting the matter).

The fifth chapter tells about Timothy; and also what happened in Ephesus to John the successor of Bassianus.

The sixth chapter, moreover, explains about the petition[3] of Timothy which he wrote to the king, which contained a censure upon Leo and his letter.

The seventh chapter tells about the replies to the Encyclical respecting the Synod, which were sent to Leo the king by the bishops; and how Amphilochius did not agree with the others in what he wrote.

The eighth chapter tells about the letter of Anatolius to the king, proving him to have influenced the bishops, as to the purport of their replies respecting the Synod.

---

[1] ܠܩܘܒܠܐܣ, "shaking cap"; again (ch. 10) ܡܠܬܪܘܩܘܒܠܐ, " crooked cap," from Σαλοφακιολος, hence I translate uniformly *Salophaciolus*.

[2] Probably ܕܒܠܣܘ has dropped out of the text, and the translation should be as in the heading of Chap. III.

[3] ܕܣܝܘܣ, *i.e.* δέησις.

The ninth chapter tells about the banishment of Timothy, and the events which happened at his departure from Alexandria.

The tenth chapter explains about the other Timothy, who was the bishop of the Proterian party, and was called Salophaciolus.

The eleventh chapter tells about the removal of Timothy from Gangra to Cherson.

The twelfth chapter tells about Isaiah and Theophilus, the Eutychians; and about the letter which Timothy wrote respecting them, and by which he exposed them.

But the time occupied by this Book is two or three years of Leo the First, and seventeen years of Leo the Second, less by two months, as the Chronicle informs us. For Timothy the Great was about two years, more or less, bishop in Alexandria; and then he was banished to Gangra, and after the lapse of eighteen years he returned to his see; and he very soon died.

This fourth Book is a narrative of the consecration of Timothy, and of the events which occurred in the days of King Leo the First, and Leo the Second.

CHAPTER I

THE FIRST CHAPTER OF THE FOURTH BOOK, TELLING
ABOUT THE CONSECRATION OF TIMOTHY THE GREAT,
SURNAMED *ÆLURUS*,[1] AND THE EVENTS WHICH HAP-
PENED THEN

The Alexandrian Church being in the condition that we
have described above, suddenly the report of the death of
Marcian reached them, and they all took courage, and consulted
with the whole order of the monks as to whom they should
make the bishop of the believing party. For[2] at that time
Dionysius the general[3] was not there, but was on a visit to
Egypt.[4] And they agreed upon Timothy, a man expert in
business[5] and of ascetic life; who had been brought from the
wilderness, by force, to Cyril, and ordained as presbyter by
him. Moreover, he was of the same faith as Dioscorus; and
he was well versed in all the truth of the faith of the doctors
of the Church. This man the people of Alexandria along
with the monks seized, and brought to the great Church which
is called *Cæsarian*. And they sought for three bishops,
according to the canonical statute, to consecrate him. And
since two Egyptian bishops were present, it was necessary that
some other bishop should be found. And on making diligent
inquiry, some of the people heard of Peter the Iberian, who
had left Palestine and was sojourning there in Alexandria.
And they ran quickly and laid hold of the man; and carried
him on their shoulders, not letting him touch the ground.
And as they were bringing him along, a voice was heard in
the minds of the clergy, and of the monks, and of the
believing citizens, like that voice which Philip heard respecting
the eunuch of Candace the queen, saying, "Consecrate him by
force, even though he be unwilling, and set him on the throne

---

[1] ܐܠܘܪܘܣ, *i.e.* αἴλουρος.　　　　[2] Evag. ii. 8; Liberat. 15.

[3] ܐܣܛܪܛܝܓܐ, *i.e.* στρατηγός.　　　　[4] *I.e.* Upper Egypt, see Evag.

[5] ܦܪܩܛܝܩܘܣ, *i.e.* πρακτικός.

of Mark." And he was weak in body through much self-mortification; so that, on account of his emaciation, the Proterian party used jestingly to style him the " Weasel." And when Dionysius the general[1] heard of the matter, he became uneasy, lest he might receive blame for there being two bishops in the city, when the king heard it. And accordingly he returned, and taking the whole Roman force with him, he made Timothy prisoner. And many were killed. And Dionysius gave orders that they should carry him off to a place called Cabarsarin.[2] And upon his departure the conflict between the citizens and the Romans became severe.[3] And there was a great tumult, and slaughters were matters of daily occurrence; more especially as he (Dionysius) kept inciting and urging on [4] the Romans called Cartadon,[5] who were passionate men and Arians. And so the custodian of the Church funds expended them upon the Romans who were contending with the people. But it happened that numbers of them and of their wives fell and perished in the conflict. And they were divided into parties, and fought one against another. And when confusion like this had prevailed in the city for many days, Dionysius was at his wits' end, so he brought a certain monk Longinus, celebrated for chastity and virtue, and he intrusted Timothy to him; that he might restore the bishop to the city and to his church, upon the condition that the fighting should cease, and that there should be no more slaughter.

And when Timothy had returned to the great church from which he had been forcibly removed, and Proterius had taken for himself the church which is called *Quirinian*, and Easter [6]

---

[1] ܩܡܛܪܛܝܣ, *i.e.* στρατηγός.

[2] ܟܒܪܣܪܝܢ, otherwise called ܩܒܘܣܪ, *i.e.* ܐܩܒܘܣܪ (Life of Peter Ib., ed. Raabe, p. 67) = Ταφοσίριον (see Euseb. *H. E.* vi. 40). Clearly then ܩܒܪ = τάφος, and the name was taken to mean " Tomb of Osiris " (Brooks).

[3] ܡܠܬܟܣܐ, MS., not ܡܠܬܟܣܡ, as L. prints.

[4] For ܡܠܟܝܘܠܣ I read ܡܠܟܝܢܘܣ.

[5] ܩܪܛܕܘ. I cannot even guess what this word may mean.

[6] ܦܛܝܪܐ, unleavened bread.

5

time came round, children without number were brought to Timothy to be baptized; so that because of their multitude those who were writing and reading out their names became weary; but only five were brought to Proterius. And the people were so devotedly[1] attached[2] to Timothy that they drove Proterius out of the church of Quirinus; and slaughter ensued.

CHAPTER II

THE SECOND CHAPTER SHOWS HOW PROTERIUS WAS SLAIN, AND DRAGGED THROUGH THE CITY; AND HOW HIS BODY WAS, AT LAST, BURNED WITH FIRE

And[3] when Proterius continued to threaten the Romans, and to display his rage against them; because they took his gold, but did not fill their hands with the blood of his enemies: then, indeed, a certain Roman was stirred to anger in his heart, and was boiling over with rage; and he invited Proterius to look round and he would show him the corpses of the slain as they lay. And suddenly and secretly, he drew his sword and stabbed Proterius in the ribs along with his Roman comrades, and they despatched him, and dragged him to the Tetrapylum, calling out respecting him as they went along, " This is Proterius." And others suspected that it was some crafty plot. But the Romans left the body, and went away. Then the people, perceiving this, became also greatly excited, and they dragged off the corpse, and burnt it with fire in the Hippodrome. Thus the end of death overtook[4] Proterius, who had done evil to the Alexandrians, just as George the Arian, and he suffered at their hands in like manner, and so was it done to him.

---

[1] ܟܣܘܢ, MS., not ܟܣܘܗ, as L.　　　[2] ܐܠܘܗܝ, MS., ܐܠܘܗܝ, L.

[3] Evag. ii. 8 ; Liberat. 15.　　　[4] ܗܠܩܗ, MS., ܗܠܩܝܗ, L.

CHAPTER III

THE THIRD CHAPTER TELLS HOW, AFTER TIMOTHY AP-
PEARED AS THE SOLE BISHOP, THE OTHER CLERGY
ALSO EXPRESSED, BY MEANS OF A LIBEL, THEIR
DESIRE TO REPENT AND BE UNITED WITH HIM ; BUT
THE PEOPLE AND THE ZEALOUS PRIESTS OF HIS
PARTY WOULD NOT ALLOW THEM

But Timothy, when he appeared before them as the only
chief priest of Alexandria, showed that he was really what a
priest should be.   For the silver and the gold that were given
to the Romans in the days of Proterius, he expended upon the
poor, and the widows, and the entertaining of strangers, and
upon the needy in the city.   So that, in a short time, the
rich men, perceiving his honourable conduct, lovingly and
devotedly supplied him with funds,[1] both gold and silver.   But
the presbyters and all the clergy belonging to the Proterian
party, since they knew all his virtues and his angelic mode of
life, and the devotion of the citizens to him, joined themselves
together and made libels in which they entreated him that they
might be received.   They also promised that they would go
to Rome to Leo, and admonish him concerning the novelties
which he had written in the Tome.   Among these persons
there were some who were ready and eloquent, and of great
wealth and dignity, and of high birth also, who had been
called to the clerical order by Cyril ; and who were honoured
in the eyes of the citizens of Rome ; and they presented the
petition on their behalf to Timothy.   And Eustace of Berytus
wrote also recommending their reception.

But the jealousy and hatred of the citizens against these
persons were great, on account of the events which had
occurred in the days of Proterius, and the various sufferings
which they had endured.   So they would not consent to their
reception, but they prepared the others to cry out, " Not one

---

[1] ܩܘܣܝܐ, *i.e.* οὐσίας.

of them shall set his foot here, neither shall the trans-
gressors be received."

CHAPTER IV

THE FOURTH CHAPTER TELLS HOW THESE MEN GOT
READY AND WENT UP TO ROME, AND GAVE IN-
FORMATION RESPECTING THE TREATMENT WHICH
THEY HAD SUFFERED

This was the reason why matters were disturbed and
thrown into confusion.   For when these men were ignomini-
ously refused, they betook themselves to Rome, and there
they told about the contempt of. the canons, and about the
dreadful death of Proterius ; and they said that he died for
the sake of the Synod and for the honour of Leo ; and that
they themselves, also, had endured many indignities ; and
further, that Timothy had come forward in a lawless manner
and taken the priesthood.   So they rendered the latter odious,
and made the whole business appear disgraceful in the eyes
of Leo ; and they stirred him up against Timothy.

CHAPTER V

THE FIFTH CHAPTER TELLS THE FOLLOWING MATTERS
RESPECTING TIMOTHY ; AND ALSO WHAT HAPPENED
IN EPHESUS TO JOHN THE SUCCESSOR OF BASSIANUS

But how it came about that Timothy was given up, I
shall now relate.   Marcian the king having died, and
Anthemius, and Severus, and Olybrius having reigned for
only short lives, in Italy and the regions beyond, Leo the
First received the kingdom in the territory of Europe in
conjunction with them and after them.   And he was both a
believer and vigorous, but simple in the faith.

And when Leo the king learned the evils which occurred in Egypt, and in Alexandria, and in Palestine, and in every place; and that many had been disturbed on account of the Synod. And also that in Ephesus there had been much slaughter, upon the entrance of John, after Bassianus had resigned and fled because he would not subscribe the transactions of Chalcedon. But this John, being inflamed with desire for pre-eminence, betrayed the rights and honours of the see; so that in Ephesus they call him "the traitor" unto this day; and they blotted his name out of the book of life. He accordingly, when he received a letter from Timothy of Alexandria, was willing to convene a Synod. But Anatolius, the bishop of the royal city, prevented him; not, indeed, that he was able to find any fault with the written statement of Timothy, but he was very uneasy lest, if a Synod were assembled, it might put an end to all the transactions of Chalcedon. And his anxiety was not for the faith, but rather for the privileges and honours which had been unjustly granted to the see of the royal city.

.Accordingly, Anatolius persuaded the king not to assemble a Synod, but by means of written letters, called *Encyclicals*, to inquire what the mind of the bishops was respecting the Synod of Chalcedon and the consecration[1] of Timothy.

And[2] the king began to write to the bishops about Timothy and the Synod of Chalcedon, in the encyclical letter, to the following effect :—

"Do ye, without fear of man or partiality, and unbiassed by influence or by favour, setting the fear of God alone before your eyes, and considering that to Him alone ye must make your defence and give your account, tell me briefly the common opinion held by you the priests in our dominion, what ye think right, after having carefully investigated the transactions of Chalcedon, and concerning the consecration of Timothy of Alexandria."

[1] ‍‍‍, *i.e.* χειροτονία.   [2] Liberat. 15 ; Evag. ii. 9.

And [1] when a letter such as this from the king was given to Leo of Rome, he wrote two letters to Leo the king; one concerning Timothy, and the other on behalf of the Proterian party, in which he also asserted of the clergy of Constantinople that they were of the same mind as Timothy; and he called Anatolius indolent; [2] and he defended the Tome which he himself wrote respecting Eutyches, and which was accepted in the Council of Chalcedon. However, in a similar strain he wrote distinctly concerning the taking of the Manhood by Christ in this letter also. And Leo the king sent it on to Timothy of Alexandria. And, upon the receipt of it, the latter wrote a petition [3] to the king as follows.

CHAPTER VI

THE SIXTH CHAPTER, DECLARING, BY HIS PETITION, THE FAITH OF TIMOTHY AND THE CHARGES THAT HE MADE AGAINST THE LETTER OF LEO

" O kind and indulgent king! Since among wise men [4] there is nothing more honourable than the soul, and also we have learned to despise the things of the flesh, and not to lose the soul; therefore, as far as in me lies and with all my might, I am careful to keep my soul, lest before the time of judgment I may be condemned as a lover of the flesh, and prepare for myself the fire of Hell. And this I think, that all who are wise concerning that which is good, desire that nothing hateful to their brethren should ever occur. And accordingly, in writing this petition I assure your Serenity that from my youth I have learned the Holy Scriptures, and I have studied the divine mysteries contained in them. And even until now, I have ever been careful to hold the true faith as it was delivered to us by the apostles, and by my

---

[1] Evag. ii. 10.

[2] For ܟܣܠܬܐ I read ܟܣܠܬܐ.

[3] ܣܘܩܣܐ, i.e. δέησις.

[4] ܚܠܒ ܢܦܐ, MS., ܢܦܫܝܢ, L.

fathers the doctors. And, being united to them by the grace of God our Saviour, I have reached my present age. And I confess the one faith which our Redeemer and Creator Jesus Christ delivered when He became incarnate, and sent out the blessed apostles, saying, ‘ Go, teach all nations ; baptizing them in the name of the Father, and the Son, and the Holy Spirit.’ [1]　For [2] the Trinity is perfect, equal of Nature, in glory and blessedness ; and there is not in It anything less or more. For thus also the three hundred and eighteen blessed fathers taught concerning the true Incarnation of our Lord and Saviour Jesus Christ, that He became man, according to His dispensation, which He Himself knows. And with them I agree and believe, as do all others who prosper [3] in the true faith. For in it there is nothing difficult, neither does the definition of the faith which the fathers proclaimed require addition. And all (whoever they be) holding other opinions and corrupted by heresy, are rejected by me. And I also myself flee from them. For this is a disease which destroys the soul, namely, the doctrine of Apollinaris, and the blasphemies of Nestorius, both those who hold erroneous views about the Incarnation of Jesus Christ, Who became flesh from us ; and introduce into Him the cleavage in two, and divide asunder even the dispensation of the only-begotten Son of God : and those, on the other hand, who say with respect to His Body that it was taken from Heaven, or that God the Word was changed, or that He suffered in His own Nature ; and who do not confess that to a human body what pertains to the soul derived from us was united.

“ And I say to any who have fallen into one or other of these heresies, ‘ Ye are in grievous error, and ye know not the Scriptures.’ [4]　And with such I do not hold communion, nor do I love them as believers. But I am joined, and united, and truly agreeing with the faith which was defined at Nicea ; and it is my care to live in accordance with it.

---

[1] Matt. xxviii. 19.　　　　　　　　[2] Migne, *Patr. Græc.* vi. p. 274.

[3] ܣܠܘܟܝܢ, MS., ܣܠܘܟܝܢ, L.

[4] Matt. xxii. 29.

" But when Diomedes, the distinguished Silentiarius, came to me and gave me the letter of the bishop of Rome, and I studied it, and I was not pleased with its contents; then lest the Church, O Christ-loving man, should be disturbed, I neither, as yet, have publicly read nor censured it.

" But I believe that God has put it into the mind of your Serenity to set right the statements in this letter, which are a cause of stumbling to the believers; for these statements are in accord, and agreement, and conjunction with the doctrine of Nestorius; who was condemned for cleaving asunder and dividing the Incarnation of our Lord Jesus Christ, in respect of natures, and persons, and properties, and names, and operations; who also interpreted the words of Scripture to mean two (natures), which are not contained in the Confession of Faith of the three hundred and eighteen. For they declared that the only-begotten Son of God, Who is of the same Nature with the Father, came down, and became incarnate, and was made man; and suffered, and rose again, and ascended to Heaven; and shall come to judge the quick and the dead. And natures, and persons, and properties were not mentioned by them, nor did they divide them. But they confessed the divine and the human properties to be of One by the dispensation.

" Accordingly, I do not agree with the transactions of Chalcedon, because I find in them divisions and cleavage of the dispensation.

" And now, O victorious king, receive me, for I am speaking this confidently on behalf of the truth; that your Highness may prosper as on earth, so also in Heaven. And accept this my petition with goodwill, for in this letter from the West there runs confusion likely to cause stumbling; for it cleaves asunder the dispensation. And I pray that this letter may be annulled, so that God Christ may be purely [1] confessed by all tongues that He truly suffered in the flesh; while He remained without suffering in His Godhead, which He has with the Father and the Spirit.

" And I entreat and [2] beseech your honoured Majesty that

---

[1] ܐܝܟܢܐܝܬ, MS., ܐܝܐܝܬ, L.   [2] ܘܡܬܟܫܦ, MS., ܘܡܬܟܫܦ, L.

orders be sent to all men to hold [1] the Confession of the faith, as defined by our three hundred and eighteen fathers, which, in a few words, declares the truth to all the Churches, and puts an end to every heresy and all false doctrine and causes of stumbling; and which itself stands in no need of correction. But the matters in this letter which appear to me to require correction" (which are not repeated) "are these—" and because they are given at length with quotations refuting them, we do not repeat [2] them here, lest the reader should be wearied. For believers may find, in all places, the censures upon them that have been made by wise men. In the first place, by Dioscorus; and after him, by this Timothy; and after him by Peter; and by Akhs'noyo of Hierapolis; and by the learned Severus, the chief priest of Antioch, in his work *Against the Grammarian*; [3] and by Cosmas; and by Simeon of L'gino; and by the letter of the Alexandrines.

CHAPTER VII

THE SEVENTH CHAPTER TELLS WHAT THE OTHER BISHOPS WROTE TO LEO; AND HOW [4] THEY ALL (WITH THE EXCEPTION OF AMPLILOCHIUS OF SIDE) MADE KNOWN THEIR VIEWS IN CONFORMITY WITH THE DOCTRINE OF THE SYNOD, AND AGREED TO IT

But Timothy wrote confidently, as above, concerning the letter of Leo and the Synod of Chalcedon. The other bishops, however, the Metropolitans of every place, having received the encyclical letter of the king, testified to what was done by them in Chalcedon, to which also they agreed. [5] And they censured the consecration of Timothy, whom Leo,

---

[1] Imperfectly written in MS. ܠܐܚܝܕ. "Mich. has 'that they hold fast,' reading ܠܐܚܝܕܘܢ; but it is hard to explain the corruption in the text" (Brooks).

[2] Read ܙܩܘܡܠܝܢ for ܙܩܘܡܝܢ.

[3] See bk. 7, ch. 10.

[4] Read ܐܝܟ? for ܐܝܟ.

[5] Mansi, vol. vii. p. 539 ff.

the bishop of Rome, even named "the Antichrist."[1]   They say, indeed, that the other bishops also were influenced to write thus by the instigation of Anatolius, and his letters to them.

But[2] Amphilochius of Side alone showed truth and uprightness without fear.   And he and the bishops of his province wrote confidently, censuring and reviling the transactions of the Synod, and the doctrine of the Tome, telling of the violence and partiality there displayed, and confirming their statements by proofs and copious testimony from the Holy Scriptures and the Fathers.   He, moreover, besought the king that the transactions of Chalcedon should be cancelled, since they were a cause of stumbling to the believers, as well as of confusion.[3]   Nevertheless, he censured the consecration of Timothy, and said that it had been done in an uncanonical manner.   This man, indeed, who testified thus confidently and truly to the king respecting the Synod, fell into danger from the Nestorian party, in consequence of the malignity and treachery which they exhibited towards him ; for he was the only one of all the bishops who had the courage to revile the Synod with its transactions, and also the Tome. But Aspar, who was general[4] at that time, although he was an Arian, pleaded and begged for him that such a truthful priest should not be exposed to danger.   And thus, indeed, Amphilochius was delivered from danger.

But[5] in his endeavour to correct the evils which were done in the days of Marcian, the king was hindered by the bishops.   And by their means also Timothy was condemned to banishment in Gangra.   Now that Anatolius of Constantinople was the one to instigate the bishops to make these statements to the king in the Encyclicals, you will learn from his letter to the king which I have written below.

---

[1] Leo, Ep. 156, ch. ii.

[2] Evag. ii. 10.

[3] Read ‏ܩܘܠܬܐ‏‎? for ‏ܩܘܠܬܐ‏‎.

[4] ‏ܣܛܪܛܝܠܛܣ‏‎, *i.e.* στρατηλάτης.

[5] Evag. ii. 11.

CHAPTER VIII

THE EIGHTH CHAPTER, INDEED, TELLS ABOUT THE LETTER
OF ANATOLIUS TO THE KING ABOUT THE SYNOD,
SAYING THAT HE HAD INFLUENCED THE BISHOPS BY
WRITING [1]

"Anatolius, bishop of Constantinople, to the believing
and Christ-loving king, victorious Augustus, Leo the emperor.
It is a subject of prayer with me, Christ-loving and believing king," etc.   And a little further on he says: "Those
audacious acts which have been committed in Alexandria, do
not suffer me to remain silent.   But, as becomes one holding
the priesthood of this your royal city, being attached to the
peaceable will of your Majesty, which desires that the canons
of the Fathers should not be despised, but that the laws
should be maintained, I have testified thus to the pious chief
priest Leo and the chaste Metropolitans of your dominion.
And I weep for the canons which have been despised by the
wicked deeds of Timothy; since the records [2] sent to your
Majesty respecting him declare that he has trampled upon the
laws of the Church and of the world; and that he has loved
vainglory, according to the saying of Scripture, that 'the
wicked man is a despiser, even when he is falling into the
depth of evils.'"[3]

And the rest of his letter will be understood [4] from this
specimen; how [5] he was the cause of the letters sent by the
bishops to the emperor, in which they agreed to the transaction of the Synod.   But many senators and citizens, having
learned this respecting Anatolius, withdrew from his communion.

---

[1] Mansi, vol. vii. p. 537.

[2] ‎ܠܐܘܦܘܡܢܐ‎, *i.e.* ὑπομνήματα.

[3] Prov. xviii. 3 (LXX).

[4] Read ‎ܡܣܬܟܠܢ‎ for ‎ܡܣܬܟܠܐ‎.

[5] MS. ‎ܗܘܝ‎, not ‎ܗܘܝܘ‎.

CHAPTER IX

THE NINTH CHAPTER TELLS ABOUT THE BANISHMENT OF
TIMOTHY, AND THE EVENTS WHICH HAPPENED AT HIS
DEPARTURE FROM ALEXANDRIA

But, because the king's order [1] respecting the departure of
Timothy was sent to Alexandria at this time, the general [2]
was consequently much distressed, and felt himself constrained
to suffer many things rather than that the city should lose
such a priest. .However, since he saw [3] the slaughter which
was threatened against him by the Proterian party, and
especially as the members of that party had taken refuge [4]
with the king, and were aided by all the bishops; this same
Stilas the general [5] thought it well that he and the bishop
should betake themselves for refuge to the Baptistery of the
great Church.   And he did so for two reasons: one was,
that they themselves might be preserved from harm; and
the other, that they might not be the cause of the loss of
life and of slaughter.

But when Timothy had taken refuge at the font of the
Baptistery, the clergy of the Proterian party paid no regard
either to the priesthood, or to the chastity, or to the age, or
to the ascetic life, or to the labours of the man, or indeed to
the place where he had taken refuge; but with an armed force,
they snatched the chief priest from the very font, and dragged
him away.   And, as soon as the report of this [6] reached
the people, they killed [7] more than ten thousand there to rescue
the priest from them.   However, after the Romans had slain
many of the Alexandrians, the man was taken; and he went
out across Egypt to Palestine, that his journey might be along
the sea of Phœnice.

[1] ‎ܟܪܘܣܛܓܡܐ, *i.e.* προσταγμα.   [2] ‎ܐܣܛܪܐܛܓܘܣ, *i.e.* στρατηγός.

[3] ‎ܗܘܐ, MS., not ‎ܠܗܘܐ, as L.   [4] ‎ܐܬܓܘܣܘ, MS., ‎ܐܬܓܘܣܘ, L.

[5] Liberat. 15 and 16.   [6] ‎ܗܕܐ, MS., not ‎ܗܘܐ, as L. prints.

[7] Perhaps we should read ‎ܘܐܬܩܛܠ, and trans. "more than ten thousand
persons were killed there in the attempt to rescue," etc.

But when the cities and the inhabitants of Palestine and the seacoast[1] heard it, they came to him to be sanctified, and that the sick among them gain healing for their diseases through the grace of God which was attached to his person ; and they snatched torn pieces of stuff from his garments, that they might have them as charms to protect them from evil.

And when he arrived at Berytus, Eustace the bishop urged the citizens there to receive him with public honour.

And he begged Timothy, upon his entry into the city, to pray for it ; and the latter stood in the midst of the city and made supplications and prayers to God for it, and blessed it.

But Auxonius, the brother of Eustace, who was at that time an interpreter of the law, acting upon the advice of his brother, spent the whole night with Timothy, speaking earnestly about the faith, and against Nestorius. And during the whole of his long discourse Timothy was a silent listener ; but when at length Auxonius, after many words, ceased speaking, Timothy said to him, " Who could persuade me that these three fingers should write upon the paper of Chalcedon ? " And, upon hearing this, Auxonius was very sad, and began to weep. Then Timothy, encouraging both him and his brother Eustace, who afterwards joined[2] them, said, " Attach yourselves to me, and let us contend together for the faith, and let us prevail ; so that either we shall recover our bishoprics, or else we shall be driven into banishment by our enemies, and live a sincere life with God." And he alleged as an excuse the dedication of a church, a great temple which Eustace built and named " Anastasia "; and Timothy said, " Shall we wait for the dedication of an earthly temple ? But if you obey me, then we shall hold our festival in the heavenly Jerusalem ? "

And Timothy received the same kind of honour along the way, until he reached Gangra.

---

[1] ܩܘܣܛܠ, *i.e.* πάραλος, the province of Phœnice Maritima.

[2] Read ܐܘܠܣܝ for ܐܘܠܣܝܗ.

CHAPTER X

THE TENTH CHAPTER EXPLAINS ABOUT ANOTHER TIMO-
THY, WHO WAS THE BISHOP OF THE PROTERIAN PARTY,
AND WAS CALLED SALOPHACIOLUS[1]

But[2] the members of the Proterian party, because of the order[3] of the king and the governors of the cities who were obedient to the command, elected one of themselves, also called Timothy Salophaciolus,[1] and placed him upon the episcopal throne. He was a man who sought popularity; [4] and was soft in his manners and feeble in his actions; as events, indeed, proved.

For when all the people of the city forsook the church, and assembled, along with the believing clergy, in the monasteries, he was neither enraged nor distressed. But when his own clergy were anxious to restrain the people by means of the Roman armed force, he would not allow them.

Now it happened that a certain woman met him carrying her child, who had just been baptized by the believers, and was being borne along in triumph according to the usual custom. And his attendants were very indignant at it. But he ordered them to bring her to him quietly; and he took up the child and kissed him, and he urged the mother to take whatever she wanted. And he said to his own followers, "Let us and these Christians, each as he thinks right, believe and honour our Lord." Nevertheless, though he did all this, he could not appease the rage of the citizens; and because he dreaded the fate of Proterius, he would not walk abroad without the Romans. And just in proportion as the people loved Timothy the believer, so they hated[5] this man. And they never ceased imploring and entreating the king that Timothy should be restored to them from banishment.

---

[1] ܩܘܠܝܣ ܡܠܛܪܘܝ, see note 1, p. 62.   [2] Liberat. 16.

[3] ܩܪܡܣܛܓܪܐ, *i.e.* πρόσταγμα.

[4] ܕܡܠܛܝܩܘܣ, *i.e.* δημοτικὸς.

[5] ܣܢܝܘ, MS., not ܣܢܝ, as L. prints.

But they say of this Salophaciolus that he tried hard to persuade the Alexandrians to hold communion with him; and, as if rejecting the Synod, he wrote in the Diptych the name of Dioscorus. And when Leo of Rome heard it, he excommunicated him.

And on one occasion, when he went up to Constantinople, he had a great dispute with Gennadius, the successor of Anatolius, in the king's presence. And he said, "I do not accept the Synod which would make your see the next in importance to Rome, and cast contempt upon the honour of my see." And the king laughed when he saw them, and heard the two priests contending for the pre-eminence.

And he wrote to tell about this dispute to the bishop of Rome; who at that time replied in writing, that the privileges of each see should be restored according to their original constitution. And he made this known to the king.

So much about this Timothy Salophaciolus.

CHAPTER XI

THE ELEVENTH CHAPTER TELLS HOW TIMOTHY WAS DRIVEN FROM GANGRA TO CHERSON, IN CONSEQUENCE OF THE HATRED WHICH THE PARTY OF CHALCEDON ENTERTAINED AGAINST HIM

But Gennadius of Constantinople and his adherents did not desist from their persecution of Timothy, even when he was in banishment. For they persuaded the king to command his removal from Gangra to Cherson, which is a region inhabited by barbarous and uncivilised men.

But the bishop of Gangra heartily consented to this, on account of the envy which he felt towards the believing, virtuous, and miracle-working Timothy, the friend of the poor; because he used to receive gifts from the believers of Alexandria and Egypt and other places, and to make liberal distribution for the relief of the needy.

And having embarked on board ship, and launched upon

the sea, though he was tossed in the midst of the winter, yet he reached Cherson without danger. And when the inhabitants of the country learned the reason, they were filled with admiration for him; and they became followers of his faith, and submitted themselves to his authority.

But the hatred which the Nestorian party entertained against him was caused by his diligence in continually writing reproaches and censures upon the Synod and the Tome, and sending them forth on all sides; thereby encouraging the believers. And he corroborated his words from the Holy Scriptures, and the doctors of the Church, from the time of Christ's preaching even to his own day.

In consequence of these writings, those persons who understood the matter left Gennadius of Constantinople and joined in communion with Acacius the presbyter and Master of the Orphans, the brother of Timocletus the composer, who joined the believers, and strenuously opposed the Nestorians; and he also set verses[1] to music, and they used to sing them. And the people were delighted with them, and they flocked in crowds to the Orphan Hospital.[2]

But the king ordered that the blessed Mary should be proclaimed and written in the book of life as *Theotokos*, on account of Martyrius of Antioch, who was an avowed Nestorian, and would not now consent to teach these things, who also was deposed.

But Gregory of Nyssa (a believing and virtuous man, the namesake of the learned Gregory) was summoned by the king to put an end to the doctrine of the Nestorians at that time; as some monks went on a mission to the king about the matter of Martyrius. And Gennadius[3] had died; and Acacius, the Master of the Orphan Hospital,[4] was appointed as his successor.

And a promise had been made by the latter that he would put an end to the Tome of Leo, and the Synod of Chalcedon,

---

[1] Read ܡܟܬܒܬܐ for ܡܟܬܒܐ.

[2] ܐܪܦܢܘܛܪܘܦܝܘܢ, i.e. 'Ορφανοτροφεῖον.   [3] Evag. ii. 11.

[4] ܐܪܦܢܘܛܪܦܘܣ, i.e. 'Ορφανοτρόφος.

and the innovations and additions which had been imposed
upon the faith in it.

CHAPTER XII

THE TWELFTH CHAPTER TELLS ABOUT THE EUTYCHIAN-
ISTS, ISAIAH, BISHOP OF HERMOPOLIS, AND THEOPHILUS,
A PRESBYTER OF ALEXANDRIA; AND ABOUT THE
LETTER WRITTEN BY TIMOTHY RESPECTING THEM, IN
WHICH HE EXPOSED THEIR ERRORS

The affairs of the Church of the royal city, indeed, were
in the condition described above.

But Timothy, when in banishment, wrote not alone against
the Nestorians, but also against the Eutychianists. And this
appears from his letters to Alexandria and Palestine, against
those who hold the opinions of Eutyches, and do not confess
Christ to be of the same nature with us in the flesh as well as
of the same Nature with the Father in the Godhead.

And it so happened that the Eutychianists, Isaiah, bishop
of Hermopolis, and Theophilus, a presbyter of Alexandria,
were sojourning in the royal city with the desire of making
money. And they circulated a report that Timothy also was
of their way of thinking. And when he heard this he wrote
a letter dealing with the doctrines of Eutyches and Nestorius,
which he sent to Constantinople signed with his own signature.
And when[1] the bearers of this letter became known, they were
treated by these men with contempt; and were exposed to
danger, because he called the followers of Isaiah " deceivers."
Whereupon he sent again another letter respecting them, confirming it by quotations from the fathers. And it was to the
following effect :—

THE LETTER OF TIMOTHY

" Our Lord and God, Jesus Christ, in order that He might
redeem us and set us free from the dominion of Satan, and

---

[1] For ܩ read ܩ; and for the defective word ܗܝ‑‑‑‑ܐܝܠܡ read ܗܝ‑‑‑‑ܐܝܠܡ.

6

make us meet for the blessings of Heaven, appointed for us, through the holy fathers, the law of those things which are pleasing to Himself. And He gave commandment that no man, thinking to honour, should insult the Merciful One; but that He should receive the dispensation for our redemption. And He said, ' Turn not aside to the right hand or to the left, but walk in the way of the kingdom.'[1] And again He said, ' Be not righteous overmuch, nor count thyself too wise, lest thou fall into error. And do not fall deeply into error, nor be stubborn, lest thou die before the time';[2] the meaning of which is, lest the evil one should infuse into thee anything contrary to My commandments, and set a stumbling-block for thee on the way of the kingdom along which thou art walking, and slay thee. For he said, ' In the way wherein I walked they laid snares[3] for me.'[4] Take heed, therefore, to thyself,[5] and do not turn aside nor depart from the way of the kingdom. For this is the desire of the evil one, who, if thou shalt fill up much wickedness, will meet thee, and thou wilt fall into danger.

" For, suppose a man seeking to enter a city surrounded by water; if he attempt to pass through on foot he will sink and be drowned in its depth; if, on the other hand, he be afraid to pass over, he cannot enter the city at all; but if there be a convenient[6] ford, and he try to cross over by it, then he can enter the city. In like manner also we being anxious to enter Jerusalem, which is above, if we do not follow the Law of God, which we have learned from the holy doctors, cannot indeed stand upon the rock of our leader Peter Kepho, the true faith.[7] ' For thou shalt indeed be called Kepho, and upon this rock I will build My Church; and the bars of Sheol shall not prevail against it.'[8] Let no man be so led astray by the evil one as to imagine that he can subvert the true faith; and if he is contending, it is against his own soul

---

[1] Num. xx. 17; Prov. iv. 27.

[2] A free quotation from Eccles. vii. 16–18.

[3] ܩܝܣܐ, MS., ܩܢܝܣܐ, L.

[4] Ps. cxlii. (Syr. cxli.) 3.

[5] ܐܠܕ, MS., ܐܠܕ, L.

[6] ܠܥܒܪܐ, MS., not ܠܥܒܪܐ, as L.

[7] ܗܝܡܢܘܬܐ, MS., not ܗܝܡܢܘܬܗ, as L.

[8] John i. 42; Matt. xvi. 18.

that he contends; but nothing can overcome the faith. And this is the meaning of the expression, 'The bars [1] of Sheol shall not prevail against it.' Wherefore, if any man stand not upon the truth of the faith, but is righteous overmuch, when he thinks to confer honour, he rather offers insult; but if he accept the Law of the Lord, which has been laid down for us by the saints, he survives visions of death and the verge of Sheol. For we have learned [2] that apart from the standard of the faith, we cannot please God.

"These things I have written, because I have heard that some persons are contentious, and are not obedient unto the Law of the Lord which has been laid down for us by the saints; and which declares that our Lord, by His incarnation, was of the same nature with us in the flesh which He took from us, which doctrine they have even rejected if they are not of this mind.

"Accordingly, let no one, thinking to honour God, insult His mercy by refusing to obey the doctrine of the holy fathers, who have declared that our Lord Jesus Christ is of the same nature with us in the flesh, and is one with His flesh. For I have heard also the holy apostle teaching and saying, 'Forasmuch as the children were partakers of the flesh and the blood, He also (partook of the same) in like manner; that by means of death He might destroy the power of death, who is Satan; and might deliver all who were held in the fear of death, and were subject to bondage, that so they might live for ever. For He did not take (the nature) from angels, but He took it from the seed of Abraham. And it was fitting that He should be made in all points like unto His brethren, and that He should be a merciful priest, and faithful with God; and that He should make reconciliation for the sins of the people. For in that He suffered being tempted, He is able to succour them that are tempted.' [3] For this expression, 'He was made like us in all points,' teaches all who desire to be meet for the blessings of heaven and to be redeemed, that they must confess [4] the Incarnation of our Lord Jesus Christ as being from Mary the

---

[1] ܡܘܟ̈ܠܐ, *i.e.* μοχλοί.   [2] ܝܠܦܢ, MS., ܝܠܦܝܢ, L.
[3] Heb. ii. 14–18.   [4] Read ܕ for ܘ before ܢܘܕܘܢ.

holy Virgin and *Theotokos*; Christ Who was of the same nature with her and with us in the flesh, and is of the same Nature with the Father in His Godhead.

"For the fathers anathematised, and we also agreeing with them anathematise in like manner, any who do not hold their doctrines.

"But we have, moreover, in our letter added some quotations from them, attesting the truth of this doctrine :—

"OF ATHANASIUS [1]

"'For this, indeed, the apostle writes expressly, that, "other foundation can no man lay (than that which is laid),[2] even Christ; but let every man take heed how he builds."[3] Now it is necessary that a foundation such as this should be in conformity and likeness with those who are built upon it. God the Word, because He is the Word and the only-begotten one, has no peers who could be the sons of the Godhead in the same manner as He. But inasmuch as He became man, of our nature, and clothed Himself with our body, we are of the same nature with Him. Accordingly, in the matter of our humanity He is the foundation; so that we may be precious stones, and be built upon Him, and be a temple for the indwelling of the Holy Spirit.

"'For, in like manner as He is the foundation and we are the stones built upon Him, so also He is the vine and we are the branches, hanging from Him and in Him; not indeed in the nature of the Godhead, for that would not be possible, but in the manhood. Now it is fitting that the branches should be like the vine, because we also are like Him in that body which He took from us.

"'And[4] we confess that He is the Son of God, and God in the Spirit, and man in the flesh. And there are not two natures in one Son, one to be worshipped and the other

---

[1] *Orat.* ii., *contra Arian.* 74.

[2] The words ܣܛܪ ܡܢ ܗܕܐ ܕܣܝܡܐ must have dropped out of the MS.

[3] 1 Cor. iii. 11, 12.

[4] De Incarn. Dei Verbi (Migne, *Patr. Græc.* vol. xxviii. p. 25).

unworthy of worship; but there is one Nature of God the
Word, Who became incarnate, and Who, along with the flesh
in which He is clothed, is to be worshipped with one worship.'

"OF THE SAME, IN HIS LETTER TO EPICTETUS [1]

"' Now there are many, hiding themselves and blushing,
who imagine that, if we affirm the body of our Lord to be
from Mary, we introduce a fourth Person into the Trinity;
but if we affirm [2] the body to be of the same Nature with the
Word, the Trinity thereby remains without the addition of
any foreign element. While if we maintain with respect to
His body that it is human; then since the body is foreign
to the Nature of God, when the Word is in it, there must of
necessity be a Quaternity instead of a Trinity, in consequence
of the addition of the body.

"' When they talk in this way they do not consider how
their own argument breaks down and fails. For even if they
deny the body to be from Mary, they, no less than those who
hold a distinct body,[3] also seem to hold a Quaternity. For
in like manner as the Son is of the same Nature with the
Father, and is not the Father but the Son in Person, yet being
of the same Nature with the Father; so also, if the body is of
the same Nature with the Word, it is not the Word, and since
there is another, the Trinity, even according to their showing,
is found to be a Quaternity.

"' But the true, indivisible and perfect Trinity can never
receive any addition. What then must be the mind of these
persons, and how can they be Christians who hold that there
is another besides Him who is God?'

"OF THE SAME, FROM THE SAME LETTER [4]

"' The body of our Redeemer, derived from Mary, was in
reality and truth human in nature, because it was like our body;

---

[1] Athan. ad Epict. 8, 9.   [2] Read ܐܟܝܬܗ for ܐܟܝܕܗ.
[3] This is the best I can make of it, the text may be corrupt.
[4] *Ibid.* 7.

since Mary is our sister, we being all descended from our father Adam.'

"OF JULIUS OF ROME [1]

"' And there is no change whatsoever in the Divine Nature, for It is not subject to diminution or increase. And when He says, "Glorify Me," that is the voice of the body, and is spoken concerning the body. For glory was affirmed with respect to His whole Being, for He is all one. And by this the " glory which I had with Thee before the world was," [2] He testified concerning His Godhead that It is always glorified, for such glory properly belongs to It, even though this affirmation was made equally concerning His whole Being. So in the Spirit He is of the same Nature with the Father invisibly ; and since the body also was united to Him in His Nature, it is equally included under the name. And again, also, His Godhead is comprehended under the name because It is united to our nature, and the nature of the body is not converted into the nature of God by the union and conjunction of the name of the nature. Just as the nature of the Godhead was not changed by the conjunction of the human body, and by the appellation of a body of our nature.'

"OF THE SAME, FROM HIS LETTER TO DIONYSIUS [3]

"' They indeed, who confess that the God of heaven became incarnate from the Virgin, and that He being joined to His flesh was one, give themselves needless trouble in contending with the maintainers of the opposite view, who affirm (as I have heard) that there are two natures. Since John proved our Lord to be one by saying, " The Word became flesh." [4] And Paul by saying, " There is one Lord Jesus Christ, through Whom are all things." [5] Now, if He Who was born from the Virgin was named Jesus, and He it is through Whom were all things ; He is one nature because He

---

[1] Migne, *Patr. Lat.* vol. viii. p. 874.   [2] John xvii. 5.
[3] Migne, *Patr. Lat.* vol. viii. p. 929.   [4] John i. 14.
[5] 1 Cor. vi. 8.

is one Person, Who is not divided into two.   For the nature of
the body was not separate, nor yet did the Nature of the Godhead remain distinct at the Incarnation ; but just as man,
composed of body and soul, is one nature, so also He, Who
is in the likeness of men, is one Jesus Christ.'

"OF GREGORY THE MIRACLE-WORKER [1]

" ' Whosoever says that Christ appeared in the world in
phantasy, and does not confess Him to have come in the
body, as it is written : let him be accursed.

" ' Whosoever says concerning the body of Christ that it
was without soul [2] and without mind, and does not confess
His humanity to be perfect, He being the same, according as
it is written : let him be accursed.

" ' Whosoever says that Christ took a part of man only,
and does not confess Him to have been in all points like as
we are, yet without sin : let him be accursed.

" ' Whosoever says that Christ was liable to change and [3]
variation, and does not confess Him to be unchanged in Spirit,
and uncorrupt in the flesh, as it is written : let him be accursed.

" ' Whosoever says that Christ was perfect man separately
(and God the Word separately), [4] and does not confess Him to
be one Lord Jesus Christ : let him be accursed.

" ' Whosoever says that there was One Who suffered and
Another Who did not suffer, and does not confess God the
Word, Himself impassible, to have suffered in His flesh, as it
is written : let him be accursed.

" ' Whosoever says that there was One Who existed before
the worlds, the Son of God, and another, who at length came
into being ; and does not confess Him to be the same Who was
before the worlds and at length came into being, according as it
is written, " Christ yesterday and to-day " : [5] let him be accursed.

" ' Whosoever says that Christ was of the seed of a man in
like manner as the rest of mankind, and does not confess Him

---

[1] Migne, *Patr. Græc.* vol. x. p. 1128 ff.   [2] ܠܒ݂ܫܐ, MS., ܠܒܫܐ, L.
[3] ܗܟܘ, MS., which L. omits.   [4] Supplied from the Greek.
[5] Heb. xiii. 8.   This quotation is not in the Greek.

to have been incarnate, and to have become man, of the Holy Spirit and also of the Virgin Mary, of the seed of the house of David, as it is written : let him be accursed.

" ' Whosoever says that the body of Christ was of the same nature as His Godhead, and does not confess Him to be God before all worlds, Who "emptied Himself and took upon Him the form of a servant," [1] as it is written: let him be accursed.

" ' Whosoever says that the body of Christ was not a created body, and does not confess the uncreated God the Word to have received incarnation and manhood from created man, as it is written : let him be accursed.

" ' For how can one affirm the body of Christ to be uncreated ; since that which is not created is not susceptible of suffering, or wounds, or contact.   But Christ Himself, after His resurrection from the dead, showed His disciples the prints of the nails and the wound of the spear, and afforded them bodily contact with Himself.   And although the doors were shut He entered, that He might display the power of His Godhead and the reality of His body.[2]   For the flesh which comes into being after lapse of time, cannot be said to be of the same nature with the eternal Godhead.[3]   For whatsoever in nature and property is incapable of change is of the same nature.

" ' And [4] He is the true incorporeal God who appeared in the flesh, a perfect Being ; He is not two persons nor two natures.   For we do not worship Four, God, and the Son of God, and a man, and the Holy Spirit ; but, on ·the contrary, we anathematise those who act so wickedly, and who would place man in the glory of God.   But we hold that God the Word became man for the sake of our redemption, and that He took òur likeness upon Him, and that He who came in our likeness is in His true Nature the Son of God, but in the flesh a man, our Lord Jesus Christ.' [5]

---

[1] Phil. ii. 7.   [2] Luke xxiv. 36–43 ; John xx. 19–27.

[3] MS. has ? before ܣܘܩܠܛܣܩ, which L. omits.

[4] Migne, *Patr. Græc.* vol. x. p. 1117.   Here Mich. has "OF THE SAME."

[5] This is only an attempt at translating the sentence ; a comparison with the Greek shows that the text is corrupt.

" OF BASIL OF CÆSAREA [1]

" ' That which is made is not of the same nature as its maker, but that which is begotten is of the same essence as its begetter. ·Accordingly, that which is created and that which is born are not one and the same.' And again, ' The children have the same nature as the parent, even though he that was born has come into being in a different fashion. For Abel, who was born as the result of copulation, was in no respect different from Adam who was not born, but was formed.' And again, ' If they who are different in the manner of their creation are different also in their essential being, then men must be unlike one another in nature. For there is one creation of Adam, who was formed out of the earth ; and another creation of Eve, who was made from a rib ; and another of Abel, who was from copulation ; and another of Him Who was from Mary, who was from a virgin alone. And, indeed, the same might be said with respect to birds and beasts.'

" OF GREGORY, HIS BROTHER [2]

" ' The nature, indeed, of those who are begotten must of necessity be like their begetters.'

" OF GREGORY OF NAZIANZUM [3]

" ' Now these are generally accepted doctrines, that He Who was exalted far above us, for our sake took our qualities upon Him and became man ; not that through the body He should thenceforth be limited to the body, for He is not so limited, since His Nature is infinite ; but that He might sanctify man by His body He became as leaven to the whole lump, and drew it to Himself. And him who was guilty he released from his guilt. He was, for our sake, in all points like as we are, sin only excepted, in body, soul, mind,

---

[1] Migne, *Patr. Græc.* vol. xxix. pp. 673, 680, 681.
[2] *Ibid.* vol. xlv. p. 601.
[3] The source of this quotation we are not able to find.

of which the ordinary mortal man is composed. He Who
manifested Himself was God in respect of His spiritual being,
but human in respect of Adam and the Virgin from whom
He was derived ; from the former as His ancestor, but from
the latter who was His mother according to the (natural) law,
and who gave Him birth in a manner superior to nature, and
not after the (natural) law.'

"OF JULIUS OF ROME [1]

" ' But, again, with respect to the dispensation of our
Redeemer in the flesh, we believe that God the Word remaining unchanged, became flesh, with the object of renewing
mankind.   And He, being the true Son of God by the eternal
generation, became man by the birth from the Virgin.   And
He, Who is perfect God in His Godhead of the same Nature
with the Father, and also perfect man of the same bodily
nature with mankind by birth from the Virgin, is one and
the same.   But whosoever says that Christ had a body from
heaven, or that His body was of His nature: let him be accursed.

" ' Whosoever denies that the flesh of our Lord is from the
Virgin, of the same nature as ours : let him be accursed.

" ' Whosoever holds concerning our Lord and Saviour
Who was from the Holy Spirit and from Mary the Virgin in
the flesh, that He was incomposite and without consciousness,
and without reason, and without mind : let him be accursed.

" ' Whosoever shall dare to say with respect to Christ that
He suffered in His Godhead, and not in the flesh, as it is
written : let him be accursed.

" ' Whosoever would separate and divide our Lord and
Saviour, and say that God the Word is one Son, and the
man whom He took another, and does not confess Him to
be one and the same : let him be accursed.'

" OF JOHN CHRYSOSTOM

" ' He Who transcends all our conceptions and surpasses

______
[1] Not in any of the extant works of Pseudo-Julius.

all our thoughts, and is exalted above angels and above all
intelligent powers, was content to become man ; and He took
flesh, which was formed from the earth and the clay. And
this He did by entering the Virgin's womb, where He was
carried for the period of nine months ; and after His birth
He sucked[1] milk ; and indeed He suffered all things per-
taining to the human lot. Why[2] was He called a Table ?
Because when I eat the mystery which is upon Him, I am
refreshed. Why was He called a House ? Because I dwell
in Him. Why was He called an Indweller ? Because I am
His temple. Why was He called a Head ? Because I am
His member. When[3] He set His love upon a harlot, what
did He do ? He did not call her up ; for He would not bring
a harlot up to Heaven. But He came down ; as she was not
able to ascend to Him, He descended to her. And coming
to her hovel, He Himself was not ashamed ; and He found her
drunk. And how did He come ? Not openly in His own
Nature ; but He became like the harlot herself in nature
though not in will ; lest, when she saw Him, she might be confounded through terror and flee. He came to her having
become man. And how did He become man ? He was conceived in the womb, and He grew gradually.'

"OF THE SAME[4]

" ' This is the day on which the Eternal One was born and
became man, a thing which never took place before, though
He did not change from being God, for it was not by a change
of the Godhead that He became man ; neither from a human
original by growth did He become God ; but the impassible
Word suffered no change in His Nature by becoming flesh.
He that is seated upon the throne high and lifted up, was laid
in the manger. He that is simple and without body, and
cannot be touched, was embraced by human hands. He

---

[1] ܣܠܩ, MS., ܣܢܩ, L.

[2] *De Capt. Eutrop.* 8. Here, and at the beginning of the next quotation, Mich.
has " OF THE SAME," which must therefore have dropped out of our text (Brooks).

[3] *Ibia.* 11.

[4] This quotation does not occur in either of the extant sermons on the Nativity.

Who severs the chains of sin, was wrapped in swathing-
bands.'

"OF ATHANASIUS [1]

"'If any man teaches doctrine contrary to the Holy
Scriptures, and says that the Son of God is One, and
he who is man from Mary is another, who became a son by
grace as we; so that there would be *Two* dwelling in the
Deity; [2] One, of the same Nature with God, and the other
who became so by grace, the man from Mary: and whosoever,
further, says that the body of our Lord was from above, and
not from the Virgin Mary; or that the Godhead was converted into flesh; or that It was confounded or changed;
or that the Godhead of our Lord suffered; or that the body
of Christ, inasmuch as it is from men, should not be worshipped, and not that the body is to be worshipped because
it is that of our Lord and God;—the man who asserts these
things we anathematise, for we obey the apostle when he says,
"Whosoever preaches to you a gospel different from that which
we have preached to you, let him be accursed."'[3]

"OF BISHOP AMBROSE

"'He is the same Persón Who speaks, though not always
in the same manner. But He had regard in it at one time to
the glory of God, and at another time to the passions of men.
As God, He teaches divine things, because He is the Word;
and as man, He teaches human things, because He speaks in
our nature.'

"OF THEOPHILUS OF ALEXANDRIA [4]

"'The Word, the living God, the Lord of all, and
Creator of the worlds, did not clothe Himself in a heavenly

[1] Migne, *Patr. Græc.* vol. xxviii. p. 28.

[2] Probably for ܒ̈ܐܠܗܐ we should read ܒܪ ܐܠܗܐ (Gk. υἱὸν Θεοῦ), and transl.
" two dwelling together, One the Son of God, of the same nature," etc.

[3] Gal. i. 8, 9.

[4] Sixth Paschal Letter, Migne, *Patr. Græc.* vol. lxv. p. 60.

body[1] as in some costly substance and come to us, but He displayed in clay[2] the greatness of the skill of His art.   For, when He would restore and renew man who was formed from the clay, He was born as man from the Virgin, who, corresponding to us in all points, sin only excepted, and coming into being by a miracle, shone upon us and blessed our human nature.

" ' However, the first man also came into being in a manner different and distinct from us, as the intercourse and association of man and woman did not minister to his creation. And if they allow, in his case, that he was formed out of the earth by the will of God, no parents having ministered to his birth by the conjunction of male and female ; why do they quarrel with the Incarnation of our Lord and Saviour, which was from the Virgin ?   And when they oppose us in this matter, we ask them whether is it easier that a man should come into being from the earth without parents, or that our Saviour Christ should be born from the Virgin, with flesh, and soul, and consciousness ?   And the first man, indeed, who was from the earth, partook of flesh and blood in all the likeness of humanity ; but our Saviour, by His own power, created and prepared from the Virgin a body for Himself with flesh, and blood, and soul, and consciousness.   And we confess that He consorted with men, even though in His holy Incarnation the sensual intercourse of man and woman had no part.'

" OF THE SAME[3]

" ' Now it was not difficult for God the Word to prepare for Himself a temple from the Virgin's body, for the purpose of our redemption.   For consider, indeed, that God also is never polluted by natural copulation[4] when He creates man ; and how much more then, by His mercy, may He become

---

[1] The Greek οὐρανίου λαβόμενος σώματος shows that for ‫ܟܐܢ‬ we should read ‫ܩܡ ܩܪܝܪ‬ or ‫ܩܡ ܩܢܐ‬.

[2] For ‫ܩܛܝܢܐ‬ read ‫ܩܛܝܢܐ‬ (Gr. πηλῷ), and for ‫ܦܘܪܩܢܐ‬ read ‫ܦܘܪܩܢܐ‬.

[3] This and the latter part of the preceding are probably from the lost part of the fifth Paschal Letter.

[4] For ‫ܐܝܟܐ‬ read ‫ܐܝܟܐ‬.

incarnate from the blood of the Virgin, for the purpose of our redemption.'

" OF CYRIL

" ' So, truly, the *Theotokos* still remained a virgin after giving birth to Christ by a miracle ; and He was partaker, in like manner as we, of flesh and blood, not of His own nature, as the heretics say, but of our nature, according to the saying, " He took the seed of Abraham." ' [1]

" OF THE SAME [2]

" ' We assert that the body of the Word was His own, and not that of some other man separately and distinctly who is held to be different from Christ the Son.   And as the body of each one of us is said to be his own, so also we believe respecting the one Christ.   And although He took the body from our race and our nature, because He was born of the Virgin ; yet it must be held and declared to be His own body. And, since God the Word is the Life in His own Nature, He declared His body to be a life-giving one.   And therefore He became to us a blessing, giving life to all.[3]   And if it be not so, how then is He like us, while yet remaining as He was before, God the Word ?   However, grant to Him that in the unity of the Person His body is not separated, and do not denude Him of His flesh.   And thus I rightly worship one Son, Who is of the same Nature indeed with the Father in the Godhead, but of the same nature with us in the manhood. And as for those who delight to believe this truth, Christ will enlighten their knowledge also of Himself by His mysteries.'

" OF THE SAME

" ' It is right, indeed, for us to say and believe that God the Word, still remaining of the same Nature with God the Father, was sent and became man, of the same nature with us.

---

[1] Heb. ii. 16.   [2] Migne, *Patr. Græc.* vol. lxxvi. p. 372.
[3] The rest is not in the Greek.   Mich. has " OF THE SAME," which must therefore have dropped out of our text (Brooks).

He is and He remains as He is, and by becoming man He
was not changed.   And He was sent to preach deliverance to
the captives and light to the blind.'

"OF THE SAME, FROM HIS LETTER TO SUCCENSUS [1]

" ' They say, if Christ be perfect God and perfect man, and
the same is of the Nature of the Father in the Godhead and
of our nature in the manhood, how [2] is He perfect if His
human nature is not seen? and how is He of our nature if that
actual and self-same nature which is ours be not seen?   The
answer which we have given at the beginning should suffice to
enlighten them.   For if,[3] when speaking of one nature of the
Word, we refrained from saying "incarnate," rejecting the dispensation, their word would be plausible when they ask, " How
can He be perfect in manhood and in Nature?"   But since
our word indeed testifies that He is perfect in manhood and in
Nature by saying that He became flesh, therefore let them
cease from these objections, and not lean upon a broken reed.'

"OF THE SAME

" ' In the might, indeed, of His Godhead He took the hand
of the daughter of Jairus, saying, " Maid, arise." [4]   And [5] He
did not give the command in word [6] merely, and the work was
accomplished according to His own will.   But [7] that we might
believe that His holy body was of the same nature with our
bodies, while it also was glorious, and divine, and raised above
our measure, it being also His own, He wrought in it.   For which
reason, also, He called His own body the " Bread of Life." ' [8]

" And so these fathers and holy men like them have with

---

[1] Cyr. *Ep.* 46. 3.

[2] We must insert ܐܢܫܘܬ ; the Greek is ποῦ τὸ τέλειον.

[3] For ܘܠܩ read ܐܠܘ, Gk. *el.*   [4] Mark v. 41.

[5] Reading ܘܠܩ for ܘܠܩܘ.   [6] ܒܩܪܒܬܐ, L., ܒܩܘܫܬܐ, MS.

[7] Pusey's *Libr. of the Fathers* (Cyr. 5 Tomes, p. 368) ; cf. Migne, *Patr. Græc.* 76,
p. 1429, where, however, the extract begins after this sentence.

[8] John vi. 48.

one consent anathematised every man who is not obedient to their doctrine.

"And I have written to Alexandria, to the clergy, to the monks, to the sisters the virgins in Christ, and to the believing people; and I have sent the letter to you, my dear friends; and that ye may know what I have written, I, Timothy, have marked the salutation with my own handwriting.

"Whosoever does not believe in the doctrine of the holy fathers, in accordance with the tradition of our Lord Jesus Christ: let him be accursed. For it is right for each one of us either to stand fast in the faith and to live in it, or else to die on behalf of it, and to live for evermore.

"My brother Anatolius the presbyter, and Theophilus, and Cyrus, and Christodorus, and Gennadius the deacons, and the members of the brotherhood who are with me, send you their greeting."

The foregoing letter, with the quotations appended thereto, we have written down here. By reading and considering it, lovers of the doctrine will find in it a sufficient refutation of the notion of Nestorius, who holds that there are two Natures in the unity of Christ; and also of the teaching of Eutyches, who does not confess that God the Word became perfect Man, and remained without change God the Word, One Person who became flesh.

And, besides this letter, we have subjoined another explaining the right method of reception in the case of those who repent and turn from heresy.

THE LETTER OF TIMOTHY WHICH HE WROTE TO ALEX-
ANDRIA, AND BY WHICH HE CUT OFF ISAIAH AND
THEOPHILUS FROM COMMUNION WITH THE BELIEVERS

"Timothy to the God-loving bishops, and presbyters, and deacons, and archimandrites, and sisters, and faithful people in the Lord, greeting—

"Inasmuch as Isaiah and Theophilus have been for a long time heretics in secret, whom I admonished by letter, urging

them to agree to the holy doctrine of the fathers, and they
have not been obedient to the letters which I wrote to them
to Constantinople, containing proofs from Scripture, and the
doctors of the Church, that our Lord Jesus Christ was of the
same nature with us in the body; and furthermore they have
shown no respect for my sufferings in being banished from place
to place, but have behaved treacherously towards the bearers
of my letter, and also informed the prefects[1] against them, and
they stirred up others, saying, 'It is a forgery,'[2] even though
they knew my signature which was on the letter. And I
waited a considerable time for them though I knew their
disposition, and they made no reply, either by word of mouth
or in writing. And upon reflection, I thought it right to
send them another letter; so I wrote urging them to come
and confess the true faith. And in my admonition I reminded
them that God does not condemn nor reject those who repent.
And I cited the examples of holy men who sinned and denied
the Lord, but who afterwards repented; and God accepted
their repentance, and accounted them worthy of their former
dignity;[3] such was the case of David, and Peter, and Paul.

" And I wrote to them that in like manner, if they would
repent and confess the body of Christ to be of the same nature
as ours, I would continue to entertain my old esteem and love
for them; and I would maintain them in the honour of their
rank. And they showed no affection for me, but treated me
with contempt.

"And after this I waited four years more for them, without
exposing them by name. And they still persevered in their
disobedience, and showed no sign of repentance, and they
neither received the doctrine of the holy fathers nor me. And
they associated with some heretics who openly deny that our
Lord took a human body, and that He became perfect man
from us. And they creep into houses, and greedily grasp at
gain,[4] which they hold as their god, while they are sojourning
in the royal city. And I wrote to them that they should

---

[1] ܩܦܘܣܝܐ, *i.e.* ὕπαρχοι.   [2] ܦܠܣܘܢ, *i.e.* φάλσον.

[3] ܩܒܠܬܗܘܢ, MS., ܩܒܠܬܗܘܢ, L.

[4] A word has been erased here from the MS.

depart from it, but they would not.   And they continued to lead simple folk astray, and to circulate other rumours respecting me, with the object of doing me great harm.   And being distressed and saddened by them, I was compelled to excommunicate them by their names lest they should cause many to stumble [1] and err.

"And I now give sentence upon Isaiah and Theophilus, who say that the body of the Lord is of His own divine Nature, and not of ours, and who deny His true humanity, thereby cutting themselves off from the fellowship of the holy fathers and mine; that no man henceforth hold communion with them.   For John the evangelist commands, saying, 'My brethren, believe not every spirit, but try the spirits whether they be of God; for indeed, many false prophets have appeared in the world.   And hereby the spirit which is from God is known, every spirit which confesses that Jesus Christ is come in the flesh is of God, and every spirit which does not confess Jesus is not from God.   And this is the spirit of the false Christ.   Because many deceivers have gone forth into the world, who do not confess Jesus Christ to have come in the flesh; this is a deceiver and a false Christ.' [2]   And again, 'If any man comes to you not preaching this doctrine, do not either receive him into the house or greet him, for he that greets him is partaker with his evil deeds.' [3]   And because of the apostle who says, 'Whosoever preaches to you a gospel different from what we have preached to you, let him be accursed.' [4]

"I am clear from their blood and from that of their associates; for I have not ceased to show them, ~~according~~ to the will of God, what is for their good.   For Paul further exhorts us, saying, 'After thou hast warned an heretic once or twice, and he has refused thine admonition, avoid him; since by continuing in his sin he is corrupted and guilty.' [5] But the blessed Dioscorus the Confessor wrote sentiments agreeable to these of the holy fathers, and after the same manner, in his letter to Secundinus." . . . And the letter goes on to say, "Now, I beseech you, brethren, by the

---

[1] ܠܟܫܠܘ, MS., not ܠܟܫܘ, as L.   [2] 1 John iv. 1–3; 2 John 7.
[3] 2 John 10, 11.   [4] Gal. i. 8.   [5] Tit. iii. 10, 11.

Lord Jesus Christ, and by the love of the Spirit, concerning those who repent and turn from the heresy of the *Diphysites*, as I wrote in a letter a year ago, that you, the bishops, and clergy, and other believers, all who are subject to you, help them, and extend the hand to them in the Lord.

"And when anyone is converted let him have one year of repentance, and after that let him be established in his former rank, and his dignity be restored to him. And if there be no believing bishop, let the clergy or the believing bishops, who from any cause happen to be in the country, fill the place in the love of God, even though those who repent are not subject to them in jurisdiction.[1]

"This same order and regulation [2] Cyril and Dioscorus observed of one year's repentance for bishops, presbyters, and deacons; after which they should be established in their former rank.

"Pray for me that God may help me in this conflict; the Lord be with you. Amen!"

Such letters he wrote advising them how they should receive converts from the Proterian party.[3]

And he became so celebrated, even with the people of India, that when their bishop died they, being of the same faith with him, sent a request to him that he would appoint a bishop for them.

But, indeed, the Alexandrians never ceased sending petitions and supplications to the king on his behalf, time after time, and stirring up popular tumult [4] for him. For as soon as they heard of the death of Leo and the succession of Basiliscus, they sent a deputation of certain chosen monks, Paul the Sophist, and James, and Theopompus.

But the chief priests who held office from the Council of Chalcedon until the time of Basiliscus, and the encyclical

---

[1] Reading ܩܘܠܬܐ for ܩܘܠܬܝ.

[2] ܩܘܢܩܐ read ܩܢܘܢܐ (or ܬܘܩܢܐ, Brooks).

[3] Reading ܠܕܝ for ܠܕܐ.

[4] ܐܣܛܣܝܣ, *i.e.* στάσις.

letters which he and Marcus wrote, and up to the reign of Zeno, who became emperor, are as follows :—

Of Rome, Leo, and his successor Hilary.

Of Alexandria, Proterius, who was killed. And his successor was Timothy the Great, who was banished. And until he returned by means of the *Encyclicals*, they appointed another Timothy, called Salophaciolus.

In Constantinople, Anatolius, and his successor Gennadius, who was succeeded by Acacius.

In Ephesus, John, who took the place of Bassian; and Paul, who was banished, and who returned by means of the *Encyclicals*, but was banished again.

In Antioch, Domnus, and his successor was Maximus, and then Martyrius, who was driven out; and after him Julian, who was succeeded by Stephen; and then another Stephen, who was driven out; and Peter, who returned from banishment two or three times.

And in Jerusalem, Juvenalis, and Anastasius his successor.[1]

Now King Leo the emperor died, and there arose after him Basiliscus, and Marcus, and Zeno, who had retired for a little time to the strongholds of Salmon; but he afterwards returned and became emperor, and Basiliscus and Marcus were driven out.[2]

---

[1] The MS. here adds ܡܟܬܒܢܘܬܐ ܕܐܪܒܥܐ, "Fourth Book."

[2] ܐܪܙܘܢܣ, MS., not ܐܪܙܘܢܣ, as L.

BOOK V

THE fifth Book (in its twelve chapters, which are written down distinctly below) tells of Basiliscus and Marcus the Illustrious ;[1] and the encyclical letter which they wrote to the bishops of their dominion, in which also they anathematised the Synod of Chalcedon and the Tome.   For after eighteen years of banishment in Gangra and Cherson, Timothy the Great returned and arrived at Constantinople ; and then he and Paul the Sophist, and James, and Theopompus, his chosen monks, persuaded Basiliscus to write the *Encyclical*.   It also tells about the petition [2] sent by the bishops of Asia, who met at Ephesus and subscribed to the *Encyclical*.

Moreover, it tells about some Eutychian monks then residing at Constantinople, who, along with Zenaia [3] the king's wife, basely conspired against Timothy to have him sent again into banishment.   Whereupon he departed to Ephesus.   And by means of a Synod, which he convened, he reinstated Paul there, and gave him the rights [4] of the Patriarchate that the Synod of Chalcedon had taken away from him, and had given to the royal city, through the flattery and treachery of John, whom they made bishop instead of Bassian.   For the latter resigned, and departed and went into banishment.   Now Timothy was received with much state.   And without any rancour he admitted to his communion the penitents from the Proterian party and from that of Timothy Salophaciolus, who was driven out [5] before him by the king's command.

---

[1] ⲟⲟⲟ⳨ⲟⲓⲟⲭⲟ], *i.e.* ἐπιφανέστατος.   "Probably ⳨ⲟⲭⲟ, καῖσαρ, has dropped out" (Brooks).

[2] ⲟⲭⲟⲟ?, *i.e.* δέησις.

[3] In ch. 4 ⳨ⲟⲭⲟⲭⲟ], really " Zenonis."

[4] ⲟⲭ?, *i.e.* δίκας.

[5] ⲭⲟ?∠], read ⲭⲟ?∠].

But this Book also relates the deeds of Acacius in Constantinople, and how he raised an insurrection and rebellion against Basiliscus; and he took possession of the Churches; and he compelled Basiliscus to write the *Antencyclical*, and to deny his former letter.   And the bishops again subscribed to this *Antencyclical*, with the exception of Amphilochius of Side and Epiphanius of Magdolum.   And then Zeno returned and became emperor, and he thrust out Basiliscus, and cancelled every law and enactment which he had made.   And when he was wishing to depose Timothy, the latter died, having retained his See to the end; and Peter, who became bishop in his stead, hid from the threats of Zeno.

Then Timothy Salophaciolus returned, and took possession of the church, and sought for Peter.   But this Book further tells about John the archimandrite, who was sent to Zeno with the petition of the party of Timothy Salophaciolus, praying for an order that, after the death of Timothy, one of their side should be the bishop in Alexandria.   Now this John coveted the see for himself.   And Zeno heard it; and, with the object of trying him, he required from him an oath in the presence of the Senate, and also of Bishop Acacius, that he would not take the bishopric.

And John then returned to Alexandria, bearing an order from the king that, in succession to Timothy, any of his party whom the citizens might desire should be appointed as bishop.   But about the same time it happened that this Timothy Salophaciolus died.   And then John transgressed his oath, and used bribery to get the bishopric there for himself.   But when Zeno heard of it, through the report of eminent believers among the monks there who went up to him and informed him of all the events which had occurred in Alexandria from the time of the Synod, he was greatly moved; and he changed his mind, and wrote a letter called the " Henotikon."

And he gave orders that Peter should return to his place, upon the condition of his receiving the Henotikon, and that John the liar should be deprived.   Whereupon John repaired to Rome, and declared that he had suffered deprivation for the sake of the Synod and the Tome. And then Zeno wrote to the Patriarch there, and exposed John.

But Peter of Antioch also returned and convened a Synod, and received the Henotikon.

And in like manner, Acacius of Constantinople and Martyrius of Jerusalem, the successor of Anastasius.

And they all, except the bishop of Rome, wrote synodical letters, and received Peter of Alexandria into their communion.

But certain zealous monks withdrew from Peter and became separatists, because he had received the Henotikon in which there was no express anathema of the Synod. And Peter thrust them out from their monasteries. Accordingly some of them went up to Zeno and persuaded him to send back with them Cosmas the *Spatharius*, to inquire[1] into their matter; and at another time he sent Arsenius the prefect, and a prolonged dispute ensued.

These, indeed, are the matters which are written expressly in the twelve chapters of this fifth Book, which (so to speak) has been translated[2] from the same Greek History of Zachariah, and has here been written in the Syriac language for the study and instruction of the diligent, that they may learn the events that occurred in former times.

CHAPTER I

THE FIRST CHAPTER OF THIS BOOK TELLS HOW TIMOTHY RETURNED FROM BANISHMENT AFTER THE DEATH OF LEO; AND THAT IT WAS HE WHO URGED BASILISCUS TO WRITE THE ENCYCLICAL LETTER

When Timothy had completed eighteen years in banishment, and Leo the emperor was dead, and Zeno, his successor, had received the kingdom, the people of Alexandria, observing this crisis in imperial affairs, sent a petition by certain chosen, and (as we may say) illustrious and noble monks, among them Amon who was called the wild bull, and Paul who had been a

---

[1] ܒܚܝܐ, MS., not ܩܚܐ, as L.   [2] ܐܬܦܫܩ, L., ܐܬܦܫܩ, MS.

sophist, and Theorion and James the miracle-workers, and Theopompus the brother of the master of the offices.

However,[1] in consequence of a rebellion that was raised against Zeno by Basiliscus, the brother of Verina the wife of Leo, who had been associated with Zeno in the command of the army[2] in the days of Leo, Zeno[3] had betaken himself to the strongholds called Salmon; and Basiliscus had assumed the crown. And he appointed Theoctistus his physician, an Alexandrian, the brother of this Theopompus the monk, as master of the offices.

Now[4] when these monks entered into the royal presence, the king, and the courtiers, and the queen were struck with admiration of them. But also Theoctistus the master of the offices and Acacius the bishop rendered them assistance.

So Basiliscus issued an order that Timothy should return from banishment.

And at first Acacius was preparing a lodging for him at the church called *Irene*; and he was setting apart some of his own clergy for his retinue and service. But afterwards, because he thought that they were forming a plan to make Theopompus bishop at the royal city instead of him, Acacius was distressed and indignant; and he endeavoured to put a stop to Timothy's coming. However, he did not succeed. For he returned, and was welcomed with great state by the Alexandrian sailors and the people who happened to be then in Constantinople. And he went to lodge in the king's palace. And large numbers were coming to him to be blessed, and to be sanctified, and to receive healing from him. And becoming intimate both with Basiliscus and his wife, Timothy,[5] along with those who happened to be there with him and on his behalf, persuaded the king, so that he consented to write encyclical letters, in which he would anathematise the Tome and the addition which was made at Chalcedon. For Paul the monk, who was a rhetorician and a sophist, drew them up. And it was he who, in a discussion with Acacius the patriarch,

---

[1] Evag. iii. 3.

[2] ܐܣܛܪܛܠܛܐ, *i.e.* στρατηγόs.

[3] ܙܢܘ, MS., an evident mistake for ܙܢܘܢ.   [4] Evag. iii. 4.   [5] Evag. iii. 4.

was able to show that the heresies of Nestorius and Eutyches
are one and the same; though they are generally thought to
be diametrically opposed to each other.   For the one, indeed,
making objection declares that it would be a degradation to
God to be born of a woman, and to be made in all points like
as we are, by becoming partaker of flesh and blood; whereas
He was only partaker by identity of name, and by power and
indwelling, and by operation.   But the other, indeed, for the
purpose of liberating and exalting God, so that He should not
suffer degradation and contempt by association with a human
body, publishes the doctrine that He became incarnate from
His own essence, and that He assumed a heavenly body; and
that just as there is no part of the seal left upon the wax, nor
of the golden signet upon the clay, so neither did there cleave
to Christ any portion of humanity whatsoever.

And when he spoke in this way, Acacius was astonished
at the solidity of his reasoning, and he assented and agreed.
And he went to Timothy and conversed with him, in a
friendly manner, respecting the rights of his see.   However,
when he was requested by Timothy to sign the Encyclical, he
hesitated.

CHAPTER II

THE SECOND CHAPTER TELLS ABOUT THE ENCYCLICAL
LETTER OF BASILISCUS AND MARCUS, WHICH IS TO
THE FOLLOWING EFFECT [1]

" The king Basiliscus, the believing, victorious, all-virtuous
ruler, Augustus,[2] along with Marcus the most illustrious
Cæsar,[3] to Timothy the reverend and God-loving archbishop of
the great city Alexandria.   Concerning all the laws justly and
righteously enacted by the believing and memorable kings who
have gone before us, for the salvation and good guidance of all

---

[1] Evag. iii. 4.

[2] Read ܐܢܝܩܘ for ܐܢܝ, and omit ܐܢܝܣܒ, and thus bring into harmony with
the Greek ἀεισέβαστος (Brooks).

[3] ܐܦܘܝܣܩܘܡܝܘܣ ܘܡܪ for ἐπιφανέστατος καῖσαρ.

the world, and in defence of the true faith as taught by the apostles and holy fathers; it is our will that all these laws should be ratified, and not lightly annulled.   Rather do we agree to them, and hold them to be of equal validity with our own.

"And earnestly desiring to honour the fear of God more than any affair of man, through zeal for the Lord Jesus Christ our God, to Whom we owe our creation, exaltation, and glory; moreover also, being fully persuaded that the unity of His flock is the salvation of ourselves and our people, and is the sure and immovable foundation, and the lofty bulwark of our kingdom; we now, moved by a wise impulse, are bringing union and unity to the Church of Christ in every part of our dominion, namely, the faith of the three hundred and eighteen bishops, who being previously prepared by the Holy Ghost, assembled at Nicea, the security and well-being of human life, the faith which we hold, like all who have been before us, and in which we believe and are baptized, that it may hold and rule[1] all the Churches with their chosen canons: the faith which is complete and perfect in all piety and true belief, and which rejects and exposes all heresies, and thrusts them out of the Church: the faith which the one hundred and fifty bishops, being assembled here to oppose and condemn the fighters against the Spirit, the Holy Lord confirmed, and with which they concurred and agreed: the faith which was also confirmed by the transactions of the two Councils at Ephesus, along with the chief priests of Rome and Alexandria, Celestine and Cyril, and Dioscorus, in condemnation of the heretic Nestorius, and all who after him have held similar opinions, and have confounded the order of the Church, and disturbed the peace of the world, and cleft asunder the unity; we mean the Tome of Leo, and the decrees of Chalcedon, whether by way of definition of the faith, or doctrine, or interpretation,[2] or addition, or whatsoever other innovation was said or done contrary to the faith and the definition of the three hundred and eighteen.

"And therefore we command that wherever, here or elsewhere, such written doctrine be found, it shall be anathematised and burnt in the fire.   For in accordance with this order, our

---

[1] ܢܪܡ, MS., not ܢܩܡ, as L.   [2] Read ܦܘܫܩܐ for ܦܣܩܐ.

blessed predecessors in the kingdom, Constantine the Great
and Theodosius, in like manner, commanded and ordained.
And also, the three subsequent Synods, that of the one hundred and fifty bishops here, and the two of Ephesus, ratified
only the faith of Nicea, and agreed to the true definition there
made.

"Moreover, we anathematise everyone who does not confess that the only-begotten Son of God truly became incarnate
by the Holy Ghost from the Virgin Mary; not taking a
body from heaven, in mere semblance or phantasy. And
also we anathematise all the false teaching of all those heresies
which are contrary to the true faith of the fathers," and so on
with the rest of the Encyclical.

To[1] this document Timothy agreed and subscribed; as
did also Peter of Antioch and Paul of Ephesus, who were
recalled from banishment, and the bishops of Asia and the
East, and Anastasius of Jerusalem, and those of his jurisdiction;
so that the number of bishops who subscribed to the Encyclical
is found to be about seven hundred, less or more. And
they anathematised the Tome of Leo and the Synod; and
they sent a petition[2] to Basiliscus and Marcus, which was as
follows :—

CHAPTER III

THE THIRD CHAPTER GIVES INFORMATION RESPECTING
THE PETITION OF THE BISHOPS OF ASIA, WHO WERE
ASSEMBLED AT EPHESUS, AND SIGNED THE ENCYCLICAL,
AND WHO WROTE TO BASILISCUS AND MARCUS TO THE
FOLLOWING EFFECT

"To[3] the believing, and Christ-loving, victorious kings
Basiliscus and Marcus the Augusti—Paul and Pergamius, and
Gennadius, and Zenodotus, and Zoticus, and Gennadius, and
Theophilus, and the other bishops assembled at Ephesus :—

[1] Evag. iii. 5; Liberat. 16.   [2] ܡܟܣܢܘܬܐ, *i.e.* δέησις.
[3] Evag. iii. 5.

In all things ye have shown yourselves to be believing and Christ-loving beings; so that when the true faith suffered persecution by the malice of men, ye also were persecuted along with it. For there are rebellious and vainglorious men, of a corrupt mind, foolish and void of the faith of the Son of God, Who humbled Himself for our sake and became incarnate, and rendered us meet for the adoption of sons. Be glad, then, and rejoice, and exult, and glory that ye have been counted worthy to suffer persecution with the faith. For there is reserved for these men the everlasting judgment of fire which devours the persecutors, and also the threat of your punishment which is upon them; because they have despised us, and slandered and belied us, and forced us with violence to agree to their doctrine.

" But now that the light of the true faith has arisen upon us, and the dark cloud of error been rolled away from us, we make known by this declaration[1] our true faith to your Majesties[2] and to all the world. And we say that freely and with willing consent, by the aid of John the Evangelist as our teacher, we have signed this Encyclical; and we agree to it and to everything in it, without compulsion, or fear, or favour of man. And if at any future time violence shall meet us from man, we are prepared to despise fire and sword and banishment and the spoiling of our goods, and to treat all bodily suffering with contempt; so that we may adhere to the true faith. We have anathematised and we do anathematise the Tome of Leo and the decrees of Chalcedon; which have been the cause of much blood-shedding, and confusion, and tumult, and trouble, and divisions, and strifes in all the world. For we are satisfied with the doctrine and faith of the apostles and of the holy fathers, the three hundred and eighteen bishops; to which also the illustrious Council of the one hundred and fifty in the Royal City, and the two other holy Synods at Ephesus adhered, and which they confirmed. And we join with them in anathematising Nestorius, and everyone who does not confess that the only-begotten Son of God was incarnate by the Holy Ghost,

---

[1] ‏ܐܠܩܪ̈ܐ‏, i.e. ἀναφορά.

[2] ‏ܡܠܟܘܬܟܘܢ‏, MS., not ‏ܡܠܟܘܬܟܘܗܝ‏, as L.

of the Virgin Mary; He becoming perfect man, while yet He remained, without change and the same, perfect God; and that He was not incarnate from Heaven in semblance or phantasy. And we further anathematise all other heresies." But they wrote down some other things. And they applauded with loud voice[1] and approved.

But the other bishops also of the various districts wrote another declaration, the beginning of which was to this effect:

"With the consent of our heart, we hold your Majesties to be in such accord with our fathers, the three hundred and eighteen bishops, as to make the three hundred and nineteenth: for you are very zealous[2] for their true faith, that it may prosper and be preached among all nations in your dominion."

CHAPTER IV

THE FOURTH CHAPTER OF THIS SAME FIFTH BOOK NARRATES THE EVENTS WHICH OCCURRED IN CONSTANTINOPLE AND EPHESUS AFTER THE PUBLICATION OF THE ENCYCLICAL

When[3] the purport of the king's Encyclical letters became generally known, certain monks holding opinions similar to those of Eutyches, who happened to be in the Royal City, came in a body to Timothy, supposing him to be of their way of thinking, and disputed with him about the terms of the Encyclical; because it anathematised everyone who affirmed that Christ was incarnate in semblance. But when he said to them, "What then is your opinion respecting the Incarnation?" then they brought up to him the illustration of the signet-ring which, after the impression, leaves no part of its substance upon the wax or the clay.

And having discovered their sentiments, he admonished and instructed them, that the Scriptures teach us that Christ

---

[1] Read ܩܳܠܰܐ for ܩܳܠܶܐ, φωνάς.

[2] ܐܝܙܝܙܘܬܗܘܢ, MS., not ܐܝܙܝܙܘܬܗܘܢ, as L.

[3] Evag. iii. 5.

was made in all points like unto us, and took our nature perfectly, yet without the motions of sin. And although He was born supernaturally[1] without copulation, nevertheless He became perfect Man, having been conceived in the Virgin Mary, and from her born, through the Holy Ghost. And being incarnate He yet remained the same and without change in His Godhead.

Then Timothy, having learned by the whole tenor of the conversation of those who came to him what their mind was, made a written statement, declaring that Christ was like unto us in everything belonging to humanity. Whereupon the monks of the place separated themselves from him, saying, "We will have no communion with the Alexandrians."

But the others, having discovered that he had no tendency to the Eutychian doctrine, attached themselves to him.

Then the Eutychianists, joining with their fellows, advised Zenona, the wife of King Basiliscus, a professor of their creed, that Timothy should be banished again. However, Theoctistus, the master of the offices, having heard what was likely to befall him, urged him to leave the city and to proceed without delay to Alexandria. And[2] he left; and having, on his journey, arrived at Ephesus, he convened a Synod, and he reinstated Paul who had formerly been the bishop there, but was in exile at that time for not accepting the decrees of Chalcedon. To him Timothy canonically restored the rights of his see, which the Council of Chalcedon had snatched from it, and had given by partiality to the throne of the royal city.

And Timothy arrived at Alexandria, and he was received with great state, with torches, and also songs of praise by the various people and languages there, and even by the members of the Proterian party, who beheld the affection for him displayed by the citizens. But the band of the priests, and the monks, and the sisters in Christ, and all the people in a body, chanting their hymns, and saying, " Blessed is he that cometh in the name of the Lord," conducted him into the great church. For Timothy Salophaciolus had by the king's command gone out before him.

[1] ܠܟܝܐ, MS., not ܠܩܝܐ, as L.   [2] Evag. iii. 6.

And inasmuch as he was a peaceable and kind man, and also gentle in his words, and by no means passionate, he remitted to the members of the Proterian party the term of repentance, which he had written and appointed for the penitents when he was in banishment.

And even Prolatius (?) himself, who had taken and dragged him from the font of the Baptistery, he received just as kindly and peaceably as the others, weeping and comforting him as to his former rebellious and insolent conduct towards himself.

For, such is the rule of the leaders of the Church, which Timothy truly showed towards the many, that brotherly charity which seeks not her own, and is not easily provoked.

But certain persons, who were ignorant of the rights of divine love, severed themselves from him on account of his gentleness and mildness towards the penitents, in that he required nothing else from them except that they should anathematise the Synod and the Tome, and confess the true faith; and because he did not hold them aloof, even for a little while, from the communion which they had made desolate.

But at the head of these persons was Theodoret[1] the bishop of Joppa, who had been consecrated by Theodosius some time before. And he was then filled with envy because he had not also been received back again to his see. And, lo! the illustrious Peter the Iberian did not return to Gaza; and he did not at all agree with this faction, but he was warmly attached to Timothy, and he proved that his conduct and actions were in conformity with the will of God. But the Separatists who sided with Theodotus fell into such error that they even practised reanointing, and they were called Anachristo-Novatians.

But the affection of the people for Timothy being great was increased the more because, by the king's command, he brought the bones of Dioscorus and of Anatolius his brother, along with him, in a silver coffin, and he buried him with great state, laying him in the place of the bishops, and honouring

---

[1] Evidently a mistake for Theodotus; see below, and Evag. iii. 6.

him as a confessor.   But his charity was so profuse that of his own free will he appointed that one denarius a day should be given by the Church, for expenditure and use, to Timothy, who was deposed, and who had been since then supporting himself by the work of his hands, by weaving baskets and selling them.

And he gave to the great men and rulers of the city a gift, assigning to[1] each of them three *paxamatia*[2] apiece.   And to King Basiliscus and to the patricians he only sent the same. And at one time the tax-gatherer[3] came to him with a royal letter, and he gave him just the same; and he answered and said, " I want a gift of denarii."   And he said, " It is the duty of the Church to expend them upon the widows and orphans."

But the people heard that the prefect there, Boetius by name, was an Eutychian ; and they cried out in the church, "Pope![4] pronounce an anathema upon Nestorius and Eutyches." And he at once anathematised them by word of mouth in the presence of the prefect.   And thereby he was cleared from the suspicion of associating with the prefect as an Eutychian.

Such were the transactions at Alexandria.

CHAPTER V

THE FIFTH CHAPTER OF THIS SAME FIFTH BOOK TELLS ABOUT THE PREPARATIONS WHICH WERE MADE BY ACACIUS OF CONSTANTINOPLE; AND ABOUT THE "ANTENCYCLICALS"; AND ALSO ABOUT PETER AND PAUL OF ANTIOCH AND OF EPHESUS, WHO WERE AGAIN DEPOSED WHEN ZENO THE KING RETURNED AND BASILISCUS WAS DRIVEN OUT

But[5] Acacius of Constantinople, having heard respecting Paul of Ephesus that the rightful authority of his see, according

---

[1] Reading ܠܒܠ for ܠܒܘ.

[2] ܩܒܣܘܡܛܝ̈ܐ ; it seems to represent παξουμάτια (παξαμάτια), but the meaning can hardly be " little cakes."

[3] ܦܪܘܩܛܪ, *i.e.* πρακτήρ.   [4] ܦܐܦ, *i.e.* παππᾶς.   [5] Evag. iii. 7.

to its former constitution, had been restored to him by Timothy; and further, that Peter had returned to Antioch; and that they were preparing to hold a Synod against him at Jerusalem with the intention of deposing himself and appointing Theopompus, brother of the master of the offices, in his stead: he, having heard all this, stirred up the monks and urged them on, and brought down Daniel from the pillar, and took possession of the churches, and raised an insurrection against Basiliscus, declaring that he was a heretic. Whereupon Basiliscus, for the report reached him at the same time that Zeno was returning with a great army, was compelled to make the "Antencyclicals," by which he cancelled his former letter.

Then Zeno, upon his return, and the ejection of Basiliscus, passed a law whereby all the proceedings of Basiliscus were to be cancelled. He also deposed Peter of Antioch and Paul of Ephesus;[1] and he uttered severe threats against Timothy. However, the latter died, departing to be with his Lord; and he was buried with great state, the obsequies being performed by Peter, who was canonically consecrated as his successor by the bishops of the country.

But the bishops of Asia made a libel to Acacius, finding fault with the "Encyclicals"; and they subscribed to the Antencyclicals. In like manner also, the Eastern bishops made a libel to Calandion, Peter's successor, whereby they, too, anathematised the "Encyclicals."

But Anastasius of Jerusalem persevered in his integrity, holding with him the three provinces of Palestine; and he would not give himself over to this party, nor would he deny the Encyclicals; although he freely associated with the bishops who came together to him.

In like manner also Epiphanius of Magdolum[2] of Pamphylia, impelled by the greatness of his soul, departed to Alexandria, and was sojourning in the monasteries there, and was honoured by Timothy and by his successor Peter.

But King Zeno was greatly enraged when he heard about Peter; and he sent threats of which Peter had previous intima-

---

[1] The text has, "Paul of Antioch and Peter of Ephesus," an evident mistake.
[2] *I.e.* Magyda.

8

tion, and he hid himself in the city by moving about from one house to another. But, by the command of King Zeno, Timothy Salophaciolus, who had been ejected, returned and took possession of the great church, and a tumult and slaughter ensued upon his entry there.

And Theoctistus, the prefect of the city, was searching for Peter to apprehend him, when a Voice was heard, saying, " I will hide him, and I will protect him, because he has known My Name; he shall call upon Me, and I will answer him; in the day of trouble I will sustain him, and I will honour him." [1]

But Timothy exerted himself by all ways and means to keep the people on his side. He preached the faith of Nicea and of the one hundred and fifty; he confessed and agreed to the transactions of Ephesus; he anathematised Nestorius; and he wrote in the diptych the names of Cyril and Dioscorus, and read them out; and he did more besides, and yet he was unable to draw the people to himself.

CHAPTER VI

THE SIXTH CHAPTER OF THIS SAME BOOK TELLS ABOUT MARTYRIUS, WHO WAS THE SUCCESSOR OF ANASTASIUS IN JERUSALEM; THAT HE ALSO WAS PREACHING THE TRUE FAITH TO THE PEOPLE, AND WAS ANATHEMAT- ISING NESTORIUS AND THE SYNOD OF CHALCEDON

And Martyrius of Jerusalem was also one of those who, following Anastasius his predecessor, separated himself from the Antencyclical, and exerted himself greatly to unite the people. And he gained over Marcianus, an excellent monk; and this man received him, and admonished the other monks to do the same. But those who did not receive him he expelled. And they say that, after his death, one of his disciples, who was quite blind, prayed to God, saying, " If the doctrine of our master be indeed the right one, when I lay mine eyes upon his corpse, let them receive their sight "; and he received his sight.

[1] Ps. xci. 14, 15.

The Public Address[1] of Martyrius

"Christ is our peace, Who hath made both one, and has taken down the middle wall of partition, and has destroyed the enmity by His flesh. For, behold, the Church is receiving back her sons, who never, indeed, of their own accord, departed far from her!   And now they have shown[2] this to us by deed, and it is time for us to say, 'Glory to God in the highest, and peace upon earth.'

"Wherefore, to their face we the God-loving bishops have blamed[3] these chaste archimandrites and the excellent clergy, in order in your presence to convince the rest of our brethren that we have no other true definition of the faith but that into which we have been and are being baptized. For thus have they been baptized, and believe as we do.

"Whosoever, then, holds or has held or learned doctrine contrary to this definition of the faith which was framed by the three hundred and eighteen holy fathers, the bishops assembled at Nicea; to which definition the one hundred and fifty believing and true bishops, assembled in the royal city, adhered, ratifying and confirming the same, as did also the Synod held in Ephesus: whosoever (I say) holds or has held or learned what is contrary to this definition, let him be accursed, if he have any other teaching or doctrine defined elsewhere, whether in Rimini, or in Sardica, or in Chalcedon, or in any other place whatsoever, according to the saying of the apostle, 'If any man preaches to you more than what we have preached to you, let him be accursed.' "[4]

And again, the same Martyrius spoke in the following terms: "If any man teaches, or brings in as new, or thinks or[5] interprets, or holds any other definition or faith contrary to this approved and orthodox doctrine of faith of the three hundred and eighteen holy bishops and the one hundred and fifty, and them of Ephesus, he is an alien to the holy Church.

---

[1] ܡܘܣܩܘܐܘܣܩܪܣ, *i.e.* προσφώνησις.

[2] ܩܘܩܣ, MS., ܩܘܘܗ, L.

[3] ܠܪܟ, MS., ܐܠܪܟ, L.

[4] Gal. i. 8, 9.

[5] ܐܘ, MS., not ܘܗ, as L. prints.

"And, behold, I adjure you in the sight of God and His Christ, and the Holy Spirit, and the elect angels, that you do not suffer any man to lead you astray from this faith! But the confession, signed with your own signatures, lo, it is recorded in Heaven above! And you shall give account before the fearful and righteous Judgment-Seat, if you accept anything more or less than the true faith. I am clear from your blood; I have not desisted from speaking unto you."

By using language such as this, the bishops were admonishing those who separated from them.

But in Alexandria not one believer would consent to hold communion with Timothy and his followers.

Then the monks and certain learned and wise men took counsel together, and they made a supplication [1] to the chiefs of the cities, begging of them that, in the event of the death of Timothy, they would not accept as bishop any other member of his party; but that they would only be satisfied with Peter the believer, who was the lawfully - appointed bishop, although he was then hidden in retirement. And [2] the partisans of Timothy having heard of this, drew up a petition and sent it to the king by John, a presbyter of the Martyr Church of St. John the Baptist, a monk, and also one of the Tabennesiots. [3] And in it they besought the king that, in the event of the death of Timothy, none but a member of his party should be made bishop, and that the people of Alexandria should not. receive Peter.

And when John was admitted into the presence of the king, the latter said to him, for the purpose of trying him, "We think it well that you should yourself be the bishop there." For the king had previously learned that he was in league with Julius [4] the general, [5] who, on account of his command over the king's army, was preparing an insurrection against the king, in conjunction with Leontius and Euprepius.

---

[1] ܐܠܘܦܣܝܣ, ἐντεύξις.   [2] Evag. iii. 12; Liberat. 16.

[3] ܐܒܐ ܕܩܘܣܝܘܬ, MS.; but in *Das Leben des Severus* (ed. Spanuth), p. 6, it is written ܐܒܐ ܕܩܘܣܝܘܬ, and said to be the name of a monastery situated in Canopus.—"Presbyter Tabennesiotis" (Lib.).

[4] *I.e.* Illus.   [5] ܣܛܪܛܝܠܘܣ, *i.e.* στρατηγός.

And John disclosed this to Julius; and he said to the king, " I am not worthy." Then he told him to take counsel upon it. And when Julius heard it he said to him, "Conceal your feelings, and be careful not to disclose them before the king." Then he took an oath in the presence of Acacius and the senators that he would never be the bishop.

And the king issued an order, and gave it to John, to the effect that any brother [1] whom the clergy and the people of the city might choose, should be the successor of Timothy.

But when he returned to the city, he delivered a letter from Julius to Theognostus the prefect there, who was one of the conspirators with Julius, and he promised that if he should become bishop he would give the royal vessels which Arcadius the king devoted to the sanctuary, and presented to Theophilus, who was the bishop at that time, and he built a church there and called it after his name.

CHAPTER VII

THE SEVENTH CHAPTER OF THE FIFTH BOOK TELLS ABOUT
JOHN, HOW HE LIED, AND OBTAINED THE BISHOPRIC BY
BRIBERY, AFTER THE DEATH OF TIMOTHY; AND ABOUT
CYRUS THE PRESBYTER, WHO WAS IN LEAGUE WITH
HIM; AND ALSO HOW PETER RETURNED TO HIS SEE

After [2] a few more days of life only, Timothy died. Then John belied his own sworn promises, and gave a bribe to Theognostus, and obtained the bishopric for himself.

But he drew over to his side Cyrus a presbyter, one of those who had formerly been in association with Dioscorus, and had afterwards forsaken him. This man also coveting the primacy, at one time [3] would attach himself to Acacius of Constantinople, and at another time to that Timothy who died; and again, he would mock [4] and revile Timothy the Great and Peter his successor. So that the Alexandrians

---

[1] For ‹‹‹ read ‹‹‹, " whomsoever " (Brooks).

[2] Evag. ii. 12; Liberat. 17.   [3] Omit ‌ before ‹‹‹.

[4] Reading ‹‹‹ for ‹‹‹, p. 42, note 5.

used to ridicule him on account of his tergiversations, holding up unripe dates before him in the public street, and charging him with vile conduct in connexion with a married woman. The blessed Dioscorus cursed this man, asying, " As God is true, Cyrus will die a layman." And so, indeed, it happened to him, as is written below.

But the king, when he heard about John, was very indignant, because the latter had belied his sworn promises, and obtained the bishopric for himself.

But there were in Constantinople at that time some chosen monks who were pleading for Peter. And they showed him, by written documents respecting them, the sad afflictions which, time after time, had occurred in Alexandria, and in Egypt, and in the other adjacent districts, on account of the Synod. And the king acceded to their request, and he issued an order that John should be ejected from the see as a liar, and that Peter [1] should be restored to the Church, upon the condition of his subscribing to the Henotikon which Zeno wrote and sent there, and to Egypt, and to Pentapolis, and of his receiving and holding communion with all the other bishops who would agree to the Henotikon ; and, moreover, with those in Alexandria called Proterians, as many of them as would confess that they agreed to the doctrines of the Henotikon, which indeed was framed by the counsel of Acacius the bishop, and was sent to Alexandria in the charge of Pergamius, the newly-appointed prefect there in the room of Theognostus.

This Pergamius,[2] upon his arrival at the city, managed the matter prudently. For having discovered that John had escaped by flight, he sought out Peter, and informed him of the king's order. And he showed him the Henotikon, saying, " You must, after having carefully studied it, subscribe and agree to it ; and further, you must receive the bishops and the other members of the Proterian party without any animosity whatsoever, if only they agree to all that the king has laid down in the same Henotikon."

And Peter, having considered the contents of this document, found that its provisions were framed faithfully and with

[1] Liberat. 18.[2] Evag. iii. 13.

all righteousness. But he hesitated somewhat, because there was no clear and express anathema of the Synod and the Tome in it, and consequently he feared that it might prove a stumbling-block to the people. However, he decided to accept it, inasmuch as it proclaimed the definition of the faith laid down by the three hundred and eighteen ; and it confessed the truth of the one hundred and fifty bishops ; and it also agreed to the twelve Heads of Cyril ; and it anathematised Nestorius and Eutyches ; and it also confessed that the body of Christ, derived from the Virgin, was of the same nature as our body. Accordingly he subscribed to it. And he also promised that, if the others would repent and accept all the provisions of the Henotikon, and persuade the people to that effect, he would receive them into communion with himself from all orders.

Then the prefect, and the duke, and the chief men, and the clergy, and the monks, and the sisters, and the believing people assembled together at the place where he was ; and they set him upon a chariot, and with pomp[1] and praise as one who kept the true faith, and doing homage before him, they brought him to the great church. And Pergamius urged him to receive the other[2] members of the Proterian party. But he first declared to the people the interpretation of the meaning of the Henotikon, and explained it, saying, " It is well and faithfully written, inasmuch as it accepts the twelve Heads of Cyril, and it anathematises Nestorius and Eutyches, and it confesses the body of Christ, derived from the Virgin, to be of the same nature as our body, and that the sufferings which He endured in the flesh, and the miracles which He wrought, belong to the same God Christ. And this document further cancels and condemns the whole doctrine of Chalcedon and the Tome, because Dioscorus and Timothy the Great also thought and expounded similarly."

And he delivered a further address[3] to the people, to the following effect: " It is right for all of us, men, women, and children, to offer with the open mouth of thanksgiving, prayer,

---

[1] ܟ, MS., not ܟ, as L.

[2] ܟ, MS., not ܟ, as L.

[3] ܟ, i.e. προσφώνησις.

and supplication to our Lord and God, on behalf of the faithful reign of the victorious King Zeno, whose noble actions and virtuous morals are urging the prudent in every place to this. For when our fathers, the chaste monks, presented a petition to him concerning the reformation of the faith, and informed him of the occurrences here, and of the tumults from which our people had suffered time after time; then he wept, and he looked up to heaven, and called God to help him, and to put it into his heart to command whatever would be in conformity with the divine will, and would conduce to the welfare of men and the unity of the people, by exerting himself to abolish the stumbling-blocks which were in all the Churches,[1] on account of all the rash innovations and additions which were made at Chalcedon.[2]

"And now, beloved children, we have the light of the true faith of the holy fathers in this written statement of his Orthodoxy, which will now be read aloud in your presence, and heard by your ears. For by confessing herein the true faith, and accepting the twelve Heads of the blessed Cyril, and anathematising Nestorius and Eutyches, and proclaiming that God the Word, Who became incarnate, is one nature, sufferings and miracles; by all this he rejects the whole teaching of the *Diphysites.* For their doctrine and that of the Tome is quite the opposite of this; and against them our holy fathers, Dioscorus and Timothy, true witnesses of Christ, earnestly contended.

"But pray for him, that the Lord may keep him in the true proportion of his love and faith. For we trust, by the mercy of Christ our God, that when your praises and prayers are heard, we shall not fail to obtain any of those other petitions which we are rightly asking of Him; but that He may freely receive your supplication and grant your requests."[3]

"Hear this honourable document, the Henotikon, which

---

[1] ܠܠܐܣܘ, MS., not ܠܠ—, as L.

[2] The rendering of this passage is somewhat conjectural, owing to defects in the MS.

[3] Or, "when the report of your praises and prayers reaches him, he will not fail us in any of the other things which we justly ask from him, but will readily receive your petition and grant your requests."

he faithfully ordained, and which will now be read in your presence."

CHAPTER VIII

THE EIGHTH CHAPTER COMES NEXT, CONTAINING THE HENOTIKON OF ZENO

"Imperial[1] Cæsar, Zeno the king, believing, victorious, triumphant, mighty, ever-worshipful, Augustus, to the bishops and the people in Alexandria, and in Egypt, and in Libya, and also in Pentapolis. Since we know that the origin and stability and invincible might[2] of our empire is the only right and true faith, which, by Divine Inspiration the three hundred and eighteen holy fathers in Council at Nicea declared, and which in like manner the one hundred and fifty holy fathers gathered at Constantinople, attested: We, by night and by day, employ constant prayers, and diligence, and enactments, that thereby the Holy Catholic and Apostolic Church in every place, which is the incorruptible and imperishable mother of the sceptre of our kingdom, may be increased. That thus the believing people, being kept in godly peace and concord, may offer up, in conjunction with the pious and holy bishops, and the God-fearing clergy, and the archimandrites and monks, acceptable prayers on behalf of our empire. For if the great God and our Saviour Jesus Christ, Who became incarnate from Mary the holy Virgin and *Theotokos*, shall approve and readily receive our unanimous praise and service, the race of enemies shall be destroyed and obliterated; and all men will bow the neck to our sway, which is next[3] to that of God; and then peace,[4] and its consequent blessings, and genial temperature, and abundance of fruits, and all those things which are adapted[5] for man's good, shall be liberally granted. This unblemished faith, then, being thus the preserver of ourselves and of the Roman affairs, petitions have been presented to us

---

[1] Evag. iii. 14; Liberat. 17.

[2] ܟܝܢܐ, MS., not ܟܝܢܐ, as L.

[3] ܒܬܪ, MS., not ܒܬܪ, as L.

[4] ܫܝܢܐ, MS., not ܫܝܢ, as L.

[5] For ܩܕܡ read ܩܕܡ = λυσιτελοῦντα (Brooks).

by God-loving archimandrites and other hermits entreating us with tears that there may be unity to the Holy Churches; and that the limbs may be joined together which the haters of good have for a long time been striving to separate; because they knew that when one makes war with the whole and perfect body of the Church he is defeated. .

"For it has happened that of the generations without number which Time, during these many years of life, has removed; some, deprived of the Laver of Regeneration, have passed away; and others, without participation in the divine Communion, have been carried off by the inevitable journey of mankind. And they have been wasted by myriads of murders; and through the profuse blood-shedding, not the earth alone, but even the very air itself has been defiled. Who would not pray [1] that this state of things may be exchanged for a good one? For which reason, then, we desired you to know that both we and the holy Churches of the orthodox everywhere, and the God-loving priests who rule them, neither hold, nor have held, nor know any man holding, any other symbol, or doctrine, or seal of the faith, or creed, than that which we have mentioned above, the holy symbol of the three hundred and eighteen holy fathers, which was also attested by the one hundred and fifty holy fathers who met in Council here. And if there be any man holding such, we account him an alien. For, as we have already said, we are confident that this only preserves our kingdom; and also all people who are counted worthy of life-giving Baptism are baptized upon the simple reception of this creed alone. And, moreover, all the holy fathers, who met in Council at Ephesus, and deposed the wicked Nestorius and all his successors in doctrine, followed the same faith.

"This Nestorius, together with Eutyches, inasmuch as they held doctrines contrary to what have been here declared, we anathematise. And we also receive the twelve Heads delivered by the ever-memorable, God-loving Cyril, formerly archbishop of the Catholic Church of Alexandria. But we confess that the only-begotten Son of God, Himself God,

[1] Reading ܠܡܨܠܐ for ܡܨܠܐ.

our Lord Jesus Christ, Who truly became man; He Who is of the same nature with the Father in the Godhead; He Who is also of the same nature with us in the manhood; He Who came down and assumed flesh, through the Holy Ghost, and from Mary the Virgin and *Theotokos*,—is *one* Son and not *two*. For we affirm that the miracles which He wrought, and the sufferings which He freely endured in the flesh, belong to one Son of God alone. Moreover, we altogether reject those who either divide or confound, or introduce the *phantasy*. For the true and sinless Incarnation from the *Theotokos* did not cause the addition of a Son. For the Trinity remained even though God the Word, Who is one of the Trinity, became incarnate.

"Since, then, you know that both the Holy Orthodox Churches everywhere and the God-loving priests who rule them, and our own Royalty, neither have received nor do receive any other symbol or definition of the faith than the holy doctrine which has been declared above; be united together without doubting. For we have written this, not to make any innovation in the faith, but to assure you.

"And here we anathematise all who have held, or hold, now or at any time, whether in Chalcedon or in any other Synod whatsoever, any different belief; but chiefly those already mentioned, Nestorius and Eutyches and all their followers in the doctrine.

"Be joined, then, to your spiritual mother, the Church, and delight in her, together with us, in divine fellowship, according to that one definition of the faith alone which was framed by the holy fathers, as we have declared above. For our all-holy mother, the Church, longs for you, that she may embrace you as beloved children. And, for a considerable time, she has been eager to hear your sweet [1] voice.

"Hasten, therefore! For by so doing you will attract to yourselves the goodwill of our God and Saviour Christ; and you will also be commended by our own Royalty."

---

[1] For ‎ܠܡܐ read ‎ܠܡܐ, *sweet*; Evag. γλυκείας; Liberat. *dulcem*. The word is written over an erasure in the MS. (Brooks).

CHAPTER IX

THE NINTH CHAPTER OF THIS FIFTH BOOK TELLS ABOUT THE SEPARATISTS [1]

These matters having been thus transacted, some of the more ardent spirits were very indignant; because in the king's document, the Henotikon, there was no express anathema of the additions imposed at Chalcedon. However, they all remained in communion with Peter because he defended himself before them; and especially as he said, " The king will not fail us in any of the requests that we shall make to him."

Then the rest of the Proterians, seeing how matters were, went off to a suburb of the city, called Canopus, and they kept crying out evil words.[2]   However, they were feeble and few, and at their head were some readers,[3] and Cyrus the presbyter, concerning whom we have already stated [4] that he was at one time a follower of Dioscorus, but he afterwards deserted him. Pergamius, hearing of this secession, sent for Cyrus to have a conversation with him. And the latter agreed to do what he was asked. So when he returned to them, he pleaded earnestly with his companions at Canopus, saying, " It is right for us to join in fellowship with the others, and to obey the king's command." But the zealous and believing priests who were on Peter's side, hearing about it, were greatly distressed. And they refused[5] to hold communion with Cyrus. And although they received a large number of his associates upon their subscribing to the Henotikon, and anathematising everyone who thought differently from what was in it; yet they refused Cyrus himself. And even when he subscribed they would not have him. For they said to

---

[1] ܐܦܘܣܟܘܦ̈ܘܬܐ for ܐܦܘܣܟ̈ܘܬܐ, *i.e.* ἀποσχίσται.

[2] ܩ̈ܘܦܣ, *i.e.* φώνας.   [3] ܐܢܓ̈ܘܣܛܐ, *i.e.* ἀναγνῶσται.

[4] Reading ܐܡܪܝܢ for ܐܡܪܝܢ.

[5] ܡܣܬܝܒܝܢ, MS., not ܡܣܬܝܒܝܢ, as L.

Pergamius that the very sight of him would be enough to bring his deeds into the remembrance of the people, and to put a stumbling-block in the way of many. So Cyrus remained a layman; and thus he died, according to the curse of the holy Dioscorus.

Then they were all associated in fellowship with Peter and Peter the Iberian, wonderfully celebrated, and the able[1] monk Isaiah, and the other Palestinians, certain blessed monks of the monasteries of Romanus and Theodore.

And Peter, the bishop of Alexandria, sent Paul, surnamed Arcadius, to the king about certain matters of one kind and another that required correction.

But John,[2] who had been bishop, went off to Rome; and there, with tears, he told Simplicius the patriarch what had befallen him; alleging that he continued in danger[3] for the sake of the Synod and the Tome. Whereupon the king, hearing of it, wrote a letter and sent it to the same Simplicius by the hand of Uranius the tax-gatherer,[4] in which he set forth to him all the wickedness and lying treachery of John, and declared that by his own command Peter had been appointed bishop there in Alexandria, with the object of bringing the people into one communion.

But Calandion[5] of Antioch, having heard about the Alexandrian affairs, was much distressed, and wrote letters to Acacius, and to Zeno the king, and to Simplicius of Rome, in which he called Peter a false teacher,[6] and he praised the Tome and the Synod. But he was closely attached to Nestorius, because in his letter he called Cyril a *fool*.[7]

However, as he took the side of Julius, and Leontius, and Euprepius, in the rebellion which they eventually raised against Zeno the king in the East, he was ejected from his place. And by the king's commands,[8] Peter, who had once and

---

[1] ܦܪܘܩܛܝܩܘܣ, i.e. πρακτικός.   [2] Evag. iii. 15; Liberat. 18.

[3] ܩܝܢܕܘܢܘܣ, i.e. κίνδυνος.   [4] ܦܪܘܩܛܝܪ, i.e. πρακτήρ.

[5] Evag. iii. 16; Liberat. 18.

[6] Literally, "an adulterer"; perhaps it is intended to express illegal occupation of the see.

[7] See Mansi, vol. iv. p. 893.

[8] ܣܘܩܘܠܝܗ, MS., ܣܘܩܘܠܝ, L.

twice contended and suffered on behalf of the true faith, was restored to his see. And the people of Antioch received him with great pomp and glory as Simon Peter. Then he convened the Synod of his province, and he healed and closed the divisions, and set matters right. The Synod also, which he convened, drew up a letter of fellowship in canonical fashion, and sent it to Peter of Alexandria. It was to the following effect :—

CHAPTER X

THE TENTH CHAPTER OF THIS FIFTH BOOK TELLS ABOUT THE SYNODICAL LETTER, WHICH WAS SENT TO PETER OF ALEXANDRIA BY THE COUNCIL THAT WAS CON-VENED AT ANTIOCH, IN THE DAYS WHEN PETER WAS BISHOP THERE

" To our Father, the God-loving, holy, Archbishop Peter, from the Synod now convened at Antioch.

" Just as Joshua the son of Nun, the leader of the host,[1] and invested with the mysteries of Jesus Christ our God, showed care and solicitude for the possession and rights of the tribes of Reuben, and Gad, and Manasseh ; when, according to the command of Moses, who delivered to him the leadership, they in conjunction with their brethren crossed the Jordan armed, and entered the land of promise to possess it ; and continued to help in the war until God caused their brethren, like themselves, to rest in peace there : in like manner we judge[2] it to be the endeavour of thine Excellency, O bishop, that we also, being the bishops from Arabia and Libanus of Phœnice, and Syria Secunda, and Euphratesia, and Cilicia, should come to Antioch armed,[3] until our Eastern brethren shall possess the inheritance of their Churches from God. But how, after the troubles and conflicts that have befallen us,

---

[1] ܣܛܪܛܝܠܛܐ, i.e. στρατηγός.

[2] ܢܕܝܢ܆, MS., not ܢܕܝܢ, as L.

[3] ܡܟܝܢܝܟ, L., ܡܟܝܢܝܢ, MS.

we are earnestly desirous of peace; and how, by the letters
of the indulgent king, we have been now called to meet at
Antioch; thy son the beloved and illustrious Uranius the tax-
gatherer will tell thee. For he, in the execution of the king's
will and command, communicated and showed to us the letter
sent by him to thy Holiness, and to the chaste monks, and to
the believing people.

"But we, having met together and been received with the
rights of divine love by our believing father Peter the
patriarch, who showed us kindness and meekness with
prudence, were in concord with him in all matters and he
with us; and we joined in fellowship one with the other in
spiritual ministration. We were honoured also by the citizens,
who met and welcomed him with joy and gladness, and with
ministering praise; and extolled him as Peter Kepho our
leader the Apostle. And, moreover, we heard about the
transactions in the royal city, how, from the jurisdiction of
the holy Archbishop Acacius, they had met together by the
king's command; and about their unity with him and with one
another; and how he wrote to thy Blessedness, showing and
explaining the will of the believing king; and that the
contents of his excellent document the Henotikon were in
complete accord with the faith of the holy fathers of Nicea;
in which also the one hundred and fifty assembled in the
royal city concurred; and which was confirmed by the
Council of Ephesus in the days of Celestine and Cyril; the
latter of whom also in the twelve Heads exposed and
anathematised all the false doctrine of Nestorius and Eutyches,
and the other heresies.

"These things, indeed, brought the Egyptians[1] into full
accord with the Easterns, or rather, we should say, with all
who in every place are devoted to peace, and who love unity
and the true faith.

"And we believe and are confident that the diligence and
prayers of Thy Holiness have tended to bring about this
happy result for the believing people everywhere, by the will
of our Lord and Brother Jesus Christ, Whom we beseech to

[1] Reading ܡܨܪ̈ܝܐ for ܡܨܪ̈ܝܐ.

preserve for us the life of thy Chastity, prospering in all virtue, and rejoicing in the Lord at what was done here upon the return of thine honourable brother our chaste father, through the diligence of this thy son Uranius, whom we commend to thy godly love, that thou mayest write and send thanks to the believing king. For he is indeed serving him with all his might, by carrying out his command, and earnestly endeavouring to promote the unity of the Churches of Christ, and to impart peace to His beloved sons."

CHAPTER XI

THE ELEVENTH CHAPTER CONTAINS THE LETTER OF ACACIUS OF CONSTANTINOPLE TO PETER OF ALEXANDRIA [1]

Acacius, indeed, desisting from his former mind, which was in favour of the Synod, and connecting himself in loving agreement with the principles of the Henotikon, also wrote a letter to Peter of Alexandria in the following terms :—

" To our pious and God-loving fellow-minister and brother Peter, Acacius sends greeting. The very name of peace, indeed, is delightful ; but its effect is very sweet. For when, in accordance with the unity and the faith of the Church, it is perfected, it imparts the more abundant grace to the prudent, and works in them joy, for it announces great things.

" Now we were blest with such joy as this in the congregations of our own city, when reports reached us respecting thy faith, which troubled us. And, moreover, they produced agitation and distress among many of the chaste monks here, and the people, and our excellent clergy. However, thine honoured letter, having been conveyed and delivered to us and to the illustrious chiefs here, exposed the entire falsehood of the rumour respecting thee, and rolled away the darkness of the cloud, and displayed the brilliancy and the purity of thy godly virtues. So that it is now time for us to

[1] Cf. Evag. iii. 16.

say, 'Glory to God in the highest.' For it is producing and manifesting the peace, which is in the land of our faith, and the goodwill amongst the men of our great God and Saviour the Lord Jesus Christ. And, therefore, that glory of which the angels from heaven in their companies were the first to sing in the ears of the shepherds over the earth, at Bethlehem, that same glory the shepherds and leaders of the sheep, His people, being joined together hand in hand in their union and concord, now ascribe in their song of praise to our Lord God, Who is the true Head and Shepherd of the flock.

"But also the triumphant Star of Christ from the East is now the believing and God-fearing king.

"And just as that star guided those of old to Christ our God, that they might repair to the cave and offer gifts for the honour of His worship ; so he also now has manifested and caused to shine forth the splendour of the true faith to the whole cave of his dominion. And he has also taken down the middle wall of partition that divided[1] and cleft asunder the unity of the members of the holy Church ; thereby making them grow into a perfect man of complete stature. So that he has displayed the body in one Person and figure, and he has made of two one. For we understand also from the thankful letter of thy Holiness that he too like David, in prophesying and in reigning, has now slain Goliath in the field[2] with the Cross alone ; and having smitten the evil one as with a sling, he has overthrown and destroyed[3] him by his faithful letter which he wrote ; and by the true sword of the Spirit which he displayed, he has cut off and taken away those heresies and stumbling-blocks which are the very heads of the Dragon ; whom also having overthrown, he has thrust into outer darkness, and has bound and imprisoned him in the lower parts of the earth.

"Accordingly Jerusalem above, the mother of the first-born, shall rejoice, and also in her daughters the Churches she shall exult and sing, giving praise to God, with prayer for

---

[1] ܡܟܣܗܝ, MS., not ܡܟܣܗ, as L.

[2] For ܟܪܒܐ perhaps we should read ܒܪܒܪܝܐ, Barbarian.

[3] ܣܚܦܗ, MS., not ܣܚܠܦܗ, as L.

the triumph of the king, and saying, 'Glory be to the Most High Lord, Who is greatly to be praised.' For we also were amazed at the triumph of God, when we learned from thy letter that the Henotikon, which in our own presence was despatched to thy Holiness by the hands of Pergamius, had reached thee, and that thou hast agreed to it. And we exult in thy faith, and we pray that the Lord may preserve[1] for us the life of this believing king who has united us to the truth. And now I, and those who are with me, sending greetings to thy Chastity, and to the excellent clergy, and to the chaste monks, and to the believing people, have written this letter of reply."[2]

The end of the letter of Acacius of Constantinople.

CHAPTER XII

THE TWELFTH CHAPTER TELLS ABOUT THE LETTER OF MARTYRIUS OF JERUSALEM, WHICH HE WROTE TO PETER WHO HAD BECOME BISHOP IN ALEXANDRIA, IN THE FOLLOWING TERMS[3]

"Martyrius of Jerusalem — to the pious and Christ-loving chief priest, my lord, and brother, and fellow-minister Peter.

"It is time for us now to say, like the prophet, ' I praise Thee, O Lord God ; and I glorify Thy Name: for Thou hast done marvellous things ; for Thy will is true of old. Amen, O Lord!'[4] For our mouth is filled with gladness and our tongue with praise ; because we have certainly seen the heart of the king in the Hand of the Lord, fulfilling His will in truth continually ; and he has united again the severed members.

"And now that we have received thine Affection's reply, our people join with this prophet in crying aloud, ' Lift

---

[1] ܟܝܢܐ, MS., not ܟܢܝܐ, as L.   [2] Read ܦܘܩܬܐ for ܦܘܩܬܐ.
[3] Cf. Evag. iii. 16.   [4] Isa. xxv. 1.

up thine eyes round about thee, and behold thy children gathering together unto thee.'[1]   For which blessing, as is right, we exult ; and we greet thy Holiness in the Lord. And, singing psalms with the prophet David, we say, ' May the Lord increase you more and more, you and your children ; blessed are ye of the Lord, Who made heaven and earth.'[2] I and those who are with me, send our best respects in the Lord also to the priests who are with thy Chastity, and to the believing people, and to the pious monks."

The end of this letter of Martyrius of Jerusalem.

[1] Isa. lx. 4.   [2] Ps. cxv. 14, 15.

BOOK VI

THE sixth Book taken from the work of Zachariah, containing seven chapters.

The first tells about the Separatists [1] from the communion of Peter, because he received the Henotikon.

The second tells of Cosmas the *Spatharius* who was sent by Zeno; and the transactions which took place in Alexandria with the seceding monks.

In the third there is an account of Peter and Isaiah the monk.

In the fourth we are told about Arsenius the prefect, who was sent to Alexandria; and how he acted towards the Separatists.

Then the fifth tells of the letter of Fravitta, who was bishop in Constantinople, to Peter.

The sixth contains a record of the letter of Peter to Fravitta.

The seventh gives information respecting the chief priests who were in the days of Zeno; and also concerning the length of Zeno's life.

[1] ܦ̈ܣܘܩܝܐ, *i.e.* ἀποσχίσται.

CHAPTER I

THE FIRST CHAPTER OF THIS SIXTH BOOK TELLS ABOUT THOSE WHO SECEDED FROM THE COMMUNION OF PETER, BECAUSE THERE WAS NO EXPRESS ANATHEMA OF THE SYNOD OF CHALCEDON AND THE TOME OF LEO, EITHER IN THE HENOTIKON OR IN THE LETTERS OF THE CHIEF PRIESTS TO HIM

Matters having been thus arranged by the king's Henotikon, and three or four of the chief priests, namely, the bishops of Ephesus, and of Jerusalem, and of Alexandria, and of Antioch, together with the bishops in their jurisdictions, being united and agreed together according to the purport of this Henotikon of Zeno, and having received and subscribed to it; then Julian and John, presbyters of Alexandria, and Helladius and Serapion, deacons, venerable men belonging to the Church there, and Theodore the bishop of Antinoe, and John and another Egyptian, and Andrew the great archimandrite,[1] and Paul the Sophist, and other illustrious monks, seceded from the communion of Peter of Alexandria. But they took this course because there was no clear and decided anathema of the Synod and the Tome, either in the Henotikon or in the letters of the chief priests to Peter. And gradually the number of these Separatists was increased, and they received a considerable accession to their numbers in the monastery. And Acacius of the royal city, having heard it, wrote to urge them to be reunited.

But Peter in his public address,[2] and the other apologies which he made before the people, continued to revile the Synod. And, at length, Acacius heard this also, and he sent his presbyter to inquire into the freedom and the faith of Peter. And there ensued an investigation[3] before the judge[4] of the

---

[1] ܐܪ̈ܟܝܡܢܕܪܝܛܐ, MS., not ܐܪ̈ܟܝܡܢܕܪܛܐ, as L.

[2] ܦܪܘܣܦܘܢܣܝܣ, i.e. προσφώνησις.

[3] ܦܪܐܩܛܝܣ, i.e. πρᾶξις.

[4] ܐܩܕܝܩܘܣ, i.e. ἔκδικος.

city on this point, that the Synod had not been expressly anathematised by Peter, and the report of this reached the ears of many and proved a stumbling-block to them. And many demands were made of him by the seceding archimandrite and bishop. Then Peter the Iberian, the bishop of Gaza, who was sojourning there, and Elijah the monk, surnamed *the potter*, were appointed to consider and examine into these matters. And having examined into them, together with the council of the monks, they selected four of Peter's discourses concerning the faith, and they said to him, " If thou dost agree to these, sign them "; and he signed them. Whereupon several of them entered into communion with him, because he thereby anathematised the Synod and the Tome, when he delivered those discourses in the ears of the people. However, the others remained unwilling to hold communion with Peter. And the latter, seeing this, took away the monastery of Bishop Theodore, and thrust out that wonderful man, who had opened the eyes of a blind man by the aspersion of water from the baptismal font. Upon which there arose a great agitation among the monks, and they sent Nephalius, who was one of those that had been ejected by Peter, and was also a disturber of the people, to Zeno the king.

CHAPTER II

THE SECOND CHAPTER OF THIS SIXTH BOOK TELLS ABOUT NEPHALIUS, WHO WENT UP TO THE KING, AND MADE A COMPLAINT AGAINST PETER ; AND HOW COSMAS THE *SPATHARIUS* WAS SENT (TO ALEXANDRIA), AND WHAT WAS DONE UPON HIS ENTRY THERE

Nephalius,[1] a monk,[2] and by his disposition and habits a disturber of the people, made preparations and went up to Zeno the king, bringing with him a letter from his fellow

---

[1] Evag. iii. 22.

[2] A similar account of him is given in *das Leben des Severus* (ed. Spanuth), pp. 26 and 27.

Separatists ; in which they testified against Peter that he had plundered[1] them, and ejected them, and taken away their monasteries.

And the king, when he heard it, was very angry with Peter, and sent Cosmas his *Spatharius* with a letter containing threats against Peter, and declaring that his Majesty had been so indulgent as to appoint him the bishop of Alexandria, with the object of uniting the people together, and not keeping them divided into two parts.

And Cosmas having arrived, in company with Nephalius, and the letter having been delivered to Peter: then the monks assembled at the Martyr Church of St. Euphemia, to the number of about thirty thousand, and ten bishops with them. But a message was sent to them, that they should not enter the city lest the people should be excited, and a tumult[2] should ensue.   However, Theodore the bishop, and John, and Julian and John the presbyters, and Palladius[3] and Serapion the deacons, and Andrew the Great, and Paul the Sophist, with about two hundred archimandrites, were selected as representatives ; and they entered the great church to have an interview with Peter.   Then they had a long conversation with Cosmas the *Spatharius* and the prefect of the city.   And the king's letter was read aloud.

Then Peter delivered an apologetic address to them, anathematising, in their ears, the Synod and the Tome.   And he further wrote in his own hand to the following effect: " I, Peter, the bishop of Alexandria, do now, as I have often before, anathematise all that was said and devised in Chalcedon against the true faith of the holy fathers, the three hundred and eighteen bishops ; and also the Tome of Leo. And I confess that these are my own works, and that anyone not agreeing with them, whether bishop, or presbyter, or deacon, or monk, or layman, is an alien.   And if I (or any other person) shall ever write in agreement with the transactions of the Synod and the contents of the Tome, I shall become thereby a castaway from the Holy Trinity."

---

[1] ܟܒ, MS., not ܟܒ, as L.   [2] ܐܣܛܣܝܣ, *i.e.* στάσις.

[3] For ܦܠܕ we should probably read ܐܠܕ, Helladius.

However, the monks would not accept this confession, for they said that Peter associated in communion with the chief priests, who had uttered no express anathema against the Synod and the Tome, as he had done.

And Peter replied, "My reason for holding communion with them is that they have accepted the king's Henotikon, which cancels all additions, and the transactions of every place, except the three holy Synods, I mean those of Nicea, Ephesus, and Constantinople. And in my public address I explained the Henotikon, and showed you how it nullified the Synod of Chalcedon, by accepting the twelve Heads of the blessed Cyril, and by anathematising Nestorius, and Eutyches, and every other who would assert the duality of the Natures . in Christ, and would ascribe the miracles to one and the sufferings to the other, and would divide the Persons in properties and in operations.

But after all this discussion, even then only a few of the monks consorted with Peter. And the others presented a libel against him to Cosmas. And they took their monasteries and dwelt in them, assembling by themselves. But they endeavoured to appoint a bishop instead of Peter. However, Theodore the bishop, being an orderly man, restrained them, saying, "It is not fitting treatment for one who believes as we do, and anathematises the Synod and the Tome (even though he may hold communion with those that have received and signed the Henotikon), lest we be blamed for rejecting him, and be accounted as disorderly persons." But they say that Theodore took this course because he was one of the bishops who laid hands upon Peter.

The people, however, since they received Peter without dispute when he anathematised the Synod, were greatly incensed against the monks. But they were restrained by the chiefs and by Peter, so that there was no public tumult.

CHAPTER III

THE THIRD CHAPTER TELLS HOW COSMAS, WHEN RETURNING TO THE KING, PASSED THROUGH TO PALESTINE, IN ORDER TO TAKE WITH HIM PETER THE IBERIAN AND ISAIAH THE MONK, ACCORDING TO THE KING'S ORDERS

But Cosmas on his return passed through Palestine, and sought for Peter the Illustrious and Isaiah the able [1] monk. However, he could not find Peter, because the latter had previous intimation of his coming, and had departed from before him.

But Isaiah prayed to God that a sickness might overtake him; lest, if he were to go up to the royal city, he might show himself a flatterer of the rich men there. And so it befell him.

And when Cosmas reached him and gave him the king's letter, he showed him his sickness and infirmity, saying, " As I am a sick man, I cannot possibly endure to embark upon the sea, lest I die at once. And then I could not appear before the king; and you would be censured both by God and the king if you were to carry a corpse round the world." And in this way he succeeded in escaping. And shortly afterwards he recovered. And he persevered in the exercise of his habits, and of his conflicts all the days of his life. This man was indeed a seer, a sharer (as we may say) in the name and in the actions of the prophet Isaiah.

[1] ܩܘܡܣܛܝܩܐ, *i.e.* πρακτικός.

CHAPTER IV

THE FOURTH CHAPTER TELLS HOW ARSENIUS WAS SENT AS PREFECT TO ALEXANDRIA BY THE KING, WHEN THE LATTER LEARNED THE STATE OF AFFAIRS FROM COSMAS RESPECTING THE SEPARATIST MONKS AND THE ORDERS THEN GIVEN BY THE PREFECT

When Cosmas [1] the *Spatharius* returned to the king, and presented a written communication informing him of the affairs in Alexandria, and about the Separatist monks, and their leaders, and the bishops; then he sent Arsenius there as prefect, and also gave him authority over the Romans. And he ordered that Theodore and John the bishops, and Agathon, and Julian, and John the presbyters, and Helladius and Serapion the deacons, and Paul and Andrew the archimandrites, and all the others should be called to unity, according to the terms of the faith laid down in the Henotikon, once or twice, by Peter the bishop of Alexandria; and that, in the event of their refusing to join in communion with him, they should be ejected from their monasteries.

And upon the arrival of Arsenius, this Nephalius, the disturber of the people, again attached himself to him. Then he brought together the bishops and the presbyters and the archimandrites; and he showed them the king's command, which he read aloud in their hearing. And Peter also readily repeated to them his explanation and anathema, at the same time entreating them to join in communion with himself. However, they would neither accept nor be satisfied with this. But Theodore the bishop said to him, " If you make a written statement abjuring the communion of the other chief priests and sign it,[2] then we will enter into communion with you." And Peter, in reply, made the same defence as before, saying, " It is right for me to associate with those who receive the Henotikon, which teaches the true faith."

[1] Evag. iii. 22.

[2] ܟܘܣܝ, L.   The MS. is indistinct, probably we should read ܟܪܗ.

Whereupon these men were compelled by Arsenius to go to the king, and personally to lay their petitions and wishes before him; so that then his command might be fully carried out. And they all went, with the exception of Theodore, who withdrew himself. And when they appeared before the king, he was astonished both at their chastity and at their reasoning with him about everything which was displeasing to them in his transactions.

But while they were there, Acacius[1] the bishop of Constantinople died. And Fravitta was appointed as his successor; a gentle and believing man, who wrote a letter, after the canonical manner, and sent it by some clergy, to Peter of Alexandria. And Peter received it gladly; and he also wrote a reply, in which he expressly anathematised the Synod and the Tome of Leo. And while this was on its way, Fravitta died. And Euphemius, a man of Apamea, who was educated at Alexandria, was appointed as his successor. However, he was tainted with the Nestorian heresy.

And when he received the letter he was very indignant. And he was even angry with Longinus the presbyter and Andrew the deacon, the clergy who conveyed this letter; and he brought an accusation against them. But they deprecated his accusation by showing the zeal of the people of Alexandria. And Euphemius severed himself from Peter's communion; and he sought to bring about the deprivation of Peter, intending for that purpose to convene a separate Synod. But Archelaus the bishop of Cæsarea, a man of wonderful learning, restrained him, saying, "It is not possible for the great bishop of Alexandria to be accused and ejected by a Synod of one province; only a General Council could do that." But when Peter heard it, he also uttered threats against Euphemius; that, just as the blessed Cyril had sent Nestorius to Oasis, so he would in like manner eject Euphemius from his see. However, Peter also departed this life. But his letter was seen[2] in Constantinople, and it convinced many that he was a believer. And John and Julian the Alexandrians, and the rest of their associates who happened to be there, the Separatists, on seeing

[1] Evag. iii. 23.   [2] The MS. has ܟܡ before ܐܬܚܙܝܬ.

his letter to Fravitta, changed their minds; and they were ready on their return to Alexandria to join in communion with him. But while they were returning, he died. And his successor [1] was Athanasius, an eloquent, believing, and peace-loving man. He, desiring and exerting himself to bring the Separatist monks into communion with the Church, in the course of his address to the people mentioned the names of Dioscorus and Timothy, but he purposely omitted to mention the name of Peter in order to try them. Whereupon they became greatly excited (and they would not be quiet) until he named Peter also in his discourse.

CHAPTER V

THE FIFTH CHAPTER OF THIS BOOK GIVES THE LETTER OF FRAVITTA OF CONSTANTINOPLE TO PETER OF ALEXANDRIA, IN THE FOLLOWING TERMS

"To our holy father, and God-loving fellow-minister, Peter, from Fravitta, who sends greetings in the Lord. When I weigh mine own natural weakness, and I wonder at the merciful acts of God towards me, I truly perceive that it is absolutely (?) that ' He raises up the poor from the dunghill to set him with the princes of the people.' [2] And it is well known that this mercy of God is not the consequence of any meritorious deeds on man's part; but that it results from the divine grace which arises, time after time, upon the sons of the Church, through the love of the Father. So that it is not the wise, nor the disputers, nor the eloquent of this world whom grace raises up as leaders by the election.

"Now, before the Law, Abel, though not learned,[3] was acceptable to God; as were also the righteous fathers who came after him. But under the Law, grace marked out shepherds and herdsmen, and gatherers of sycamore fruit,[4] and raised them up as prophets. And after the Law, the same

---

[1] Evag. iii. 23.   [2] Ps. cxiii. 7, 8.

[3] So MS. ܩܘܣܝܐ, not ܩܘܣܝܐ, as L.   [4] Amos vii. 14 (Syriac).

grace appointed fishermen, and a tent-maker, to be the preachers of the living word from heaven. That thus the power of God might be truly known to be made manifest and perfect in the weak. And such are the mysteries of Christians who hold fast the Incarnation of Christ; according to His own word in the Gospel, 'I thank Thee, O Father, Lord of heaven and earth, that Thou hast hidden these things from the wise and prudent, and hast revealed them unto babes: even so, Father, for such is Thine own will.'[1]

"For Jesus Christ our God is the foundation and the corner-stone of the Holy Church. And therefore these blessings, which we have received, are not a strange display of His mercy. But we hope[2] that from them we shall understand His equal mercy towards other men; and we shall show ourselves gentle and kind to our brethren in the flesh and in the faith, and to the priests who are our fellow-ministers and Christ-loving brothers. Thus we shall endeavour[3] to rule the Holy Church everywhere in the same right faith, and in perfect love. And by the events which are taking place (the Lord helping us) we shall show the rational flock which has been intrusted to our care in all places to be one; that of the Great Shepherd, Who has appointed us to be the leaders of His flock. And we shall drive out those grievous wolves, the accursed heresies, more especially of Nestorius and Eutyches, by preaching and holding the faith of the holy fathers, who maintained the truth and preserved the order of the Church, and in our day teaching the right faith to the people and to mankind, as well as they.

"But, using brotherly love and concord in my salutation, I now present to thy Holiness the pledge of my affection, by the hands of Longinus the presbyter and Andrew the deacon. And to complete what is right, I send my greetings to all the pastors, and the honourable priests, and the chaste monks, and the believing people of thy jurisdiction. We,

---

[1] Luke x. 21.

[2] For ‫ܠܐ‬ I read ‫ܐܠܐ‬, and for ‫ܡܣܒܪ‬ I read ‫ܢܣܒܪ‬. The whole passage is difficult to translate, owing to defects in the MS.

[3] ‫ܢܬܚܦܛ‬, MS., not ‫ܢܬܚܦܦ‬, as L.

moreover, entreat thy Holiness to pray along with us, that we may show ourselves wise men and rulers in all matters, like Solomon, and like Paul and Peter and the rest of the apostles, in preaching the truth to the sons of the Church; and that in everything about which you refer to us, we may be able, to the best of our ability, to render fitting aid to the other Churches; and also in those matters taking place in the Christ - loving city, through the enactment of the Christ - loving and indulgent king, who is watchful and studious and desirous to bring · about the peace of the Churches, and the concord of the priests, and the unity of the people.

"I and the brethren with me send our best respects to thy Chastity, and to the brethren with thee."

CHAPTER VI

THE SIXTH CHAPTER OF THIS SIXTH BOOK TELLS ABOUT THE LETTER OF PETER THE BISHOP OF ALEX-ANDRIA, WHICH HE WROTE IN REPLY TO FRAVITTA OF CONSTANTINOPLE, IN THE FOLLOWING TERMS

"To my pious and God-loving brother and fellow-minister, my lord Fravitta, from Peter, who sends greetings in the Lord.

"In consequence of the election of thine Eminence, it is time now for us to say, 'Ye heavens above be glad, and let the earth with her fulness rejoice, and let her sing with [1] joy,' according to the word of the prophet.[2]

"For also, our Lord Jesus Christ, Who is the one only-begotten Son of God the Father, has not redeemed [3] us with corruptible things, as silver and gold; but He rather laid down His life for us, as a lamb without blemish; and He offered a sacrifice of sweet savour to God His Father; and

---

[1] For ܐܪܥܐ I read ܐܪܥܐ.

[2] It seems to be a free quotation from Isa. xliv. 23 or xlix. 13.

[3] Reading ܩܒܠ for ܩܢܐ.

gave His body as a substitute for the life of the whole
human race. He Who is honoured by all creation, and is
equal to the Father, God the Word, became incarnate; yet
He suffered thereby no variation nor change; but He as
man remains the same, and He is in truth alive for ever, the
Word of His Father, and of the same nature. Come then,
as with one tongue and one believing, Christ-loving mind, let
us offer to Him thanksgiving, and say with the blessed Baruch,
' This is our God, there is none other beside Him. He found
out the whole way of wisdom, and gave it to Jacob His servant, and to Israel His beloved. And afterwards, He appeared
upon the earth, and had converse with men.'[1] For there was
not indeed One the Son of God, Who existed before the times
and ages, through Whom all things were made; and another
who, in the last time, was born in the flesh from the *Theotokos*;
according to the notion of Nestorius. But rather He, being
the same, took the seed of Abraham, according to the word of
the blessed Paul;[2] and also He was partaker of our flesh and
blood, and was made like us in all points, sin only excepted.
For neither do we say that the body of our Lord Jesus Christ
is from heaven, as Eutyches in his folly affirms; nor that He
became incarnate in semblance or imagination; on the contrary, we anathematise all such teachers. But we confess one
only - begotten Son of God the Father, Who is our Lord
Jesus Christ. And we know that He, God the Word of
the Father, Who became incarnate for our redemption, in
His divine nature took the likeness of a servant, by the
dispensation.

" This is the faith of the Church of Alexandria, by which
we are all adorned, both we, and the God-fearing bishops and
clergy, and the monks, and all the people of God. And the
congregation of the people grows and multiplies exceedingly
in the Churches, while we are obedient to the apostle, who
says, " If any man shall preach to you any other gospel than
what we have preached, let him be accursed.'[3]

" But the cause of all these blessings so dear and acceptable to us, was the election of thy Piety's Eminence, which

[1] Bar. iii. 35-37.   [2] Heb. ii. 16.   [3] Gal. i. 8 and 9.

has been mentioned above; and also the goodwill of the believing and Christ-loving King Zeno, who consented to thine
election.   And he also, for the ·sake of the unity of the
people, and that we might be established in power and in the
truth, by what he wrote so faithfully in the Henotikon, anathematised all the rash thoughts and words of Chalcedon and
the Tome of Leo.

"And we consent to this same document; and we preach
it, by word of mouth and by writing, to the believing nations;
as also our ever-memorable and holy brother and fellow-
minister Acacius was seen to hold and teach until his death,
when the Alexandrians testified to us his true faith, as thy
Holiness is also persuaded.   For it is right for the Christ-
loving king, not only to subdue enemies, and to set the
Barbarian races beneath his feet; but also to expose the
snares of these intellectual enemies, and to cause the true
faith to shine upon the believing people.   For thy Holiness
has risen up and bloomed forth for us like the plant of peace.
And this is the gift of the believing king to us, by the
will of God, Who chose him before, as we have already said.
And, therefore, we are delighted at this, that such a good
priest should arise and appear for the believing nations.
May God keep him, and may He adorn him with the
heavenly crown by His own rich Hand, as we hope and
pray that he may be found walking in the whole way of
the truth, in the footsteps of the holy fathers, a believing
chosen priest, by the mercy of our Saviour Christ, through
Whom, to the Father, with the Holy Spirit, be glory for evermore!

"But we welcomed affectionately the bearers of the letter
of thy Righteousness the excellent Longinus the presbyter and
Andrew the deacon; and we now send them back in peace
to thy Holiness."

But Athanasius[1] also wrote in the same strain, two years
afterwards, to Palladius, who was Peter's successor in Antioch,
expressly anathematising the Synod, and quoting freely from
the Henotikon.[2]

---

[1] Evag. iii. 23.   [2] Or using more freedom of speech than the Henotikon.

And John [1] was appointed as the successor of Athanasius; and when anyone would ask [2] him to give an anathema of the Synod and the Tome in writing, he would give it cheerfully and without fear. Now Flavian, who was the successor of Palladius in Antioch, sent Solomon, a presbyter of his Church, to this John of Alexandria. And Solomon asked John for a letter to Flavian, concerning the concord in the faith. But John would not consent to do this for him, until he should receive from him a sworn statement that he would send him a letter from Flavian in which there would be an anathema of the Synod and the Tome. And John, his namesake and successor, was believing and acting in like manner.

Now after Zeno had reigned seventeen years, and matters had been thus carried on in the Church; and also the tyrants Basiliscus and Marcus had risen up against him, and been driven out, as we have related above; and again, Illus and Leontius and Euprepius had rebelled against him and been slain in the East; and again, in his days, one Theodoric a tyrant had taken captives from Thrace and many other places, and had gone to Rome and subdued it, because Odoacer [3] the Anti-Cæsar there fled before him to Ravenna a city of Italy; Zeno died in the year eight hundred and two, according to the Greek mode of reckoning.

And Anastasius, his successor, received the kingdom on the fourth day of the Great Week; when Euphemius was the bishop of Constantinople; and Flavian of Antioch; and Athanasius of Alexandria; and Sallustius, the successor of Martyrius, of Jerusalem; and Felix, the successor of Simplicius, of Rome.

CHAPTER VII

THE SEVENTH CHAPTER TELLS WHO WERE THE CHIEF PRIESTS IN THE DAYS OF ZENO

But the following were the chief priests in the days of Zeno. In Rome, after Hilarus, Simplicius, the author of the

---

[1] Liberat. 18.　　　　　[2] ܟܬܒ, MS., for ܟܬܒ, L.

[3] Text, "Arcadius," from the confusion between ܪ and ܕ.

10

letter to Zeno respecting John the liar, who was ejected from Alexandria; and after him Felix, who was still living when Anastasius became the emperor.

In Alexandria, Timothy the Great, who was recalled from banishment; and Timothy Salophiaciolus; and John, who was forthwith ejected; and Peter; and his successor, Athanasius.

In Jerusalem, Anastasius; and. Martyrius; and Sallustius.

In Antioch, Martyrius, who was ejected; and Julian; and Stephen; and the other Stephen; and Peter the Believer; and Calandion, who was ejected; and Palladius; and Flavian, his successor, who was ejected in the days of Anastasius.

In Constantinople, after Gennadius,[1] Acacius; and Fravitta, his successor; and Euphemius, his successor, who was ejected in the days of Anastasius.

But in this sixth Book and in the fifth Book preceding it, which have been translated concisely and briefly (so to speak) in contracted style, for the information of. the Syriac reader, from the Greek History of Zachariah the Rhetorician; which he wrote thus far, in protracted style, after the manner of Greek amplification;[2] there is a period of seventeen years, comprising only the life of the Emperor Zeno.

---

[1] For ܝ read ܝ.

[2] ܩܘܒܠܘ, *i.e.* πλάτος.

BOOK VII

THIS seventh Book, in the fifteen chapters which are contained in it as given below, tells about the events that occurred in the reign of Anastasius; in the first chapter, about the beginning of his reign, and how Epiphanius the bishop was ejected; and in the second chapter, about the Isaurians who rebelled and were subdued, and the tyrants at the head of them were killed; and in the third chapter, about Theodosiopolis and Amida, the cities which were subdued; and in the fourth, about the manner in which the city of Amida was subdued; and the fifth, about the famine that was in it, and how the Persians departed from it; the sixth, about Dara, how the city was built; the seventh, about the expulsion of Macedonius, who was ejected from Constantinople; the eighth, containing the letter of Simeon the presbyter, giving information concerning his expulsion; the ninth, about his successor Timothy, and how the expression, "Who was crucified for us," was proclaimed in Constantinople in his days; the tenth, about the Synod which was held in Sidon in the days of Flavian and Akhs'noyo the bishops, in the fifth year,[1] the eight hundred and twenty-third year of the Greeks; the eleventh, about the petition which was framed by the monks of the East and Cosmas of Antioch, and presented to the Synod; the twelfth chapter, about the Synod that was held in Tyre in the days of Severus and Akhs'noyo, which anathematised the Council of Chalcedon and the Tome of Leo with great freedom of speech; the thirteenth chapter, about Ariadne the queen, who died, and about Vitalian the tyrant, who took Hypatius prisoner in war; the fourteenth chapter, about Timothy, who died, and his

---

[1] *I.e.* of the Indiction = A.D. 512.

successor was John ; and about demons that entered into the Egyptians, and Alexandrians, and Arabians who came to the dedication festival at Jerusalem, and barked at the Cross and then ceased ;[1] the fifteenth, telling who were chief priests in the days of Anastasius the king. Anastasius, then, died in the eight hundred and twenty-ninth year of the Greeks, in the three hundred and twenty-fourth Olympiad.

CHAPTER I

THE FIRST CHAPTER OF THIS SEVENTH BOOK TREATS OF
THE REIGN OF THE EMPEROR ANASTASIUS WHO
RECEIVED THE KINGDOM AFTER ZENO, AND OF
EUPHEMIUS[2] THE BISHOP THERE, WHO WAS EJECTED

Zeno,[3] having reigned seventeen years, as is recorded above in the sixth Book and its chapters, died in the three hundred and seventeenth Olympiad, in the eight hundred and second year by the reckoning of the Greeks, the fourteenth Indiction, on the fourth day of the Great Week. And Anastasius, who was silentiary decurion, received the kingdom. This man was from the city of Dyrrhachium, and was powerful in aspect, vigorous in mind, and a believer. When he was a soldier he had confidential friendship with Ariadne the queen, who desired and agreed to make him king.[4] To this man a few days before he became king [it happened as follows].[5] There was a certain person named John the Scholastic, brother of Dith, a native of Amida, a valiant man, and just and upright, fearing God and forsaking evil ; but by his own accord and freewill

---

[1] The text has ﹍﹍﹍, which cannot be translated ; for it I read ﹍﹍﹍, which is almost identical in meaning with the word ﹍﹍. See ch. 14, where the full expression is ﹍﹍ ﹍﹍ ﹍﹍, "and then were silent and went out."

[2] Called Epiphanius in the Introduction to this Book.

[3] Here begins an extract in Cod. Rom.

[4] ﹍﹍ ; the reading of the Cod. Rom. is ﹍﹍, which may be rendered "his accession."

[5] The words in brackets are not in the Syriac, but they must be understood.

he was constant in the ministry, being a scholastic of the Church.   And when he was in Constantinople on a confidential mission[1] on behalf of his city, he saw a vision once, and again a second time, showing that Anastasius the silentiary should be made king.   And he called him, and said to him, " In accordance with the rectitude and the virtues and the honour of thy soul, that thou mayest fulfil the goodwill of God, do thou be peaceable and gentle and modest and upright, and show thyself towards everyone quiet and kind for the benefit of all men, who are thy kindred.   It is not because I want anything from thee, or because I would flatter thee, that I reveal to thee that thou shalt be made king very soon."   And because this John was celebrated and honoured for his merits, and was known also to many, and, moreover, because he was a learned man,[2] Anastasius believed him, and took it as true ; and he was constant with him there in the vigil of the church.   But it happened that when he received the kingdom, and he was desirous of rewarding his friend with gifts of gratitude such as are sought after by[3] and visible to men, this John would not take anything at all from him ; but he soon left the city and returned to his own country : being content with the documents[4] which Zeno had drawn up, he only took assurance from Anastasius that they should be received.

But Euphemius the bishop there had been threatening Peter of Alexandria that he would decree his deprivation, because he wrote expressly a reply to Fravitta the predecessor of Euphemius, and also because in his synodical letter which was sent by some clergy, Longinus the presbyter and Andrew the deacon, he had anathematised the Synod of Chalcedon and the Tome.   But at that time Euphemius was prevented from doing this by the advice of Archelaus, bishop of Cæsarea,

---

[1] Or, "with liberty to treat on behalf of his city" ; the Syriac is ܒܦܪܗܣܝܐ, i.e. ἐν παῤῥησία.

[2] ܕܝܠܩܛܝܩܐ, "skilled in dialectics."

[3] ܡܬܒܥܝܢ, MS., not ܡܬܚܙܝܢ, as L.

[4] ܟܪܛܝܣ, i.e. χάρτης, perhaps the Henotikon. Cod. Rom. has ܕܐܬܩܢ ܙܢܘܢ, and Mai translates, "quæ Zeno pro Christianis constituerat." Here the extract in Cod. Rom. ends.

a wise man who happened to be there. And when Peter died, Euphemius maintained the same hatred against Athanasius, Peter's successor in the bishopric of Alexandria, who more openly and authoritatively anathematised the Synod and the Tome; against him Euphemius was making preparations to depose him, and called in Felix of Rome to his aid. And when his machination became known to Athanasius through his *Apokrisiarioi* there, who wrote and also sent to him a copy of the letter which had been sent by him[1] to Felix, then Athanasius made preparation, and wrote to Sallust of Jerusalem, and received a reply from him concerning the agreement of the faith. And they both informed Anastasius the king respecting Euphemius that he was a heretic, and showed a copy of his letter in confirmation (of their charge). And when his deeds were examined by certain bishops who happened to be in Constantinople, and also by believing monks from Alexandria and the East, he was banished and ejected from his see; and Macedonius, who also was ejected fifteen years later, as is recorded below, became bishop in his stead.

CHAPTER II

THE SECOND CHAPTER OF THIS BOOK TELLS US HOW ISAURIA REVOLTED

Now the Isaurians prospered in the days of Zeno (who withdrew before Basiliscus and Marcus the tyrants, and dwelt[2] as a refugee in the strongholds there called Salmon); and they also had free intercourse[3] in the kingdom in his days, and he was their rewarder, and he counted them worthy to receive good things of all kinds from him; and on that account they could not bear their good fortune, but were proud[4] and insolent when Anastasius became king. And they raised a rebellion against him, and they appointed a

---

[1] *I.e.* by Euphemius.   [2] For ܩܡܠܝ, MS., ܩܠܟܝ, L., read ܩܠܝ.
[3] Or, "great influence"; the word is ܦܪܗܣܝܐ, *i.e.* παρρησία.
[4] ܡܟܘܐܒܝ; see p. 199, note 4.

tyrant for themselves, and they refused the gifts which were sent to them by Anastasius, and they would not consent to give him tribute, but they even raided the provinces[1] round about them. And when an outcry[2] and accusation[3] against them was brought to the king, he sent an army and made preparations against them. And the Isaurians were defeated in battle; and they showed themselves to be weak, and were subdued, and the tyrants were killed.

But an earthquake occurred. And locusts invaded 'Arab[4] of Mesopotamia. And there was a famine in the year nine,[5] of which James the doctor of Batnæ wrote an account, in the eleventh (year) of the reign of Anastasius. And many of the Arabs died, both in Amida, whither they retired, and in various other places.

CHAPTER III[6]

THE THIRD CHAPTER OF THIS SEVENTH BOOK MAKES KNOWN HOW THEODOSIOPOLIS OF ARMENIA WAS SUBDUED, AND CONCERNING THE CITY AMIDA OF MESOPOTAMIA

When[7] Piroz, king of the Persians, was reigning in his own country, in the thirteenth (year) of Anastasius, the Huns issued forth from the gates that were guarded by the Persians, and from the mountainous region there, and invaded the territory of the Persians. And Piroz became alarmed, and he gathered an army and went to meet them. And when he inquired from them the reason of their preparation and . invasion of his country, they said to him, " What the kingdom of the Persians gives to us by way of tribute is

---

[1] ܩܘܒ̈ܪ̈ܝܣܘܗܝ, *i.e.* ὑπαρχίας (meaning ἐπαρχίας).

[2] ܩܒܣ̈ܩܒܐ, *i.e.* ἐκβόησις.

[3] ܩܒܝܣܐ (ܐܒܝܣܐ), *i.e.* ἀναφορά.

[4] "'Arab," a name applied to certain districts in Mesopotamia.

[5] 501.

[6] This and the three following chapters are contained in Cod. Rom.

[7] Mich. fol. 156 v ff. ; Greg. p. 75 ff.

not sufficient for us Barbarians, who, like rapacious wild beasts, reject God in the North-West region; and we live by our weapons, our bow and our sword; and we support ourselves by flesh-food of all kinds; and the king of the Romans has promised by his ambassadors to give us twice as much tribute whenever we shall dissolve our friendship with you Persians; and accordingly we made our preparations,[1] and we have come here, that either you shall give us as much as the Romans, and we will ratify our treaty with you, or else if you do not give it to us, take war." And when Piroz perceived the determination of the Huns, although they were much fewer in number than his own army, he thought it well to play them false and deceive them; and he promised them to give it. And four hundred of the chief men of the Huns assembled, and they had with them Eustace, a merchant of Apamea, a clever man, by whose advice they were guided. But Piroz also and four hundred men with him met together. And they went up into a mountain; and they made a treaty, and they ate together, and they swore, lifting up their hands to heaven. And when few remained along with the four hundred men who were to receive[2] the tribute money which was being collected, and the rest of the Huns had dispersed to return to their own country; after ten days Piroz broke faith with them, and prepared war, both against the Huns who had dispersed, and against the four hundred who remained and those with them. But Eustace the merchant encouraged the Huns that they should not be alarmed even though they were very much fewer. And[3] in the place where the oaths were made, they cast musk and spices upon coals of fire, and made an offering to God according to the advice of Eustace, that he might overthrow the liars. And they joined battle with Piroz, and killed him and a great number of his army; and they pillaged the Persian territory, and returned to their own country. And the body of Piroz was not found; and in his country they call him *the liar*.

But Kawad, who succeeded him in the kingdom, and his

---

[1] ܐܬܛܝܒܢ, MS., not ܐܬܛܝܒܘ, as L.　　[2] Cod. Rom. has ܢܣܒܘܢ.

[3] There is a ܘ before ܩܘܡܐ in the MS., which L. does not print.

nobles cherished hatred against the Romans, saying that they
had caused the incursion of the Huns, and the pillage and the
devàstation of their country.   And Kawad gathered an army,
and went out against Theodosiopolis in Armenia of the
Romans, and subdued the city ; and he treated its inhabitants
mercifully, because he had not been insulted by them ; but
he took Constantine, the ruler of their city, prisoner.

And in the month of October[1] he reached Amida of
Mesopotamia.   (But though he assailed it) with fierce assaults
of sharp arrows and with battering-rams,[2] which thrust the
wall to overthrow it, and pent-houses,[3] which protected those
who brought together the materials for the besiegers' mound [4]
and raised it up and made it equal in height with the wall,
for three months, day after day, yet he could not take the city
by storm ; while his own people were suffering much hard-
ship through work and fighting, and he was constantly hearing
in his ears the insults of disorderly men on the wall, and their
ridicule and mockery, and he was reduced to great straits.
And indignation [5] and regret took possession of him, because
the winter came upon him in its severity, and because the
Persians, being clad in their loose garments,[6] showed themselves inefficient ; and their bows were greatly relaxed by the
moisture of the atmosphere ; and their battering-rams did not
hurt the wall or make any breaches in it, for (the defenders)
were binding bundles[7] of rushes[8] from the beds[9] with chains,
and receiving upon them the violence of the battering-rams,
and thus preventing them from breaking the wall.   But they
themselves made a breach in the wall from inside, and
they carried the material of the mound from without into

---

[1] The text has merely ܬܫܪܝ, not stating whether it was the first or the second
Theshri ; but from Josh. Styl. 50 we know that it was the first, *i.e.* October.

[2] ܪܫܝ ܕܟܪ̈ܐ, rams' heads.   [3] ܩܪ̈ܡܐ ܕܓܠܕܐ, roofs of skin, testudines.

[4] ܟܘܕܢܬܐ, lit. "mule."

[5] Read ܐܘܝܐ for ܐܢܝܘܐ, with Cod. Rom.

[6] ܣܪ̈ܒܠܝܢ, perhaps from ܣܪܒܠܐ (σαράβαλλα), "loose trousers" ; but see
p. 229, note I.

[7] ܩܘܕܪܐ, *i.e.* κόδρα, quadra.   [8] ܐܒܨܠ, not ܐܒܨܠ, as L.

[9] ܐܩܘܒܝܬܘ, *i.e.* ἀκκούβιτον, accubitum.

the fortress within, and they gradually propped up the cavity with beams from beneath. And when chosen Persian warriors ascended the mound and laid beams upon the wall to effect an entrance (now they were clad in armour, and the king was near with his army outside, and was supporting them with display of strength[1] and shooting of arrows, and encouraging them with shouting, and stimulating them and urging them forward by his presence and appearance, they being about five hundred men), the defenders threw strings of skin just flayed from an ox, and soaked vetch mixed with myrrh-oil from the wall upon the beams, and poured the liquid from the vetch upon the skins to make them slippery, and they placed fire among the props which were beneath the mound. And when they had engaged in a conflict with each other for about six hours, and (the besiegers) had failed to effect an entrance, the fire blazed up and consumed the wood of the props, and immediately also the rest of the material[2] was reduced to ashes by the violence of the fire, and[3] the mound was destroyed and fell.[4] And the Persians who were on the top of it were burned, and they were also bruised, being struck with stones by those on the wall. And the king retired with shame and grief, being more than ever mocked and insulted by those daring, proud, and boastful men. For there was no bishop in that city to be their teacher and to keep them in order. For John the bishop, a chaste and noble man of honoured character, had died a few days before. This man was called from the monastery of Karthamin, and he, having been elected, came, and he became their bishop. However, he did not change his asceticism and self-mortification and habit of life, but was constant (in them)[5] by day and by night. And he

---

[1] ܦܐܪܐ, "pomp." Cod. Rom. has ܙܝܢܐ, "arms."

[2] So Cod. Rom. ܠܐܗܘܐ for ܗܘܐ of MS. and L.'s text.

[3] Cod. Rom. has ܘ before ܐܬܢܩܙ.

[4] There appears to be some confusion in both texts; by a few slight alterations it might be made to yield this meaning, "and consumed the wood of the props, and immediately it was reduced to ashes; and the rest of the mound which escaped the violence of the fire was loosened and fell."

[5] Cod. Rom. has ܒܬܫܡܫܬܐ, "in the service."

warned [1] and rebuked the rich men of the city at the time of
the famine and the incursion of the Arabs [2] and the pestilence,
saying that they should not keep back the corn in the time of
distress, but should sell it and give to the poor; lest if they
kept it back, they might be only hoarding it for the enemy,
according to the word of Scripture. And so, in fact, it
happened.   To him an angel appeared openly, standing
beside the altar[3]-table, and he foretold to him the incursion
of the enemy, and that he should be taken away as a righteous
man from the face of the enemy; and he revealed the saying,
and published it in the presence of the people of the city, that
they might turn and be saved from the wrath.

CHAPTER IV

THE FOURTH CHAPTER OF THIS SEVENTH BOOK TELLS
HOW THE CITY OF AMIDA WAS SUBDUED, AND WHAT
BEFELL ITS INHABITANTS

When Kawad and his army had been defeated in the
various assaults which they made upon the city, and a large
number of his soldiers had perished, his hands were weakened;
and he asked that a small gift of silver should be given to
him, and he would withdraw from the city.   But Leontius, the
son of Pappus, the chief councillor, and Cyrus the governor,[4]
and Paul Bar Zainab the steward, by the messengers whom
they sent to Kawad, demanded from him the price of the
garden vegetables which his army had eaten, as well as for
the corn and wine which they gathered and brought away
from the villages.   And when he was greatly grieved at this,
and was preparing to withdraw in disgrace, Christ appeared
to him in a vision of the night, as he himself after-

---

[1] Reading ܡܙܗܪ, with Cod. Rom.

[2] So the text; but it may be corrupt, and the reference be to the invasion of
"'Arab" by locusts (see ch. 2).

[3] ܡܕܒܚܐ, MS., not ܡܕܢܚܐ (east), as L. prints it.

[4] ܗܓܡܘܢܐ, *i.e.* ἡγεμών.

wards[1] related it, and said to him, that within three days He would deliver up to him the inhabitants of the city, because they had sinned against Him; and this took place as follows:—On the western side of the city by the *Tripyrgion* was a guard of monks who were told off from the monastery of John of Anzetene,[2] and their archimandrite was a Persian. And on the outside, right opposite this watch-tower, a certain Marzban,[3] named Kanarak the Lame, was encamped. And day after day, vigilantly watching by night and by day, he was diligent and clever in devising plans for the subjugation of the city. For there was one whom they called in the city Kutrigo,[4] a turbulent and thievish fellow; this man was very daring in all kinds of attacks upon the Persians, and he used to make raids and snatch away from them cattle and goods; so that they also, being accustomed to hear the men on the wall crying out, used to call him Kutrigo. Kanarak observed this man, and perceived that he went out by the aqueducts adjoining the *Tripyrgion*, and snatched up spoil, and went in again. And for a time the Persians let him accomplish his will, marking and examining his actions, and they ran after him and saw the place from which he came out and where he went in.

But it happened on that night on which the city was subdued, that there was darkness, and a dense cloud sending down soft rain; and a certain man gave a friendly entertainment to the monks who guarded the *Tripyrgion*, and he gave them wine to drink late in the night, and consequently sleep overtook them, and they did not watch diligently upon their guard, according to their usual custom. And when[5] Kanarak and a few soldiers came up, pursuing Kutrigo, and drew near

---

[1] So Cod. Rom. The other text has [Syriac] for [Syriac], meaning, "as he himself related the sight."

[2] [Syriac]. Mr. Brooks points out that in Jo. Eph., *de Beat. Orient*, 58 (Land, *Anecd. Syr.* ii. p. 279), this word is definitely identified with " Anzetenian."

[3] [Syriac]. See Payne Smith's *John of Ephesus*, 121, note.

[4] *I.e.* "the accused," from καтηγορέω; after Kutrigo Cod. Rom. has the words [Syriac] [Syriac] [Syriac]. The meaning of [Syriac] is uncertain; Dean Payne Smith suggests λῃστρικός.

[5] For [Syriac], MS., Cod. Rom. has [Syriac].

to the wall, the monks did not cry out nor cast stones; and the man perceived that they were asleep, and he sent for scaling-ladders and for his troops; and his followers went in by the aqueducts, and climbed the tower of the monks, and killed them. And they took the tower and also the battlement[1]; and they set up the scaling-ladders against the wall, and sent to the king.

But when those who were in charge of another tower, their neighbours, heard it, they cried out, and tried to come to the monks who were being killed, and were not able; but some of them were wounded by arrows from the Persians, and died. And when the report reached Cyrus the governor, and he came up and[2] torches were held close to him, he was easily struck by an arrow from the Persians, who stood in the darkness and were themselves unhurt by the archers; and he withdrew wounded. But when it was morning, and the king and his army reached the place, they set scaling-ladders against the wall; and he ordered his troops to go up; and many of those who went up perished, being[3] wounded by arrows and by stones, and[4] driven back by spears. And those who through fear turned and fled down the scaling-ladders were killed by the king's command, as cowards and fugitives from the battle. Whereupon the Persians took courage and set themselves either to gain the victory by conquering and subduing the city, or being smitten in the actual conflict to escape reproach and slaughter from their king; for he was near, and was a spectator of their struggle. But the citizens tried to loose from beneath the keystone of the arch of the tower in which the Persians were, and they were engaged in loosening the supports; and while this was taking place, another tower was subdued, and another and another in succession, and the guards of the wall were killed.

But Peter, a man of huge stature, a native of 'Amkhoro,[5]

---

[1] ܦܪܘܿܣ, *i.e.* πεδατοῦρα, the walking space in a fortification.

[2] Cod. Rom. has ܘ before ܢܩܘܡܝܢ.   [3] Inserting ܕ with Cod. Rom.

[4] The MS. has ܘ before ܕܢܡܠܘܢ, which L. omits.

[5] This translation is conjectural. From the text it would rather seem as if ܥܡܟܘܪܐ was an adjective qualifying ܓܒܪܐ, and meaning "formidable"; but the Lexicons give no such word.

being clad in an iron coat of mail, held the battlement of one side alone by himself; and did not allow the Persians to pass, and repelled and hurled back with a spear those who assailed him from without and within, holding his ground and standing like a hero : until at length, when five or six towers on another side were subdued, he also fled and was not killed. And the Persians first got possession of the whole wall and held it ; and they spent a night and a day and the following night in killing and driving back the guards. And at last they descended and opened the gates, and the army entered, having received the king's command to destroy the men and women of all classes and ages for three days and three nights. But a certain Christian prince of the country of Arran pleaded with the king on behalf of a church called the Great Church of the Forty Martyrs; and he spared it, being full of people. And after three days and three nights the slaughter ceased by the king's command. And men went in to guard the treasures of the Church and of the great men of the city, that the king might have whatever was found in them. But the order also was given that the corpses of those who were slain in the streets and of those whom they had crucified should be collected and brought round to the northern side of the city, so that the king, who was on the south side, might enter in. And they were collected, and they were numbered as they were brought out, eighty thousand ; besides those that were heaped up in the taverns, and were thrown into the aqueducts, and were left in the houses. And then the king entered the treasury of the Church, and seeing there an image of the Lord Jesus, depicted in the likeness of a Galilean, he asked who it was. And they answered him, " It is God " ;[1] and he bowed his head before it, and said, " He it was Who said to me, ' Stay, and receive from Me the city and its inhabitants, for they have sinned against Me.' " But he took away a quantity of silver and gold of the holy vessels, and costly garments formerly belonging to Isaac Bar Bar'ai, a consul[2] and a rich man of the city, which came to the Church by inheritance a few years before. But he found there also good wine dried into its dregs, which

---

[1] Cod. Rom. and Mich. add "of the Nazarenes."   [2] ܩܘܣܠܘܣ, i.e. ὕπατος.

used to be brought out and placed in the sun for seven years together, and at last it became dry ; from this the stewards, when on their journeys, were accustomed to take some, ground to dust, in clean [1] linen pouches. And they would put a little of it into water so as to make a mixture, which, when they drank it, afforded the sweetness and flavour of wine. And they told the ignorant that it was " h'nono." [2] And the king admired it greatly, and took it away. And the art of making this agreeable beverage was lost to the sons of the Church from that time.

But the gold and silver belonging to the great men's houses, and the beautiful garments, were collected together and given to the king's treasurers. But they also took down all the statues of the city, and the sun-dials, and the marble ; and they collected the bronze and everything that pleased them, and they placed them upon wooden rafts that they made, and sent them by the river Tigris, which flows past the east of the city and penetrates into their country. But the king sought for the chiefs and great men of the city ; and Leontius, and Cyrus the governor, who was wounded by the arrow, and the rest of the great men, were brought to him ; but the Persians had killed Paul Bar Zainab the steward, lest he should make known to the king that they had found a quantity of gold in his possession. But they clothed Leontius and Cyrus in filthy garments, and put swine-ropes on their necks, and made them carry pigs, and led them about proclaiming and exposing them, and saying, " Rulers who do not rule their city well nor restrain its people from insulting the king, deserve such insult as this." But at last the great men, and all the chief craftsmen,[3] were bound and brought together, and set apart as the king's captives ; and they were sent to his country with the military escort which brought them down. But influential men of the king's army drew near and said to him, " Our kinsmen and brethren were killed in battle by the inhabitants of the city," and they asked him that one-tenth

---

[1] ܢܩܐ, MS., not ܢܩܝܐ, as L.   [2] ܚܢܢܐ, " mercy."

[3] For ܗܘܠܐ ܕܚܣ ܘܐܘܡܢܐ, which cannot be translated, I adopt Mr. Brooks' suggestion, and read ܟܘܠܗ ܪܝܫ ܐܘܡܢܐ.

of the men should be given to them for the exaction of vengeance.   And they brought them together and counted them, and gave to them in proportion from the men ; and they put them to death, killing them in all sorts of ways.

But the king bathed himself in the bath of Paul Bar Zainab, and after winter he departed from the city.   And he left in it Glon the general as governor, and two *Marzbans*, and about three thousand soldiers to guard the city, and John Bar Habloho, one of the rich men, and Sergius Bar Zabduni, to rule the people.

And then in the summer the Romans came, and their leaders were Patrick the commander-in-chief, an old man, upright and a believer, but deficient in mental power, and Hypatius, and Celer the master of the offices, and at length also Areobindus ; moreover, Count Justin, who received the kingdom after Anastasius, accompanied them.   And they met together, and they attacked [1] the city with wooden towers and excavations, and all kinds of engines ; and they set fire also to the gate of the city, which was called the gate of Mâr Z''uro, to effect an entrance upon the Persians ; however, they were hindered because they were resting, and they did not rush in, for the Persians shut the gate.   And the Romans did not subdue it nor take it from them by assault ; although the inhabitants were reduced to misery from famine, day after day, until at last the people there were eating one another.   But how this happened, although the story is horrible and wretched, yet because it is true, I shall relate how [2] in the following fifth chapter of this seventh Book.

CHAPTER V

THE FIFTH CHAPTER OF THIS SEVENTH BOOK TELLS ABOUT THE FAMINE WHICH OCCURRED WHEN AMIDA WAS BEING SUBDUED, AND HOW THE PERSIANS WENT OUT FROM IT AND DEPARTED TO THEIR OWN COUNTRY

King Kawad, as stated above, on his departure with his army from Amida to his own country, left in it Glon, a

---

[1] For ܟܘܠ, MS., I read ܟܠ, with Cod. Rom.

[2] Read ܐܝܟܢܐ݂, with Cod. Rom., for ܘܐܝܟܢܐ.

general, and two *Marzbans*, and about three thousand soldiers to guard the city; and also two or three rich men and some private inhabitants. These the Roman generals did not overcome, nor did they subdue and take the city. But at last Patrick went down to Arzanene [1] of the Persians, and carried off captives, and subdued fortresses there. And Areobindus and Hypatius went down to Nisibis and did not subdue it, although the citizens were favourably inclined towards the Romans, and showed themselves lazy [2] in the fight. However, the king of the Persians hearing of it, came with an army against the Romans; and they fled before him, and they left their tents and the heavy baggage which they had with them. Areobindus fled from Arzamena and Aphphadana,[3] and Hypatius and Patrick and others from Thelkatsro. And they lost many horses and their riders, who fell from the cliffs of the mountains, and were bruised, and perished, and were mangled.

But [4] Farzman alone, a warlike man, prospered in battle several times; and he was celebrated and dreaded amongst the Persians, and his very name terrified them, and his exploits wasted and weakened them; and they proved themselves to be cowards in his presence, and fell before him. This man at last came to Amida with five hundred horsemen, and he watched the Persians who went out to the villages, and he killed some of them, and he took the animals [5] which they had with them, and also their horses.

Now a certain crafty fellow, Gadono by name, of the town of Akhorè, whom I myself know, introduced himself to him, and made a compact with him, that he would beguile and bring out to him, on some pretext, Glon, the Persian general, and three or four hundred horsemen. And because this aforesaid Gadono was a hunter of wild animals, and partridge, and fish,[6] he used to go in freely to Glon, carrying in his hands a

---

[1] Cod. Rom. has ܐܪܥܗܘܢ, *i.e.* "the country of the Persians."

[2] For ܡܬܟܝܢ of L.'s text (ܡܬܟܢܝ, MS.) read ܘܡܬܟܝܢ, with Cod. Rom.

[3] For ܩܢܐ, MS., Cod. Rom. has ܐܦܪܝ. [4] Mich. fol. 158 *v.*

[5] The MS. has ܚܐܘܬܐ, "butter"; for it I read ܚܝܘܬܐ.

[6] For ܢܩܘܢ Cod. Rom. has ܝܘܢܐ, "pigeons."

II

present of game for him; and he ate bread in his presence, and received from him out of the property of the city what was equal in value to the game.

And at last he told him that there were about one hundred Romans and five hundred horses nearly seven miles away from the city, at a place called 'Afotho Ro"en;[1] and as a friend he advised him to go out and take possession of the beasts, to kill the Romans, and make a name for himself.

And he sent scouts, who saw a few Romans and the horses, and returned and gave him the information. Then he made preparation and took with him four hundred horsemen, and this Gadono upon a mule; and he led him and set him in the midst of the ambush of the Romans, who were on the watch for him. So the Romans cut the Persians to pieces, and they brought away the head of Glon to Constantia.[2]

Upon this, distress and rage seized the son of Glon and the Marzbans, who used to allow[3] the inhabitants who happened to be shut up in the city to go out to the market, which was held beside the wall by peasants from the villages. These peasants brought wine and wheat and other produce, and sold them both to the Persians and to the citizens, while horsemen were stationed close to them, and escorted them, a certain number at a time, and conducted them in. And by an excellent law of the Persians, no one dared to take anything from the villagers, who sold what they liked and received the price in money and kind from the city; consequently they attended the market diligently. However, in consequence of the slaughter of Glon and the horsemen, the market was held no more. And the great men who were left in the city, and about ten thousand persons besides, were arrested and shut up in the Stadium, and they were kept there without food; and they ate their shoes, and they also ate and drank their excrements. And at last they attacked one another; and now when they were almost perishing, those who were left in the Stadium

---

[1] ܥܢ̈ܐ ܕ perhaps means "the fold of the shepherds."

[2] ܠܐܛ, MS. and Cod. Rom., not ܠܛܠ, as L. prints.

[3] After ܡܪ̈ܙܒܢܐ Cod. Rom. inserts the words ܐܬܙܗܪܘ ܗܘܡܢ ܘܠܐ, "the Marzbans who were there became cautious, and would not allow."

were let loose like the dead from their graves in the midst of the city.   And famishing women, who were found there in troops, laid hold of some of the men by means of blandishments and guile and artifices, and overcame them, and killed and ate them ; and more than five hundred men were eaten by women.   And the famine which was in this city being so grievous, the distress surpassed the blockade of Samaria and the destruction of Jerusalem, which is recorded in Scripture and Josephus relates.

But at last Farzman came to the city, and he made a treaty with the Persians there, for they, too, were weak.   And the chiefs of the Romans and the Persians sat by the gate of the city, while the Persians went out carrying as much as they could, and they were not searched.[1]   And if any of the citizens accompanied them they were asked whether they desired to remain or would like to go with the Persians.   So the evacuation of the city took place.

But eleven hundred pounds of gold were given to Kawad by Celer, the master of the offices, for the ransom of the city and for peace.[2]   And when the documents were drawn up they brought the drafts[3] to the king for his signature.   And the king fell asleep, and it was told him in a vision that he should not make peace ; and when he awoke he tore up the paper, and departed to his own country, taking the gold with him.

But Farzman remained in the city to govern its inhabitants and the country.   (Now a remission of tribute was granted by the king for seven years.)   And he dealt kindly with the inhabitants of the city.   And he bestowed gifts lavishly on those who returned from captivity, and he received them peaceably, every man according to his rank.   And the city was at peace and was inhabited.[4]   And building was added to the wall.   And, by the advice of Dith, a merciful bishop was sent again to the city, a quiet and affable man, a monk, and a councillor,[5] Thomas

---

[1] For ⲥⲟⲇ Cod. Rom. has ⲥⲟⲇ, "decorated" or "armed."

[2] For ⲥⲟⲇ read ⲥⲟⲇ with Cod. Rom.

[3] ⲥⲟⲇ, i.e. ὑπογραφάς for ἀπογραφάς.

[4] ⲥⲟⲇ, MS., not ⲥⲟⲇ, as L. prints it.

[5] ⲥⲟⲇ, i.e. βουλευτής.

by name.   And, besides, the providence of God summoned and conveyed thither Samuel the Just, from the monastery of the *Katharoi*, a miracle-worker and a "dissolver of doubts";[1] and he also sustained the city by his prayers, and aided its inhabitants.

CHAPTER VI

THE SIXTH CHAPTER OF THIS SEVENTH BOOK TELLS ABOUT THE TOWN OF DARA OF MESOPOTAMIA, HOW IT WAS BUILT ON THE BORDER OF THE ROMAN AND PERSIAN TERRITORIES IN THE DAYS OF ANASTASIUS THE KING, AND THOMAS THE BISHOP OF THE CITY OF AMIDA

Anastasius[2] the king brought severe censures[3] against the Roman generals[4] and commanders who betook themselves to the royal city after the conflict with the Persians, because they did not, according to his will, under the Lord, prosper and succeed in the war, and conquer the Persians or drive them out from Amida, except by the gifts and the gold that were sent from him.   And they alleged in their defence to him, that it was hard for generals to contend with a king who according to the word of God, although he was an Assyrian and an enemy, was sent by the Lord to the country of the Romans for the punishment of sins, and, moreover, on account of the greatness of the army which he had with him; and that it was no easy matter for them in his absence also to subdue Nisibis; because they had no engines ready, nor any refuge in which to rest.   For the fortresses were far away and were too small to receive the army, and neither the supply of water in them nor the vegetables were sufficient. And they begged of him that a city should be built by his command beside the mountain, as a refuge for the army in which they might rest, and for the preparation of weapons, and to guard the country of the Arabs from the inroads of the

---

[1] Dan. v. 12.   [2] Mich. fol. 158 *r*.   [3] ܟܐܢ̈ܐ, Cod. Rom., not ܟܐܒ̈ܐ, MS.
[4] ܐܣܛܪܛܓܘ̈, *i.e.* στρατηγός.

Persians and Saracens.   And some of them spoke to him in
favour of Dara, and some in favour of Ammodis.   Then he
sent a message to Thomas the bishop of Amida, and he despatched engineers[1] who drew up a plan,[2] and this holy Thomas
brought it up with him to the king.   And the king and
the great men agreed that Dara should be built as a city.
And at that time Felicissimus was commander,[3] an energetic
and wise man; and he was not at all covetous, but was
upright, and a friend of the peasants and the poor.   Now
King Kawad was fighting with the Tamuroye and other
enemies of his country.   And the king gave gold to Thomas
the bishop as the price of the village which belonged to the
Church; and he bought[4] it for the treasury.   And he liberated
all the serfs who were in it, and granted to each of them his
land and his house.   And for the building of the church of
the city he gave several hundred pounds of gold.   And he
promised with an oath that he would give with liberal hand
whatever the bishop might expend, and that he would not
disown the obligation.   And at last he issued a royal decree,[5]
and in full detail,[6] providing that the work of building the
city should be carried out according to the direction of the
bishop without delay, gain and profit thereby accruing to the
craftsmen and slaves and peasants who were required for the
collection of material there.[7]   And he sent a number of stone-
cutters and masons; and he commanded that no man should
be deprived of the wages he earned, because he rightly perceived and cleverly understood that by that means a city
could quickly be built upon the frontier.   And when they
began by the help of the Lord and commenced the work,
there were there as overseers and commissaries over it Cyrus
'Adon and Eutychian the presbyters, and Paphnout and
Sergius and John the deacons, and others from the clergy of
Amida.   And the bishop himself paid frequent personal visits

---

[1] ܡܟܢܝܩܘܣ, *i.e.* μηχανικούς.   [2] ܣܩܪܝܦܣ, *i.e.* σκάριφος.

[3] ܕܘܟܣ, *i.e.* dux.   [4] Cod. Rom. has ܐܒܢܗ for ܒܢܗ.

[5] ܣܩܪܐ ܐܡܪܡܢܝܬܐ, *i.e.* σάκρα είμαρμένη.

[6] ܕܠܐ ܣܘܢܦܣܝܣ, without *synopsis*.

[7] ܒܢܝܢܗ ܕܗܘܝܐ, Cod. Rom. for ܒܢܝܢܐ ܕܒܗ.

to the place.[1]   And gold was given in abundance without any stint to the craftsmen and for work of every kind, at the following rate, the regular sum of four *keratin*[2] a day for each workman, and if he had an ass with him, of eight.   And consequently many grew rich and wealthy.   And since the report was published abroad that the work was honest and that the wages were given, from the East to the West workmen and craftsmen flocked together.   And the overseers who were over the work also received a · liberal allowance,[3] and their wallets were filled ; for they found the man generous, gentle, and kind ; and, moreover, he believed in the just king, and in his promises which he made to him.   And in two or three years the city was built, and, as we may say, suddenly sprang up on the frontier.   And when Kawad heard of it, and sought to put a stop to the work, he was unable, for the wall was raised, and built high enough to be a protection for those who took refuge behind it.   And a large public bath[4] and a spacious storehouse were built.   And a conduit was constructed which passed along the lower part of the mountain, and wonderful cisterns within the city to receive the water. And persons to hasten the work were frequently sent from the king to the bishop, and they all brought back excellent reports of his integrity and justice to the king; and he was greatly pleased with the man, and sent gold in answer to the man's requests, and fulfilled them without delay.   And at last the number of hundred pounds which he sent was counted, and the bishop forwarded a written statement to the king, that, speaking in the presence of God, the money had been expended upon the work, and that no part of it remained in his hand or had been given to his Church.   And he readily sent him a royal decree containing a receipt of the exchequer[5]

[1] So Cod. Rom.   The MS. has ܣܩܘܼܐ‎ (see p. 13, note 6), "showed himself diligent in attendance there."

[2] 1½ *obols*.

[3] For ܐܠܝܢܐ Cod. Rom. has ܐܠܝܢܐ, which might perhaps be rendered "were very active."

[4] ܕܡܘܣܝܘܢ, *i.e.* δημόσιον.

[5] So the MS. ܟܘܬܐ, not ܟܘܬܐ, as L. prints.

to the effect that all the gold which had been sent by him
had been expended upon the building in the city.   And Dara
was completed, and it was named Anastasiopolis, after the
name of the just king.   And he swore by his crown that no
statement of accounts [1] should be required from Thomas or
from his Church, either by himself or by any of his successors
in the kingdom.   And he [2] appointed there and consecrated
as first bishop Eutychian the presbyter, a zealous man, and
accustomed to the transaction of business ; and he gave the
privilege of certain rights to his Church, taken from the jurisdiction of the Church of Amida.   And attached to him was
John, one of the Roman soldiers from Amida.   Him Eutychian
tonsured, and made him a presbyter and master of the
hostelry ; [3] and when he went up to the royal city this John
accompanied him.   And the king, upon his being presented to
him, gave him an endowment [4] for his church.   But Abraham
Bar Kili of Thel-midè was notary at that time, who was the
son of Ephraim of Constantia, and he also attached himself to
Eutychian the bishop, who made him a presbyter.   And he
was sent as overseer of the work and the building of the bath ;
and at last he became steward of the Church.

But the king gave Eutychian gifts of holy vessels and
gold for the building [5] of the great church,[6] and sent him away.
And the bishop having lived but a little longer, died.   And
his successor there was Thomas Bar 'Abdiyo of Resaina, who
had been a Roman soldier, and had been appointed steward of
the Church of Amida ; and he also was vigilant and well
versed in business.   And John the master of the hostelry,
being an honourable and chaste man, was faithful to him and
beloved by him.   And when this holy Thomas withdrew from
his see on account of his zeal for the faith, this believing John

---

[1] ܠܝܣܘܬܐ, i.e. λογοθεσίαι.

[2] Thomas, bishop of Amida, seems to be the subject of this sentence, not the king.

[3] ܟܣܢܕܟܪܐ, i.e. ξενοδοχάριος.   [4] ܐܘܣܝܐ, i.e. οὐσία.

[5] Reading ܒܢܝܢܐ for ܩܢܝܢܐ.

[6] Here Cod. Rom. inserts the words ܕܒܬܪܐ ܒܡܕܝܢܬܐ, "which was to be built in the city."

joined him, and he appointed him as his suffragan;[1] and for about seventeen years he lived in exile in different places. And he sent him (John) to Berroea,[2] where he died in the year three[3] (when Khosrun went up to Antioch), having joined the monks who had withdrawn from Marde before the enemy; and he was buried in the monastery of Beth-Thiri; and he was laid beside his bishop, who entered into rest before him.

CHAPTER VII

THE SEVENTH CHAPTER OF THE SEVENTH BOOK CONCERNING THE EXPULSION OF MACEDONIUS THE HERETIC FROM THE ROYAL CITY

Macedonius, who was bishop of Constantinople, omitted no intrigue of heart to conceal his opinions. But, like the fruit which bursts open in its day, according to the saying of Job,[4] and " what is covered shall be revealed, and what is done in the secret chamber shall be proclaimed upon the house-tops,"[5] as is said, again, in the Gospel. This man (was attached) to the monks of the monastery of the *Akoimetoi*, of whom there were about one thousand, and who lived luxuriously in baths and in other bodily indulgences, and outwardly appeared to men honourable, and were adorned with the semblance of chastity, but were inwardly like whited sepulchres, full of all uncleanness. And they agreed to the mind of Macedonius; and he used to celebrate the memory of Nestorius every year, and they used to celebrate it with him in their monastery and in the other monastic dwellings where the same opinions were held. And consequently they had great freedom of intercourse with this Macedonius. And they were continually reading the writings of the school of Diodorus and Theodore; and Macedonius himself com-

---

[1] ܟܘܪܐܦܣܩܘܦܐ, *i.e.* χωρεπίσκοπος.   [2] 540.

[3] I read ܢܚܠܒ for ܐܚܠܦ. However, as both MSS. have the latter, it may be that we should render it " Ahlaf."

[4] Job xxxii. 19 (Syr.).   [5] St. Luke xii. 2, 3.

piled a book of quotations from them, and from the work which was drawn up by Theodoret concerning the Acts of the Synod (not the one that is translated into the Syriac language); and he ornamented it with gold; and he said, " It is from the holy fathers and the doctors of the Church." And when he showed it[1] to the king, he would not receive it; and he said to him, " You have no need of such things, go rather and burn this."   And when he saw the mind of the king he formed a plan[2] for actually raising a rebellion against him; and he was in the habit of calling him a heretic and a Manichæan.   And the Master of the Offices, because he was lavishly supplied with gifts by him, was favourably inclined towards him.   And the report was brought to the king by some true men who were no framers of flattering words.   And he held a Council;[3] and in the presence of his patricians he told of the insult which had been offered to him by Macedonius; and he was distressed, and wept, and adjured them not to be influenced by fear ; but if, in truth, their king was displeasing to them, or if they knew that he was infected with the deceit of heresy, they should take his dominion from him, and he should be cast out as an unbeliever.   And they fell upon their faces before him, weeping.[4]   And they inveighed against the audacity of Macedonius, crying out and reviling him ; and they praised the king; and they decreed the bishop's banishment.   And in order that the Master of the Offices,[5] who aided him, might be humiliated, he was commanded to expel him, so that he should be sent to Oasis.   And also Pascasius the deacon, who was attached to and beloved by Macedonius, was arrested (and he wrote, in the presence of the prefect, in the records[6] of the Acts,[7] all his deeds), he and certain monks and others who caused a tumult in the city to prevent the words, " God Who was crucified for us," being proclaimed there, as they had been proclaimed in the whole jurisdiction of Antioch from the days of Eustace the bishop.

---

[1] ⲟⲩⲟⲛ, MS., not ⲟⲓⲟⲩⲛ, as L.

[2] See p. 245, note 5.

[3] [Syriac], i.e. σιλέντιον.

[4] [Syriac], MS., not [Syriac], as L.

[5] Text, " Magisterian."

[6] [Syriac], i.e. ὑπομνήματα.

[7] [Syriac], i.e. πρᾶξις.

And to show when and how these things were done, behold I have written down accurately, for the instruction of the readers, the letter of Simeon the presbyter and his brethren the monks who were with him, who happened to be at that time in the royal city having come from the East, and who wrote to Samuel their archimandrite concerning the expulsion of Macedonius, as follows:—

CHAPTER VIII

THE EIGHTH CHAPTER OF THIS SEVENTH BOOK TELLS ABOUT THE LETTER THAT WAS SENT FROM CONSTANTINOPLE CONCERNING THE EXPULSION OF MACEDONIUS

"To the virtuous, elect, and God - loving presbyter and archimandrite Samuel, and to the presbyters and deacons, together with all the other brethren, from Simeon the presbyter, in the royal city, and the brethren who are with him, greeting. After we wrote the former letter to your Holiness concerning all that Macedonius did in the monastery of Dalmatus against the whole truth, God stirred up the spirit of the believing king like a lion to the prey, and he roared, and made the whole faction of the enemies of the truth to tremble; for it is said, 'As a watercourse in the hands of the gardener, so is the heart of the king in the hands of the Lord.'[1] May He Who has not turned away from the prayer of His elect, and Who has not suffered the desire of those who worship man instead of God to come to pass, grant that the matter may receive a righteous fulfilment through your prayers; yea and amen! We testify to you that after Macedonius did that of which we sent[2] information to your Piety, and anathematised those reprobate persons and the accursed Council on the 20th of July, there was on the 22nd (the sixth day of the week)[3] a dedication festival at

---

[1] Prov. xxi. 1.   The words ܟܐܬܒܝ ܘܓܢܬܐ are not in the Peshitto.

[2] ܡܫܠܚܝܢ, MS., not ܡܫܟܚܝܢ, as L.

[3] ܥܪܘܒܬܐ, "the preparation."

the Martyr Church in the Hebdomon; and the king himself
was present.   And neither he nor the queen would receive the
oblation from him; on the contrary, he even addressed him in
severe terms.   But on the 24th (the first day of the week) the
monks of this place went in and communicated in the church
with Macedonius, and the king was vexed with them for
going in.   And on the 25th (the second day of the week) a
few brethren, who seceded from these monks, entered in and
went to Mâr Patrick the general,[1] and gave him a libel to
present to the king, saying, 'We declare that he celebrated
the memory of Nestorius, and that he used to send orders to
us, and we also did the same in our monasteries every year.'
And they wrote other things against him, testifying that transactions such as these took place in their monasteries.   On that
same day the king commanded, and the water which supplied
the baths was cut off from their monasteries, and only that
which they drank was left to them.   And also he took
away the denarii[2] which they used to receive from the
treasury.[3]   And on the 26th, one of the senators called
Romanus went in to the king and gave him a written
statement of all the things which were done at the bishop's
house; and he said to the king that Pascasius the deacon,
along with Macedonius, was the author of all the mischief;
and he said besides, 'They have made a certain large book
containing extracts from all the heresies, and it is overlaid
with gold.'   And the king sent for it, and took it to himself, that he might see all its blasphemies.   But on the 27th
the king convened a Council; and when the patricians went
in the king said to them, 'Have you not seen what this
Jew who is amongst us did, for in my presence and that of
your excellencies he did what he did, and he anathematised
the accursed Synod and those reprobate persons; and when,
to avoid great trouble, we accepted his act, he then went off,
and in the monastery of Dalmatus reversed everything which

---

[1] ‏ܐܣܛܪܛܝܠܛܣ‎, *i.e.* στρατηλάτης.

[2] The word ‏ܕܝܢܪ‎ in the text is manifestly wrong; it should be written ‏ܕܝܢܪܐ‎, *i.e.* δηνάριον.

[3] ‏ܩܘܠܐ‎, *i.e.* ταμιεῖον.

he himself had done, and he contradicted the whole truth, and lied unto God and before me and unto you. Is this a fair statement?' And at once Clementinus the patrician said before them all, 'May God Himself cast him out from his priesthood who has lied unto God!' And forthwith the king commanded the great prefect to go out into the city and bring together all the orthodox who were wounded when they cried out, 'Who was crucified for us,'[1] that he might learn who their assailants were. And the prefect went out and did as he was commanded. And on the 28th he took the names of all the Nestorians who were the life of Macedonius, and brought them in to the king; and the king commanded that they should be arrested.

"And on the 29th the king assembled all the commanders of the forces and all the officers of the Scholarians[2] and the patricians, and he said to them, 'According to my regular custom I wish to give a *donative*.'[3] For so it had been his practice to give it once in five years ever since he became king, at the same time requiring oaths from all the Romans to the effect that they would not act treacherously against the kingdom. But on this occasion he required them to take the oath in the following manner: A copy of the gospel being placed for them, they went in and received five *denarii* each, and they swore as follows, 'By this law of God and by the words which are written in it, we will contend[4] with all our might for the true faith and for the kingdom, and we will not act treacherously either against the truth or the king.' In this manner, indeed, he required them to take the oath, because he heard that Macedonius was trying to raise a rebellion against him.

"On the 30th of July the king gave a largess[5] to the whole army. On the same day the presbyters and deacons, who separated from his clergy lest they should be implicated

----

[1] ܐܣܛܘܪ̈ܘܬܝܚ ܕܢܗܘܣܠܡܚ, σταυρωθεὶς δι' ἡμᾶς.

[2] ܘܣܟܠܪܗܘܢ ܕܢ̈ܝ ܣܚܬܐ, MS., for ⊙ L. has ?. ܣܟܠܐ, *i.e.* σχολάριος.

[3] ܐܘܢܛܝܒܐ?, *i.e. donativum.* Payne Smith's *John of Ephesus*, p. 185, note.

[4] For ܣܠܬܠܬܘ I read ܣܠܬܠܬܚ, which is most probably the reading of the MS., here somewhat rubbed.

[5] ܪܘܓܐ, *i.e.* ῥόγας.

in his wickedness, presented a libel[1] against Macedonius to the king, charging him, in addition to all his other wickedness, with calling his Majesty a Manichæan and a Eutychianist.   And on the 31st of July (the first day of the week) they went in to the king's presence with great fear, and found him filled with rage and agitation.   And when they had waited a long time, and everyone was watching in fear to see what commands would issue from him, he opened his mouth and began to speak thus, ' Do you not know that from my childhood I have been brought up in the faith; have any of you ever seen in me any departure from the truth?'   And they said, ' Far be it from us, lord.'   And at once he rejoined to them, ' Since Macedonius calls me a Manichæan and a Eutychianist, behold! before God the Judge of all I make my defence, affirming that I neither have held nor do hold any opinion foreign to the faith of the three hundred and eighteen holy fathers, and of the one hundred and fifty ; and I confess that One of the Persons of the Trinity, God the Word, came down from heaven, and became incarnate from Mary the *Theotokos* and ever virgin ; and He was crucified for us, and He suffered and died; and He rose again in three days, according to His own will; and He is the Judge of the dead and of the living.   I adjure you by the Holy Trinity, that if you know anything else in me, or if you are not persuaded of the truth of what I have said, you take this robe[2] and crown off me and burn them in the midst of this city.'   And when he said this there was great weeping; and all the patricians cast themselves down before him, and Patrick the general[3] said, ' God will not forgive, nor will your Majesty and the canons of the Church have mercy on him who has done this.'   And the king said, ' Everyone, then, who goes to confer with[4] Macedonius or to hold communion with him, is thereby alienated from me.'   And while they stood before him, he spoke against the Master of the Offices, saying, ' The riches and the honour which God gave us were not sufficient,

---

[1] ‎ܠ‍ܒ‍ܩ‍ܘ‎ here is an evident mistake for ‎ܠ‍ܒ‍ܠ‍ܩ‍ܘ‎, *i.e.* λίβελλον.

[2] ‎ܟ‍ܠ‍ܡ‍ܝ‍ܣ‎, *i.e.* χλαμύς.   [3] ‎ܐ‍ܣ‍ܛ‍ܪ‍ܛ‍ܝ‍ܠ‍ܛ‍ܘܣ‎, *i.e.* στρατηλάτης.

[4] ‎ܣܘܢܛ‍ܘ‍ܟ‍ܝ‎, *i.e.* συντυχία.

but we must needs take a bribe in a matter of the life of all men, and we shall lose our own life.' And while he was speaking he looked at the Master of the Offices, who had inflicted many evils upon the believers ; and the Lord, forasmuch as He is the Judge of the dead and the living, rewarded him according to his works. And on the same day the king set guards of Romans at the gates of the city and the harbours, lest any of those monks here should come in to the city. And on the first of August Pascasius the deacon was arrested, and he went in before the prefect and confessed everything which was done in the bishop's house, saying that Macedonius was even trying to raise a rebellion against the king. And on the day after some Nestorians were arrested, and they affirmed that they had some forged [1] books of this heresy ; and the prefect sent and brought them to the Prætorium, and he showed them to the king and to the Senate.

" And on the sixth day of the month there was a General Council,[2] and the orthodox and the Nestorians who undertook the defence of Macedonius came in before them. And they found the king standing, because some bishops belonging to our party had entered. And the king said to these clergy of Macedonius, 'Why have you come?' and they replied, 'If your Majesty commands, your servant will come to your Clemency.' And he said, 'Let him go to those before whom he proclaimed his wickedness, and who obeyed him ; for, at one time, he had a certain ornamented book, and he affirmed it was taken from the fathers, and that they taught two Natures after the Incarnation ; and I said to him, 'There is no need for you to use this, go and burn it.' And he said to the clergy, 'What are the two Natures and the Synod of Chalcedon which God has overturned from its very foundations? Ye are accursed Jews, I declare to you that there is not one God-fearing man among you who is grieved for what has been done in His Church.' And they went out from his presence in great fear and distress. And the orthodox were

---

[1] ‎ܠܒܘܬܐ‎, i.e. πλαστά.

[2] ‎ܣܠܢܛܝܢ ܩܘܡܒܢܛܘܢ‎, i.e. σιλέντιον κομβέντον.

loud in his praises.   And when the clergy returned to Macedonius they said to him, 'The lord of the world has, in the presence of the Senate, anathematised the Synod of Chalcedon and everyone who says two Natures.'   And he replied to them, 'I, in my turn, anathematise everyone who does not receive the Synod, and say two Natures.'   And his archdeacon cried out, 'Far be it from us, then, ever to have any more part or communion with you.'

" And on the first day of the week, which was the seventh of the month, the believers came and entered the church, and it was filled from end to end.   And when the passage from the apostle was read, all the people began to cry out together, 'Let not him who has taken away from the Trinity enter the church; let not him who has blasphemed against the Son of God come in hither; no one wants the Jewish bishop; where Nestorius went, there let his disciples also go. Long live the king, the second Constantine, the upholder of the faith; the gospel to the throne!'   And at that instant the clergy took the gospel and placed it on the throne.   And when the clergy saw the whole congregation of the church crying out together, they also showed themselves, and cried out, shaking their stoles,[1] and saying, 'The victorious king has gained the victory for our Church.'   And as soon as they ceased, the great prefect delivered an address[2] to them in the following terms: 'We accept your goodwill and your zeal on behalf of the truth; and the lord of the world is, as you know, very solicitous for the preservation of orthodoxy and the peace of all the Churches; and your acclamations on behalf of the true faith we·will bring to his hearing.'   And when the deacon made the proclamation and did not mention his name, and it was not read in the Diptych, the mysteries were celebrated: and as[3] our Lord willed that he should go out, the king commanded, and his banishment was decreed.   And, with the object of humiliating[4] the Master of the Offices, he sent him to expel

---

[1] ܐܘܪ̈ܪܐ, *i.e.* ὡράρια αὐτῶν, ὡράριον = *orarium*.

[2] ܦܪܘܣܦܘܢܣܝܣ, *i.e.* προσφώνησις.

[3] Jo. Eph. ap. "Dion."

[4] So the MS. ܠܡܒܣܪܗ ; there is a mistake in L.'s text.

him ; and he found him in the church, whither he had fled, sitting down, with his head between his knees ; and he said to him, ' The lord of the world has decreed your banishment ' ; and the other asked, ' Whither ? ' and he replied, ' Where your comrade[1] went.'   And the stewards of the Church interposed, saying to him, ' We entreat your Lordship, have pity on his old age, and let him not depart in the daytime, lest the people of the city strike him and stone him, but in the evening time let him go.'   And when they swore that they would keep him, then he (the Master of the Offices) also left an auxiliary force[2] with them.   And they said to him, ' The king has commanded you to give up that book of the Synod which you have with you ' ; and he replied, ' I will not give it.'   But, being forced to do so, he laid it on the table ; and the clergy took it up and gave it to the Master's officer,[3] and he brought it to the king.   And in the evening of the seventh day of the month the Master of the Offices arrived with a military force[4] and expelled him, and gave him up to those who were appointed to carry him away.   And all the orthodox were in great fear.[5]

" Now, my lord, we have truly informed[6] your Holiness of what has occurred,[7] and we shall declare to you hereafter whatever the Lord may bring to pass.   Pray for us, O elect of God ! "

But the former defence made by the king proves to us that Akhs'noyo, the believing doctor, the bishop of Hierapolis,

---

[1] Probably Euphemius, who was also banished to Euchaita.

[2] ܒܐܠܬܐ, i.e. βοήθεια.   "Dion." ܚܝܠܐ.

[3] " Magistrian," an attendant upon the Master of the Offices.   The whole passage is a troublesome one, and I am much indebted to M. Nau, who has published an analysis of the unedited parts of the Chronicle attributed to Dionysius of Tellmahrè, and who, through Mr. Brooks, kindly supplied a MS. extract from fol. 147 of the account of the expulsion of Macedonius.

[4] The corresponding expression in the Chronicle of " Dionysius " is ܣܘܝܥܐ ܣܓܝܐܬܐ, " a large auxiliary force."

[5] In Chron. " Dion." ܣܘܝܥܘܬܐ (sic) ܢܦܩܬ ܣܓܝܐܬܐ ܒܟܠܗ ܥܕܬܐ ܕܐܪܬܕܘܟܣܘ, " and it (or he) caused great trouble in the whole Church of the orthodox."

[6] ܐܘܕܥܢܝܟ, MS., not ܐܘܕܥܝܢܟ, as L. prints.

[7] ܗܘܐ, MS., not ܗܘܝ, as L.

who was a zealous man, having learned that Macedonius
was a heretic, sent a written statement of the true faith to
the king (as he had done also in the days of Zeno),[1] and it
was read before the Senate ; and he showed that opinions
in opposition to it were held by the school of Diodorus
and Theodore, and by Nestorius, their disciple, who was
ejected, and by Theodoret, and Hibo, and Andrew, and John,
and Ætheric—the men who set up the Synod of Chalcedon
and received the Tome, and cleft asunder the unity of God the
Word, Who became incarnate, dividing it into two natures with
their properties, by what they taught concerning Christ after
His Incarnation.   And at the same time he (Akhs'noyo) urged
the king, saying, " It is right that they should be anathematised
by all who make a public boast of their own orthodoxy,[2] and
of agreeing to the faith of your Majesty."   And when Macedonius was required to do this, he anathematised them under
compulsion ; but after that he used secretly to celebrate their
memory in the monastery of Dalmatus, as has been written
above.

CHAPTER IX

THE NINTH CHAPTER OF THIS SEVENTH BOOK TELLS ABOUT
TIMOTHY THE SUCCESSOR OF MACEDONIUS, AND HOW
IN THE DAYS OF ANASTASIUS THE KING, THE WORDS,
" WHO WAS CRUCIFIED FOR US," WERE PROCLAIMED IN
THE ROYAL CITY [3]

After [4] Macedonius, Timothy became bishop in Constantinople ; and he was a believing man, and his deeds were in
conformity with his name, for it means " God-honouring."
And in his days there was one Marinus of Apamea, a vigilant
and clever man, well-versed in business, wise and learned, who
was, moreover, true in the faith, the friend and confidant of the
king, and a *chartularius* and his counsellor.   And when he was

---

[1] Assem., *B. O.* vol. ii. p. 34.

[2] The MS. has ܂ before ܐܝܠܝܢ ܕ ܡ ܘ ܪ ܣ, which L. omits.

[3] This chap. is in Cod. Rom.   [4] Mich. fol. 156 *r.*

12

walking in the street or sitting anywhere, he would tell his secretaries[1] to commit in concise form whatever thought he had to writing. And at night also, he had a pen-and-ink stand[2] hanging by his bedside, and a lamp burning by his pillow, so that he could write down his thoughts on a roll; and in the daytime he would tell them to the king, and advise him as to how he should act. And accordingly, as he was from the district of Antioch, all of which ever since the days of Eustace the bishop had been so full of zeal that it was the first to proclaim, "Who was crucified for us," he also vehemently[3] urged and advised King Anastasius to do the same. And[4] when some heretics heard of his ardour, they went to him together, and said to him, " You desire and incite men on earth to go beyond the holy hymn of praise which the angels offer to the Trinity, saying, ' Holy, Holy, Holy, mighty Lord, of whose praises heaven and earth are full.'" Immediately, God the Word Himself, Who in the flesh was crucified for us men, prepared a defence in his mouth to this effect, " The angels, indeed, offer the hymn of praise, which contains their confession to the adorable and co-equal Trinity, rightly, and do not proclaim that He was crucified for them; but we, on the other hand, in the hymn of praise, which contains our confession, rightly say that He was crucified for us men, for He became incarnate from us, and did not invest Himself with the nature of angels." And so he put them to silence, and he instructed the king, who thereupon commanded that the words, " Who was crucified for us," should be proclaimed in the royal city as in the district of Antioch. And at the same time a wonderful sign occurred, proving to wise men that Christ, Who was crucified in the flesh at Jerusalem, was God; namely, an eclipse[5] of the sun, which took place in those days,[6] and produced darkness from the sixth hour unto the ninth hour.

---

[1] ܢܘܛܪܐ, i.e. νοτάριος. Cod. Rom. has ܠܡܢܛܪܘܬܗ, "to preserve it."

[2] ܩܠܡܪܐ, i.e. καλαμάριον.

[3] ܚܡܝܡܐܝܬ, see p. 13, note 6.

[4] Greg. *H. E.* i. p. 185.

[5] For ܠܩܘܠܝܦܣܝܣ we must read ܠܩܠܝܦܣܝܣ, i.e. ἔκλειψις.

[6] MS. ܘܒܗܠܝܢ. Omit ܘ with Cod. Rom. and L.

CHAPTER X

THE TENTH CHAPTER OF THIS SEVENTH BOOK GIVES IN-
FORMATION RESPECTING THE SYNOD WHICH WAS HELD
AT ZIDON IN THE YEAR FIVE, THE EIGHT HUNDRED
AND TWENTY-THIRD YEAR OF THE GREEKS, AND OF
THE ANTIOCHENES THE FIVE HUNDRED AND SIXTIETH

Akhs'noyo,[1] a learned man and a Syriac doctor, and zealous
in the faith, the bishop of Hierapolis, in the days of Zeno sent
a written statement of the faith, and asked Zeno some questions
about his faith, and received a reply. And it was he who
exposed Calandion of Antioch, and ejected him from his See.
But he had his suspicions also about Flavian, that he was a
heretic; and he sent a letter and urgent messengers to King
Anastasius, begging that a Synod should be held at Sidon.
And the king gave the order, and the Synod assembled in the
five hundred and sixtieth year of the Antiochene era.[2]   And
he urged the believing and zealous monks of the East, and
Cosmas a learned man from the monastery of Mâr 'Akiba at
Chalcis, who was residing in Antioch, and they drew up a
petition and presented it to Flavian and to the Council of
bishops who were with him at Sidon.   And they wrote, in an
able and logical manner, a list of censures in seventy-seven
Heads, with many quotations from the holy doctors confirming
the censure upon the Synod of Chalcedon and the Tome of
Leo, and they presented this also to the Synod, at the same
time begging and adjuring the priests to effect reforms, and
take stumbling-blocks out of the way of the Church and purge
it, by openly anathematising the Synod.   But Flavian the
chief priest and some of the priests who were with him deferred
the matter, saying, " We are content with a document anathematising the school of Diodorus, the censures of certain persons
upon the twelve Heads of Cyril, and Nestorius, lest we should
arouse the sleeping dragon [3] and corrupt many with his poison."
And so the Synod was dissolved.

---

[1] Mich. fol. 160 *r* ff.   [2] 512.
[3] The MS. has ܠܝܘܬܐ; there is a mistake in L.'s text.

But the zeal of Akhs'noyo urged the monks again, and they went up to Anastasius and informed him of what had occurred in the Synod, and concerning Flavian, that he was a heretic; and having received an order for his ejection, and returned to the East, they assembled at Antioch against him. And some of them were wounded, and others were killed; but nevertheless Flavian was ejected from his See. And his successor was Severus, a learned and well-tried monk from the monastery of Theodore the ex-pleader [1] at Gaza, who was *apokrisiarios* at the royal city, and was a confidant and friend of Probus, and his kinsmen. This man had previously written the *Philalethes*, and also he had made a solution of the seven questions of the *Diphysites*. And he was ready in dispute with the heretics, and he was well known to the king by means of Probus; and he was appointed chief priest of Antioch. And afterwards, when there was a Synod in Tyre, he joined with Akhs'noyo, and the priests of his district, and those of Phœnice Libani, and Arabia, and Euphratesia, and Mesopotamia in expounding the Henotikon of Zeno, showing that its effect was to abrogate the Council of Chalcedon. And the bishops assembled at Tyre openly anathematised the Synod of Chalcedon and the Tome. And they wrote to John of Alexandria and to Timothy of the royal city; and received replies from them and from Elijah of Jerusalem, who was eventually ejected, and was succeeded by John. And because Sergius, a grammarian there, composed shortly afterwards a book of censure upon that Synod, and gave it to the monks from Palestine who were of his way of thinking, this holy Severus, hearing about it, wrote a refutation of it at great length, and by quotations and proofs derived from the true doctors of the Church he confirmed his doctrine in three volumes, entitled, *Against the Grammarian*. But the other treatises of this doctor Severus, and his commentaries, and his *Catechism*, and his work, *Against Julian the Phantasiast*, and his wonderful *Dogmatic Letter*, afford great profit and instruction to the lovers of doctrine.

---

[1] ‎. I have taken it as the Syriacised form of ἀπὸ δικανικῶν; but I give this explanation with diffidence. The word ‎ = δικανικός, is found in *Leben des Severus*, p. 3.

CHAPTER XI

THE ELEVENTH CHAPTER OF THIS SEVENTH BOOK TELLS ABOUT THE PETITION WHICH WAS DRAWN UP BY MONKS OF THE EAST AND COSMAS OF CHALCIS, AND WAS PRESENTED TO THE COUNCIL WHICH MET AT ZIDON IN THE DAYS OF FLAVIAN AND AKHS'NOYO THE BISHOPS, IN THE FIVE HUNDRED AND SIXTIETH YEAR OF THE ANTIOCHENE ERA

"Before all things we give thanks to Christ, Who is God over all, and we also thank our merciful Christ-loving king, who has aroused you all to zeal for religion, and called this your holy Council to one meeting place, in the name of one only Christ the Son of God, that in Him you may bring all men together to the one faith, which the Holy Scriptures have delivered and the fathers have ever kept, standing steadfastly in one mind, and being united and agreeing together in one good man,[1] and teaching all men the divine doctrine through the Holy Spirit, Who spoke by them.   For our Lord has accounted you to be worthy,[2] and chosen you at this time for the sake of the unity of his holy Churches, not that you should make a new faith for them; because that written definition, which was made by the three hundred and eighteen holy fathers who assembled at Nicea, is sufficient for the affirmation of the Holy Scriptures; but that you should build up[3] the faith which has always existed, and which many persons have rashly sought to destroy, speaking 'not from the mouth of the Lord,' as the prophet[4] says, but 'from their own belly,' and by their wicked artifices they have severed from one another those who in the simplicity of their hearts kept the tradition of the holy fathers and were united together in the true faith.   For Christ is He, O holy men! Who is divided by them; and, therefore, as long as He is denied, it is not possible for the Church ever to come to any

---

[1] [Syriac]. Mich. has "in one good work," reading [Syriac].

[2] MS. [Syriac], not [Syriac], as L.   [3] For [Syriac] I read [Syriac].

[4] Jer. xxiii. 16.

agreement; seeing that it is rent asunder by these persons through the inventions of different words. For it is written, 'No kingdom that is divided against itself shall stand';[1] and again, 'If ye bite and devour one another, take heed lest ye be consumed one of another.'[2] Since, then, we are one body in Christ, and we are members of His members, according to the word of the divine apostle,[3] we draw near to your Holinesses with confidence as to pastors, entreating you to keep the true faith for the whole world, without spot, like the fair dove spoken of in the Song of Songs; and that you separate it from all heresies which have the outward appearance of religion, and stand around it like queens and concubines and damsels, and are anxious to associate and to be one and the same with it, and through it to be received as true. But by doing this you shall receive a reward, and you shall hear the Lord saying, 'Him that confesses Me before men, will I confess before My Father Who is in heaven.'[4] Separate, then, as stewards of the divine words, between the pure and the corrupt, as He says;[5] and cast out those who mingle[6] the tares with the pure wheat, and their evil doctrine along with them, for He says, 'Put away the evil-doer from the congregation, and victory shall go forth with it.'[7]

"Now, though what has been said is manifest and well known,[8] it was necessary to explain it above and prove it clearly, even as the holy fathers agreeing in one true faith bound all men together in one concord. But the heretics have mingled lawless wranglings with the words of the holy fathers, and confound[9] with them schismatical[10] impieties, and have separated the holy Churches; whom the prophet rebuked, saying, 'Thy tavern-keepers[11] mingle water with wine.'"[12]

---

[1] St. Mark iii. 24.　　　[2] Gal. v. 15.　　　[3] Rom. xii. 5.

[4] St. Matt. x. 32.　　　[5] Mal. iii. 18.

[6] The MS. has ܣܚܒܩ, not ܣܚܒܩ, as L. prints.

[7] This is probably a general reference to Josh. vii. rather than an exact quotation.

[8] ܝܕܝܥܐ, MS., not ܝܕܥ, as L.

[9] ܘܡܚܠܛܝܢ, MS., not ܘܡܚܠܛ, as L. prints.

[10] MS. ܣܟܠܝܘܬܐ, not ܣܟܠܝܘܬܐ, as L.

[11] ܢܦܩܬܝܟܝ, MS., not ܢܦܩܝܟܝ, as L.

[12] Isa. i. 22. The rendering in the Peshitto is remarkable, and no doubt suggested the above: it is ܢܦܩܬܟܝ ܡܠܟܝ ܡܝܐ.

And so the petition goes on, and has many quotations from the fathers in proof of the seventy-seven censures upon the Council of Chalcedon.

CHAPTER XII

THE TWELFTH CHAPTER, WHICH TELLS ABOUT THE SYNOD THAT WAS HELD IN TYRE, IN THE DAYS OF SEVERUS AND AKHS'NOYO THE DOCTORS, AND THE BISHOPS WHO WERE WITH THEM, WHO EXPRESSLY AND OPENLY ANATHEMATISED THE SYNOD AND TOME

Now Severus, who succeeded Flavian in Antioch, was a learned man by reading the wisdom of the Greeks, and he was an ascetic and a well-tried monk, and he was also zealous for the true faith and well-versed in it, and he had read the Holy Scriptures with understanding and the expositions made by the ancient authors who were disciples of the apostles, namely, Hierotheus, and Dionysius, and Titus, and also Timothy; and after them Ignatius, and Clement, and Irenæus, and such writers as Gregory, and Basil, and Athanasius, and Julius, and the other chief priests and true doctors of the holy Church. And like a "scribe who is instructed for the kingdom of heaven, who brings from his treasures things old and new,"[1] so also he had thoroughly studied many histories, and they were rooted in his mind clearly to be seen.

And this Akhs'noyo, also, was a Syriac doctor, and he had diligently studied the works existing in that language, and besides these he was well-versed in the doctrine of the school of Diodorus and Theodore and the others; but, nevertheless, as his actions proved to the wise, this old and zealous man was truly a believer.

These men gave full and clear information to King Anastasius, who rejected the Council of Chalcedon with all his heart; and he commanded that, for the purpose of effecting needed reforms, a Synod of Orientals should be assembled at

[1] Matt. xiii. 52.

Tyre.   And it was assembled, consisting of the bishops of the districts of Antioch, and Apamea, and Euphratesia, and Osrhoene, and Mesopotamia, and Arabia, and Phœnice Libani.

And, making the true faith clear, he (*i.e.* Severus) expounded the Henotikon of Zeno as meaning the abrogation of the transactions of Chalcedon; and he openly there anathematised the addition which it had made to the faith.   And the bishops in Council assembled, along with Severus and Akhs'noyo the believers and doctors who zealously stood at their head, proclaimed the whole truth; and they wrote letters of agreement both to John of Alexandria, and to Timothy of the royal city, and also Elijah of Jerusalem at that time assented to the letters, although shortly after he was ejected, and was succeeded by John. Consequently the priests were again united in this concord of the faith, with the exception of the see of Rome.   (And the reason of this exception was) that Alimeric[1] was the anti-Cæsar there, and he had rebelled against Anastasius in the Western region, and he held the kingdom in Rome.   And he was a warlike man; and in his day he rendered great service to the people of Italy, by delivering them from the barbarians and Goths.   And he also conferred many benefits upon his city, Rome, erecting buildings and granting privileges.[2]   However, he was a *Diphysite*, having been converted from the heresy of Arius.   Consequently there could not be any assent on the part of Symmachus and his successor Hormisda, the chief priests of Rome, to what was done in the East.   And zealous persons can gain information respecting these matters from the letter which Akhs'noyo wrote after his expulsion.[3]

[1] "Theodoric, called ὁ Οὐαλαμήρου, hence the form above" (Brooks).

[2] ⟨Syriac⟩, *i.e.* προνόμια.

[3] Cf. p. 207, and note 4 there.

CHAPTER XIII

THE THIRTEENTH CHAPTER OF THIS BOOK TELLS ABOUT
ARIADNE THE QUEEN, WHO DIED, AND HOW THE
TYRANT VITALIAN CAME UPON THE SCENE, WHO
TOOK [1] HYPATIUS PRISONER IN WAR

Ariadne [2] the queen, the wife of Zeno, was allied to this
Anastasius after the death of her husband, and she made him
king; and she held the kingdom for many years, as many as
forty, in the state of first and second marriage; and she died in
the year eight hundred and twenty-four of the Greeks. And
her husband remained on, keeping the holy truth; even though
he was advanced in years, and he was occupied with the
business of his kingdom. [3]   And he had anxiety and trouble,
because of one Vitalian a Goth, who was a general, [4] and warlike,
and courageous and daring, and cunning in war. To this man
many savage people attached themselves; and he gave them
gold with a liberal hand, and, besides, they enriched themselves with the spoil which they took from the dominions of
Anastasius.   And when he had been for a long time at
peace, Vitalian broke his word; and he rebelled and injured
the Roman dominions, and oppressed the kingdom, and treated
it with contempt; and he haughtily advanced to the very
suburbs of Constantinople without any fear. And at one time
troops, with Hypatius at their head, were sent against him by
Anastasius; and they were routed by him, and Hypatius was
taken prisoner; and he treated him with great indignity, and
to insult him he even shut him up in a pig-sty. [5]   And upon
one occasion he put him to open shame, carrying him about
through the army in the most humiliating fashion, because
Hypatius once took the wife of this Vitalian prisoner and
treated her insultingly. And in consequence of this Vitalian's
indignation against him was very strong. For in the impetu-
osity of his youth this Hypatius was carnal and wanton in
lust after women. And at last he was ransomed by a large

---

[1] MS. ܣܘܪ, not ܣܘܪ, as L.   [2] Here begins an extract in Cod. Rom.

[3] Here an extract in Cod. Rom. ends.   [4] ܐܣܛܪܛܝܠܛܐ, *i.e.* στρατηγός.

[5] For ܚܙܝܪܐ read ܚܙܝܪܐ.

sum of gold that was sent for him, and he returned from captivity with Vitalian, possessing the wisdom that results from punishment.[1]

CHAPTER XIV

THE FOURTEENTH CHAPTER OF THE SEVENTH BOOK TELLS ABOUT TIMOTHY, WHO DIED, AND WHOSE SUCCESSOR WAS JOHN; AND OF SOME PEOPLE WHO CAME TO JERUSALEM FOR THE FESTIVAL, AND THEY WERE POSSESSED BY DEMONS, WHO BARKED AT THE CROSS DURING THE DEDICATION[2]

Timothy, having lived six or seven years, died[3] in the year eleven.[4]   And John succeeded him.   And in the year in which Anastasius the king died, there were some Egyptians and Alexandrians and men from beyond the Jordan, Edomites and Arabians, who came to the festival of the dedication[5] which is the making of the Cross at Jerusalem, which was held on the fourteenth of September; and demons took possession of many of them, and they barked at the Cross, and then ceased and went out.   And this caused anxiety and distress to the prudent; they did not, however, accurately[6] understand the reason, until the event occurred, and it signified the wrangling about the faith, and the stumbling-block afterwards caused thereby.   This God made known beforehand, that we might consider the temptation[7] and be proved by it;[8] and by our enduring it and persevering in the faith we might have joy; as James the apostle says, "Let it be all joy to you, my brethren, when you enter into divers and many temptations; for you know that the trial of faith procures patience for you.   But let patience have its perfect work, that you may be complete and perfect, wanting nothing."[9]

[1] Or literally, "And punishment is wisdom."

[2] This chap. is in Cod. Rom.

[3] Cod. Rom. has the word ܩܒܝܼܬ; it is omitted in the MS.

[4] 518.   [5] ܐܢܩܢܝܐ, i.e. ἐγκαίνια.

[6] Cod. Rom. has ܚܝܬܐܝܬ here.   The other reading, ܚܕܬܐܝܬ, "recently," could hardly be made to give sense.

[7] So Cod. Rom.   The MS. has "the event."

[8] So Cod. Rom. ܘܢܬܒܩܐ ܒܗ.   [9] Jas. i. 2–4.

Now Anastasius died on the ninth day of July.   And his successor was Justin, who went down with the army [1] in company with the generals,[2] at the time that Kawad, king of the Persians, came to Amida.   And he was a handsome old man with white hair, but he was unlearned;[3] and he shared [4] in the opinions of the people of Rome respecting the faith, because he belonged to that jurisdiction, being from the camp [5] called Mauriana,[6] the water [7] of which is bad, and turns to blood when it is boiled.

There is in this Book a period of twenty-seven years, three months and a half, the lifetime of Anastasius.

CHAPTER XV

THE FIFTEENTH CHAPTER OF THE SEVENTH BOOK, STATING
  WHO WERE CHIEF PRIESTS IN THE DAYS OF ANASTASIUS
  THE KING

Now the following were the chief priests in the days of Anastasius.   Of the Diphysites:—Of Rome—Felix, and Symmachus his successor, and Hormisda who is still living.

Of Alexandria, the believers—Athanasius, and John his successor, and again another John, and Dioscorus who now occupies the See.

In Antioch—Flavian who was ejected, and Severus the believer.

In Constantinople—Euphemius, and Macedonius who was ejected, and Timothy the believer, and John his successor, who received the Synod in the beginning of the reign of Justin and died shortly after, and Epiphanius was his successor.

Of Jerusalem—Sallust, and Elijah his successor who was ejected, and John who received the Synod in the days of Justin, and Peter his successor.

---

[1] ‏ܐܣܪܩܛܘܐ‏, i.e. ἐξέρκετον, or *exercitus*.   [2] ‏ܐܣܛܪܛܝܓܐ‏, i.e. στρατηγός.

[3] Mai takes ‏ܣܘܩܝ‏ as part. from ‏ܣܘܩ‏, "to shave," and translates "prolixo capillo"; but Jo. Mal. p. 410, has ὀλοπόλιος, εὔμορφος . . . ἀγράμματος (Brooks).

[4] Cod. Rom. has ‏ܟܪ ܕܝܢܝܐ‏ for ‏ܟܪܕܝܢܝܐ‏ of MS.

[5] ‏ܩܣܛܪܐ‏, i.e. κάστρα.   [6] Or Bederiana, as Mai writes here.

[7] ‏ܡܝܗ‏, MS., not ‏ܡܝܗ‏, as L.

BOOK VIII

THE eighth Book in the chapters, as given below,[1] gives information, the first about the accession of Justin and about Amantius the provost, who was killed in the palace, and about Theocritus his domestic, and Andrew the chamberlain; in the second it treats of Vitalian the tyrant, who was killed in the palace, he and Paul his notary and Celer his domestic; in the third chapter it tells the story of the martyrs who were killed in Nagrin, in the royal city of the land of the Homerites, by the Jewish tyrant; in the fourth chapter it describes the flood of water which entered Edessa, and how the flow of the waters of Shiluho in Jerusalem was stopped, and how Antioch was overthrown[2] by an earthquake, and the temple of Solomon in the city of Heliopolis was burnt;[3] in the fifth chapter it gives an account of the negotiations which were held on the frontier, and of Mundhir, king of the Saracens, who invaded the Roman territory, and of the bishops who were banished; the sixth chapter, stating who were chief priests in the days of this king Justin; the seventh chapter, concerning the prologue of Moro the bishop.

[1] The MS. has ܐܚܝܕܐ, not ܐܚܝܕ, as L. prints.

[2] MS. ܐܬܗܦܟܬ, not ܐܬܗܦܟ, as L.

[3] The word ܘܩܐ has dropped out before ܗܝܟܠܐ, as appears from the heading of the chapter below.

THE EIGHTH BOOK

CHAPTER I

THE FIRST CHAPTER OF THE BOOK, CONCERNING THE ACCESSION OF JUSTIN

In[1] the year eight hundred and twenty-nine according to the reckoning of the Greeks,[2] on the tenth of July, when the year eleven was already drawing to an end, on the death of Anastasius, Justin[3] became king after him ; and he was an old man of a handsome presence with white hair and was *cura palati*, and he was illiterate.   This man Marinus of Apamea, an able man, who was chartulary,[4] depicted in the public baths,[5] as he had come from the fortress[6] of Mauriana in Illyricum to Constantinople with all the history of his entry into Constantinople, and how he had been advanced from step to step until he became king.   And, when this same Marinus was accused on this ground and came into danger, trusting in his astuteness, he readily rendered an answer, saying, " I have represented these things in pictures for the consideration of the observant and the understanding of the discerning, in order that magnates and rich men and men of high family may not trust in their power and their riches and the greatness of their noble family, but in God, who raises the poor man out of the mire and places him as chief over the people, and rules in the kingdom of men to give it to whom He will, and to set the lowest among men over it, and chooses men of low birth in the world, and men that are rejected, and men that are not, that he may bring to naught men that are." And he was accepted, and escaped from the danger.

Now[7] Amantius the provost,[8] he and Andrew the chamber-

---

[1] vii. 14.   [2] 518.

[3] vii. 14 ; Mich. fol. 161 *r* ; cf. Jo. Mal. p. 410.

[4] The MS. has ܟܬܘܒܘܬܐ, not ܟܬܘܒܘܬܐ, as L. prints.

[5] δημόσιον.   [6] κάστρον.

[7] Cf. Jo. Mal. pp. 410, 411.   [8] πραιπόσιτος, *i.e. præpositus sacri cubiculi.*

lain, his associate, favoured and cherished Theocritus his domestic; and after the death of Anastasius he gave a large sum of gold to this old man, the *cura palati* Justin, for the purpose of making largesses[1] to the scholarians and the other soldiers, in order that they might make Theocritus king. But he by giving the gold to these men gained their favour, and they made him king, because the Lord willed it. And,[2] because he shared the opinions of the inhabitants of Rome, he gave strict orders that the Synod and the Tome of Leo should be proclaimed. And this Amantius tried to prevent it, saying, "The signature of the three patriarchs and the principal bishops of your dominions, who have written and anathematised the Synod, is not yet dry." And,[3] because he spoke with freedom, this same Amantius the provost was immediately put to death, and so were Theocritus his domestic and Andrew the chamberlain.

Now a year afterwards John,[4] the bishop of the city, died, and Epiphanius succeeded him. And, since Severus withdrew from Antioch for fear of the threats of the king, who[5] had ordered his tongue to be cut out, Paul succeeded him, who was called "the Jew." And, because he celebrated the memory of Nestorius, he was driven out, and Euphrasius succeeded him, who was burnt in a cauldron blazing with aromatic wax during the earthquake of Antioch.

CHAPTER II

THE SECOND CHAPTER OF THE EIGHTH BOOK TREATS OF VITALIAN THE TYRANT, HOW HE WAS KILLED IN THE PALACE, HE AND PAUL HIS NOTARY AND CELER HIS DOMESTIC.

Vitalian[6] the tyrant was general[7] in the days of Anastasius; and he was a Goth and a stout-hearted warrior, and barbarians[8] followed him. Of him it was said that he

---

[1] ῥόγας. [2] Mich. *loc. cit.* [3] Cf. Jo. Mal. *loc. cit.*
[4] Cf. Theoph. A.M. 6012. [5] Cf. Evag. iv. 4.
[6] vii. 13. [7] στρατηγός.
[8] There is no ‍O before ܩܘܦܣ‍, as L., but the letter must be inserted.

wished to raise a rebellion against Anastasius; and he exacted an oath from him, and he did not keep it, but rebelled and induced barbarian tribes to follow him, and made an attack upon the dominions of Anastasius, and took cities and their villages; and he marched forward as far as the royal city, and blockaded it,[1] and he annoyed the king in many ways; and he caused him anxiety, because he had taken Hypatius, who had gone out against him, prisoner and routed his army, and carried him about with him, treating him with indignity and insult, and exposing him to contumely; but for a large sum of gold which he received for him he sent him back.

And, when Anastasius was dead, a letter was written to him by this old man Justin, entreating him and appeasing him,[2] in order that he might not again act unjustly and rebel in his days, as he was accustomed to do. And then various tribes also followed him, and the Goth came confidently;[3] and the king went out to the Martyr's Chapel of Euphemia at Chalcedon, and they swore oaths to one another and entered the city; and he became one of the generals[4]-in-chief; and in the fulness of power he went in and out of the palace, and presided over the conduct of affairs. And he was united by a spiritual relationship[5] to Flavian of Antioch, who was driven out; and he nursed great resentment against the holy Severus, who succeeded Flavian, but he was not able to injure him in the days of Anastasius. However, at the beginning of the reign of this old man Justin an order was issued that, wherever he was caught, his tongue[6] should be cut out, they say, by the advice of Vitalian.

[1] ܢܣܝܗܝ. The usual meaning of this word is "take," which is here impossible. The word sometimes, however, means "shut," and the rendering in the text seems justified by the use in vii. 5 (p. 212, l. 23, L.).

[2] Cf. Jo. Mal. p. 412; Evag. iv. 3.

[3] It is very probable that we should insert ܡ before ܢܩܝܦܝܢ, translating, "various tribes also and Goths following him, he came confidently."

[4] στρατηγός.

[5] In bk. 3, ch. 4 this word means "godfather"; but, since this meaning seems to be here out of place, I have given it the indefinite rendering above. The relation meant is that of the σύντεκνος, which we can hardly express in English (Smith, *Thesaurus*, col. 4342).

[6] Cf. Evag. iv. 4.

Now it happened some days afterwards that, while Vitalian was bathing in the royal city, he received a command from the king to come to a banquet, he and Justinian the general,[1] his colleague; and he was coming from the baths, he and Paul his notary and Celer his domestic, and, men having been posted ready to stab him as he was going from one house to the other, he was killed, he and his notary and his domestic; and God requited him for the evil which he did in the days of Anastasius and the violation of his oaths; and his army did no injury.

CHAPTER III

THE THIRD CHAPTER OF THE BOOK TREATS OF THE MARTYRS WHO WERE KILLED IN NAGRIN, THE ROYAL CITY OF THE COUNTRY OF THE HOMERITES, IN THE YEAR EIGHT HUNDRED AND THIRTY-FIVE OF THE GREEKS, THE SIXTH YEAR OF THE REIGN OF JUSTIN, AS SIMEON, BISHOP AND *APOKRISIARIOS*[2] OF THE BELIEVERS IN THE LAND OF THE PERSIANS, WROTE TO SIMEON, ARCHIMANDRITE OF GABBULA, AS FOLLOWS[3]

"We[4] inform your affection that on the twentieth of January in this year eight hundred and thirty-five of

---

[1] στρατηγός.

[2] There is probably some mistake in the heading, as a bishop could not be an *apokrisiarios*.   Jo. Eph. (ap. "Dion.") omits the word, while *Mart. Areth.* speaks of a Συμεωνίτου πρεσβυτέρου καὶ ἀποκρισιαρίου.

[3] This chapter is contained in Cod. Rom.   Mai's text is, however, not taken from the MS. but is a copy of that of Assemani (*B. O.* vol. i. p. 364 ff.), taken not from our author, but from John of Ephesus (ap. "Dion."). The letter also exists in a much longer form in Brit. Mus. Add. MS. 14,650, fol. 155, and in a MS. in the Museum Borgianum at Rome, which has been edited by Prof. Guidi (*Atti dell' Accademia de' Lincei*, Ser. 3, Tom. 7, 1881). It exists also in Brit. Mus. Add. MS. 14,641, fol. 157, where the text is not a copy of 14,650, as Guidi states on the authority of Wright, but is similar to that in our author and in Jo. Eph., and, being followed by the later history of the little boy, as in Jo. Eph., is plainly derived from that author. A Greek account of the same events, derived in part from this letter, is contained in the *Martyrium Arethæ* (Boissonade, *Anecd. Græc.* vol. v.), and a slightly different one in Simeon Metaphrastes (Migne, *Patr. Græc.* 115, p. 1249 ff.).

[4] Jo. Eph. ap. "Dion." (Assem., *B. O.* p. 364 ff.); Mich. fol. 166 ff.

the Greeks[1] we left the camp of Nu'man in company
with Abraham the presbyter, the son of Euphrasius, who had
been sent to Mundhir by Justin the king to make peace, of
which we wrote also in our former epistle; and here we,
even all the believers, express our thanks to him for his
assistance to our side; and he knows what we wrote formerly
and what we are writing now.   For we travelled ten days'
journey through the desert towards the south-east, and we
came upon Mundhir over against the hills called 'the hills
of sand,'[2] and in the Saracen language 'Ramlah.'[3]   And, as
we were entering the encampment of Mundhir, some Saracens,
heathens and *Ma'doye*,[4] met us, and said to us, 'What can
you do? for, behold! your Christ has been expelled by the
Romans and the Persians and the Homerites.'   And when
we were insulted by the Saracens it distressed us; and in
addition to the distress sorrow also fell upon us, because, while
we were present, there came an envoy, who had been sent by
the king of the Homerites to Mundhir, and gave him an
epistle full of boasting; and in it he had written to him as
follows: 'The king whom the Ethiopians set up in our
country died; and, because the winter season had begun,
they were not able to march out into our country and appoint
a Christian king, as they generally do.   Accordingly, I became king over the whole country of the Homerites, and I
resolved first to slay all the Christians who confessed Christ,
unless they became Jews like us.   And I killed two hundred
and eighty men, the priests who were found, and besides them
also the Ethiopians who were guarding the church.   And I
made their church into a synagogue for us.   And then with
a force of 120,000 men I went to Nagrin, their royal city.
And, when I had sat down before it[5] for some days and was
not able to take it, I swore oaths to them, and their chiefs

---

[1] 524.   [2] Read ܠܡܐ for ܠܡܐ, with Cod. Rom.

[3] Read ܪܡܠܗ for ܪܡܠܗ, with Cod. Rom. (marg.), Jo. Eph., 14,650, and
Cod. Borg.

[4] *I.e.* emigrants or nomads, a name applied to certain Arab tribes: Ar. *Ma'addiyya*.

[5] Read ܥܠܝܗ for ܥܠ, with Cod. Rom., "Dion.," 14,650, and Cod. Borg.
14,641 agrees with 17,202.

13

came out to me; but I judged it right not to keep my word to the Christians, my enemies. And I arrested them, and required them to bring their gold and their silver and their possessions; and they brought them to me, and I took them. And I asked for Paul their bishop; and, when they told me that he was dead, I did not believe them, until they showed me his grave: and I dug up his bones and burnt them,[1] as well as their church and their priests and everyone who was found seeking refuge there. And the rest I urged to deny Christ and the Cross, and become Jews; and they would not, but, confessing that He is God and the Son of the Blessed, they even chose to die for His sake. And their chief said many things against us,[2] and insulted us. And I ordered all their magnates[3] to be put to death. And we fetched their wives, and told[4] them, now that they had seen their husbands put to death for Christ, to deny, and have mercy on their sons and on their daughters. And we urged them, and they would not; but the nuns strove hard to be put to death first; and the wives of the magnates were angry with them, and said,[5] "We ought to die after our husbands." And they were all put to death by our order except Rhumi, the wife of the king who was to have reigned there, whom we would not permit to die; but we kept requiring her to deny Christ and live, having mercy upon her daughters, and retaining everything which she possessed by becoming a Jew. And we bade her go and take counsel, attended by guards from our army. And she went out, going round the streets and squares of the city with her head uncovered, a woman whose person no one had seen in the street since she grew up. And she cried and said, "Women of Nagrin, my Christian companions, and the rest of you also who are Jews and heathens, listen![6] My

---

[1] The MS. has ܐܠܗ, not ܐܠܝ, as L. prints.

[2] The MS. has ܟܘܘܟ, not ܟܘܘܟ, as L. prints. So Cod. Rom., which, however, has ܟܕܘܪ instead of ܟܕ.

[3] The MS. has ܪܒܘܬܗܘܢ, not ܪܒܘܬܗܘܢ, as L. prints.

[4] The MS. has ܐܡܪܝܢ, not ܐܡܪܝܢ, as L. prints.

[5] The MS. has ܐܡܪ, not ܐܡܪ, as L. prints.

[6] The MS. has ܫܡܥܝ, not ܫܡܥ, as L. prints.

birth and my family, and whose Christian daughter I am, you know; and that I have gold and silver and slaves, male and female, and[1] many lands and revenues; and, now that my husband has been put to death for Christ's sake, if I wish to be married to a husband, I have 40,000 *denarii*, and gold ornaments, and much silver and pearls and raiment, splendid and magnificent, besides the treasures of my husband; and that these things have not been falsely spoken by me you know of yourselves; and that to a woman there are no days of joy like the days of her marriage; for from that time forward there are distresses and lamentation, at the birth of children, and when[2] she is deprived of them, and when she buries them; but I from this day forward am free from them all. And on the days of my first marriage I was full of joy, and now, behold! it is in the gladness of my heart that I have adorned my five virgin daughters for Christ. Look[3] upon me, my companions, for, lo! you have twice seen me,[4] at my first marriage, and at this second one; for it was with my face exposed before you all that I went to my former bridegroom; and now it is with my face exposed that I am going to Christ, my Lord and my God, and the Lord and God of my daughters, even as He in His love humbled Himself and came to us and suffered for our sake.

"'"Imitate[5] me and my daughters, and consider that I am not inferior to you in beauty; and, behold! I am going to Christ my Lord resplendent in that beauty, undefiled, as it is, by Jewish denial, that my beauty may be a witness before my Lord that it could not lead me astray to commit the sin of denial, and my gold and silver and all that I have may be witnesses that I did not love them as I loved my God. And

---

[1] Omit ܘ, with Cod. Rom., "Dion.," 14,650, and Cod. Borg. 14,641 agrees with 17,202.

[2] Insert ܘ before ܟܕ, with Cod. Rom., "Dion.," 14,650, and Cod. Borg. 14,641 agrees with 17,202.

[3] Read ܚܘܪ̈ܝ for ܚܘܪܝ, with Cod. Rom.

[4] Insert ܠܟܝ after ܐܝܬܝܟܝ, with Jo. Eph. 14,650 and Cod. Borg. have ܒܦܪܨܘܦܝ, "my face."

[5] Read ܐܬܕܡܝ̈ܝܢ for ܘܐܬܕܡ̈ܝܢ, with Cod. Rom. and Jo. Eph.

that rebellious king permitted me to deny and live. Far be it from me, my companions, far be it from me to deny Christ my God in whom I have believed! and I and my daughters have been baptized in the name of the Trinity, and I worship His cross, and for His sake I and my daughters joyfully die, even as[1] He suffered in the flesh for our sake. Behold! I resign everything that is pleasant to the eyes and to the bodily senses on the earth and passes away, that I may go and receive from my Lord that which does not pass away. Blessed are you, my companions, if you will hear my words and know the truth and love Christ, for whose sake I and my daughters die. Then shall there be rest and peace to the people of God. The blood of my brothers and my sisters who have been slain for Christ shall be a wall to this city, if it hold fast to Christ my Lord. Behold,[2] with my face exposed I pass away from this city, in which I have been as in a temporary tabernacle, that I may go with my daughters to an everlasting city, for it is there that I have betrothed them. Pray for me, my companions, that Christ my Lord may receive me and may pardon me for having remained alive these three days after my husband."[3]

"'And, when we heard a cry of lamentation from the city, and those who had been sent came back and, when[4] asked, told us that, as we have written above, Rhumi had gone round the city, speaking to the women her companions and encouraging them, and a cry of woe was being raised[5] in the city, then we were enraged with the guards, so much so that, had we not been persuaded not to do so, we would have put them to death for allowing her to act in this manner. But at last she came out from the city like a madwoman, with her head uncovered, accompanied by her daughters; and she came and stood before me without shame, and holding

---

[1] Omit ‏ܘ‎ before ‏ܐܝܟ‎, with Cod. Rom., 14,650, Cod. Borg., and "Dion."

[2] Insert ‏ܗܘ‎ before ‏ܒ‎, with Cod. Rom., "Dion.," 14,650, and Cod. Borg.

[3] The MS. has ‏ܒܥܠܝ‎, not ‏ܒܥܠܝ‎, as L. prints.

[4] Insert ‏ܘ‎ before ‏ܒ‎, with Cod. Rom., Jo. Eph., 14,650, and Cod. Borg.

[5] Insert ‏ܘ‎ before ‏ܗܘܐ‎, with Cod. Rom. and Jo. Eph.

her daughters, who were attired as for marriage, by the hand. And she loosened the bands of her hair and turned them round with her hands, and stretched out her neck, and bowed her head, crying, " I am a Christian, and so are my daughters ; for Christ's sake we die.   Cut off our heads, that we may go and find our brothers and our sisters and the father of my daughters."   But after all this madness I exhorted her to deny Christ, and only to say that He was a man ; and she would not, but one of her daughters insulted us for saying this.   And, since I saw[1] that it was not possible to induce her to deny Christ, for the sake of striking terror into the other Christians I gave orders, and they threw her to the ground, and her daughters' throats were cut, and their blood ran down into her mouth, and afterwards her head was cut off.   And by Adonai I swear that I was much distressed because of her beauty and that of her daughters.   Now the chief priests and I thought that in accordance with the purport of the laws children ought not to die because of parents ; and I distributed them, both the boys and the girls, among the army to bring them up ; and, as soon as they are grown up, if they become Jews, they shall live ; and, if they confess Christ, they shall die.   And these things[2] I have described and related to your Majesty, and I beg you not to suffer a Christian among your people, unless he denies and stands on your side.   Now, as for the Jews also, my brethren, who are in your dominions, treat them kindly, my brother, and write and send me word what you wish me to send you in return for this.'

"All these things were written to him after we had reached[3] the place :[4] and he assembled his army, and the epistle was read before him, and the envoy related how the Christians had been put to death and banished from the land of the Homerites.   And Mundhir said to the Christians in his army, ' Behold ! you have heard what has happened.   Deny Christ ;

---

[1] The MS. has O before ܐܝܠܝܢ?, which L. does not print.

[2] Insert O before ܗܠܝܢ, with Cod. Rom., Jo. Eph., 14,650, and Cod. Borg.

[3] The MS. has ܐܙܠܢܢ, not ܐܙܠܢܢ, as L. prints.

[4] The MS. has ܠܬܡܢ, not ܠܬܡܢ, as L. prints.

for I am no better than the other kings who have persecuted the Christians.'   And a certain man of high position in his army, who was a Christian, was moved with zeal, and boldly said to the king, ' It was not in your time that we became Christians, that we should deny Christ.'   And Mundhir was enraged, and said, ' Do you dare to speak in my presence ? ' And he said, ' Because of the fear of God I speak without fear, and no one shall stop me ; for my sword is no shorter than the swords of others, and I will not shrink [1] from fighting unto death.'   And because of his birth, and because he was a great and distinguished man and valiant in war,[2] Mundhir was silent.

"And, when we returned to the camp of Nu'man in the first week of the fast, we found a Christian envoy,[3] who had been sent by the king of the Homerites before he died. This man, when he heard about the people who had been slaughtered by this Jewish tyrant, immediately hired a man from the camp of Nu'man, and sent him to Nagrin to bring him intelligence of what he saw and learned as to the events which had happened there.   And, when he returned, he also in our presence related to the former Christian envoy the things which are recorded above, and that three hundred and forty of the magnates had been put to death,[4] who had come out to him from the city, and he swore to them, and perjured himself to them ; and as to their chief, Harith the son of Khanab, the husband of Rhumi, that the Jew insulted him, and said to him, ' Trusting [5] in Christ, you have rebelled against me ; but have mercy upon your old age and deny Him, or else you shall die with your companions.'   And he answered and said to him, ' Truly I am distressed for all my companions and my brothers, because they would not listen to me when I told

---

[1] The MS. has [Syriac], not [Syriac], as L. prints.

[2] After [Syriac] insert [Syriac] [Syriac], with Cod. Rom. and Jo. Eph.

[3] Read [Syriac] for [Syriac], with Cod. Rom., Jo. Eph., 14,650, and Cod. Borg.

[4] The MS. has [Syriac] before [Syriac], which L. does not print.

[5] Read [Syriac] for [Syriac], with Cod. Rom.

them that you were lying, and said that we should not[1] go out
to you nor trust your words, but fight with you. And I
trusted in Christ that I should have overcome you, and the city
would not have been taken, for there was nothing lacking in it.
And you are not a king, but a perjurer: and I have myself
seen many kings who are truthful and do not lie. And I will
not deny Christ my God to become a Jew like you, and a liar.
And now I know that He loves me; and I have lived[2] long in
the world, and have had children and grandchildren, and I
have daughters[3] and many kinsmen, and I have won renown
in wars by the power of Christ. And I am sure that, even as
a vine which is pruned and gives forth much fruit, so shall our
Christian people be multiplied in this city; and the church,
which has been burnt by you, shall increase and be built up,
and Christianity shall have dominion and give commands to
kings, and shall reign, and your Judaism shall be blotted out,
and your kingdom shall pass away, and your dominion shall
come to an end. Boast not that you have done anything, nor
be puffed up[4] with glorying.'[5]

"And, when the great Harith the son of Khanab, the
venerable old man, had said these things, he turned round and
said in a loud voice to his believing companions who surrounded him, 'Did you hear, my brothers, what I said to this
Jew?' And they said, 'We heard everything which you
said, father ours.' And again he said, 'Is it true or not?'
And they cried, 'It is true.' And he said, 'If any man
fears the sword and denies Christ, let him be separated from
among us.' And they cried, 'Far be it from us! Be of

---

[1] Insert O before ܠܒ?, with Cod. Rom. and 14,641.   "Dion." has ܠܒܘ.

[2] The MS. has ܚܝܝܬ, not ܚܝܝܬ, as L. prints.

[3] Read ܒܢܬܐ for ܒܢܝܐ, with Cod. Rom. and Jo. Eph.

[4] ܬܬܪܝܡܘܢ. This word occurs again in 1. 7 (p. 73, 1. 7, L.) and 9. 3 (p. 257,
1. 14), where the meaning seems to be as above, not "vafer fuit," as Payne Smith.
Cf. also 3. 1 (p. 123, 1. 12) and 3. 10 (p. 130, 1. 22). In 7. 2 (p. 203, 1. 3)
ܡܬܪܝܡܢܐ, from the cognate ܐܪܝܡ, seems to bear the same meaning.

[5] Read ܒܫܘܒܗܪܐ for ܒܫܘܒܗܪܐ, with Cod. Rom. Jo. Eph. has
ܒܫܘܒܗܪܐ, which gives the same sense.

good cheer, father ours: we are all like you,[1] and with you will we die for Christ's sake, and no one amongst us will remain after you.' And he cried and said, ' Ye Christian people [2] who surround me, and ye heathens and Jews, hear. If any man of my family and my relations and of my kin denies Christ and joins this Jew, he has no part with me, and he shall not inherit anything that is mine, but all that belongs to me shall go to the expenses of the church that shall be built. But, if any man of my kin does not deny Christ and survives me, he shall inherit my property ; but three fields, whichever the Church shall choose [3] in my estate,[4] shall go to the expenses of the Church.' And, when he had said these things, he turned to the king and said, ' You and everyone who denies Christ I deny. Behold! we stand before you.' And his companions were emboldened, and said, ' Behold! Abraham the patriarch will look upon you and us with you ; but every-one who denies Christ and remains alive after you we deny.' And he ordered them to be taken to the gully called *Wadiya*, and their heads to be cut off and their bodies thrown into it. And they stretched out their hands to heaven and said, ' Christ, our God, come to our aid, and put strength within us, and receive our souls. And may the blood of Thy bond-servants, which is shed for Thy sake, smell sweet unto Thee ; and make us worthy of Thy sight ; and confess us before Thy Father, as Thou promisedst. And may the church be built, and may a bishop be appointed in the stead of Paul, Thy bond-servant, whose bones they burnt.' And they bade one another farewell ; and the old man Harith made the sign over them, and he bowed his head and received the sword. And his companions rushed forward and crowded together and smeared themselves with his blood ; and they were all martyred.

"And a child of three years old, whose mother was coming

---

[1] Read ܐܟܘܬܝ for ܐܟܘܬ, with Cod. Rom.

[2] Omit ܠ before ܢܨܪ̈ܝܐ, and read ܠܟܘ for ܠܗ, with Cod. Rom. and Jo. Eph. 14,650 and Cod. Borg. also give the same sense.

[3] Read ܢܓܒܐ for ܢܓܒܐ, with Cod. Rom.   [4] οὐσία.

out to be put to death and was holding him [1] with her hand, ran up (and it happened that, when he saw the king sitting clad in royal apparel, he left his mother and ran up and kissed the king on the knees); and the king took hold of him and began to caress him and to say to him, 'Which would you like, to go and die with your mother, or to stay with me?' The boy said to him, 'By our Lord, I would like to die with my mother; and for this purpose I am going with my mother; for she said to me, "Come, my son, let us go and die for Christ's sake." But release me, that I may go to my mother, lest she die and I do not see her, because she says to me, "The king of the Jews has commanded that everyone who does not deny Christ shall die," and I will not deny Him.' And he said to him, 'Whence [2] do you know Christ?' The boy said to him, 'Every day I see Him in the church with my mother, whenever I go to the church.' And he said to him, 'Do you love me, or your mother?' [3] And again he said to him, 'Do you love me, or Christ?' He said to him, 'Christ more than you.' And he said to him, 'Why did you come and kiss my knees?' The boy said to him, 'I thought that you were the Christian king, whom I used to see in the church, and I did not know that you were the Jew.' He said to him, 'I will give you nuts and almonds and figs.' And the boy said, 'No, by Christ, I will not eat the Jews' nuts; but let me go to my mother.' And he said to him,[4] 'Stay with me, and you shall be a son to me.' And the boy said, 'No, by Christ, I will not stay with you, because your smell is foul and fetid, and not sweet like my mother.' And the king said to those that were standing by, 'Look at this evil root, whom from his boyhood Christ has deceived so as to make him love

---

[1] The MS. has ܠܗ, not ܠܐ, as L. prints.

[2] The MS. has ܐܝܡܟܐ, not ܐܝܟܐ, as L. prints.

[3] After ܠܐܡܟ there follow in Jo. Eph., 14,650, and Cod. Borg. the words ܐܡܪ ܠܗ ܡܪܢ ܐܡܝ, "He said to him, 'By our Lord, my mother.'" This answer (absent in both MSS.) seems to have been accidentally omitted by our author.

[4] Insert ܠܗ after ܘܐܡܪ, with Cod. Rom., Jo. Eph., 14,650, and Cod. Borg.

Him.'[1] And one of the magnates said to the boy, 'Come with me, and I will take you, that you may be a son to the queen.' And the boy said to him,[2] 'You are smitten on the face. My mother, who takes me to the church, is more to me than the queen.' And, when he saw that they held him tight, he bit the king on the thigh, and said, 'Release me, you wicked Jew, that I may go to my mother and die with her.' And he gave him to one of the magnates, and said, 'Take care of him until he grows up; and, if he denies Christ, he shall live; and, if not, he shall die.' And, while this man's slave was carrying him off, he struggled with his feet and cried to his mother, 'My mother, come and take me, that I may go with you to the church.' And, crying out[3] before him, she said, 'Go, my son; you are intrusted to Christ's care; do not weep; wait for me in the church in Christ's presence till I come.' And, when she had said this, they cut off her head.

"And owing to this letter and the reports that have been received distress has fallen upon all the Christians here. And, in order that the things which have happened in the land of the Homerites may be made known to the pious believing bishops, and that they may celebrate the memory of the illustrious martyrs, we have written[4] these things; and we beg your affection to let them be made known at once to the archimandrites and bishops, and especially to the chief priest of Alexandria, in order that he may write to the king of the Ethiopians to come at once and help[5] the Homerites. But let the chief priests of the Jews in Tiberias also be arrested, and be compelled to send to this Jewish king, who has appeared, and tell him to put an end to the tribulation and persecution in the land of the Homerites." And so the rest, consisting of

---

[1] ܚܣܝܒܘܗܝ?. So Jo. Eph. (not ܚܣܝܒܘܗܝ?, as Assem. prints) and Mich. (ܚܣܝܒܟ).

[2] Insert ܠܗ after ܘܐܡܪ, with Cod. Rom., Jo. Eph., 14,650, and Cod. Borg.

[3] The MS. has ܓܥܝܐ, not ܓܥܝܐ, as L. prints.

[4] Omit ܕ before ܟܬܒܢ, with Cod. Rom. and Jo. Eph.

[5] Read ܢܥܕܪ for ܢܥܕܘܪ, with Cod. Rom. and Jo. Eph.

salutations to the chief priests and bishops of that time and
the believing archimandrites, which are contained in the
epistle.

CHAPTER IV

THE FOURTH CHAPTER OF THE EIGHTH BOOK TREATS
OF THE FLOOD OF WATER WHICH ENTERED EDESSA,
AND HOW THE FLOW OF THE WATERS OF SHILUHO
IN JERUSALEM WAS STOPPED, AND ANTIOCH WAS OVER-
THROWN BY AN EARTHQUAKE, AND THE TEMPLE OF
SOLOMON IN THE CITY OF HELIOPOLIS WAS BURNT

While Asclepius Bar Malohe,[1] the brother of Andrew and
of Demosthenes the prefect,[2] held the see of Edessa, having
become bishop there after Paul, who showed an outward appearance of being orthodox,[3]—(Now this man was ostentatious in his
person, and polished. And, when he was a bishop in Edessa in
the days of Flavian, before Asclepius, he drew up a written
statement for him, which did not anathematise the Synod,
because he had been [4] his *synkellos*: and this book came into
the hands of the holy Severus, who succeeded Flavian; and,
when this Paul went up to salute him, he gave it him, and in
divine love forgave him his offence, that is, on his assurance
that he was a believer; and this wise man, who kept knowledge
hidden, as it is written,[5] did not expose him. And in the days
of this king he at first firmly refused to accept the Synod,
while the people of Edessa supported him, and even suffered
loss and outrage on his account every day; however, on being
banished to Euchaita he conformed, and returned to Edessa;
and after surviving a short time he was struck with shame
and soon after died, and Asclepius succeeded him. And he

---

[1] *I.e.* " son of sailors."   [2] ὕπαρχος.

[3] Here the sentence breaks off, being taken up again lower down.

[4] We should probably insert another |ܘܐ in order to express the pluperfect,
which is necessary for the sense, since a bishop could not be a *synkellos*.

[5] Prov. x. 14.

was a Nestorian; but he was just in his deeds, and showed kindness to the tillers of the soil, and was gentle towards them, and was not greedy after bribes. In his body he was chaste, and in outward matters he did much good to his church, and paid its debts. But he was active and violent against the believers; and many were banished by him and outraged with every kind of torture, or died under the hard treatment inflicted on them at the hands of Liberius, a Goth, a cruel governor, who was called "the bull-eater.")

And,[1] while affairs in Edessa were in this position, in the year eight hundred and thirty-six of the Greeks, the year three,[2] on the twenty-second of April, the river Scirtus, which enters and passes through the city, rose and overflowed, and overthrew two sides of the wall, and drowned many persons; for it was supper-time, and while their food was in their mouth the waters rushed in upon them, the flooded Scirtus. But this Asclepius escaped, and so did Liberius. And[3] the flow of the waters of Shiluho, which are in Jerusalem, in the southern quarter of it, was stopped for fifteen years; and the temple of Solomon in the city of Heliopolis in the forest of Lebanon, as to which Scripture mentions that Solomon built it and stored arms in it[4] [was burnt].[5] And to the south of it are three wonderful stones, on which nothing is built, but they stand by themselves, joined and united together and touching one another; and all three are distinguished by effigies, and they are very large. And in a mystical sense they are set, as it were, to represent the temple of the knowledge of the faith in the adorable Trinity, the calling of the nations by the preaching of the gospel tidings. There came down lightning from heaven, while the rain fell in small quantities: it struck the temple and reduced its stones to powder by the heat, and overthrew its pillars, and broke it to pieces and destroyed it. But the three stones[6] it did not touch, but they remain perfect; and now a

---

[1] Mich. fol. 161 *r*, 164 *v*.　　　　　　[2] 525.
[3] Mich. fol. 164.　　　　　　[4] 1 Kings ix. 18, 19.

[5] The word ܩ has dropped out of the text, and must be supplied from the heading. The verb is also omitted in Mich.

[6] The MS. has ܟܐܦܐ, not ܟܐܦܐ, as L. prints.

house of prayer has been built there, dedicated to Mary the
Holy Virgin, the *Theotokos*.

And a year afterwards, in the year four,[1] Antioch was
overthrown by a great earthquake of unwonted severity,
and countless myriads of people perished in it. For it was
summer time; and, while they were feasting, and their food
was in their mouth, their houses[2] were thrown down upon
them, as upon the sons of Job in the proving of Satan. And
Euphrasius was chief priest there, who succeeded Paul who
was called "the Jew"; and he fell into a boiling[3] cauldron of
wax, and perished.

And his successor[4] was Ephraim of Amida, who was *Comes
Orientis*[5] at that time. And this man in the authority which
he exercised in various countries was a man just in his deeds,
and was not greedy after bribes, and was able and successful.
And[6] for years he had been infected with the teaching of the
Diphysites through some books which his mother Mako (?)
had inherited from a certain Bar Shalumo of Constantia, of the
school of Diodorus and Theodore; and he corrupted and
won over many persons, some by subtilty and moderation,
and some by the threats of the king, who was fond of him,
and paid attention to what he wrote to him.

[1] 526.

[2] The MS. has ⟨Syriac⟩, not ⟨Syriac⟩, as L. prints.

[3] MS. ⟨Syriac⟩, not ⟨Syriac⟩, as L.

[4] Mich. fol. 165 *v*; Greg. *H. E.* i. p. 201.   [5] κόμης ἀνατολῆς.

[6] Two leaves in the MS. have here been transposed.   I pass on from p. 244, l. 26
(Land) to p. 246, l. 16.   The intermediate portion has nothing to do with the subject
of this chapter, but belongs to the next.   This is also evident from a comparison with
Michael and Gregory.

CHAPTER V

THE FIFTH CHAPTER OF THE SAME EIGHTH BOOK TREATS
OF THE NEGOTIATIONS WHICH WERE HELD UPON
THE FRONTIER; AND OF MUNDHIR, KING OF THE
SARACENS, WHO WENT UP INTO THE TERRITORY OF
EMESA AND APAMEA, AND TOOK A LARGE NUMBER
OF CAPTIVES AND CARRIED[1] THEM AWAY WITH
HIM; AND OF THE BELIEVING BISHOPS OF THE EAST
WHO WERE BANISHED AND WITHDREW FROM THEIR
CHURCHES

Kawad,[2] king of the Persians, kept making pressing
demands for the payment of the tribute of 500 lbs. weight
of gold which was paid to him by the king of the Romans on
account of the expense[3] of the Persian force which guarded
the gates facing the land of the Huns; and for this reason he
used from time to time to send his own Saracens into the
territory of the Romans, and they plundered and carried off
captives. The Romans also invaded Arzanene, a country
which belonged to him, and the district of Nisibis, and did
damage. On this account negotiations[4] were held, and the
two kings sent envoys, Justin sending Hypatius and the old
man Farzman, and Kawad Asthebid;[5] and much discussion
took place on the frontier, which was reported to the two
kings by their magnates through couriers;[6] and no peaceful
message was sent by them, but they were hostile to one
another.

And Mundhir, the Saracen king, went up into the territory
of Emesa and Apamea and the district of Antioch on two
occasions; and he carried off many people, and took them
away with him. And four hundred virgins, who were sud-

---

[1] Insert ܘ before ܐܢܘܢ.

[2] Mich. fol. 164 r; Greg. p. 78.

[3] ἀνάλωμα.

[4] τράκτατον.

[5] The name meant is *Spahpat* ('Ασπεβέδης), the title of the Persian commander-in-chief (Josh. Styl. 59, and Wright's note). Cf. also 9. 4.

[6] βερηδάριοι.

denly made captive [1] among the congregation in the church of
Thomas the Apostle at Emesa (?),[2] he sacrificed in one day
in honour of 'Uzzai. Dodo also the anchorite, an old man,
who was made captive among the congregation, saw it with
his eyes, and told me.

Now of the bishops of the East, and especially those in
the jurisdiction of the learned Severus, some [3] were banished,
and others withdrew to Alexandria and various other countries,
walking in the footsteps of the chief priest, Severus the doctor.
And Akhs'noyo [4] of Hierapolis had been sent into exile at
Gangra ; and he was imprisoned over the kitchen in the
hospital [5] there, and was suffocated [6] by the smoke, as he
states in his epistle ; [7] and at last he died. And [8] Antoninus
of Berrhœa, and Thomas of Damascus, and Thomas of Dara,
and John of Constantia, and Thomas of Amrin (?),[9] and Peter
of Rhesaina, and Constantine of Laodicea, and Peter of
Apamea, and others withdrew, and lived in hiding wherever
it was convenient for them. But the see of Alexandria had
not been disturbed, and Timothy [10] succeeded Dioscorus ; and he
did not withdraw nor accept the Synod in the days of Justin ;
and the fugitive believing priests who sought refuge with

[1] Omit ܕ before ܐܘܠܕܒܢ.

[2] ܐܘܡܣܩ seems to be corrupt. There is no authority for the form ܐܘܡܣܩ for
Emesa, and only a few lines above our author writes ܚܡܣ ; but it may be an
accidental corruption. Mich. has ܕܗܡܣܩܘ (δῆμιος ?), but a name of a town
seems to be required.

[3] Mich. fol. 162 *r*.

[4] Jo. Eph. ap. Mich. fol. 161 *v*, Greg. *H. E.* pp. 195, 197, from Philox. *Ep. ad
Mon. Sen.* (Brit. Mus. Add. MS. 14,597, fol. 35 ff.).

[5] ξενοδοχεῖον.

[6] Read ܩܢܚܝܠܬܩ for ܩܝܕܬܠܩ, with Greg. and Mich. So also Philoxenus
himself (fol. 89 *v*).

[7] Cf. 7. 12.

[8] Cf. Jo. Eph. *l.c.*

[9] I cannot identify this place. ܐܘܡܪܝ should stand for Amorium ; but, as
it is mentioned among the Mesopotamian sees, this is out of the question. John of
ܐܘܡܪܝ is mentioned among the Mesopotamian bishops in Mich. fol. 161 *v*. In a
chronicle of the ninth cent. in Brit. Mus. Add. MS. 14,642, fol. 29 *r*, he is called
Thomas of ܐܘܡܪܝ, as here ; cf. Assem., *B. O.* 2, *Diss. de Monoph.* lxiii.

[10] Mich. fol. 162 *r*.

him he received affectionately, and honoured and encouraged them.

Now [1] Nonnus [2] of Seleucia, who came from Amida, had withdrawn to his own city and taken up his abode in his mansion there, because he came of a wealthy family, and had been governor [3] and great steward of the Church in his city in the days of John the bishop, who came from the monastery of Karthamin, a righteous man. He in his days blessed Nonnus, and said, " I am confident in my Lord that you will die as bishop in my see." And the event was delayed, inasmuch as after the captivity of Amida the gracious Thomas became bishop there, who built Dara. He, when the couriers [4] came to seïze him, in order that either he might accept the Synod or they might drive him out, fell ill [5] in accordance with his prayer, and died suddenly and at once while in possession of his see, the couriers being in the city ; and this caused many to marvel. Accordingly, in order that the blessing of John might be fulfilled, the men of Amida seized Nonnus and appointed him bishop there ; and he lived a few months, and departed. [6]

And in succession to him again, in the presence of three bishops, as the canons require, Nonnus of Martyropolis, Arathu (?) of Ingila, and Aaron of Arsamosata, who were on the spot, they ordained Moro Bar Kustant, the governor, [3] who was steward of the Church, an abstemious man and righteous in his deeds, chaste and believing ; and he was fluent and practised in the Greek tongue, having been educated in the monastery of St. Thomas the Apostle of Seleucia, which in zealous faith had removed [7] and had settled at Kenneshre on the river Euphrates, and there been rebuilt [8] by John the

---

[1] Jo. Eph. ap. " Dion." (Assem., *B. O.* 2, pp. 48, 49) ; Mich. *l.c.*

[2] Read ⲗⲟⲩ for ⲗⲟⲩ. The former form occurs twice lower down.

[3] ἡγεμών.　　　　　　　　　　　　　[4] βερεδάριοι.

[5] Logically, we require ⲗⲟⲩ, " ill," for ⲗⲟⲩ, " illness " ; but the meaning is clear.

[6] At this point we go back to fol. 140 (see p. 205, note 6).

[7] The MS. has ⲗⲟⲩ?, not ⲗⲟⲩ, as L. prints.

[8] Read ⲗⲟⲩ for ⲗⲟⲩ.

archimandrite, a learned man, who was at that time an ex-pleader (?),[1] a native of Edessa, the son of Aphthonia.[2]   And this Moro had been trained up in all kinds of right instruction and mental excellence from his boyhood by Sh'muni and Morutho, his grave, chaste, and believing sisters.[3]   And after remaining a short time in his see he was banished to Petra, and from Petra to Alexandria ; and he stayed there for a time, and formed a library there containing many admirable books ; and in them there is abundance of great profit [4] for those who love instruction, the discerning and studious.   These were transferred to the treasury of the Church of Amida after the man's death.   And in every matter which I record, in order not to cause annoyance by blaming one man or praising another, I have related whatever the truth of the matter is without any falsehood.   However, the man progressed more and more in reading in Alexandria, and there he fell asleep. And his body was conveyed by his sisters, who were with him and ministered to him, comforting him in affliction, as it is written,[5] and laid in his own Martyrs' Chapel in the village of Beth Shuro.[6]   And as a record of the eloquent expression of his love of instruction I will set down at the end of this Book the prologue composed by him in the Greek tongue and inserted in his Tetreuangelion.

Now [7] the believing cloistered monks in the East had also, moreover, been expelled and had withdrawn from the year three until the year nine,[8] one week, that is, of years, from their cloisters in the district of Antioch and in Euphratesia, and also in Osrhoene and Mesopotamia.   And the cloister of Thomas at Seleucia with the brotherhood came to Kenneshre

---

[1] ܐܦ ܕܩܘܕܝܩܘܩ. This seems to represent ἀπὸ δικανικῶν, as in 7. 10 ; but the meaning does not suit this passage very well.

[2] Not Aphthonius ; see John's life in Brit. Mus. Add. MS. 12,174, fol. 84.

[3] The MS. has ܐܣܝܬܗ, not ܐܣܝܬܐ, as L. prints.

[4] The MS. has ܕ before ܢܘܬܪܢܐ, not ܘ, as L. prints.

[5] 2 Cor. i. 4 (?) ; I Thess. iii. 7 (?).

[6] In Jo. Eph. (Land, *Anecd. Syr.* ii. p. 110, l. 3) " Beth Shur'o."   " Dion." " in the temple of Beth Shilo."

[7] Mich. fol. 163.

[8] 525–531.

14

on the Euphrates, and was there settled by the learned John the archimandrite, the son of Aphthonia.   And Cyrus, archimandrite of the Syrians in Antioch, was expelled, together with the brotherhood of the monastery[1] of Thel 'Addo, and the monastery of Romanus,[2] and Simeon of L'gino, and Ignatius, archimandrite of the monastery of 'Akibo at Chalcis, and the monastery of S'nun, and John, archimandrite of Khafro d'Birtho,[3] and the monastery of my lord Bassus, and John of the Orientals, and the monks of the Arches, and the monastery of Magnus (?),[4] and Sergius of the Quarry, and Thomas of the house of Natsih, and Isaac of the house of "bedyeshu', and the cloisters of 'Arab[5] in Mesopotamia and Izlo and Beth Gaugal, and five metropolitan cloisters in Amida, Hananyo and Abraham called "the humble," a worker of miracles, and Daniel, visitor of the cloister of Edessa, and Elijah of the house of Ishokuni, and Simai and Cosmas of the foundation of John the Anzetenian,[6] and Maron of the Orientals, and Solomon of the house of my lord Samuel, and Cyrus of Sugo, and the monks of the Watch-tower and of Thiri, near Rhesaina.

Now for this reason four or five communities of hermits also settled in the desert: at Ramsho Mori, a chaste man and of honourable character; and at Natfo Sergius, a plain and simple man, and after him Antony, a mild and peaceful man, and that kindly old man Elijah, our countryman, and Simeon of Chalcis, and Sergius, who has now rebuilt Sodakthe (?), and the community on the Harmosho (?),[7] the

---

[1] Mich. "was expelled together with the brotherhood, and the monks of the monastery . . ."

[2] Of ܟܝܪ܇ I can make nothing, and take the meaning from Mich. (ܕܪܘܡܢܘܣ). Read either ܕܪܝܐ or ܕܟܝܬ. Dr. Hamilton proposes ܕܡܟܝܒ, "that of my lord Romanus."

[3] Read ܟܦܪܐ ܕܒܝܪܬܐ for ܟܦܪܐܙܕܒܬܐ. Cf. Wright, *C. B. M.* pp. 605, 755, etc.; Mich. ܟܦܪ ܐܟܬܒܝܗ.

[4] Text, "Magos"; so Mich.

[5] The last letter of this word, left blank by L., is ܒ.

[6] See bk. 7, ch. 4 (p. 156, note 2).

[7] Or, "near Harmosho."   I find no trace of either of these names, and suspect both to be corrupt.   Mich. omits both, writing merely "Sergius, and the monastery . . . Hauro."

monastery founded by my lord John at Hauro.[1]   And Simeon, archimandrite of the monastery of my lord Isaac at Gabbula, which is now polluted[2] with the heresy of Julian the Phantasiast, was at that time zealous in the faith, he and those who were with him ; and Bar Hakino of the house of my lord Hanino, a worker of miracles, was similarly moved with zeal, insomuch as to go up to the royal city and in his own person admonish and reprove the king, although he was not received ; and this is witnessed by Akhs'noyo's epistle of thanks which he wrote to him from Gangra ; and similarly with the monks of the house of my lord Zakhkhai at Callinicus, and of the foundation of my lord Abbo, and of Beth R'kum.

And so the desert was at peace, and was abundantly supplied with a population of believers who lived in it, and fresh ones who were every day added to them and aided in swelling the numbers of their brethren, some from a desire to visit their brethren out of Christian love, and others again because they were being driven from country to country by the bishops in the cities.   And there grew up, as it were, a commonwealth[3] of illustrious and believing priests, and a tranquil brotherhood with them ; and they were united in love and abounded in mutual affection, and they were beloved and acceptable in the sight of everyone ; and nothing was lacking, for the honoured heads of the corporation, which is composed of all the members of the body, accompanied them, the pious John of Constantia, a religious and ascetic man, (he would not even partake of the desirable bread, " the foundation of the life of man,"[4] and so he progressed in the reading of the Scriptures and became a gnostic and a theoretic;[5] for he used to raise his understanding upwards by the study of spiritual things for the space of three hours, marvelling and meditating on the wisdom of the works of God ; and for three hours more, from the sixth to the ninth, he continued in joy

---

[1] At this point we return to fol. 142.
[2] Mich. has the masculine, " who is now polluted."
[3] πολιτεία.   [4] Sir. xxix. 21.
[5] *I.e.* learned in the inner or allegorical meaning.

and peace with every man, in intercourse with those who came to him upon necessary business)—and Thomas of Dara again, while undergoing many labours, conversed much upon physics.

Now in the year nine,[1] in the fifth year of the reign of this serene king, Justinian, the king of our day, being moved by God our Lord, who had foreknowledge of his deeds, he distributed justice, and ordered that all orders should return from exile and from the countries to which they had withdrawn in zeal for the faith, while he summoned the believing bishops to come up to him.   And, after this had happened in the year nine, in the year ten[2] a multitude of Huns entered the Roman territory and massacred those whom they found outside the cities; and they crossed the river Euphrates, and advanced as far as the district of Antioch.   Accordingly, under the direction of God, as he said, " My people, enter thou into thy chambers, and hide thyself until My indignation be overpast,"[3] and by order of the king, the believers in the East again retired into hiding.   But John the hermit of Anastasia, a man of honourable character, had been killed in the desert by the Huns; but Simeon the hermit, who was called " the horned," had not been hurt.

CHAPTER VI

THE SIXTH CHAPTER OF THE EIGHTH BOOK, STATING WHO WERE CHIEF PRIESTS IN THE DAYS OF JUSTIN, WHO, AFTER REIGNING NINE YEARS DIED IN THE YEAR FIVE, AND THIS JUSTINIAN OF OUR DAY, HIS SISTER'S SON, BECAME KING AFTER HIM

The chief priests[4] in the days of Justin are as follows:—Of Rome, Hormisda ; of Alexandria, Timothy ; of Jerusalem, Peter, who succeeded John ; and of Antioch, Paul the Jew, who was driven out, and after him Euphrasius, who was

---

[1] 531.   [2] 531-2.
[3] Isa. xxvi. 20.   [4] Cf. Mich. fol. 167 v.

burnt in the earthquake of Antioch in the year four,[1] and after him was Ephraim of Amida; of Constantinople, Epiphanius. There is comprised in this space of time[2] a space of nine years.

CHAPTER VII

THE SEVENTH CHAPTER.   IN IT IS CONTAINED BELOW THE PROLOGUE COMPOSED BY MORO, BISHOP OF AMIDA, IN THE GREEK TONGUE IN THE *TETREUANGELION*[3]

" In order[4] to gather together the sense of a long treatise a man stores up a knowledge of these things succinctly under a few heads in his mind and memory[5] and understanding. And we may understand these things from the heads[6] which are set down in this book; and these again cause the inner meaning[7] of all that is in them to pass rapidly and succinctly into the mind, when heard and considered[8] in due order. For, if a man gathers together the record of the Gospels, he will learn from it that God became incarnate, and that divine[9] as well as human properties are His, by which He made[10] the

---

[1] 526.

[2] We should probably read ⲥⲫⲣⲟ, "book," for ⲕⲃⲁⲗ.

[3] This chapter is contained in Cod. Rom., where the heading is, " The prologue composed concisely under heads by the holy Moro, bishop of Amida, a man deserving of blessed memory, upon the Gospel and the dispensation of Christ in the flesh."—Cf. p. 221.

[4] Mich. fol. 162 ff.

[5] The MS. has ⲟ, not ⲓ, as L. prints, before ⲕⲃⲁⲥⲟⲛ.

[6] The MS. has ⲣⲫⲁ, not ⲣⲫⲁ, as L. prints.

[7] θεωρία.

[8] Instead of ⲕⲁⲣⲓⲝ, Cod. Rom. has ⲕⲁⲥⲓ, "repeated." Mich. agrees with Cod. Brit.

[9] After ⲕⲃⲁⲥⲓⲓ insert ⲕⲃⲟⲛⲁⲓ, with Cod. Rom.   So Mich.

[10] Cod. Rom. seems to have ⲣⲥⲃⲟ, not ⲣⲥⲃⲟ, as Mai prints; and, as Mich. also has "made," this must be the right word. The participle, however, cannot here stand alone, so that we must either read ⲥⲃⲁ or suppose ⲓⲟⲟⲓ to have dropped out.

foundations of the world, which at His second coming He will make clearly to appear. And so everyone who examines these things severally will find first a notice of the census before His Incarnation, and then next the birth of John the Baptist for a testimony to the God of Israel, which happened in accordance with the previous annunciation of the angel; and he will find that the supernatural birth of Jesus, who is God, took place in the Virgin Mary and from her, and that every man has his beginning from the earth according to the saying of the Baptist,[1] but He who is not from the earth is Jesus from heaven.

" Now the testimonies to His Incarnation mentioned [2] in the book of the Gospel are those spoken in the spirit by Elizabeth and by the angel to the Virgin and Joseph and the shepherds at the annunciation of His birth by the assembly of watching angels; and again the prophecy of Zachariah, and the rising of the star, which betokened [3] the indestructible reign of the Son of God, who was born; and the prophecy of Simeon the priest and Anna about the coming of Christ for the salvation of the world and of Israel; and besides these also the proclamation of the Baptist, who testified that he was from earth and our Saviour from heaven. And, further, in the Gospel-record a man will understand His divine dispensation, which was effected by infinite wisdom, and not through book-wisdom and the pursuit of learning; and His power of performing wonderful mighty works in deed and word, and His knowledge about everything, and that He did no sin; and again that it was at His own pleasure to suffer in His own time and not to suffer when it was not time; and that it was in His power [4] to destroy sufferings by His voluntary sufferings in the body, and to do away death by His Resurrection and to ascend to heaven. And the record plainly states that He became incarnate of the Virgin in flesh endowed with a soul and an intellect; it states His nine months' human conception, His natural and

---

[1] John iii. 31.

[2] Read ܐܡܟܢ̈ܝ for ܐܡܟܢ̈ܝ, with Cod. Rom.

[3] Insert ܕ before ܣܘܩܒ, with Cod. Rom.

[4] Cod. Rom., " that it is now in His power."

supernatural[1] birth, and that He was wrapped in swaddling-clothes and sucked milk, and was also circumcised according to law ; and, further, that He fled before the threats of Herod into Egypt, carried by His mother, and that He came up from Egypt for the renovation of Israel and after the manner of Israel ; and again,[2] that He increased in stature, and was subject to His mother and to Joseph her husband, and was baptized with water by John to signify the renovating birth of mankind, which is in him renewed in a figure, because[3] His baptism bestowed upon us the holy birth of the Spirit ; and He was tempted by the devil as a man, but as God easily overcame the tempter in the contest and the argument ; and He was ministered to by angels ; and He gave peace to our race by restoring us to Paradise ; further, He associated with the disciples in human fashion, and withdrew at one time from the persecutors, and hungered[4] and thirsted[5] and was weary ; but He showed that He did not submit to these things merely from the necessity of nature[6] in human fashion, as though He were not God,[7] by the fact that it is testified that He verily fasted forty days and was afterwards hungry (in a similar manner He also slept ; but, because He was on a mountain in quiet, He kept watch in prayer, and this prayer He made to the Father in human fashion on behalf of men ; but on the sea and in the storm He slept in the ship for the instruction of the disciples, that they might believe that it is He who stills the storms of the seas and the sound of their waves) ; and, further, that, when they sought to throw Him down from the brow of the hill they could not do so, but, while[8] they stood all around Him, He passed through the midst of them and went His way ; and,

---

[1] Insert ◦ before ‎‎, with Cod. Rom.

[2] Insert ◦ before ‎‎, with Cod. Rom.

[3] Insert ‎ after ‎‎, with Cod. Rom.

[4] Read ‎‎ for ‎‎, with Cod. Rom.

[5] Insert ◦ before ‎‎, with Cod. Rom.

[6] After ‎‎ insert ‎‎, with Cod. Rom. So. Mich.

[7] Insert ‎ before ‎‎, with Cod. Rom. So Mich.

[8] Read ‎‎ for ◦, with Cod. Rom. So Mich. (‎‎).

when wounded by the lance on the Cross, His life did not pass away of necessity, but He bowed His head and gave up the ghost ; and in every respect divine and human qualities are His.   But the reforms which Christ effected in the world are His rebuke of the deceiver, and the demons which He drove out, and the fiends which He ejected, and the sore diseases which He healed, and the dead which He raised, and the divers temptations which He thrust away, and certain passions which He brought to naught ; which reforms were types and figures of the future world, which shall be far removed from evil, the world which is looked for by us with hope and faith and love.   And the teaching of our Saviour draws men away from the passion [1] of the love of money and the love of glory and pleasure, and raises them up that they may serve God in uprightness of will."

Now there was inserted in the Gospel of the holy Moro the bishop, in the eighty-ninth canon, a chapter which is related only by John in his Gospel, and is not found in other manuscripts, a section running thus : " It happened [2] one day, while Jesus was teaching, they brought Him a woman who had been found [3] to be with child of adultery, and told Him about her.   And Jesus said to them (since as God He knew their shameful passions and also their deeds), ' What does He command [4] in the law ? '   And they said to Him, ' That at the mouth of two or three witnesses she should be stoned.'   But He answered and said to them, ' In accordance with the law, whoever is pure and free from these sinful passions, and can bear witness with confidence and authority, as being under no blame in respect of this sin, let him bear witness against her, and let him first throw [5] a stone at her, and then those that are after him, and she shall be stoned.'   But they, because

---

[1] Insert ? ܣܝ݀ܡ before ܪܚܡܬܐ, with Cod. Rom.   So Mich.

[2] John viii. 1–11.

[3] Read ܐܬܕܟܚܬ for ܐܬܕܟܚ, with Cod. Rom.

[4] Cod. Rom., like Cod. Brit., has ܦܩܕ, not ܡܦܩܕ, as Mai prints.

[5] Read ܢܕܪܐ for ܪܡܐ, with Cod. Rom.   L. prints ܪ̈ܡܐ, but there is no point either above or below the letter in the MS.

they were subject to condemnation and blameworthy[1] in respect of this sinful[2] passion, went out one by one from before Him and left the woman.   And, when they had gone, Jesus looked upon the ground and, writing in the dust there, said to the woman, ' They who brought thee here and wished to bear witness against thee, having understood what I said to them, which thou hast heard, have left thee and departed. Do thou also, therefore, go thy way, and commit not this sin again.' "

[1] Cod. Rom. has ܡܚܝܒܝܢ, as Cod. Brit., not ܡܟܣܢܝܢ, as Mai prints.

[2] Read ܟܝܢܝܬܐ ܚܛܝܬܐ for ܟܝܢܝܬܐ ܚܛܝܬܐ, with Cod. Rom.   The reading of Cod. Brit. is doubtful.

BOOK IX

ALSO this ninth Book, concerning the reign of Justinian, states
how he became Anti-Cæsar [1] on the fifth day of the week in
the last week of the fast; and, after he had governed for three
months in conjunction with Justin his uncle, who died at the
end of July, when the year five was now ending,[2] this Justinian
became emperor,[3] in the year eight hundred and thirty-eight of
the Greeks, in the three hundred and twenty-seventh Olympiad.
And the events which happened during his reign down to the
year fifteen,[4] a space of ten years, which is contained in the
sections below, are set down in this ninth Book, consisting of
twenty-six chapters. Behold! they are set down below, and
are as follows :—

The first chapter of the ninth Book deals with the fighting which went on in the summer of the year five before Nisibis
and Thebetha, a Persian fortress.

The second chapter of the Book treats of the battle which
was fought in the desert of Thannuris.

The third chapter of the Book gives an account of the
battle which was fought before the city of Dara on the frontier.

The fourth chapter of the Book gives information about
the battle which was fought on the Euphrates in the year nine.

The fifth chapter tells of Gadar the Kadisene, a Persian
general, how he was killed; and Izdegerd, who was with him,
a nephew of the *Ptehasha* of Arzanene, was taken prisoner.

The sixth chapter deals with the battle which was fought
before Martyropolis on the frontier, and the large numbers

---

[1] Cf. bk. 6, ch. 6.   [2] 526–7.

[3] αὐτοκράτωρ.   [4] 537.

of Huns who invaded the territory of the Romans in the year ten.

The seventh chapter explains how in the summer of the year eleven peace was made between the Romans and the Persians by the ambassadors, Rufinus and Hermogenes, the master of the offices.

The eighth chapter of the ninth Book treats of the Samaritans who rebelled and set up a tyrant of their own in the country of Palestine.

The ninth chapter of the Book, concerning the heresy of Julian the Phantasiast, bishop of the city of Halicarnassus,[1] how it appeared.

The tenth chapter sets forth the first epistle of Julian to Severus, with a question about the body of Christ our God.

The eleventh chapter of the Book treats of the answer to the epistle of Julian, which the doctor Severus, the chief priest, wrote to him.

The twelfth chapter of the Book imparts information about the second epistle of Julian,[2] which he wrote to Severus.

The thirteenth chapter tells of the answer made by Severus the patriarch to this second epistle of Julian.

The fourteenth chapter of the Book treats of the riot which took place in the royal city, and describes how Hypatius and Pompeius were put to death, and large numbers of the people were massacred in the circus in the year ten.

The fifteenth chapter treats of the request contained in the petition which the believing bishops who had been summoned from exile to the royal city presented to King Justinian concerning their faith.

The sixteenth chapter of the ninth Book sets forth the defence made by Severus the chief priest in his epistle to King Justinian, refusing to come, when summoned by him to the royal city.

The seventeenth chapter of the ninth Book treats of Carthage, the chief city of the country of Africa, how it was

---

[1] The text has "Alexandria," but Halicarnassus is obviously meant, as in the heading of the chapter below.

[2] Read ‏ܩܠܘܣܝܢ‎ for ‏ܩܠܘܣܢ‎.

taken by Belisarius the general and a Roman army, and made subject to King Justinian.

The eighteenth chapter of the ninth Book deals with Rome and Naples in the country of Italy, and how they were taken by Belisarius the general and a Roman army.

The nineteenth chapter of the ninth Book again treats of Severus the patriarch, who went up[1] to the royal city and appeared before the king, and was received in the palace, and remained there till the end of the month of March in the year fourteen, and then departed.

The twentieth chapter of the ninth Book treats of the epistle of Severus the patriarch to the order of priests and the society of monks in the East, dealing with his expulsion from the royal city.

The twenty-first [chapter][2] of the ninth Book sets forth the canonical epistle of union and concord which was sent by Anthimus, chief priest of the royal city, to Severus the patriarch.

The twenty-second chapter of the ninth Book treats of the epistle of concord and union canonically sent by Severus in answer to Anthimus, chief priest of Constantinople, the royal city.

The twenty-third chapter of the ninth Book introduces the epistle of concord and union which was canonically sent by Severus to Theodosius of Alexandria.

The twenty-fourth chapter of the ninth Book treats further of the canonical epistle of union and concord which was sent by Theodosius the patriarch in answer to Severus the doctor.

The twenty-fifth chapter of the ninth Book gives information about the canonical epistle of concord which was sent by Anthimus, chief priest of the royal city, to Theodosius, patriarch of the great city of Alexandria.

The twenty-sixth chapter of the ninth Book records[3] the answer to the epistle, which was canonically sent by

---

[1] The MS. has ܐܠܟ‍‍ܝ, not ܐܠܟ‍ܝ, as L.

[2] The word ܪ‍ܝܫܐ seems to have dropped out of the text.

[3] For ܡܫܟ‍ܚܕܗ‍ܝ read ܡܫܟ‍ܚܕ or ܡܫܟ‍ܚ.

Theodosius, archbishop of Alexandria, to Anthimus, chief priest of the royal city, in concord and brotherhood.

There is inserted also in it, at the end of this ninth Book, the prologue given above,[1] which was composed concisely under heads by the holy Moro, bishop of Amida, a man deserving of blessed memory, upon the Gospel and the dispensation of Christ in the flesh, and also a story which is contained in the eighty-ninth canon, taken from the Gospel of John and mentioned [2] by him alone, about a woman with child by adultery, who was brought to Him by the Jewish doctors.[3]

CHAPTER I

THE FIRST CHAPTER OF THE NINTH BOOK, TREATING OF THE ACCESSION OF JUSTINIAN, AND OF THE FIGHTING WHICH WENT ON BEFORE NISIBIS AND THE FORTRESS OF THEBETHA

In the year five,[4] when Justin was king, that old man of whom we related above [5] that he came from the country of Illyricum, he made his sister's son, who was general,[6] Anti-Cæsar;[7] and Justinian became Anti-Cæsar on the fifth day of the week in the last week of the fast. And,[8] after he had governed for three months, his uncle died, at the end of July, and he became emperor,[9] in the year eight hundred and thirty-eight of the Greeks,[10] in the three hundred and ·twenty-seventh Olympiad. And[11] as to his own Castra Mauriana he gave orders, and a great city was built, and privileges [12] were granted to it, and a military force was also stationed in it; and water was brought into it from a distance,[13] because its own water was bad.

---

[1] Insert ? before ܘܟܠ. Without this the meaning will be, "there is inserted above," which seems contradictory.

[2] Read ܐܘܟܠܝ̈ܐ for ܐܘܟܠܝ.

[3] This seems to refer to the MS. from which the scribe was copying, as the prologue of Moro is not inserted at this place in our MS.

[4] 527.

[5] Bk. 7, ch. 14; 8, 1. } Mich. fol. 167 v, 168 r; Greg. p. 78.

[6] στρατηγός.

[7] See bk. 6, ch. 6.

[8] Mich. fol. 167 v, 168 r.

[9] αὐτοκράτωρ.

[10] 527.

[11] Mich. fol. 162 r.

[12] προνόμια.

[13] Mich. fol. 161 r.

And, behold! from the beginning of his reign down to this day he has indeed devoted attention to building, refounding [1] cities in various countries, and repairing walls in various places for the protection of his dominions.

But, since the Persians and the Romans were at enmity with one another in those times, while Timus [2] (?), the master of the soldiers,[3] was duke on the frontier, the army with its officers was mustered round him to fight against Nisibis; and they fought, but could not take it, and retired thence to the fortress of Thebetha; and the army came close up to the wall and made a breach in it; and it was the hottest part of the summer. And through some cause or other they were prevented from effecting their purpose, and did not get possession of the fortress, which was about fifteen parasangs from Dara. And the army was ordered to return to Dara; and, because they greedily ate honey and the flesh [4] of large numbers of swine, some of the infantry [5] died of thirst on the march and were lost to the army, and others threw themselves into the wells of the desert and were drowned, and the rest were burnt up by the heat on the march, but the cavalry reached Dara; and so the army was broken up.

CHAPTER II

THE SECOND CHAPTER OF THE NINTH BOOK, CONCERNING THE BATTLE WHICH WAS FOUGHT IN THE DESERT OF THANNURIS

During the lifetime of Justin [6] the king, who had learned that Thannuris was a convenient place for a city to be built as a place of refuge in the desert, and for a military force to be stationed to protect 'Arab against the marauding bands of

---

[1] Read ـــــ for ـــــ.

[2] Probably Timostratus (Wright, *C. B. M.* p. 559). ـــــ might well fall out before ـــــ.

[3] στρατηλάτης.

[4] Insert ‌ܘ‌ before ـــــ.   [5] Insert ـــــ after ـــــ.

[6] The text has "Justinian," but clearly Justin must be meant.

Saracens, Thomas the silentiary, a native of Aphphadana, had been sent to build such a city. And, when he had made but inconsiderable progress, then the works which had begun to be carried out were destroyed by the Saracens and Kadisenes from Singara and Thebetha. Now, because the Romans, as we have stated above, had taken the field and fought against Nisibis and Thebetha, therefore afterwards [1] the Persians also similarly came and made an entrenchment (?) [2] in the desert of Thannuris. And, Duke Timus, the master of the soldiers,[3] having died, Belisarius had succeeded him ; and he was not greedy after bribes, and was kind to the peasants, and did not allow the army to injure them. For he was accompanied by Solomon, a eunuch from the fortress of Edribath (?) ; [4] and he was an astute man, and well-versed in the affairs of the world ; and he had been notary to Felicissimus the duke, and had been attached to the other governors ; and he had gained cunning through experience of difficulties.

Accordingly, a Roman army was mustered for the purpose of marching into the desert of Thannuris against the Persians under the leadership of Belisarius, Cutzes,[5] the brother of Butzes, Basil, Vincent, and other commanders, and Atafar, the chief of the Saracens. And, when the Persians heard of it, they devised a stratagem, and dug several ditches among their trenches,[6] and concealed them (?) [7] all round outside by triangular [8] stakes of wood, and left several openings. And, when the Roman army came up, they did not perceive the Persians' deceitful stratagem in time, but the generals entered the Persian entrenchment [6] at full speed, and, falling into the pits, were taken prisoners, and Cutzes was killed. And of the Roman army those who were mounted [9] turned back and returned in

---

[1] Read ⲥⲓⲗⲟ for ⲓⲗⲟ. [2] ⲗⲟⲟⲟⲟ (?). [3] στρατηλάτης.

[4] Perhaps Hieriphthum (Gelzer, *Geo. Cypr.* p. 159).

[5] Insert ⲟ before ⲥⲓⲥⲓⲗⲟⲟ. [6] φόσσα.

[7] ⲟⲟⲟⲟⲓ. Brockelmann quoting this passage gives doubtfully " erexit " ; but, as ⲟⲟⲗⲟⲓ = was wrapped up (" involutus est," Brock.), I take it as above. In Smith's *Thesaurus* it is proposed to read ⲟⲟⲟⲟⲓ, but this could only mean " beat " or " dashed."

[8] τρίγωνος. [9] Read ⲗⲟⲓⲟ for ⲗⲟⲓⲟ.

flight to Dara with Belisarius; but the infantry, who did not escape, were killed and taken captive. And Atafar, the Saracen king, during his flight was struck (?)[1] from a short distance off, and perished; and he was a warlike and an able man, and he had had much experience in the use of Roman arms, and in various places had won distinction and renown in war.

CHAPTER III

THE THIRD CHAPTER OF THE NINTH BOOK, CONCERNING THE BATTLE BEFORE DARA

The Persians were proud and puffed up[2] and boastful; and, indeed, the *Mihran* and the marzbans assembled an army and came against Dara and encamped at Ammodis, being fully confident in the expectation of taking the city, because the Roman army had been diminished by their sword. And their cavalry and infantry approached and came up on the south side of the city, intending to encompass it all round for the purpose of blockading it; but a Roman force met them by the help of our Lord, who chastises but does not utterly deliver over unto death. For a certain Sunica, a general, who was a Hun,[3] and, having taken refuge with the Romans, had been baptized, and Simuth (?),[4] a Roman tribune,[5] and their armour-bearers with twenty men each drove the whole Persian army away from the city several times, passing boldly and vigorously from one part of the field to another, and cutting men down right and left with the lance. And they were practised in the use of the sword; and their cry was loud and terrific, and made them appear terrible to the Persians, so

---

[1] The MS. seems to have ܐܝܚܘ؟, not ܐܝܚܘ܄, as L. prints. The word is a rare one, and generally means "to be shaken."

[2] The MS. has ܐܝ؟ܣܒܩ, not ܐܝ؟ܣܒܩ, as L. prints. For the meaning of the word see p. 199, note 4.

[3] Insert ؟ before ܗܘܢܝ.

[4] Perhaps the "Simas" of Procopius (*Bell. Pers.* i. 13). ܣܝܡܘܬܐ is probably corrupt, the scribe having taken it for a common noun.

[5] χιλίαρχος.

that they fell before them : and two of their leaders were killed, besides no small number of horsemen ; while of the *faige*, who are the Persian infantry, many were cut down and hurled back by the Helurians,[1] under Butzes, to the east of the city.

And the Persians, when they saw how great the number of the dead was, acted craftily, and sent to Nisibis, asking them to bring as many baggage-animals as possible and come at once to Dara, and take as much spoil as they could.   And, when large numbers came, they laded them with the bodies of their slain, and then they returned in shame.   However, the rest of the Persian force invaded [2] Roman 'Arab, and burned it with fire.

CHAPTER IV

THE FOURTH CHAPTER, CONCERNING THE BATTLE WHICH
WAS FOUGHT ON THE EUPHRATES IN THE YEAR NINE [3]

The Persians, having learned wisdom by experience through the great injury which they had suffered from the attacks of the Romans whenever they approached the city and went out against them, went up into the desert portion of the Roman territory and encamped on the Euphrates ; and according to their usual practice they made a trench.[4]   And Belisarius at the head of a Roman [5] force and tribunes [6] came up against them to battle ; and they arrived in the last week of the fast.   And the Persians were found to be as a little flock, and so they appeared in their eyes : and Asthebid [7] their commander was afraid of them, and those who were with him ; and he sent [8] to the Romans, asking them to respect the feast,

----

[1] Read ܠܥܘܪ̈ܐ for ܠܩܘܪ̈ܐ ; cf. Proc. *l.c.*   The Herulians, whom the Greeks frequently called Ἔλουροι, are meant.

[2] The MS. has ܠܥܪ̈ܒ, not ܥܪܒܟ, as L. prints.   [3] 531.   [4] φόσσα.

[5] The MS. has ܪ̈ܗܘܡܝܐ, not ܪ̈ܗܘܡܝܐ, as L. prints.   [6] χιλίαρχοι.

[7] The MS. has ܐܣܛܒܝܕ, not ܐܣܛܒܝܕ, as L. prints.   See bk. 8, ch. 5 (p. 206, note 5).

[8] Mich. fol. 168 *r*; Greg. pp. 78, 79.

15

" for the sake of the Nazarenes and Jews who are in the army that is with me, and for the sake of yourselves, who are Christians." And, when Belisarius the general[1] had considered this, he was willing to agree; but the commanders murmured greatly, and would not consent to wait and respect the day. And, when they went out to battle on the eve of the first day of the week, the day of unleavened bread, it was a cold day, with the wind in the face of the Romans; and they showed themselves feeble, and turned and fled before the Persian attack; and many fell into the Euphrates and were drowned, and others were killed; but Belisarius escaped, while the nephew[2] of Butzes was taken prisoner (for he himself was ill at Amida, and did not go to the battle, but sent his army to Abgersatum under Domitziolus), and went down to Persia, but eventually returned: and how this happened I will relate in this next[3] chapter.

CHAPTER V

THE FIFTH CHAPTER OF THE NINTH BOOK, CONCERNING GADAR THE KADISENE, A PERSIAN GENERAL, HOW HE WAS KILLED; AND IZDEGERD, WHO WAS WITH HIM, AND WAS NEPHEW OF HORMIZD, *PTEHASHA* OF ARZANENE, WAS TAKEN PRISONER

The Romans, when Belisarius was duke, in the year five,[4] having been prevented from building Thannuris on the frontier, wished to make a city at Melebasa; wherefore[5] Gadar the Kadisene was sent with an army by Kawad; and he prevented the Romans from effecting their purpose, and put them to flight in a battle which he fought with them on the hill of Melebasa. And he was high in the confidence of Kawad,

---

[1] στρατηγός. [2] Syr. " sister's son."

[3] The MS. has ܐܝܠܝܟ, not ܐܝܠܬ, as L. prints.

[4] 527.

[5] Read ܟܪܝܟܐ for ܒܪܘܟܐ, as proposed by Prof. Nöldeke (*Zeitschr. Deutsch. Morgenländ. Gesellsch.* vol. xxxiii. p. 159, note 1).

and had been stationed with an army to guard the frontier eastwards from Melebasa in the country of Arzanene as far as Martyropolis. And this man uttered many boasts and vain words against the Romans, and blasphemed like Rab Shakeh, who was sent by Sennacherib. And he brought about seven hundred armed cavalry, and some infantry, who accompanied them for the sake of amassing plunder ; and they crossed the Tigris into the district of Attachæ in the territory of Amida. And Bessa was duke in Martyropolis ; and it was summer time in this year nine.[1] And with Gadar was Izdegerd, the nephew[2] of the *Ptehasha*,[3] who, as a neighbour, knew the region of Attachæ. And when Bessa heard of it he went out against him with about five hundred horsemen from Martyropolis, which was about four (?)[4] stades distant. And he met him at Beth Helte and routed his army on the Tigris, and killed Gadar, and took Izdegerd prisoner and brought him to Martyropolis. This man after the peace, which was made in the year ten,[5] was given in exchange for Domitziolus, who returned from Persia. But Bessa the duke after routing Gadar and the Persian cavalry, who were guarding the frontier of Arzanene, entered the country and did much damage there ; and he carried off captives and brought them to Martyropolis.

CHAPTER VI

THE SIXTH CHAPTER INFORMS US IN THIS NINTH BOOK ABOUT THE FIGHTING WHICH WENT ON BEFORE MARTYROPOLIS, AND ABOUT THE GREAT HOST OF HUNS WHICH INVADED THE TERRITORY OF THE ROMANS

The villages in the country of Arzanene are the property of the Persian crown, and no small[6] sum is collected as poll-tax

---

[1] 531. [2] Syr. "sister's son."

[3] The native title of the tribal chief : Arm. *bdeashkh*. See Nöldeke, *l.c.* note 2.

[4] This number cannot be right, as Martyropolis was N. of the Tigris, 240 stades from Amida and 100 from Attachæ (Proc. *Bell. Pers.* i. 21).

[5] 532. [6] The MS. has ܐܟܘܕ, not ܓܘܟܘ, as L. prints.

from their inhabitants for the king's treasury and for the office [1] of the *Ptehasha*, who is stationed there (he is the king's prefect).[2]   To this country, as related above, Bessa the duke did much injury; who took the nephew of the *Ptehasha* captive, and also kept him prisoner in Martyropolis. And King Kawad was much distressed when he heard from the *Ptehasha* about the devastation of the country: which same Hormizd left no stone unturned,[3] using force and cunning (?)[4] against Martyropolis,[5] in order to get possession of it, for it acts as an ambush and a place of refuge for a Roman army, enabling it to ravage Arzanene.   And an army was, so to speak, equipped by the Persian army:[6]   Mihr Girowi was sent to hire a large number of Huns and bring them to their assistance.   And they came and were gathered together against Martyropolis at the begining of the year ten;[7] and they made a trench[8] against it, and a " mule "[9] and many mines; and they made assaults upon it, and pressed it hard.   And in it was Butzes and a Roman force of no small size, and they drove large numbers of Persians back in battle. But Nonnus also, the bishop of the city, had died.

Now Belisarius, being held culpable by the king on account of the rout which had been inflicted on the Roman army by the Persians at Thannuris and on the Euphrates, had been dismissed from his command, and went up to the king; and he was succeeded at Dara by Constantine.

And a large Roman army was mustered, and Sittas was general;[10] and Bar Gabala, the Saracen king, was with them. And they reached Amida in November[11] (?) of the year ten;[12] and John, the hermit of Anastasia, a man of honourable character, who had been elected to the bishopric, accompanied

---

[1] ἀξία.   [2] ὕπαρχος.   [3] Lit. "was moving all the stones."

[4] ܩܠܬܐ ܕܡܠܟܗ. I can make nothing of this, and only guess at the meaning. The literal rendering is " a palace which he filled," and it is perhaps just possible that the idea of bribery is concealed under it; but more probably the text is corrupt.

[5] Omit ܠ before ܡܝܦܪܩܛ.   [6] Read ܚܝܠܐ for ܚܝܠܗ.

[7] 531-2.   [8] φόσσα.

[9] See bk. 7, ch. 3 (p. 153).   [10] στρατηγός.

[11] Or October.   It is not stated whether it was the 1st or the 2nd *Theshrin.*

[12] 531.

them.   And, when they had gone to Martyropolis and the winter came on (and the country is northerly and cold), the Persians were impeded[1] by rain and mud, and underwent[2] hardships, while they were also afraid of the numbers of the Roman army; and Kawad their king also had died while they were there; and they made a compact with the Romans to withdraw from the city.

And, soon after they had withdrawn and Martyropolis had been freed from blockade, and the Roman army had returned, the Huns,[3] who had been hired by the Persians, arrived.   This great people suddenly attacked the territory of the Romans, and massacred and slew many of the tillers of the soil, and burned villages and their churches; and they crossed the Euphrates and advanced as far as Antioch; and no one stood before them or did them any harm except only the same Bessa, the duke of Martyropolis, who fell upon a detachment of them during their retreat and killed them, and captured[4] about five hundred horses and much spoil; and the man became rich.   And at the fortress of Citharizon the duke there repulsed a party of them, consisting of about four hundred men, and captured their baggage-animals.

Now[5] after Kawad Khosru his son became king.   His mother during the lifetime of Kawad her husband had been vexed by a demon; and all the magians and sorcerers and enchanters, who had been summoned by Kawad her husband, who loved her greatly, did her no good, but, to say the truth, added demons to demons in her.   She in the year four,[6] in the days of Liberius the duke, was sent to the blessed Moses, who was a monk close to Dara, about two parasangs' space distant, and was a famous man.   And she was with him a few days, and was cleansed, and returned to her own land,

---

[1] ܐܠܨ, from the root ܪܒܐ, "to swell."   This form occurs only here, but the Shaf'el is found in 7. 3, (p. 205, l. 5, L.).   See Smith's *Thesaurus*, col. 3795.

[2] The MS. has ܚܫ, not ܚܫ, as L. prints.

[3] The rest of this chapter and the following chapter are contained in Cod. Rom.

[4] Read ܒܕ for ܚܕ.   Cod. Rom. ܐܕ.   Cod. Brit. is indistinct; the ܘ seems to have been obliterated.

[5] Mich. fol. 168 *r*.   [6] 526.

having received from this holy Moses of the monastery called Tarmel an amulet taken from the bones of Cyriac the martyr to protect her, that in it she might find refuge, so that the spirit should not return upon her. And, to do him honour, she, under a certain symbolical form (?),[1] built him a house of prayer in her own country, and he is worshipped there. And, remembering the grace wrought in her through this blessed Moses of Tarmel, she did a service to the land of the Romans in the manner and on the occasion set forth below.

CHAPTER VII

THE SEVENTH CHAPTER OF THE NINTH BOOK, HOW PEACE WAS MADE BETWEEN THE ROMANS AND THE PERSIANS, AND LASTED SIX OR SEVEN YEARS, IN THE DAYS OF RUFINUS AND OF HERMOGENES, THE MASTER OF THE OFFICES.

Justinian the king, considering the things which had happened in his dominions between the rivers, and the forces which had at various times been destroyed by the Persians, and the tillers of the soil who had been slain and made captive by the Huns, and the land which had been burnt with the villages upon it, was not inclined again to send an army to contend in war with Khosru, who became king after Kawad his father. And, since this man was friendly to Rufinus, and it was he who had advised his father to make him his successor, he used to make assertion to the king, and encourage him, and to undertake that, if he showed himself before him in his own country, he would for the sake of the

---

[1] ܟܐܪܙ ܡܪܝܙ. In bk. 3, ch. 4 (p. 244, l. 11, L.), ܟܐܪܙ means "in a mystical sense" (the word ܐܪܙ being practically equivalent to μυστήριον), and I therefore here translate as above. Other possible renderings are "with certain mysterious rites" and "with some secrecy." I understand the meaning to be that Moses (or Cyriac?) was worshipped under the outward forms of Magism. Mich. adds, "and it was called the monastery of Moses of Tarmel."

peace desired by the king accept what he justly asked of him.[1] And so this Rufinus and Hermogenes, the master of the offices, were sent as ambassadors[2] to Khosru in the year eleven;[3] and they had much speech with him. And, because this Rufinus was well known there, inasmuch as he had been several times sent to Kawad, and was his friend, and used to give many presents to the magnates of his kingdom, and the queen, the mother of Khosru, was friendly to him, because he had advised Kawad to make her son king, and she owed gratitude to Moses the blessed monk of Tarmel after God for her healing, she earnestly entreated Khosru her son, and on consideration of a sum of gold which he received, which was sent by King Justinian according to the message transmitted to him by Rufinus and Hermogenes his ambassadors, he made peace; and a written treaty was drawn up and ratified. And[4] the stars in the sky had appeared dancing in a strange manner, and it was the summer of the year eleven.[5] And it lasted about six or seven years, until the year three.[6]

CHAPTER VIII

THE EIGHTH CHAPTER OF THE NINTH BOOK, CONCERNING THE SAMARITANS, WHO REBELLED AND SET UP A TYRANT OF THEIR OWN IN THE COUNTRY OF PALESTINE.

The Samaritans in the country of Palestine who live near the city of Neapolis, not far from Cæsarea, having heard that

---

[1] Read ܡܟܝܚ for ܡܟ ܐܠܗܐ, with Cod. Rom. The meaning of the reading of Cod. Brit. is "of God."

[2] Cod. Rom. has the meaningless ܐܓܪܬܐ, "epistle."

[3] 532-3.   [4] "Dion." fol. 182 v*; cf. Jo. Mal. p. 477.
[5] 533.   [6] 540.

---

* In the Paris transcript. I take the reference from the analysis of "Dionysius," published by M. Nau in the *Revue de l'Orient Chrétien, Suppl. trim.* 1897, fasc. 4.

the Persians had from time to time attacked and invaded the Roman territory, and supposing that they had shown themselves weak before them, were emboldened by the thought that they had been sent from Khuth and Babylon,[1] and from 'Awa and from Hamath and from S'farwayim by Shalman-'asar, king of Assyria, and settled in the land of Samaria; and, having rebelled, they set[2] a tyrant at their head; and they entered Neapolis, and killed Mommuno the bishop there; and they made an insurrection, and wrought havoc in the country, wishing to help the Persians, because it was out of their country that they had been settled in the territory of the Romans; and they burnt many temples of the saints; and they occupied the city and amassed spoil.

And, when the king heard of this, he sent Hadrian the tribune;[3] and there were gathered together also the duke of the country, who was with him, and an army of Romans, and the Saracens of Arabia; and they marched against the Samaritans. And they were cut to pieces by the Romans; and they killed the tyrant, and took the city and restored it to its former normal condition of subjection to their authority. And a bishop was also appointed in it; and a military force was stationed there, to guard it and to keep order among the inhabitants of the country.

CHAPTER IX

THE NINTH CHAPTER OF THE NINTH BOOK, CONCERNING THE PHANTASIASTIC HERESY OF JULIAN OF HALICAR-NASSUS, HOW IT APPEARED

Julian,[4] bishop of the city of Halicarnassus, withdrew from his see through zeal with the other believing bishops; and he was an old man, and he was zealous in the faith: and in his desire to avoid speaking of two natures he, like Eutyches and

---

[1] Insert O before ܠܘܬ.   [2] Mich. fol. 168 r; Greg. p. 79.

[3] χιλίαρχος.   [4] Mich. fol. 181 r; Greg. H. E. p. 211.

the monks who have not a right knowledge of the true order
of things, fell into the heresy of Eutyches.   (And he was an
acquaintance and a friend of the learned Severus the chief
priest; and once this same Julian on being questioned by
someone composed a treatise against the Diphysites, and he
produced it (?)[1] at no great length without cause of offence.)
However, though that wise combatant[2] Severus had heard of
it, he had kept this knowledge hidden,[3] fearing lest, if he
corrected it, house should be divided against house, and he
should cause a division in love, which no man had been able
to separate, being patiently determined to accept his poverty,
which is according to right (?).

And, when in this way[4] reason was added to reason, as our
Lord brought it about, in order, that is, that the learning of
Severus might be made manifest, the beauty of his true faith,
for the benefit of the discerning and of those who love instruction, [he was compelled to expose the matter].[5]

And, to show the nature of the original subject of contention,[6] I insert some epistles, which, taken in order, supply
information to the reader, in the following chapters of this
ninth Book.

[1] ܣܘܩܒܗ (so MS., not ܢܩܒܗ, as L.).   Mich. has ܐܬܒܣܟܗ, "followed it,"
which points to a reading ܢܩܒܗ.   All the remainder of this chapter is exceedingly obscure and probably corrupt.

[2] ἀγωνιστής.

[3] ܟܣܐ ܕܝܕܥܬܐ, from Prov. x. 14; cf. bk. 8, ch. 4 (p. 243, l. 17, L.).

[4] Perhaps something has fallen out before this sentence.   Mich. has "but, after
Julian had written that it was his opinion, and the holy man had answered him
twice, and he would not obey."

[5] I supply these words from Mich.   [6] ὑπόθεσις.

CHAPTER X

THE TENTH CHAPTER, CONCERNING THE FIRST EPISTLE OF
JULIAN TO SEVERUS, WITH A QUESTION ABOUT THE
BODY OF CHRIST [1]

"Certain [2] men have appeared here who say that the body
of our Lord was corruptible, making use of testimony from the
holy Cyril; in the first place from what he wrote to Succensus,
saying, 'After the Resurrection it was the body which had
suffered, though it no longer supported human infirmities but
was incorruptible'; [3] and from this they wish to prove that
before the Resurrection it was corruptible, inasmuch as it
was of our nature, but after the Resurrection it received
incorruptibility: and in the second place from what he
wrote to Theodosius the king, saying, 'It is a marvel and a
miracle that a body naturally subject to corruption rose without
corruption.' [4]

"And they quoted such things as these by way of extracts;
but I, who set down the whole passage, [5] made it my endeavour
to show the opinion held by numerous doctors. But they
brought me also his sixty-seventh treatise, which was written
by him on the subject of the holy Virgin, the *Theotokos*, and
in it are contained the words, 'The body of our Lord was in
no way subjected to the sin which belongs to corruption, but
was susceptible of death and of true burial, and He destroyed
them in it.' [6]   And I indeed considered it to be an error in

---

[1] These letters are contained in Add. MS. 17,200 and in *Cod. Syr. Vat.* 140,
from which last extracts are given by the Assemani (*Bibl. Vat. MSS. Catal.* vol. iii.
p. 323 ff.).   Both these give the Syriac translation of Paul of Callinicus.   Our
author's translation is independent.

[2] Mich. fol. 181 *r*.

[3] Cyr. *Ep.* 45 (Migne, *Patrol. Græc.* vol. lxxvii. p. 236).

[4] Cyr. *de Rect. Fid. ad Theod. Imp.* 22.

[5] ܒܠܗ ܦܘܩܐ ܣܘܟܠܐ. Mich. has ܘܬܝܒܬ ܒܠܗ ܘܚ ܘܬܠܝ, and therefore probably read ܦܘܩܒܐ, "set down the whole matter in a sentence." Paul.
Call. has ܠܫܘܕܥܐ ܒܠܗ ܣܘܟܠܐ, which determines the sense of ܦܘܩܐ.

[6] I cannot find this in the *Quod Beata Maria Sit Deipara.*

writing.   And so, in order that the dispute may be solved by our being examined by you, I have also sent what I have written,[1] and I am convinced that our fathers agree with it. And write to me at once, that I may know what opinions to hold on these matters, because I do not consider it right that we should again say that that which was not corrupted was susceptible of corruption.   And pray that our life may be in unison with the grace of God."

CHAPTER XI

THE ELEVENTH CHAPTER, THE RESPONSE[2] TO THIS EPISTLE OF JULIAN, WHICH SEVERUS WROTE TO HIM, AS FOLLOWS

" When [3] first I received your piety's epistle, I rejoiced in accordance with my custom at your greeting, with which I was well pleased.   Since in it you urge me to read the tome composed by you, which you sent with it, written to those who, you say, think and say concerning the body of our Lord and God, Jesus Christ our Saviour, that it was corruptible, and you ask me to write a criticism of it and send it to the love of God that is you, in obedience to you I have readily done this, I, a man who change about from one place to another and have no convenient time even for other things that are required.   Still, so far as it was possible for it to be written, I have written it, partly by collecting in my memory passages from the teaching of the fathers, partly also from the few volumes of their works which were here.   For I know well that there was a similar question in the royal city also, and by means of the proofs from the fathers drawn up by me the controversy and dispute were brought to an end.   And so, since there appeared to me to be something unseemly in the things written by you,

---

[1] Possibly something has dropped out here.   See the quotation in ch. 13 (p. 238); and so Paul. Call. Mich., however, has the same as our text, so that no alteration should be made in it.

[2] ἀντίγραφον.   [3] Mich. fol. 181 v.

since I find that the doctors of the holy Church, who have been from time to time, have instructed me[1] differently on these matters, I have delayed sending what I have written to your piety (as indeed was right), lest some in ignorance should suppose that the controversy conducted in these words was a strife between us, and, although a discussion such as I knew it was would abound in love, yet some might suppose it to be hostility. Accordingly, let me know at once what your pleasure is upon these things, for I am ready to perform whatever is agreeable to your affection, holding as my warrant the saying of the apostle, who said, ‘ Let everything that is done by you[2] be done in love.’ ”[3]

CHAPTER XII

THE TWELFTH CHAPTER, THE SECOND EPISTLE OF JULIAN
TO SEVERUS, WRITTEN IN ANSWER TO THE PRECEDING,
AS A RESPONSE[4] TO IT

“ You[5] write that there appeared to you to be something unseemly in the things which I have written ; and you ought to have informed me at once in the epistle, and released me from anxiety. But I believe that in all that I have written I have truly confessed the Incarnation derived from us, and I have exerted myself to prove that the fathers were in accord with one another ; for I do not consider it possible for us to believe and hold that which is corruptible and that which is incorruptible to be the same. And, while we confess Him who by His stripes healed all men to be passible, yet we also know Him to be raised and exalted above passions ; and, if He was mortal, yet we also confess that He trampled on[6] death, and gave life to mortals through His death. Accordingly you have only caused me anxiety by saying that I have written

---

[1] The MS. has ܣܒܠܩܘܠܝ, not ܣܒܠܩܘܠܝܗܝ, as L. prints.

[2] Read ܡܠܝܟܘܢ for ܡܠܝܗܘܢ.   [3] 1 Cor. xvi. 14.

[4] ἀντίγραφον.   [5] Mich. fol. 181 v.

[6] Read ܦܝܗ for ܦܝܗ. The MS. has no dot, either above or below the letter.

something that is unseemly, and not telling me what it is, that I may defend it.　But condescend to write and tell me what is stated by the fathers, by Athanasius [1] and Cyril and others, for I wish to know your mind also.　But [2] I believe that I have followed the intention of the fathers, who are not at variance with themselves or at variance with one another, even as Paul, who says that salvation is not by works but by faith, is not at variance with James, who says that faith without works is dead.　They did not say these things in opposition to one another, but in concord. [3]

"But pray that we may be enlightened by God, and may not through passion yield to our own wills, while at the same time you cause the word in 'a brief compass to shine upon us.

"The holy Cyril writes, 'It is not easy for us to say that corruption can ever take hold of the flesh which was united to the Word'; [4] and five lines lower down, 'It is a wonder and a miracle that a body [5] naturally subject to corruption was raised.' [6]　And what is the idea which he wishes to bring out (for he is not at variance with himself in these things), if he was not in these words thinking of the corruption of universal nature?　For He bore our infirmities of His own will and not by compulsion of nature; and He took up our sins in His body on the tree, dying for our sin."

CHAPTER XIII

THE THIRTEENTH CHAPTER, THE RESPONSE [7] TO THIS EPISTLE, ADDRESSED TO THE SAME JULIAN BY SEVERUS

"It [8] seems to me a very strange thing, when I call to

---

[1] Text, "Theodosius."　Paul of Callinicus, however, has "Athanasius," and so Mich.

[2] Here begins a short extract in Cod. Rom.

[3] Here the extract in Cod. Rom. ends.

[4] Cyr. *de Rect. Fid. ad Theod. Imp.* 21.

[5] Insert ? before ‎. So Paul of Callinicus.

[6] Cyr. *op. cit.* 22.　　　[7] ἀντίγραφον.　　　[8] Mich. fol. 181 ff.

mind the few words which I wrote, that the love of God that is in you says that you were in great anxiety; since I performed your request for no other reason than to free you from anxiety and disturbance. For, if you had sent me a small question and problem, then I might perhaps have used [1] few words in making answer; but, since it is a tome of many lines and a fully-completed [2] work that you have sent me to examine, after considering the things contained in it every day according to my ability, I will make my opinion clear to you.

"Now in respect of what is fitting I have found much which I will do readily for [3] your piety; and, to show that I am not speaking falsely, listen to what you wrote, as follows: ' In order to bring about an understanding of the matter in dispute, I have sent what I have written; but test it to see whether it is in accord with the Holy Scriptures, because I believe that our fathers were in accord with these. Write and tell me what opinion I am to hold.' Since, therefore,[4] you have given me matter for much discussion, how is it that in your second epistle you have required me to treat of many matters in a few lines and in a single utterance, as you say, a thing which needs many words and proofs from the fathers, who spoke under the inspiration of God? For the Holy Scripture says, ' It is the Lord that teacheth intelligence and knowledge';[5] and again in another place, ' The Lord giveth wisdom; and from His presence cometh knowledge and understanding. And He giveth salvation to the righteous.'[6] For, if your piety and we endeavour in this way to prove with respect to these fathers that they are not in opposition to one another, there is nothing to prevent us from examining the matter carefully and knowing that they have never in anyway shown

---

[1] Insert ܒ before ܟܬܒܝܢܢ.

[2] ܐܬܡܠܠܬ seems to be a denominative verb from ܡܠܠܐ (Hamilton). Paul. Call. ܟܠܝܬ.

[3] Insert ܕ before ܠܟ. But the sentence seems to be corrupt.

[4] Read ܡܟܝܠ for ܡܟܕܘ (ܗܫܐ, Paul. Call.).

[5] Job xxi. 22.   [6] Prov. ii. 6, 7.

themselves to be in opposition either to one another or to themselves.

"For [1] you rightly and justly [2] say that the doctors are not in opposition to one another, even as Paul is not in opposition to James when the one says, 'By faith is a man justified without works,' [3] while the other wrote, 'Faith without works is dead'; [4] because Paul spoke of faith before baptism, which is the perfection of confession out of a pure heart, when it has not previously displayed good works in the world, [5] but such a man is justified by believing and confessing and being baptized; while James referred to faith after baptism, when he said that it is dead without works, if a man does not confirm it by right action. [6] For baptism is the earnest of a good conversation; since even our Lord, who was to us an instructor, after He had hallowed [7] the water and been baptized [8] by John and given us [9] the institution of baptism, went up to the mountain and underwent a struggle with the tempter and destroyed all his power, thereby guiding us, that we might know that after the divine cleansing we ought to display a contest in deed and to struggle according to law with the adversary, therein displaying our virtues.

"But someone will object, and say, 'Behold! Paul took Abraham as a proof that a man is justified by faith without works, saying, "Therefore they that are in the faith are blessed with the believing Abraham"; [10] and, "To him that hath not worked but hath believed on Him that can justify sinners his faith is reckoned for righteousness"; [11] while James proved by the case of Abraham that a man is not justified

---

[1] Here begins an extract in Cod. Rom.

[2] After ܂܂܂ insert ܐܠܗܝܐ, with Cod. Rom. and Paul. Call.; so Mich.

[3] Rom. iii. 28.   [4] Jas. ii. 20.

[5] After ܐܦ insert ܒܥܠܡܐ, with Cod. Rom.; so Mich.

[6] The MS. has ܩܘܠܣܝܢ, not ܩܘܠܣܝܢ, as L. prints.

[7] The MS. has ܩܕܫ, not ܩܕܝܫ, as L. prints.

[8] After ܡܝܐ insert ܘܥܡܕ, with Cod. Rom.; so Mich.

[9] Read ܠܢ for ܠܗ, with Cod. Rom. (Paul. Call. ܢܡܘܣܐ ܕܠܢ); so Mich.
[10] Gal. iii. 9.   [11] Rom. iv. 5.

by faith only, but by works confirmed by faith.[1] And how are these not contradictory? for the same[2] Abraham is an example of those who have not worked but believed, and of those who have shown faith by works.'

"I am ready to explain from the Holy Scriptures. For he who examines the periods of Abraham's life [will see][3] that he is an instance of both, of the faith which before baptism confesses salvation by believing in Christ, and of that after baptism which is joined with works, which is a reproduction[4] of the old circumcision of the flesh, which drives away[5] the denial of uncircumcision and brings to us the adoption as sons by God; wherefore Moses also was ordered to say thus to Far'oh; 'And say thou unto Far'oh, "Israel is my son, my firstborn."'[6] Wherefore Paul writes to the Colossians and says, 'In whom ye were circumcised with a circumcision not made with hands, in the putting off of the flesh of sins and in the circumcision of Christ, and ye were buried with Him in baptism.'[7] Wherefore he said of[8] Abraham also that he was justified by faith without works while he was in un-circumcision, before he was circumcised, thus pointing to confession before baptism without works, writing to the Romans, 'To Abraham his faith was reckoned for righteous-ness. How? Not through circumcision, but in uncircum-cision.'[9] And he did not speak falsely; for the words of Moses are witness, which say of God that He said to Abraham, 'Look toward heaven and tell the stars, if thou be able to tell them'; and He said, 'So shall thy seed be':

[1] Jas. ii. 21–24. With Cod. Rom. insert ܒ before ܗܝܡܢܘܬܐ; so Mich. Paul. Call. agrees with Cod. Brit., giving the meaning "which confirm faith."

[2] Read ܕ for ܘ before ܗܘ, with Cod. Rom.

[3] This must be supplied in order to make sense. Paul. Call. has ܗܘ ܚܝ ܕܝܢ ܐܒܪܗܡ ܕܟܕ ܠܙܒܢ̈ܐ ܡܬܦܠܓ, "for the one Abraham, when divided into periods." Mich., like our text, omits the verb.

[4] Insert ܕ before ܬܚܠܘܦܬܐ, with Cod. Rom.

[5] The MS. has ܣܚܝ?, not ܣܚܝ?, as L. prints.

[6] Ex. iv. 22.   [7] Col. ii. 11, 12.

[8] Read ܥܠ for ܐܦ, with Cod. Rom.; so Mich.

[9] Rom. iv. 9, 10.

and Abraham believed God, and it was reckoned to him for righteousness.[1]

"But again our master James also took the same Abraham as an example in the faith which saves[2] by works after baptism, he being then circumcised and not in uncircumcision. And we may learn from the Scripture; for he writes thus: 'Wilt thou know, O man, that faith without works is dead? For our father Abraham was justified by works, when he offered Isaac his son as a burnt-sacrifice. Thou seest that faith wrought with his works, and by works was made perfect. And the Scripture was fulfilled which saith, "Abraham believed God, and it was reckoned to him for righteousness: and He was called his friend."'[3] It is[4] easy again for one who reads the writings of Moses to learn from the book of Genesis that Abraham, after he was circumcised, offered Isaac as a burnt-sacrifice[5] and fulfilled the commandment and was justified by works, giving us an instance of faith after baptism, which is a spiritual circumcision, justifying a man by works; for it is written, 'Abraham was circumcised, and Ishmael his son, and those born in his house, and those bought with his money from strange peoples';[6] and then God, trying Abraham, said to him, 'Take thy son, whom thou lovest, even Isaac, and get thee to the high land; and offer him there as a burnt-sacrifice.'[7] Accordingly these words of the apostles and those written in the old law do not seem to be in opposition[8] to one another, but to be one, and to have been spoken by one spirit concerning faith before[9] baptism, which justifies the man who presents himself upon a short[10] confession[11] only without action,[12] baptism

---

[1] Gen. xv. 5, 6.   [2] Read ⟨Syriac⟩ for ⟨Syriac⟩, with Cod. Rom.   So Mich.

[3] Jas. ii. 20-23.   [4] Read ⟨Syriac⟩ for ⟨Syriac⟩, with Cod. Rom.

[5] Read ⟨Syriac⟩ for ⟨Syriac⟩, with Cod. Rom.

[6] Gen. xvii. 26, 27.   [7] Gen. xxii. 2.

[8] The MS. has ⟨Syriac⟩, not ⟨Syriac⟩, as L. prints.

[9] Read ⟨Syriac⟩ for ⟨Syriac⟩, with Cod. Rom.

[10] The MS. has ⟨Syriac⟩, not ⟨Syriac⟩, as L. prints.

[11] Insert ⟨Syriac⟩ before ⟨Syriac⟩, with Cod. Rom.

[12] The MS. has ⟨Syriac⟩, not ⟨Syriac⟩, as L. prints.

being full salvation if a man depart from the world forthwith, and another faith, which is after baptism, which requires the proof of good works and also raises the man to the measure of perfection and to high place.[1] And so also [2] James very properly says of it that faith is made perfect by works; since the wise Paul also in another place gives similar teaching respecting faith, saying that it is made perfect through works: for the Galatians,[3] after they had been baptized and been reckoned sons of God through the Spirit, were perverted to Judaism and were circumcised, since they vainly supposed that by the circumcision of their flesh they gained something in Christ beyond the uncircumcised; and he wrote to reprove them, saying, 'In Jesus Christ neither circumcision nor uncircumcision availeth anything; but faith which is worked out by love.'[4] From this also, therefore, it is plain that that kind of faith after baptism is of avail and saves with which work is joined and united in love; and [5] what work done in love is Paul declares and says, 'Love is long-suffering and kind; love is not envious and excited and puffed up, nor is it ashamed; and it seeketh not its own, and is not provoked; and it imputeth no evil; and rejoiceth not in iniquity, but rejoiceth in the truth; and it hopeth all things, and endureth all things. Love doth not quickly fail.'[6] These things are for the direction of action[7] and labour and toil, that many may be profited and be saved, when united to faith. And who will dare to find fault? for respecting this our Lord also said, 'If ye love Me, keep My commandments.'[8]

---

[1] Cod. Rom. here inserts in the margin a sentence from bk. 10, ch. 9 (see p. 313), which Mai prints as if it were part of the text.

[2] Insert ‬ before [Syriac], with Cod. Rom.

[3] There is no [Syriac] before [Syriac] in Cod. Rom., as Mai prints.

[4] Gal. v. 6.

[5] After [Syriac] insert with Cod. Rom. [Syriac], which has dropped out in Cod. Brit. through homoioteleuton.

[6] 1 Cor. xiii. 4–8.

[7] The MS. has [Syriac], not [Syriac], as L. prints.

[8] John xiv. 15.

"As, therefore, the Holy Scriptures and our fathers have been consistent in the teaching given to us, so upon this question too they are in accord in teaching those who do not read negligently: wherefore, as it is written, ' Everything is known[1] to the understanding, and plain[2] to them that find knowledge ';[3] which knowledge I have endeavoured to send in a discreet manner to your affection, as is the duty of Christians.[4]

" But, since I have learned from several quarters that you have published the tome containing your work, which was addressed[5] to me, not only in the great city of Alexandria but also in various places, in accordance, as I am persuaded, with Christ, even God the Lawgiver, I have in love again sent and written to our brother the presbyter Thomas not to publish my work, but to keep it to himself, because I hoped that by the counsel of two persons, as by one mouth and soul, my writings and those of your Holiness might be made known. For after this fashion I once and again examined the teaching of the memorable Akhs'noyo[6] and Eleusinus the bishops, and the books which they composed upon abstruse matters[7] concerning the faith; and I never found in their case any declaration of the relations which we had with one another in love during our discussions, when by the help of our Lord we were alike of one mind. For I never produced either book or treatise in order to gain distinction with men, or to win renown beyond the measure of my feebleness, but in the rectitude of the Gospel in accordance with the teaching and legislation of the apostles. However, it is also unseemly that at such a time as this we should abandon the struggle against the heretics and contend and write against one another, lest the saying of the apostle be

---

[1] Read [Syriac] for [Syriac], with Cod. Rom. So Paul. Call. ([Syriac]) and Mich.

[2] Read [Syriac] for [Syriac], with Cod. Rom. So Paul. Call. and Mich.

[3] Prov. viii. 9.   [4] Here the extract in Cod. Rom. ends.

[5] Insert [Syriac] before [Syriac].

[6] Paul. Call. has " Felicissimus."

[7] θεωρία, the inner or allegorical meaning of a book.

fulfilled against us, who says, 'If ye bite and devour one another, take heed that ye be not consumed one of another.'[1] Such contentions it is the duty of those who love our Lord to shun with all their power, and to love one another, that peace may abound and may visit the Israel of God. Greet the brotherhood that is with you. The one that is with me salutes you in our Lord."

When Julian received this epistle also from this learned Severus, he was very indignant, and was moved with anger; and he wrote, saying that his request had been refused by him for a year[2] and a month, and he had not received[3] the respect due to him, and he had been tricked (?).[4] And then Severus again wrote a long treatise abounding in proofs from the true doctors of the holy Church, who say that the body of Christ which He received from us was susceptible of innocent passions except sin until the Resurrection.[5] And for this reason, in order that it may be known, I have set down the above epistles for the discerning.

There were many books addressed to Julian and Felicissimus and Romanus and others who shared his opinions, and in them there is also much material for profit in study for those that love instruction. And they became known to the sagacious and intelligent of the true party of the faith concerning the Incarnation of our Saviour, and the simple were preserved and enlightened so as not to become Eutychianists, and especially the monks.

[1] Gal. v. 15.　　　　　　　　　　[2] *Ep. III. ad Sev.* (Add. 17,200, fol. 9 *r*).

[3] ܩܛܠ, "felt." Mich. has ܣܒܠ, "bound," and therefore read ܩܛܠ.

[4] ܐܬܦܢܝ "was answered" (?), is unintelligible, unless we insert a negative. Mich. has ܐܬܓܢܒ, "was stolen," and therefore read ܐܬܓܢܒ. This reading I adopt. Both renderings, however, are very doubtful in grammar.

[5] Add. 17,200, fol. 38 ff. (Latin translation in *Mai Spicilegium Romanum*, x. p. 169).

CHAPTER XIV

THE FOURTEENTH CHAPTER OF THE NINTH BOOK, CON-
CERNING THE RIOT WHICH HAPPENED AT CONSTAN-
TINOPLE, AND HOW HYPATIUS AND POMPEIUS WERE
KILLED, AND LARGE NUMBERS OF THE PEOPLE[1] WERE
MASSACRED IN THE CIRCUS

In the year ten[2] the slaughter wrought by the many Huns
who invaded the territory of the Romans, and harried it, and
killed many people who were in the country, and burned, as
recorded above, was not enough, but in the royal city also
many persons perished there in a riot[3] which broke out. For,
when John of Cæsarea in Cappadocia was prefect[4] there, by
sedulously inventing pretexts against persons by the use of
trickery[5] and cunning, there and in various cities, he amassed
a large quantity of gold for the royal treasury from all classes,
both magnates and craftsmen; and he was listened to with
attention in the palace, and was formidable to everyone, since
he stood so high in the confidence of the king that he made
false accusations against many persons; and he was surrounded
by flatterers[6] and informers.[7] And there were present in the
royal city no small number of people from every quarter who
had complaints against him, and favoured[8] and supported one
of the factions.[9] Wherefore there were constant outcries[10]
against him and against the king; and the factions united
and were in accord with one another for several days; and
the workshops were shut, and they began to plunder everything that came in their way, and to burn. And the king

---

[1] δῆμος.　　　　[2] 532.　　　　[3] στάσις.　　　　[4] ὕπαρχος.

[5] ܣܘܟ̈ܠܠܐ. This word apparently occurs only here and in 7. 7 (p. 217, l. 11, L.).
It is not given in Payne Smith's *Thesaurus*, and Brockelmann, who refers only to
p. 217, 11, renders it "cogitavit, spectavit"; but from this passage it seems clear that
the meaning is as above.

[6] Read ܚܢܘܦ̈ܐ for ܚܢܘ̈ܦܐ.

[7] MS. ܠܘܕܪ̈ܐ, not ܠܘܕ̈ܪܐ, as L. The dictionaries give this word as = λουδάριος,
"gladiator" or "brigand," but here and in ch. 16 (pp. 257, 258) it seems clear that
the meaning is as above (=λοίδορος (?)).

[8] Or, "and he favoured . . ."　　　　[9] μέρος.　　　　[10] ἐκβόησις.

was alarmed; and at last the palace was shut. And the parties collected in the circus [1] and raised a great riot; and they kept crying out that Hypatius should be king; and, if not, they would burn the city. And Hypatius was compelled to come out, and Pompeius accompanied him. And they took a necklace belonging to one of the soldiers and set it on his head and enthroned him king, and they cried out at him and praised him.

And, when this happened, by the advice of certain persons they set fire to the great church of the city, in order that upon receiving the news of the disaster the assembled people might be scattered; for King Justinian was in distress and alarm in the palace. And Mundus, a general,[2] and his troops were present there; and he and the Scholarians and all the troops who were at hand received orders, and they shut the door of the circus, and they massacred and slew all classes of people who were present there; and there were no means of fleeing and escaping from the massacre. And more than 80,000 persons perished there in this riot. And Hypatius and Pompeius were at last arrested, and came in before the king. And, when he understood the state of the case, he wished to spare the men's lives; but he was not able to do so, for his consort was enraged, and swore by God and by him, and adjured him also to have the men put to death. And they were sent to the seashore and killed and thrown into the sea.

CHAPTER XV

THE FIFTEENTH CHAPTER, CONCERNING THE BELIEVING BISHOPS WHO WERE RECALLED FROM EXILE TO THE ROYAL CITY AND PRESENTED A SUPPLICATION [3] TO THE KING CONCERNING THEIR FAITH, WHICH RUNS AS FOLLOWS

"Various [4] other men crown your believing head, O victorious king, with a crown of praises—men who take

---

[1] ἱππικός.

[2] στρατηγός.

[3] Read ⌂ for ⌂.

[4] Mich. fol. 171 ff.

occasion from the case of other persons to write words about your favours towards them ; but we, who have been ourselves judged worthy to experience your virtues, render thanks to you with a crown of laudation, which we weave with splendour. And, while in the desert, and, so to speak, at the end of the world, we have been this long time dwelling in quietness, praying to the good and merciful God during such days as those on behalf of your Majesty and on behalf of our sins : and your tranquillity has inclined towards our vileness and in your believing letters summoned us to come to you.   And the thing is a wonder to us that you did not receive this our request with scorn,[1] but, with the kindness innate in you, sympathised with us, so as to bring us[2] out of affliction, making the pretext that this or that man had interceded for us.

" Now we, since it is our duty to obey when commanded, immediately left the desert, and, journeying quietly along the road in peace without our voice being heard, have come before your feet ; and we pray God, the bountiful giver, on our behalf to reward your serenity and the God-loving queen with good gifts from on high, and to bestow peace and tranquillity upon you, and to set every rebellious people as a stool beneath your feet.

" However, now that we have come, we present a supplication to your peacefulnesses containing our true faith, not wishing to hold an argument with any man on any matter that is not profitable, as it is written,[3] lest we annoy your ears ; for it is very hard for a man to convince persons of a contentious disposition, although he make the truth manifest.   And so, as we have said,[4] we refuse to engage in a dispute with the contentious, who will not receive instructors ; for our master[5]

---

[1] Read ‌ܟܣܘܠܝ‌ for ‌ܟܣܘܒܝ‌.   Mich. has ‌ܟܠܐܘܠܟܣ‌, "expecting," which represents ‌ܟܣܘܒܝ‌ ; but I cannot see any meaning in it.

[2] At Dr. Hamilton's suggestion I read ‌ܠܢܬܝ‌ for ‌ܠܢܝ‌.   Mich., however, has ‌ܠܟܣܩܘܝ‌, "because you (it)," and must therefore have read ‌ܠܢܝܗ‌.

[3] Tit. iii. 9.   [4] Read ‌ܐܘܡܪ‌ for ‌ܐܡܪ‌.   Mich. "the apostle said."

[5] Read ‌ܗܘܕܢܝ‌ for ‌ܗܪܝܢܝ‌.

the apostle said, 'We have no such custom, neither the Churches of God.'[1]

"Accordingly, victorious king, we do now also declare the freedom of our faith, although in the desert, when we received your edict at the hands of Theodotus the duke, we wrote and declared what we think, and your Majesties gave us a message of truth free from affliction in that you were graciously moved and summoned us to your presence. And, since we have been judged worthy of the mercies of God, we do in this supplication inform your orthodoxies that by the grace of God we have from our earliest infancy received the faith of the apostles, and have been brought up in it and with it, and we think and believe even as our three hundred and eighteen God-inspired holy fathers, who drew up the faith of life and salvation, which was confirmed by our one hundred and fifty holy fathers who once met here, and ratified by the pious bishops who assembled at Ephesus and rejected the impious Nestorius.   And so in this faith of the apostles we have been baptized and do baptize, and this saving knowledge is grounded in our hearts, and this same doctrine alone we recognise as a rule in the faith, and beyond it we receive no other; because it is perfect in all points, and it does not grow old nor need renovation.

"Now we acknowledge a worshipful and holy Trinity of one nature, power, and honour, which is made known in three persons; for we worship the Father and His only Son, God the Word, Who was begotten of Him eternally beyond all times, and is with Him always without variation, and the Holy Spirit,[2] which proceeds from the Father, and is of the nature of the Father and of the Son.   One of the persons of this holy Trinity, that is, God the Word, we say by the will of the Father in the last days for the salvation of men took flesh of the Holy Spirit and of the holy Virgin the *Theotokos* Mary in a body endowed with a rational and intellectual soul,[3] passible after our nature, and became man,

---

[1] 1 Cor. xi. 16.

[2] We require ܠ for ܒ before ܪܘܚܐ.   Mich., however, also has ܒ.

[3] Read ܒ for ܕ before ܢܦܫܐ.

and was not changed from that which He was. And so we confess that, while [1] in the Godhead He was of the nature of the Father, He was also of our nature in the manhood. Accordingly He Who is the perfect Word, the invariable Son of God, became perfect man, and left nothing wanting for us in respect of our salvation, as the foolish Apollinaris said, saying that the Humanisation of God the Word was not perfect, and deprives [2] us, according to his opinion, of things that are of prime importance in our salvation. For, if our intellect was not united with Him, as he absurdly says, then we are not saved, and in the matter of salvation [3] have fallen short of that which is of the highest consequence for us. But these things are not as he said; for the perfect God for our sake became perfect man without variation, and God the Word did not leave anything wanting in the Humanisation, as we have said, nor yet was it a phantom of Him, as the impious Mani supposes, and the erring Eutyches.

"And, since Christ is truth and does not know how to lie and does not deceive, because He is God, therefore God the Word truly became incarnate, in truth again, and not in semblance, with natural and innocent passions, because of His own will He for our sake among the things which He took upon Himself in the passible flesh of our nature of His own will endured also our death, which He made life for us by a Resurrection befitting God, for he first restored incorruption and immortality to human nature.

"And, indeed, as God the Word left nothing wanting and was not phantasmal in the Incarnation and Humanisation, so He did not divide it into two persons and two natures according to the doctrine introduced by Nestorius the man-worshipper and those who formerly thought like him, and those who in our day so think.

"And the faith contained in your confession refutes the doctrine of these men and contends with it, because in your

---

[1] Insert ܕ before ܒ.

[2] Read ܟܣܝܘܗܝ for ܟܣܝܘܗ; so Mich. ܣܒܪܘܗܝ.

[3] After ܘܦܘܪܩܢܐ the MS. has ܠܢ, not ܠܐ, as L. prints.

earnestness [1] you said thus: 'God appeared, Who became incarnate. He is in all points like the Father except the individuality of His Father. He became a sharer of our nature, and was called Son of Man. Being one and the same, God and man, He showed Himself to us, and was born as a babe for our sake; and, being God, He for men and for the sake of their salvation became man.' [2]

"If those who dispute with us adhered to these things in truth and were not content to hold them in appearance only, but rather consented to believe as we do and you do and as our holy God-inspired fathers did, they would have abstained from this stirring of strife. For that Christ was joined by composition, and that God the Word is joined by composition with a body endowed with a rational and intellectual soul the all-wise doctors of the Church have plainly stated. Dionysius, who from the Areopagus and from the darkness and error of heathendom attained to the supreme light of the knowledge of God through our master Paul, in the treatise which he composed about the divine names of the Holy Trinity says, 'Praising [3] it as kindly, we say, as is right, that it is kindly,' [4] because it in truth partook perfectly of our attributes in one of its persons, drawing to itself and raising the lowliness of our manhood, out of which the simple Jesus became joined by composition in a manner that cannot be described; and He who was from eternity and beyond all times took upon Him a temporal existence, and He who was raised and exalted above all orders and natures became in the likeness of our nature without variation and confusion.' [5] And Athanasius again in the treatise upon the faith named the unity of God the Word with soul-possessing flesh a composition, speaking thus: 'What is the relationship to the unbelief of those who

---

[1] The MS. has ܩܘܠܘܬܟܘܢ, not ܩܘܠܘܬܟܘܢ, as L. prints. Mich. has ܒܟܬܒܝܟܘܢ, "in your writings."

[2] I do not know whence this is taken.

[3] The MS. has ܡܫܒܚܝܢ, not ܡܫܒܚܝܢ, as L. prints.

[4] The words ܐܝܟܢ ܕܝܣܩܐ ܐܝܟ are accidentally repeated in L.'s text, but not in the MS.

[5] Dion. Areop. *de Div. Nom.* i. 4.

call it an indwelling instead of an Incarnation,[1] and instead of a union and composition a human energy?'[2]

"If, therefore, according to our holy fathers, whom your peacefulnesses have followed, God the Word, who was before simple and not composite, became incarnate of the Virgin, the *Theotokos* Mary, and united soul-possessing and intellectual flesh to Himself personally and made it His own and was joined with it by composition in the dispensation, it is manifest that according to our fathers we ought to confess one[3] nature of God the Word, who took flesh and became perfectly[4] man. Accordingly God the Word, who was before simple, is not recognised to have become composite in a body, if He is again divided after the union by being called two natures. But, just as an ordinary man, who is made up of various natures, soul and body and so forth, is not divided into two natures because a soul has been joined by composition with a body to make up the one nature and person of a man, so also God the Word, who was personally united and joined by composition with soul-possessing flesh, is not divided into or in two natures because of His union and composition with a body. For according to the words of our fathers, whom the fear of God that is in you has followed, God the Word,[5] Who was formerly simple, consented for our sake to be united by composition with soul-possessing and intellectual flesh and without change to become man. Accordingly one nature and person of God the Word, Who took flesh, is glorified, and there is one energy of the Word of God which is made known, which is exalted and glorious and fitting for God, and is also lowly and human. How is it that some are not corrected?"[6]

And they are urgent and refuse to accept what Leo wrote in the Tome in opposition to these things, he and those of his opinions; and they produced quotations from him, and from

[1] Omit ? before ܩܬܠܘ.

[2] This is not in the extant portions of the *Sermo de Fide.*

[3] Insert ܒ before ܟܝܢ.

[4] Insert ܘ before ܡܫܡܠܝܐܝܬ.   [5] Omit ? before ܐܠܗܐ.

[6] Read ܡܬܬܪܨܝܢ for ܡܬܬܪܨܝܢ. Mich. ܐܬܬܘܣܦܘ.

Nestorius and Theodore and Diodorus and Theodoret and the Synod of Chalcedon,[1] who speak of two natures after the Incarnation of God the Word, and two persons; and they provided a copious refutation of these with proofs drawn from the fathers who have at various times held opinions contrary to these and taught one nature and person in the Church, saying that God the Word was in truth humanised without change and became perfect man, and the same remained perfect God, besides things which I forbear to record here on account of their length, and because they were everywhere to be found in works against the Diphysites.

And at the end of their petition[2] they said thus: "And for this reason we do not accept either the Tome or the definition of Chalcedon, O victorious king, because we keep the canon and law of our fathers who assembled at Ephesus and anathematised and deprived Nestorius and excommunicated any who should presume to compose any other definition of faith besides that of Nicæa, which was correctly and believingly laid down by the Holy Spirit. These we reject and anathematise. And this definition and canon those who assembled at Chalcedon deliberately set at naught and transgressed, as they state in the Acts[3] of that Synod;[4] and they are subject to punishment and blame from our holy fathers in that they have introduced a new definition of faith, which is contrary to the truth of the doctrine of those who from time to time have been after a pure manner doctors of the Church, who, we believe, are now also entreating Christ with us, that you may aid the truth of their faith, honouring the contests undergone by their priesthoods, by which the Church has been exalted and glorified. For thus shall peace reign in your reign by the power of the right hand of God Almighty, to whom we pray on your behalf[5] that without toil or struggle in arms He will set your enemies as a stool beneath your feet."

And, when the letter of defence for the faith, as given

---

[1] After ܣܘܪܘܣ insert with Mich. ܘܛܝܩܣܘ ܣܘܪܘܣ.
[2] δέησις.   [3] πεπραγμένα.
[4] Mansi, vii. pp. 456, 457.
[5] The MS. has ܢܘܠܦܟܘ, not ܢܘܠܦܟܘ, as L. prints.

above, had been presented to the king and been read, and
many words had been spoken during the no small space
of one year and more by the believing bishops who had
come thither to the royal city by the king's command, as
recorded above, with whom was the learned John the archimandrite, the son of Aphthonia, (and he wrote a record of
the discussions), the king would not banish the Synod of
Chalcedon from the Church, while he summoned by letter
the holy Severus the chief priest, who was hiding in various
places.   And, since he rejected the king's request and
refused to come to him, the believing bishops who were in
Constantinople returned each one of them to any place he
chose to hide himself, according as he judged convenient
for him.

And[1] then after a time, in the year thirteen,[2] after many
letters from the king, the holy Severus also came to him and
was received, and he was in the palace till March of the year
fourteen,[3] while the Diphysite bishops everywhere were disturbed and annoyed and also alarmed, and especially Ephraim
of Antioch, until in their anxiety they stirred up Agapetus,
chief priest of Rome, who shared their opinions, and invited
and brought him to the royal city.   Moreover, how it came
about and what happened will be made known in a chapter
which I am going to write below.

The end of the petition contained in the fifteenth [chapter][4]
concerning the monks who assembled at Constantinople.[5]

---

[1] Jo. Eph. Frag. (*Anecd. Syr.* ii. p. 386).   [2] 534–5.
[3] 536.   [4] This is not in the text.
[5] According to the heading the petitioners were not monks but bishops. In
Mich., however, they are called "bishops and monks."

CHAPTER XVI

THE SIXTEENTH CHAPTER OF THE NINTH BOOK TREATS OF THE DEFENCE, WHICH SEVERUS, WHEN REFUSING TO COME TO THE ROYAL CITY, WROTE IN AN EPISTLE TO THE KING, AS FOLLOWS

"The[1] eternal Word of the Father, the Son of God, Who had in the end taken flesh and was not changed, and, moreover, became perfectly man by the Holy Spirit and Mary the holy Virgin, the *Theotokos*, and in everything was truly made like unto us except sin, fulfilling the teaching of salvation in parables, [sowed][2] the seed from it in His disciples, that they too and all throughout the whole world who by their means received the word, if anything that was good sprang up from it in the way of righteousness and pious deeds, might ascribe this not to themselves but to the power of that which He sowed in the beginning, as by grace, and, when among valleys and boulders[3] and stone rocks in the wilderness, might with loud and strong voices cry out, making utterance. Similarly, therefore, has your serene Mightiness also sown[4] the seed of kindliness that is in my vileness, and has caused this letter to spring forth from me; not as the offspring of presumption, for how was it possible that in answer to the powerful and strong voice of your Majesty, which reached my ears, an utterance should not be emitted by me? For, when those who bitterly despised my vileness thought that they had everywhere shut the doors in my face without mercy, then indeed, as by an unexpected miracle, you by your letter summon me to yourself, me, a man who am, as it were, driven about and banished by enemies. And this same thing is like God, who to them that were pursued[5] by foemen, when they thought themselves

---

[1] Cf. Evag. iv. 11.

[2] ܐܘܪܥ seems to have dropped out before ܠܬܘܪܥܐ.

[3] MS. ܩܘܦ̈ܐ, not ܩܟ̈ܐ, as L.

[4] Read ܐܘܪܥ for ܐܘܟܥ.

[5] Read ܩܘܪܕܝ for ܩܘܪܕܝ.

shut in and caught by them, provided a broad way of safety, worthy of His wisdom and His great might; a way which worked a miracle upon Far'oh, who had let them go after their long time of subjection, and again [1] pursued after them to bring them into subjection to his hard yoke, and with his horsemen surrounded them in the wilderness of the Sea of Rushes and barred the way, thinking in his heart and saying, 'These men are entangled in the land, for the wilderness hath shut them in.' [2]   But the marvellous God to those who thought themselves hemmed in by warriors made a way of grace over the sea dry, that they might cross it on foot; who commanded Moses to raise his staff over the sea and cause it to be divided.   And so in close resemblance to these things you also with your Majesty's wand of peace have divided the sea in the wilderness which hemmed me in; and the way which, it was thought, could not be traversed you have again caused to be traversed by me.

"And it is a great proof of your gentleness that you unhesitatingly indited your letter to me even with oaths, promising me immunity from injury; in this also after the manner of God, because He too, condescending to the weakness of men, oftentimes sent forth His promises with oaths, as Scripture teaches, and Paul made mention of it, saying, 'When God made promise to Abraham, because He had none greater than Himself by whom He could swear, He sware by Himself and said, " Blessing, I will bless thee; and multiplying, I will multiply thee."' [3]   But I, the vile one, am bold to say that I was in no need of such security,[4] since I trust the word that comes out of your mouth only, believing it to be a perfect safeguard to me, even as the wise Koheleth said, 'Observe the mouth of the king, and be not anxious in regard to the word of the oaths of God.' [5]   But I have confidence in the test which springs from the deeds which in truth bear witness more than oaths to your peacefulness as well as [6] to your inclination to the mercies which belong to a gentle

---

[1] Insert ◯ before ܘܠ.   [2] Ex. xiv. 3.   [3] Heb. vi. 13, 14.
[4] Read ܠܣܘܠܢ (ἀσφάλεια) for ܠܣܘܢܠ.   [5] Eccles. viii. 2.
[6] ܘܠ is crossed out in the MS., but a copula of some kind is required.

soul.   For, as soon as you have taken upon yourself the cares of the kingdom, you release from sorrow all classes of men sentenced to exile, chief priests and magnates and common people, having regard to that which is equally esteemed by all men, the light of the sun,[1] and rain, and the temperate air which it brings, and the other things which are required for and conduce to the life of men.

"But I will not, by drinking from the copiousness of this rich stream of your gentleness, cause myself to err, and be rendered proud ; but I have determined to declare what is in my mind. For I am afraid lest, if my meanness be openly seen in the royal city, many persons may be alarmed, and, though I am in truth nothing but merely a vile person bound under this heavy yoke of sins, when they hear of this, many persons may be roused to anger and inflamed by this paltry anxiety, as by a little coal of fire, so as to trouble and annoy even your Mightiness [2] owing to your affection towards me : and I think that it will not seem to you fitting nor to others profitable. Now this I say, not as though I had any power against your Majesty's Mightiness, for it is written, 'When a righteous king sitteth upon a throne, no evil riseth up against his eyes,'[3] but because I am persuaded that, as this power [4] belongs to you by grace from on high, so you are clad in understanding and wisdom, and make it your endeavour to do[5] many things, not by this sword, but by sagacity befitting kingship.   And this we are taught by the Scripture, which says, 'A wise king winnoweth and scattereth the wicked.'[6]   And, just as it is easy for those who are winnowed by the wind, which blows away the chaff, to hold aloof from sinners,[7] so also is it simple for your serenity, my lord, with the all-considering heart and with

---

[1] Read [Syriac] for [Syriac].

[2] Read [Syriac] for [Syriac].   [3] Prov. xx. 8.

[4] The MS. has [Syriac], not [Syriac], as L. prints.

[5] The MS. has [Syriac], not [Syriac], as L. prints.   [6] Prov. xx. 26.

[7] For [Syriac] we should perhaps read [Syriac], "grains of wheat" (Hamilton). In this case we should probably read [Syriac] for [Syriac], and render "easy for them (the reapers) to separate the things that are winnowed . . . from the wheat."

the mercy of a gracious [1] father, to separate those that are under subjection to you from those of the contrary part, in order that the Churches in union may be reckoned worthy of friendship. For I know that it was for this reason also that you judged it right that my feebleness too should come to your feet, because, when also you reckoned this same thing [2] worthy of a letter from you to the pious bishops of the East, who are men that pray for the safety and preservation of your Majesty, they also, after they had written to you what they thought, informed my feebleness of this your will, urging us according to the custom of the Church to help you [3] by prayer on your behalf.

"Now in your great city of Alexandria nothing has been done by me of the things falsely asserted against me. And it is easy for me to show the folly of the informers ; [4] for they have slandered me, saying that by means of a large sum of gold which I distributed there, I stirred up riotous contention. And this same thing is known to those who hate me greatly that, though involved in the passions of other sins, I do not seek hastily to amass money ; and this by no light reasons, but my life [5] is habitually frugal, insomuch that not even the renowned bishopric drew me away from this habit. For, as it is the approved custom for a priest to perform priestly functions, [6] in the same way it is the approved custom for him to be poor : wherefore also the law given by Moses ordained that the chosen tribe of Levi should have no inheritance in the land, but for their necessary food the appropriated oblation [7] should be sufficient, being associated in this with

----

[1] The MS. has ‏ܠܡܚܣܝܐ‏, not ‏ܠܡܚܣܝܐ‏, as L. prints.

[2] This sentence is very awkward and obscure. The general sense I owe to Dr. Hamilton, and I arrive at it by omitting ‏ܟܡ‏.

[3] Only ‏ܘ‏ . . . is visible. Read ‏ܠܟܘܢ‏.

[4] ‏ܠܡܘܪ̈ܝ‏. See p. 245, note 7.

[5] βίος.

[6] The MS. has ‏ܠܒܗ‏, not ‏ܠܒܚܣ‏, as L. prints. Logically we require another ‏ܕ‏ before ‏ܕܠܒܗ‏.

[7] Omit ‏ܠ‏ before ‏ܩܘܪܒܢܐ‏. It is doubtful whether the letter is really in the MS.

17

the widows and the needy and the orphans, because they are accustomed to poverty, saying, ' And the Levite shall come (because he hath no part or inheritance with thee), and the stranger and the orphan and the widow, which are in thy villages, and they shall eat and rejoice; that the Lord thy God may bless thee in all thy works which thou doest.'[1]   But, since, as it is written, ' Righteous lips are acceptable to the king, and he loveth upright speech,'[2] your Mightiness may learn from the governors who have been at any time in Alexandria, and now from their officials,[3] whom nothing escapes, whether anything of the kind has been done by me even in word, or has been reported to have been done, as they have falsely and maliciously asserted of me.   But about these informers[4] I will not say anything, because it does not escape your knowledge what kind of men they are: but I await a judgment with them, after we have been separated from this world of toil, before the tribunal of Christ, where we shall give an account for idle words and for vain thoughts ; and especially shall we bishops, to whom much has been intrusted, be judged, although here we delight in bodily things and dally in them.[5]

" But, if some apply the term turbulence to what I wrote to Julian, bishop of Halicarnassus, who has been perverted to the heresy of the Manichees and reckons the voluntary saving passions of Christ, the great God, as a phantasy, I do with ten thousand mouths and tongues confess and do not deny what I wrote, even as no one will hastily order me to deny my faith: for this is the opinion of your orthodoxy also, who more than the affairs of the world care to hold fast the things which belong to the Spirit.   And I was not impelled to do this by my own will or my own motion, but I was greatly pressed by him to write, because he thought that I agreed with his doctrine.   For, when I had gone through what he sent to me (and I am[6] far away from Alexandria), in the things which

---

[1] Deut. xiv. 29.   [2] Prov. xvi. 13.
[3] τάξις.   [4] See above, and p. 245, note 7.
[5] Read ܒܩܘܝ for ܒܩ.
[6] For ܐܝܬܝ, " I am," we should perhaps read ܐܝܬܝ ܗܘܐ, ܐܝܬܝ ܗܘܐ, or ܐܝܬ ܗܘܐ, " I was."

he wrote I found that under the name of incorruptibility he covered, as it were with a sheepskin, the blasphemies [1] of Mani, because there are many things which I will forbear to mention.

"This foolish man, who confesses the passions with his lips only, hiding his impiety, wrote thus: 'Incorruptibility was always attached to the body of our Lord, which was passible of His own will for the sake of others.'   And in brotherly love I wrote and asked him: 'What do you mean by "incorruptible," and "suffered of His own will for the sake of others," and "was attached to the body of our Lord," [2] if without any falsehood you confess it to be by nature passible?   For, if by the incorruptibility possessed by it you mean holiness without sin, we all confess this with you, that the holy body from the womb which He united to Himself originally by the Holy Spirit of the pure Virgin, the *Theotokos*, was conceived and born in the flesh without sin and conversed with us men, because "He did no sin, neither was guile found in His mouth," [3] according to the testimony of the Scriptures.   But, if you call impassibility and immortality incorruptibility, and say that the body which suffered in the flesh on our behalf was not one that was capable of suffering with voluntary passions and dying in the flesh, you reduce the saving passions on our behalf to a phantasy; for a thing which does not suffer also does not die, and it is a thing incapable of suffering.' [4]   And upon receiving such remarks as these from me he openly refused to call the holy body of Emmanuel passible in respect of voluntary passions; and therefore he did not hesitate to write thus, without shame and openly: 'We do not call Him of our nature in respect of passions, but in respect of essence. [5]   Therefore, even if He is impassible, and even if He is incorruptible, yet He is of our nature in respect of nature.'"

[1] Read ܠ for ܒ before ܝܗܘܦܪܘ.

[2] I owe the translation of this difficult passage to Dr. Hamilton.   For ܢܩܝܦ ܗܘܐ we should have expected ܠܗܘܐ ܢܩܝܦܐ.

[3] I Pet. ii. 22.

[4] Quoted shortly from the third letter of Severus to Julian (Add. MS. 17,200, fol. 17).

[5] οὐσία.

And the rest of the erring fatuity of Julian, which is contained at great length in the epistle, I forbear [1] to record now, matters which are to be found in the many books which this holy Severus composed against Julian.

But at the end of the epistle he wrote, saying thus: " I therefore entreat you and take hold of your feet, again repeating the request that you will leave my meanness alone, and not again bring me forth among men, because I am enfeebled in my body and in my mind; wherefore also I am weak, since true are the words of Scripture which say, ' The mind falleth among blows (?).' [2]   And there are now many white hairs on my head, which bear witness to me of death, the departure from this weary life, and it appears to me to be a thing very good and beneficial to sit hidden in a corner and bear in my mind the separation of soul from body, awaiting my grave; [3] for ' the earth is the home of everyone that dieth,' [4] as Job said; because in the case of other animals who live on the earth their hair does not change, but in the case of this rational animal, man, because he was destined to come to judgment and have his deeds examined in the future world, as soon as he reaches old age, the hair of his head turns white, such appearance making announcement to him and inciting him, as far as those who have delayed are concerned, to prepare his deeds for his departure; and the Scripture also bears testimony to him, saying, ' Lift up thine eyes and look on the fields, for they are white and prepared for harvest '; [5] for the separation of the soul from the body is in truth a harvest, and, as with a sickle, He cutteth it away from it, and it is bereft. So I beg that your Mightiness will grant me this simple request, [6] that I may dwell hidden where I am, because the

---

[1] Read ܠܟܪ for ܠܟܪ.

[2] If ܐܘܒܫܐ is right, it would seem to be connected with ܐܒܫ, "to impel." Cf., however, p. 73, l. 8, 21 (L.), where the verb seems to mean "to revile." I cannot find the source of the quotation.

[3] For ܟܒܐ ܩܒܪܘ we must read either ܟܒܐ ܩܒܪܘ or ܟܒܐ ܩܒܪܘ?.

[4] Job xxx. 23.   [5] John iv. 35.

[6] For ܩܦܣܘ I read ܩܦܣܘ.

rest of my days in the world I am determined to live in secret, as in a corner; for such is the life of a monk.

"May Christ, who is God over all, give you dominion over your enemies, with perfect peace and concord among the Churches, that you may be crowned with this also.   And, if I am committing any fault or presumption in this my letter of petition, I entreat you to forgive me, as on other points; for it is very becoming in a Christ-loving king to overcome evil with good, as the apostle said,[1] a duty which you display in deed, and are therefore rightly called victorious."

The signature of Severus to the epistle—

"May the only Trinity, for that is our God, preserve [2] your orthodoxy many years, keeping the dominion of the common-wealth [3] of the Romans in peace, and may He bring every nation of Romans and barbarians into subjection to you, and grant to the holy Churches [4] by your means perfect concord in sound faith; and may He reckon you worthy to receive a crown in the kingdom of heaven."

Now after this epistle the holy Severus remained till the year thirteen,[5] and then came to the royal city, because he was pressed by letters from the king.

CHAPTER XVII

THE SEVENTEENTH CHAPTER, CONCERNING AFRICA, WHICH
WAS CONQUERED BY BELISARIUS THE GENERAL [6]

When in the summer of the year eleven [7] Rufinus and Hermogenes, the master of the offices, had by the help of our Lord made peace between the Romans and the Persians on the terms contained in the written treaty, and the Roman generals [6] and army in the East had come to the royal city, they received blame from the king and incurred his displeasure, ·

---

[1] Rom. xii. 21.   [2] The MS. has ܪܚܡ, not ܪܚܡ, as L. prints.

[3] πολιτεία.   [4] Insert ܠ before ܥܕ̈ܬܐ.

[5] 534-5.   [6] στρατηγός.   [7] 533.

because they had not acted worthily of the high honour and rank which he had bestowed on them by showing themselves brave and astute [1] in the struggle against the Persians, and especially Belisarius, because of the loss of the army under his orders, which had been defeated in battle at Thannuris and on the Euphrates; and he made his defence to the king on the ground of the impatience of the army, and the lack of discipline [2] among the men under him.

Now there were in Constantinople certain magnates from Africa, who, owing to a quarrel which they had with the prince of the land, had left their country and taken refuge with the king, and they gave him information about the country and incited him, saying that it was very extensive and very peaceful, and that it had no thought [3] of a war with the Romans, but was engaged in a struggle with the Moors, a people who are settled in the desert and live by robbery and devastation like the Saracens. And they pointed out to the king that this country had been torn and snatched from the Roman Empire since the days of Zirzeric, who took Rome, and also carried off valuable objects of gold and silver and other precious substances, and withdrew to Carthage in Africa, a distinguished [4] city, which he took and occupied; and he settled there, and stored and placed the treasures in it.

And so the king made ready an army under Belisarius and Martin and Archelaus the prefect,[5] and many ships carrying [6] arms and accoutrements (?) [7] for the army; and they sailed over the sea; and, because God willed this expedition and assisted it, they arrived in a few days and suddenly appeared before the royal city of Carthage. And the prince of the land was not there,[8]

---

[1] ‎ܟܪܝܐ‎. See bk. I, ch. I (p. 16, note 8).

[2] The negative ‎ܠܐ‎ has fallen out of the text.

[3] The MS. has ‎ܡܬܪܥܝܐ‎, not ‎ܡܬܪܥܝܐ‎, as L. prints.

[4] Read ‎ܡܫܡܗܬܐ‎ for ‎ܡܚܡܬܐ‎.   [5] ὕπαρχος.

[6] Read ‎ܕܛܥܝܢ‎ for ‎ܛܥܝܢ‎.

[7] ‎ܢܚܬܐ‎, "outer garments," can hardly be right.

[8] We must either insert another ‎ܬܡܢ‎ or omit ‎ܘ‎, rendering "the prince was not there."

but was engaged in war with the Moors in the desert; but a small force, which was in the city, which came out and met the Romans, was defeated in battle and was vanquished and retreated. And the city was surrendered, and the Romans entered and occupied it. And they collected spoil; and the prince's treasure was kept for the king of the Romans.

Now the Romans also occupied a few of the cities of the country, because they were betrayed [1] to them by certain men who were with them, who betrayed the country and knew it well; and it [2] is a spacious land, extending over about fifty days' journey, and contains more than one hundred and thirty cities, and is rich and fertile. But the king and the chief priests of the land and the magnates of the people were Arimenites. [3]

Now, when the prince heard it and came with an army, it was found to be small and contemptible before the Romans; and, when he understood that his kinsmen had been taken, and his magnates had surrendered, and his treasure had been carried away, he was weakened, and on condition that his life should be spared he surrendered. And he was taken away in company with Belisarius in the year twelve, [4] and was publicly presented to the king in the circus [5] before the people, [6] with the treasure [7] and his kinsmen and his magnates. And an ambassador of Khosru, king of the Persians, was there and was present and saw these things. And from that time Africa has been subject to the Romans. And gradually the other cities in the region of Africa were reduced: only the Moors continue their accustomed hostilities there.

[1] Read ܟܣܘ̈ܒܝ for ܟܣܘܪ̈ܝ.

[2] The rest of this sentence is contained in Cod. Rom. Instead, however, of "and is rich and fertile," it has "and the chief city and capital of the country is called Carthage."

[3] *I.e.* Arians—followers of the Synod of Ariminum.

[4] 534.   [5] ἱππικός.   [6] δῆμος.   [7] Cf. Jo. Mal. p. 479.

CHAPTER XVIII

THE EIGHTEENTH CHAPTER OF THE NINTH BOOK, CON-
CERNING ROME, WHICH WAS TAKEN BY BELISARIUS

Alimeric[1] the tyrant held possession of Rome by rebellion
in the days of Zeno and Anastasius; and he was a warlike
man and an able, and he added great strength to the country
of Italy, and he rebuilt Rome and kept the barbarians out of
it.   And he had died, and his successors one after another
held and governed the country of the Romans in rebellion
against the kingdom of Constantinople.

Now a certain Dominic,[2] one of the chief men of the
country, had a quarrel with the tyrant, and took refuge with
King Justinian, and gave him information about the country.
And he was an old man, well read in the Scriptures,[3] a
Diphysite; and he often engaged in disputation, and I know
him.   Now the king, having conquered Africa in the manner
described above, was eager to conquer Rome also.   And,
observing that Belisarius had been successful in the war in
Africa without doing any injury to the population of the
country or diminishing it by bloodshed, but had been content
with the necessary demands of tribute, taxes, and subjection,
he made ready an army for him and sent him to Rome.
And John the chief priest there had died during those days,
and Agapetus had succeeded him.

And, when the army had reached a place called Naples, a
celebrated city, not far from Rome, and had taken it, the
Senate[4] in Rome and their council,[5] together with their chief,[6]
were disturbed and afraid, because they had already heard
how Carthage and the tyrant of that country of Africa had
been conquered; and, observing these things, they anticipated

---

[1] *I.e.* Theodoric; see bk. 7, ch. 12.   [2] Or Demonicus.
[3] Lit. "from the reading of the Scriptures."   Possibly some words have fallen out.
[4] σύγκλητος.   [5] βουλή..
[6] If the singular is genuine, the Gothic commandant, or possibly the king, would
seem to be meant; but perhaps we should read ܩܫܝܫ̈ܐ, "their chief men."

matters by sending a petition, asking for peace, and promising to surrender the city; and later they also sent hostages. And afterwards Belisarius arrived there with the army and was received in the city with the praises of its inhabitants, and he occupied it and did no injury in it. And he was there for a time, while occupying the other cities also and bringing them into subjection to the king, without doing any hurt by slaying or destroying the population. And the king gained renown by these things and rejoiced in the year fourteen.[1]

CHAPTER XIX

THE NINETEENTH CHAPTER, CONCERNING SEVERUS, WHO AGAIN WENT UP TO CONSTANTINOPLE AND APPEARED BEFORE THE KING

Now[2] the well-tried Severus, after receiving pressing summonses from the king, at last came to Constantinople in the year fourteen,[3] and was received in a friendly manner in the palace by the king, who was disposed[4] and incited thereto by Theodora the queen, who was devoted to Severus, and he was honourable and venerable in her eyes. And, Epiphanius, the chief priest of the city, having died, Anthimus had succeeded him; and he was an ascetic man and a practiser of poverty, and a friend of the needy and a believer. He was bishop of Trebizond, and, happening for some reason to be present there, and being a man of virtuous character and known to the king and the magnates for his chastity, he was appointed patriarch; and he would not receive the Synod of Chalcedon into the faith.

---

[1] 536. The text is ⟨Syriac⟩, which is a confusion between "Τρισκαιδέκατον" and "τεσσαρεσκαιδέκατον." Read ⟨Syriac⟩, which is the nearer to historical fact.

[2] Jo. Eph. Fragm. (*Anecd. Syr.* ii. p. 386).

[3] 535-6. In chs. 15 and 16 the date is rightly given as the thirteenth year of the Indiction (534-5). "τρίς" (⟨Syriac⟩) and "τέσσαρες" (⟨Syriac⟩) are easily confused: see note 1 above.

[4] Cf. Evag. iv. 10.

And in Alexandria, after Gaian had been driven out, who was a Julianist, and was there for three months after the death of Timothy, Theodosius became bishop, a man of conspicuous faith and learned and kind and gentle; and he was an acquaintance and a friend of the holy Severus.

When these three chief priests were joined together in love, and in faith [1] were not divided from one another, Ephraim [2] of Antioch was alarmed and greatly disturbed, and yet more so because [3] Peter of Jerusalem was not of his own inclination a lover of discord [4] or a heretic, although through weakness and lack of energy and vigour he conducted himself according to the times.

Now [5] it happened that in those days Sergius, [6] an *archiatros* of Rhesaina, went up to Antioch to make a complaint against Asylus, [7] the bishop of that city, telling Ephraim the patriarch [8] that he had been injured by him. And this man was a man of eloquence and practised in the reading of many books of the Greeks and in the teaching of Origen, while for some time he had been reading commentaries on the Scriptures by other doctors in Alexandria (and he was skilled in the Syriac tongue, reading and speaking) and books [9] of medicine. And of his own inclination he was a believer, to which evidence is also borne by the prologue and the very apt translation of Dionysius which he made [10] and the treatise composed by him on the faith in the days of the illustrious Peter, the believing bishop. However, as regards his character, this Sergius was very

---

[1] Insert ܒ before ܗܝܡܢܘܬܐ. [2] Mich. fol. 170.

[3] Insert ܕ before ܦܛܪܘܣ. So Mich. ܠܦ.

[4] Read ܗܪܛܝܩܐ for ܗܪܛܝܩܐ. Mich. ܡܣܟܠܬܐ.

[5] What follows is contained in an abbreviated form in Add. MS. 12,154, fol. 151.

[6] Mich. *l.c.*; Greg. *H. E.* p. 205 ff.

[7] 17,202 has ܐܣܘܠ, and 12,154 ܐܣܘܠ, while Mich. and Greg. have ܐܣܘܠ. Asylus of Rhesaina is mentioned in Elijah's life of John of Constantia (ed. Kleyn, p. 59), whence I follow the reading of 17,202.

[8] After ܦܛܪܝܪܟܐ insert ܕܐܘܪܫܠܡ ܦܛܪܘܣ, with 12,154 : similarly Mich. and Greg.

[9] The MS. seems to have ܒܒܠܝܐ (βιβλία), not ܒܒܠܐ, as L. prints.

[10] Wright, *C. B. M.* pp. 493–501.

wanton in the lust of women, and he was incontinent and not chaste, while he was greedy in respect of the love of money.

Of this man Ephraim made trial, and, finding him to be a man of experience, promised to do for him anything that he asked, if he would go as his emissary to Rome with an epistle to Agapetus, the chief priest there, and return.   And he accepted.[1]   And he was furnished with presents by Ephraim, and received a letter for the man, while he was accompanied by a lad named Eustace, an architect, from Amida,[2] who spreads about a strange story about Sergius; but, lest it should do harm to the reader, I do not record it.

These men also accordingly came to Rome to Agapetus, and they delivered the epistle and were received; and the man was pleased with their epistle, in which he found agreement with his opinions.   And he came with them to Constantinople in the month of March in the year fourteen;[3] and Severus was there, and Anthimus was chief priest.   And the whole city was disturbed at the arrival of Agapetus;[4] and the earth with all that is upon it quaked; and the sun began to be darkened by day and the moon by night, while ocean was tumultuous with spray (?)[5] from the 24th of March in this year till the 24th of June in the following year fifteen.[6]   And Agapetus, when he appeared before the king, had a splendid reception from him, because he spoke the same language[7] and was chief priest of the country of Italy, which had been

---

[1] After ـܝܘܣܦܘܣ insert ܗܘ ܕܝـ ܩܒܠ, with 12,154.   Similarly Greg.

[2] Read ܐܡܝܕ for ܐܡܝܕ.   [3] 536.

[4] This sentence is not in 17,202, but, being in 12,154 (which, however, omits the portents following) and in Mich., it must be presumed to have formed part of the original text.

[5] ܟܝܼܦ ܒܿܐܝܟܘܬܐ, a very awkward phrase, the rendering of which I owe to Dr. Hamilton.   The usual meaning of ܟܝܼܦ is "to be anxious," or "to neglect"; but, as ܠܥܪܘܦܐ means "a storm," and Mich. has ܬܗܘܡܐ, we may fairly render as above.

[6] 537.

[7] Instead of the rest of this sentence 12,154 has ܘܡܢ ܠܬܪܒܝܬܗ, "and had been brought up with him," which is probably an error for ܘܡܢ ܠܬܪܥܝܬܗ, "and shared his opinions."

conquered and brought into subjection to him.   And he was instructed in the outward words of Scripture but did not understand its meaning ; and he held an ignoble opinion upon the Incarnation of Jesus, our Lord Christ, God the Word, and he would not consent to call the Virgin Mary the *Theotokos*, and divided the unity into two natures, since he held the priority of the conception of the babe, like those of the school of Diodorus and Nestorius.   And he abstained from communion with Anthimus and Severus, and they yet more from communion with him ; and one of them he called an adulterer and the other a Eutychianist : and he perverted the love of the king towards them and made him hostile to them ; and he drove them from the city.

And[1] Anthimus and Severus and Theodosius of Alexandria made union with one another[2] in epistles, which we have set down below ; and Anthimus and Severus left the city to live each of them in hiding wherever was convenient for him.

Now Menas became bishop[3] in the royal city after Anthimus.   And Sergius the *archiatros* died suddenly there, and Agapetus died after him in those days by a miracle, his tongue being eaten away and rending him in his lifetime ;[4] and Silverius became bishop in Rome after him.

CHAPTER XX

THE TWENTIETH CHAPTER, THE EPISTLE OF SEVERUS TO
THE ORDER OF PRIESTS AND MONKS IN THE EAST,
TREATING OF HIS EXPULSION FROM THE ROYAL CITY

" To[5] the God-loving presbyters and deacons and archi-

---

[1] Cf. Evag. iv. 11.

[2] Here the extract in 12,154 breaks off owing to the loss of a leaf in the MS.

[3] The MS. has ܠܘܐ, not ܠܘܐ, as L. prints.

[4] This passage is repeated in a ninth cent. chronicle in Brit. Mus. Add. MS. 14,642, fol. 29 *v*, which, however, in place of ܒܢܣ̈ܘܗܝ has ܒܫܢ̈ܘܗܝ, " and he tore it with his teeth."

[5] Mich. fol. 178.

mandrites and priors and all the holy order of monks in the
East Severus greeting in our Lord.

"That I have passed outside the city which is ruler among
cities and beyond the pursuit of men, some of you, O holy
ones, being present, have seen with their own eyes, I who
have reckoned it right to indite this short letter on my part
and to stir you up to the expression (?)[1] of thanksgiving for
what I even reckon as my glory (?),[2] and to state clearly that
the actions of the divine providence towards us[3] are in truth
beneficial to us for the preservation of the orthodox faith and
the formation of a new will, with which, as one may say, it is
right to clothe oneself after the fashion[4] of a new garment,
and for shunning every heretical opinion and contention. For
Jacob also the patriarch, the great in endurance of labours
and in trust in God, when he fled from intercourse with the
barbarians in Sh'khem and from the dangers that surrounded
him there, urged those that dwelt with him to the same course
to which I have urged you, as he says in Scripture: 'And
Jacob said to his household and to all them that were with
him, Put away from among you the strange gods, and be clean,
and change your garments: and let us arise and go up to
Beth El and build there an altar unto God, who answered me
in the day of distress and delivered me in the way which I
went.'[5] For he has in truth delivered me from all the
expectation of the adversaries, who hate me without a cause,
and mocked at me and wagged their heads and said, as in
Job, 'His foot hath fallen into a gin, and he hath been caught
in a net. Let gins come upon him, and they shall prevail
against him, as thirsting[6] for him. His noose is hid in the

---

[1] For ⟨Syriac⟩ I read ⟨Syriac⟩, but the sentence is extremely obscure. Mich.
has ⟨Syriac⟩, "bringing." Dr. Hamilton suggests ⟨Syriac⟩, "strength."

[2] Read ⟨Syriac⟩ for ⟨Syriac⟩. With the MS. reading we must render
"desertion."

[3] This sentence is hopelessly corrupt in the text. I take the sense from Mich.,
who seems to have omitted ⟨Syriac⟩, and read ⟨Syriac⟩ for ⟨Syriac⟩, and ⟨Syriac⟩ for ⟨Syriac⟩.

[4] Logically the ⟨Syriac⟩ before ⟨Syriac⟩ should be omitted.

[5] Gen. xxxv. 2, 3.

[6] The MS. has ⟨Syriac⟩, not ⟨Syriac⟩, as L. prints.

ground, and the net is over his paths.'[1]   But, as for the wickedness of these men, it is not sated with blood; the Christ-worshipping queen was a sufficient protection for me, and God, who through your prayers directed her to that which is good in His sight, even as He cries in Isaiah the prophet to those that trust in Him, 'Fear not, because I have delivered thee. I have called thee by thy name, because thou art Mine. If thou pass through water, I am with thee, and rivers shall not overflow thee; and in fire thou shalt not be burned, and flame shall not scorch thee. Because I am the Lord thy God, the Holy One of Israel, that delivereth thee.'[2]

"And He that said these things has not only given me a marvellous deliverance, but has further also added an addition to the portion of the believers, to say truth, to the portion of the Lord and to the possession of His inheritance, Israel, that it may not be as those whom the Scripture blames, saying, 'Ye shall sow your seed in vain.'[3] For the pious Anthimus, archbishop of the royal city, who received the chief chair, even when he was in possession of it, would not retain it, but in upright fashion and with true judgment and knowledge hated the impiety of these men, and accepted the communion of us and of Pope Theodosius of Alexandria and of all the pastors who belong to our confession. Accordingly they vainly lead men astray who say that they do not receive the Synod of Chalcedon in respect of the definition of faith, but in respect of the rejection of Eutyches and Nestorius, clokes which Flavian also used but did not succeed in leading your zeal astray, and you were not overreached by Satan, and are able to say like Paul, 'His devices do not escape us.'"[4]

And so on with the rest of the epistle.

[1] Job xviii. 8–10.   [2] Isa. xliii. 1–3.
[3] Lev. xxvi. 16.   [4] 2 Cor. ii. 11.

CHAPTER XXI

THE TWENTY-FIRST CHAPTER, THE EPISTLE OF ANTHIMUS
TO SEVERUS OF ANTIOCH

"To[1] our pious and holy brother and fellow-minister, the patriarch, my lord Severus, Anthimus greeting in our Lord.

"Bearing in my mind the utterance of the Lord which says, 'To whomsoever much has been committed, from him shall much be required,'[2] and the saying[3] of the Psalmist, 'Who shall ascend into the hill of the Lord? and who shall stand in His holy place?'[4] and the apostle, who ordains of what sort a man must be who is set apart for God, I have been in no small fear. For, if those great patriarchs called themselves, one 'dust and ashes'[5] and another 'a worm and no man,'[6] what shall I say, the small and contemptible, who have attained to the height of this ministry without being worthy of it? For the disturbance of the holy Churches also agitates my soul greatly; for certain men, being held fast in sins and, as if displaying an appearance of avoiding variation and confusion, which does not exist, wantonly[7] divide God the Word, who is one and indivisible, and became incarnate without variation. And for this reason I am in great sorrow, as it is said in the Psalmist, 'Sorrow hath taken hold upon me because of the sinners that have forsaken Thy law.'[8] But trust in God gives me joy, and I believe that He will surely perform His promises and will give us all that we mean creatures need, not because we are His friends but because of importunity, and He will make requisition for all His elect; who has also for a long time preserved your Holiness from sins

---

[1] Mich. fol. 174.

[2] Luke xii. 48.

[3] Insert O before]ܠܟܘ.

[4] Ps. xxiv. 3.

[5] Gen. xviii. 27.

[6] Ps. xxii. 6.

[7] To get this sense we should probably read ܡܟܘܪ for ܡܟܘܪ. Mich., however, has ܦܠܓܐ, "part," which points to a reading ܡܟܘܪ. With the MS. reading the meaning will be " mock and divide."

[8] Ps. cxix. 53.

through your apostolic [1] contests and labours and your spiritual teachings, which by grace have been vouchsafed unto you, as a stone that cannot be moved, as well as us, His holy Churches, to be an invariable foundation of the faith. It is therefore the same God who assigns exaltation to the lowly and greatness to the small and strength to the weak, as the divine apostle says, ' By grace are we all justified.' [2] And these things, being by divine power made strong in weakness, have by an ineffable judgment brought our weakness also to be ruler in the holy Church in this royal city. Acknowledging therefore His grace, we beg you, pious one, to entreat Christ our God to assist our worthlessness ; and, because different men [3] have different marks, the mark of priests is also the preaching of the gospel, for, ' Speak,' He says, ' priests, and, when you go up upon the high mountains, make proclamation.' [4]

" In this first spiritual and love-abounding [5] greeting I communicate with you, O holy one ; for, while rejoicing in union and also in conjunction with you and in spiritual ties in accordance with the laws of the Church, I declare that I cleave to the one only definition of faith, that which was laid down by the three hundred and eighteen holy fathers who assembled at Nicæa under the direction of the Holy Spirit, and to this I pray that I may cleave unto the end ; which definition was ratified [6] by the Synod of one hundred and fifty holy fathers which assembled in this royal city against the impious fighters against the Spirit ; and not only so, but also by the holy Synod which assembled at Ephesus against the impious Nestorius, the leaders of which were the archbishops, memorable for piety and love of God, Celestine of the Romans and Cyril of Alexandria, who in his twelve chapters overthrew Nestorius the man-worshipper. To these chapters I assent together with all his writings and embrace

---

[1] Read ‏ܩܠܝܡܐ‎ for ‏ܩܠܡܐ‎.

[2] Tit. iii. 7.

[3] Read ‏ܣܘܪ̈ܝܐ‎ for ‏ܣܘܪ̈ܝܐ‎. The sentence is awkward, but the sense is clear from Mich. ‏ܐܝܟ ܕܠܟܠܢܫ ܐܝܬ ܐܦ‎.

[4] The reference seems to be to Isa. xl. 9.

[5] Read ‏ܚܘܒܬܠܝܬ‎ for ‏ܚܘܒܐ‎.

[6] Read ‏ܚܬܝܡܬܐ‎ for ‏ܚܬܝܡܬܐ‎, as in the parallel passage in ch. 25 (p. 289).

them as a holy law, while together with these holy teachings of Cyril I receive also the formula of Zeno uniting the Churches, which aims at the consummation of religion for the annulling of the Synod of Chalcedon and the impious Tome of Leo. I confess that God the Word, who was begotten before the ages of God the Father, the only Son, connatural and coeternal with the Father, through whom all things were made and through whom all things were established, the Light of Light, the invariable image and invisible will of the Father, in the last days became incarnate and became perfectly man of the Holy Spirit and of the holy *Theotokos* and ever-virgin Mary, and united to Himself personally flesh of our nature, having a rational and intellectual soul, and without variation and confusion and sin took our resemblance upon Him. For He remained immutable as God, and even in assuming our attributes He did not at the same time also diminish His own divine properties; and that which was derived from us He made His own by dispensation by a junction[1] consisting in a natural union. For He who was begotten without time and without a body of God the Father, the same submitted to a second[2] birth in a body; and, after He had in an ineffable manner become incarnate of a virgin mother, she that bore Him also continued a virgin even after the birth. Wherefore also we truly confess her to be the *Theotokos*, and that He who was born of her in the flesh is perfect God and perfect man, the same out of two natures one Son, one Lord, one Christ, and one nature of the incarnate Word ; and He became perfectly man, while each one of the natures remained without confusion in its sphere of manifestation, the natures which combined to form an indivisible unity. So also He is very rightly one of the holy and connatural Trinity, before the Incarnation and after the Incarnation, inasmuch as He did not add a number to the Trinity, the number of a quaternity ; and He is impassible in that He is of the nature of the

---

[1] MS. not ܟܝܢܐ, as L., but ܟܝܢܐ, changed into ܟܝܢܐ. Perhaps read ܟܝܢܘܬܐ.

[2] The MS. has ܬܪܝܢ, not ܬܪܝܢ, as L. prints.

18

Father, but passible in the flesh in that He is of our nature. For God the Word did not suffer in His own nature, but in flesh [1] of our nature; and He who personally united this to Himself suffers in our likeness.   And Gregory the Theologian defined the matter and called Him impassible in the Godhead, passible in the assumption of flesh.[2]   And He is one and the same in the miracles and also in the passions; and by dispensation He made our passions His own, voluntary and innocent ones, in flesh which was passible and mortal and of our nature, intellectually and rationally possessed of a soul.   And this all the time of the dispensation He allowed to be passible and mortal for the purpose mentioned above with respect to His Humanisation, I mean that He suffered not in semblance but in reality.   For in the flesh that was capable of suffering He endured voluntary and natural and innocent passions and the death by the Cross; and by a miracle befitting God, that of the Resurrection, He made and rendered it impassible and immortal and in every way therefore incorruptible, since it came from the union and existence [3] in the womb, which [4] was holy and without sin.   While recognising, therefore, the distinction between the elements which have combined[5] to form the unity of nature, I mean the divine and the human nature, we do not separate them from one another; also we do not cut the One and ineffable into or in two natures, nor yet do we confound Him by rejecting the distinction between the Godhead and the manhood, but we confess Him to be one out of two, Emmanuel.

"And, thus believing and taking my stand upon this belief, as upon a rock, I also anathematise the deviations from the truth which have been made by both sides, and the impious and erring men who went before them as their

---

[1] Read ⏑ for ⏑ before ⏑⏑, as in the parallel passage in ch. 25 (p. 290).

[2] Greg. Naz. *Or.* xl. 45.

[3] For ⏑⏑⏑ read ⏑⏑⏑ or ⏑⏑⏑.

[4] If "the womb" is the antecedent we must read ⏑⏑ for ⏑⏑; but possibly the antecedent is "the union."   Cf. p. 290, note 4.

[5] ⏑⏑⏑, "ran," here and in the parallel passage in ch. 25 seems to be used to represent συνέδραμον, though no such meaning is recognised in lexicons.

leaders [1] (I refer to Valentine and Marcion and Arius and Macedonius and Eunomius and Apollinaris and Eutyches), and those also who owing to the union with the Word have vainly and impiously confessed the flesh which was derived from us and was personally united to God the Word to be impassible and immortal, and have introduced a semblance and a phantasy as belonging to the great mystery of the immutable and veritable Humanisation of the Lord; and I anathematise also Paul of Samosata and Photinus and Diodorus and Theodore and Nestorius, and also Theodoret and Andrew and Hibo and Eutherius and Alexander of Hierapolis and Irenæus the twice-married and Cyrus and John [2] and Bar Tsaumo the Persian and the Synod of Chalcedon and the Tome of Leo and those who say that He is made known and exists in two natures, *i.e.* our Lord Jesus Christ after the ineffable union, and do not confess that there is one aspect,[3] one person and nature of God the Word, who became incarnate and became man. On the basis of these apostolic and divine and blameless doctrines, holy brother ours, I give you the right hand of communion, a communion which I will hold fast till my last breath, while I will not consent to hold communion with any man who thinks differently from this, because Basil says, ‘He who[4] communicates without discrimination with the foolish [5] is separated from the freedom [6] of Christ.’[7] For I know that you also, pious one, hold these things [8] fast, and have [9] for a long time laboured. For who is there who in our times has undergone such a contest, removing from place to place, that his faith may not be shaken? And in you I see the doctors of the Church, because you have duly set the lamp

---

[1] MS. ‍‍‍‍‍, not ‍‍‍‍‍, as L.

[2] After this name the names of Theodoret and Andrew are accidentally repeated in the MS.

[3] πρόσωπον.   [4] Insert ? before ‍‍‍   [5] ἰδιώτης.

[6] For ‍‍‍ (παῤῥησία) Mich. has ‍‍‍ (παράδεισος).

[7] I do not know from what part of Basil's works this quotation is taken.

[8] The MS. has ? before ‍‍‍, which L. does not print.

[9] There seems to have been another letter before ‍‍‍, and I insert ‍. So Mich.

visibly on a stand, shining, as you do, in deed and word. It will be worthy therefore of your piety in consideration of these things to gladden us by instruction in return for our letter." And the rest, consisting of the greeting of the epistle.[1]

CHAPTER XXII

THE TWENTY-SECOND CHAPTER, THE EPISTLE OF SEVERUS TO ANTHIMUS

" To[2] our all-pious and all-holy brother and fellow-minister, the patriarch Anthimus, Severus greeting in our Lord Jesus Christ our God.

" For the letter[3] of your chastity Paul the apostle shall give me a precedent for crying aloud in very opportune time, ' Thanks be unto God for His ineffable gift ' :[4] for immediately upon your accession to the see of the patriarchal throne of the Church in the royal city you determined in the exaltation of the primatial see for the sake of the right religion to despise that which to others is an occasion for betraying their faith. For in those who wish to follow the divine commandments and, as it is written, to go after the Lord, the wisdom of the Most High places fitting thoughts, in deacons and presbyters and patriarchs according to the order of their priesthood; insomuch that the patriarch Abraham, after he had settled in many and divers countries, came to a certain country and drank copiously from a well that sprang from it, which was named the Well of Oaths, because[5] he made oaths and treaties with the barbarians who lived near the country, and he planted fair and fruitful plantations ; and, lest his thoughts should be dissipated in them, he called there upon the name of the Lord, the everlasting God, and, as he said to Him, ' Thy thoughts shall not go after the beauty of things that are seen and forget God in the pleasant delight of the sight,

---

[1] Given by Mich.   [2] Mich. fol. 174.

[3] The sentence, as it stands, is ungrammatical, but this is clearly the meaning; there is the same difficulty in Mich.

[4] 2 Cor. ix. 15.   [5] Omit O before ܘܐܠܘ.

for He alone is from everlasting, and hath made the things
that are seen bright to the eyes and pleasant to the taste':
and Scripture goes on to relate thus: 'Abraham planted a
piece of land by the Well of·Oaths and called there on the
name of the Lord, the everlasting God'[1] (and some have
explained it to be wood-land and some plantation-land).   In
the same way, therefore, your piety after having settled in
other countries has come to the head of the oaths,[2] as to a
piece of land fair in produce, I mean the see of the royal
city, which is rich in the pomp[3] of the world, and drinks
from the plentiful abundance of the stream.   And, when
you perceived that certain men wish to be perverted to a
reprobate mind, differing[4] from the pure unadulterated
coinage, well tried in the orthodox faith, you did not allow
the eyes of your mind to go astray through the beauty of the
world and the splendour of its vanities, which pass away;
but, after the pattern of the patriarch Abraham, you called
there upon the name of the Lord, the everlasting God,[5]
whose merciful Word became incarnate[6] and became man,
that is, in order that the second Adam might in truth die
the death that had prevailed over us[7] and overthrow its
eternal dominion, a death which it was not possible for
impassible and immortal flesh to endure, because that which is
impassible and immortal is not capable of suffering and dying.
For, if He did not die our death for our sins and destroy this

---

[1] Gen. xxi. 33.

[2] ܪܹ̈ܫ ܩܰܘ̈ܡܳܬܐ. Perhaps the original Syriac translator of this letter wrote
ܪܹ̈ܫ ܩܰܘ̈ܡܳܬܐ, the chief see; but Mich. has the same as our text, and, as the
divergences between him and our text in these letters show that he drew not from
our author but from a common source, we must not emend.

[3] φάντασις.   [4] Read [ܦ.]ܠܰܚ.

[5] What follows in Mich. is entirely different from our text.   Moreover, not only
is the transition at this point abrupt, but the sentence is of doubtful grammar, the
personal ܩܢܽܘܡܐ being used with a feminine pronoun.   Probably, therefore, a leaf
has been lost; but, as what follows is not in Mich. and cannot easily be joined on
to his text, I leave the text as it stands.   A leaf ends at this point.

[6] The MS. has ܐܬܒܣܪ, not ܘܐܬܒܣܪ, as L. prints.

[7] The MS. has ܥܠܝܢ, not ܥܠܘܗܝ, as L. prints.

death in flesh resembling our passions [1] when He rose from the dead, we are strangers and alien to the benefit of the Resurrection. For 'Christ died for our sins,'[2] cries Paul; and again, 'Since by man came death, by man came also the resurrection of the dead. For, as in Adam all die, so in Christ shall all live';[3] and again, 'Since the children partook of flesh and blood,[4] He also in like manner partook of the same, that through death He might bring to naught him that had the power of death, that is, Satan, and might deliver them who through fear of death were all their lifetime under subjection to bondage. For He received not of angels, but of the seed of Abraham did He receive. Wherefore it was right that in all things He should be made like unto His brethren.'[5] Now the seed of Abraham was the passible body of our race, which God the Word, the Ruler of All, united to Himself personally from the Holy Virgin, in order that with Him He might raise our race, which had fallen under the power of death, inasmuch as He was the firstfruits of our race. So also, since He is one nature and person, it is manifest that the incarnate Word of God of His own will endured the assay and assault of human [6] and natural and innocent passions. And the signs, even the human ones, He utters in a divine fashion (?),[7] and performs some of them in a manner befitting God and some in human fashion. And we do not on account of the difference of the energies and the utterances and the miracles [8] and the passions fall into the division of the two natures after the ineffable union and divide these things, the utterances and tokens and energies,[9] forasmuch as we know that it is the same who wrought the miracles and who suffered and spoke in a divine manner and after the dispensation.

[1] This is an awkward construction, and we should perhaps insert a word, rendering "resembling us in our passions."

[2] 1 Cor. xv. 3.   [3] 1 Cor. xv. 21, 22.   [4] Insert ‍O before ‍‍ܡܕ.

[5] Heb. ii. 14–17.   [6] MS. ‍‍ܐܢܫܐ‍, not ‍‍ܐܢܫ‍, as L.

[7] Probably some words have dropped out in this sentence.

[8] Read ‍‍‍ for ‍‍‍

[9] It would accord better with the following clause if instead of ‍‍ܟܠܗܝܢ ‍ܘܡܟܬܒܢܘܬܐ we read ‍ܟܠܗܝܢ ‍ܘܬܕܡܪܬܐ, "the passions and miracles."

"These, to speak briefly, are the foundations on which the faith and confession of Christ rest, and 'to them nothing can be added, and from them nothing can be taken away.'[1] I[2] use opportunely in connexion with these things the holy words of Koheleth, and with application to those who have swerved from the king's highway and have gone in a crooked way and rejoice in evil perversity, but,[3] as the Scripture said, 'in the Spirit which speaks parables,'[4] according to the law which was before delivered unto the Church by the apostles."

And again a little lower down in the epistle he says,[5] "On these terms I undertake to participate in communion and also in inseparable conjunction with your piety and with those only who hold and also preach these things with you, and those who hold or say anything different I reject as strangers and aliens to our communion; and I avoid the foolishness that is in these men, as also your messenger said, as a thing that makes us alien to the boldness[6] of Christ and supplies many with an occasion to sin. But, as one of those men of wisdom in divinity also says, 'By reason of foolishness many have sinned.'[7] For, if so be that we stand upon this watch-tower and place of observation and proclaim this to those who are under our power, we shall hear from them combs of honey, even good words, and the sweetness of them is healing to the soul.

"Since therefore you have chosen for yourself to contend in a good struggle and have confessed a good confession, cry out like the prophet Habakkuk, 'I will stand upon my watch

---

[1] Eccles. iii. 14. I owe this reference and the translation of the difficult sentence which follows to Dr. Hamilton. I can scarcely think that this sentence represents what Severus wrote, but, as Mich. has practically the same, any corruption must be older than our author. See p. 277, note 2.

[2] Mich. fol. 175.

[3] Mich. omits "but," and in place of ܡܬܠܐ, "parables," has ܟܬܒܐ, "the Scripture," making the clause run, "as is said in the Scripture in the spirit of Scripture, saying."

[4] The reference is probably to 1 Cor. xiv. 2, as Dr. Hamilton suggests.

[5] A fragment of the letter not contained in our author is found in Add. MS. 12,155, fol. 110, and the whole intervening portion, including this fragment, is given in Mich.

[6] Insert ܠ before ܦܪܗܣܝܐ.

[7] Sir. xxvii. 1.

and walk upon a rock,'[1] and despise them that strive below. And, if so be they place you under curses and anathemas, say to God with David with great fitness, 'They shall curse,[2] and Thou shalt be blessed: let them that rise up against me be ashamed, but Thy bond-servant shall rejoice.'[3] For also those who profess a sound faith according to the utterance of the apostle 'are come unto Mount Tsiyon,[4] and unto the city of the living[5] God, unto Jerusalem in heaven, and to innumerable companies of angels, and to the Church of the firstborn, which are written in heaven.'[6] Now, how can a man, shooting from the earth, hit those that are in the Church that is in heaven and mingle with it? For in vain will he toil and without profit will he stretch his bow, even if he dare to shoot upwards; for upon himself will the arrows that are shot come down: for we listen also to one of the wise men, who says thus: 'He that casteth a stone upwards casteth against his own pate';[7] only if so be we continue unto the end, armed in the breastplate of the right faith and girt about in every place with all kinds of spirits.[8] Now of this conjunction with your piety, which has been brought about for us by this canonical letter, tending both to unity of spirit and to be a bond[9] of peace, as the apostle said,[10] I will send information to our fellow-minister my lord Theodosius, the holy Pope and archbishop of the great and Christ-loving city of Alexandria, who labours in apostolic fashion, and undergoes a contest and stands in danger on behalf of the true word, and increases the efficacy[11] of the talents intrusted to him every day by means of industry, and rejoices constantly in the manifestation of them. And do you write to him,

---

[1] Hab. ii. 1.

[2] Read [Syriac] for [Syriac].

[3] Ps. cix. 28.

[4] Read [Syriac] for ? before [Syriac].

[5] The MS. has [Syriac], not [Syriac], as L. prints.

[6] Heb. xii. 22, 23.

[7] Sir. xxvii. 25.

[8] Mich. has [Syriac], "with the arms of the Spirit," and therefore probably read [Syriac] instead of [Syriac]. The former, no doubt, represents what Severus wrote.

[9] Read [Syriac] for ? before [Syriac].

[10] Eph. iv. 2.

[11] The MS. has [Syriac], not [Syriac], as L. prints.

even as you have written to us, and grasp him with the same hands of concord, and write and enter into communication with him by a communicatory letter in accordance with the rules and laws of the holy Church. Wherefore the love of God that is in you should take care to perform your part towards him also, and it shall be to you, according to the prophecy of Isaiah, ' a wall and an outwork ' ;[1] as shall come to pass. And greet your brotherhood. That which is with me greets you in our Lord."

CHAPTER XXIII

THE TWENTY-THIRD CHAPTER, THE EPISTLE OF SEVERUS TO THEODOSIUS

" To[2] our all-pious and all-holy brother and fellow-minister, the chief priest, my lord Theodosius, Severus greeting in our Lord.

"In the Book of the Judges, which is the Book of the Tribes, he said that the tribe of Judah invited the tribe of Simeon his brother to community of lots, urging him, as to brotherly assistance, in these words: ' And Judah said unto Simeon his brother, Come with me into my lot, and let us fight with the Canaanites; and I likewise will go into thy lot. And Simeon went with him.'[3]   But I invite your person, holy brother, not to the community of war and fighting and to give a helping hand for the sake of lots of inheritance, but rather to the community of peace and concord, and[4] on account of a gain made by the Church which Christ, even God, purchased with His own blood, a wonderful addition.   For the holy Anthimus, the chief priest, who has been judged worthy to tend the Church of the royal city, severing the bonds and snares of the bitterness of the heretics, and repelling now their deceitful arts, now his open attacks,[5] has embraced our com-

---

[1] Isa. xxvi. 1.   [2] Mich. fol. 175 ff.   [3] Judg. i. 3.

[4] The MS. has O before ܥܠܝ, which L. does not print.

[5] Severus must have written "their open attacks"; but, as Mich. also has the singular possessive, we must not emend.   See p. 277, note 2.

munion, holding the sound and pure faith. And to my meanness he has sent a letter, containing a covenant of communion upon a perfectly orthodox confession, and he has anathematised by name everyone who is a heretic and an alien; and his mind is not estranged from the commandments and ordinances of the Lord, which our spiritual fathers left as holy laws, upon which[1] we all ought to gaze earnestly and say, like the enduring Job, 'Gazing upon righteousness, I will not turn away.'[2] So I eagerly and with goodwill welcomed this event which has happened as the gift of God, and I repeated the saying of the divine Scripture, 'This day we know that the Lord is with us, that all the peoples of the earth may know that the power of God is mighty.'[3] For this is written in Joshua the son of Nun.

"And it would indeed have been right that the[4] holy archbishop Anthimus should first apply to your evangelical[5] throne and offer to you the firstfruits of concord; but the necessity of this time and the distance of the country and the hurry of events changed the due order of things; and because this was done in secret; for as a wise doctor of divine doctrines you know what is written in the record by John the Theologian rather than Evangelist,[6] that the disciples were assembled with the doors shut for fear of the Jews, and that the great God and our Saviour, Jesus Christ, while the doors were shut, appeared inside by a miracle, and stood in the midst and said, 'Peace be with you.'[7]

"I have therefore attached to this letter a copy of my own letter of concord and that of the God-loving chief priest, the man above mentioned, which were composed under fear of the Jews, and have sent them to your Holiness. But the religious presbyter and steward, Theopompus,[8] also has certainly[9] already given you an account of this proceeding (for he also has communicated with you[10] in this counsel and

---

[1] Read ‏ܒܗܘܢ‎ for ‏ܒܗ‎.   [2] Job xxvii. 6.

[3] Josh. xxii. 31, iv. 24.   [4] Read ‏ܗܘ‎ for ‏ܗܘܐ‎.

[5] The MS. has ‏ܐܘܢܓܠܝܐ‎, not ‏ܐܘܢܓܠܝܘܢ‎, as L. prints.

[6] Mich. "beyond the other evangelists."   [7] John xx. 19.

[8] MS. Theopomptus.   [9] πάντως.   [10] Mich. "with us."

action), because I believed that the love of God that is in you would rejoice and exult over it, especially when you met with the canonical letters containing the covenants.

"But know, O pious brother, beloved by me above all things, that these demands of the Chalcedonians [1] differ in no way whatever from the promised covenant of Nahash the Ammonite, which he wished to make with the Children of Israel, who said to him, 'Make a covenant with us, and we will serve thee'; but he cruelly and barbarously returned answer, 'On this condition will I make a covenant with you, that you pluck out all your right eyes; and I will lay a reproach upon Israel.' [2] We are therefore in need of much watching and of immutable faith, and of prayers and entreaties that He that keeps Israel will not slumber nor sleep, and that He will turn the reproach upon those that are rich and boastful, and we may not become 'a scorn and a reproach to them that are round about us,' [3] as David somewhere sings, while falling from divine things, they also confess human things; for no trust is to be placed in unbelievers and enemies of God. But to you, who are understanding in divine things, what is here said is matter of knowledge."

CHAPTER XXIV

THE TWENTY-FOURTH CHAPTER, THE EPISTLE OF THEODOSIUS TO SEVERUS

"To [4] our all-pious and all-holy brother and fellow-minister, the patriarch, my lord Severus, Theodosius greeting in our Lord.

"O being beloved by me above all things, rock of Christ, and guardian of the pure faith who cannot be shaken, very excellent is the blessing granted to our time, which has displayed your spiritual constancy to the holy Churches of God. We are also in good hope and are confident that the blameless pattern of your virtue, which we possess, will be preserved

---

[1] Insert � before ‎ܟܠܩܝܕܘܢ‎. [2] I Sam. xi. I, 2.
[3] Ps. lxxix. 4. [4] Mich. fol. 176, 177 r.

for you.[1]   But I do not know which of your virtues to admire; for what is there among your qualities which is either defective or which stands in need of superfluous description? If so be I admire the severe manner of your lovely life, the virtue of chastity attracts me to it, and the glorious purity of right faith, which justly demands to be placed before them all, and your life[2] of labours endured for a long time for God's sake, and your flight from place to place, and the fact that in everything you have chosen to suffer, in order that we may not be perverted from the right faith.   In the same faith how many times have you under stress of events boldly cried with Paul, 'Who shall separate me from the love of Christ?   Shall tribulation or distress or persecution?'[3]   But in what category shall we place the exactitude of your teaching, whereby those that err are reproved and deceit is plucked out by the roots, while those that believe are delivered and are planted into the right faith?   And it seems to me as if I heard Christ, even God, saying to you what He said to Jeremiah the divine prophet: 'Behold! I have put My words in thy mouth.   Behold! I have this day set thee over nations and over kingdoms, to root out, and to pull down, and to destroy, and to build, and to plant';[4] and again what He said about Paul: 'He is a chosen vessel unto Me, to bear My name before the nations, and before kingdoms, and before all Israel.'[5]

"These are your qualities, O divine father,— qualities which it is perhaps easy to admire, but difficult to carry fully into action, even as now also by the watchful labours of your pious soul good deeds have been done to the Church of God. For in Christ Jesus those who were before far off have become near.   The pious Anthimus, who will be henceforth renowned for character and faith, the chief priest and true pastor of the Church of the royal city, has of his own will become a communicator with you, pious one, and with us, and walked after our right faith; who has banished and rejected snares and disturbances, and has trampled on transitory and unstable

---

[1] Possibly we should read ‎ܠܢ‎, "for us"; so Mich.

[2] Read ‎ܩܘܒܠܗܘܢ‎ for ‎ܥܘܒܠܗܘܢ‎.   [3] Rom. viii. 35.

[4] Jer. i. 9, 10.   [5] Acts ix. 15.

profit, inasmuch as he has learned to believe that human greatness is nothing,[1] and has boldly proclaimed the right and unfailing faith ; so that on account of this which has happened how we rejoiced and how we gave thanks to God and what spiritual festival we celebrated, O honoured father ours, it is not possible to say in words.

" Now he has made a firm covenant in a canonical letter and sent it to our evangelical throne, as indeed your Holiness also has already stated even in your honoured letter. And in the things which he has written he has declared the whole exactitude of the sound and right faith, while he has spurned with the anathemas everything that is deceitful and heretical, professing that he holds and proclaims these things with us, and says these things, since he is a communicator with those in whose communion our holy Church also rejoices, and professing that from those from whom we turn away he also turns away. He has therefore mentioned by name and anathematised those other names of the impious heresy, and the impious Synod held at Chalcedon, and the epistle of Leo. And, when we had with all possible care considered [2] the things written to us by the pious man and minutely examined them all, and had found that nothing in them was alien from the right faith, and we saw that there also everyone who is opposed to us was attacked,[3] we all the more admired your judgment upon them ; for with the things which were canonically written to you, holy one, by the pious Anthimus upon the divine doctrines we found [4] those also which were written to us to be in accord. Since, therefore, we have found the letter of concord and communion of the holy Anthimus to be of such sort, I will, like the prophet, cry out in due season, ' Let the heavens rejoice from above, and let the clouds sprinkle righteousness,'[5] because the Lord has had mercy on His people, and such good reforms have been brought to pass for the holy Church of God.

" With outstretched hand, therefore, we have accepted the event, and on our own part also hasten to conclude similar

---

[1] Insert ܀ before ܠܟܐ܂

[2] Read ܐܬܟܠܣ for ܐܬܟܣ.

[3] Lit. "shot at with arrows."

[4] Omit ܀ before ܐܬܟܣܡܗ.

[5] Isa. xlv. 8.

covenants; and we have admitted the pious man to the closest communion with us, and have indited[1] a return letter to him, in which we have clearly set forth the right faith of the fathers and exposed the evil character of the faith which pollutes feeble understandings. And of the document on account of which we have entered into communion with him, and will give it to any who shall be hereafter, of this we have sent a copy to your fatherhood, because we did not wish that any of your rights should cause you jealousy,[2] and especially those which have to do with our holy Church. And then of necessity I say that the fact that you observe towards the evangelical see the prime honour which is due to it, and express the same in writing, as the things written to me declared you to do, was in truth worthy of your holy soul, which is careful to do everything with judgment and in accordance with the will of God. But I plainly declare my feeling that my chief honour, and one which gives me great joy, is that honour which is justly paid to you by everyone. With confidence, therefore, pious father ours, I unhesitatingly assent to whatever[3] rightly seems good to you with regard to the holy Church, considering that, as[4] befits your fatherhood, you will not cease from action and advice which will be of benefit to the Church.

"But so much for these things. But as to ourselves, O honoured father ours, by what distresses and human humiliation we are now surrounded, every kind of plot[5] being concerted against us, in order that we may either flee of our own accord, or that we may be expelled by force by others, while they may be granted time[6] here also to do their own deeds and lead astray the holy Church, I wished to declare in this letter

---

[1] The MS. has ܐܬܝܣܒܢ, not ܐܬܝܣܒܢ, as L. prints.

[2] Mich. "to deceive you in any of our affairs." He read therefore ܕܚܣܘܪܟ for ܕܝܩܪܟ, ܠܝܬ for ܠܟܘܢ, and ܠܟܠܢ for ܢܟܠܟ, which probably represents what Theodosius wrote.

[3] Read ܥܠ for ܕ before ܐܠܟ.   [4] Insert ܕ before ܠܚܡܐ.

[5] I read ܥܘܠܙܐ for ܥܘܠܙܐ. No point either above or below the letter is visible in the MS. Mich. ܠܟܠܐܘܗܝ ܠܟܘܢܕܐ.

[6] The MS. has ܐܬܒܐ, not ܐܬܒܝ, as L. prints.

also (for thus especially should we incite you, who sympathise with us, to prayer on our behalf), but it is not right for us to add load to load and burden to burden. But by only saying this much about the greatness of the stress [1] I make it plain that we are in very truth in need of your pious prayers."

And so on with the rest of the epistle. [2]

CHAPTER XXV

THE TWENTY-FIFTH CHAPTER, THE EPISTLE OF ANTHIMUS
TO THEODOSIUS OF ALEXANDRIA

" To [3] our all-pious and all-holy brother and fellow-minister, the patriarch, my lord Theodosius, Anthimus greeting in our Lord.

" Christ Jesus our God, who called simple and unlearned men and fishermen to be apostles and teachers, and called those who were before these from feeding a flock to be kings and prophets, who has chosen weak things and despised things, as the divine apostle said, [4] He it is who has now called me also, the mean one, to the work of this spiritual ministry in the judgments which He knows, to be the head of this holy Church of Constantinople. I therefore, the sinner, remembering the utterance of the Lord spoken [5] through Ezekiel, ' As for thee, son of man, I have given thee as a watchman unto them of the house of Israel ; and, if thou hear [6] the word at My mouth, and give forewarning [7] from Me, saying unto the sinner, If thou sin, thou shalt die the death, and thou tell not the sinner, that he may take warning, nor yet the impious, that he may turn from his way and live, the wicked man shall die in his wicked-

---

[1] ἀνάγκη.

[2] Given in Mich.

[3] Mich. fol. 177.

[4] 1 Cor. i. 27, 28.

[5] Read]ܐܡܪ[for]ܐܡܪ[, and so it appears to be corrected in the MS.

[6] The MS. has ܬܫܡܥ, not ܬܫܡܥ, as L. prints.

[7] The MS. has ܘ before ܬܙܗܪ, not ?, as L. prints. So Mich., though it cannot represent what Anthimus wrote.

ness, but his blood will I require at thine hands,'[1] and the commandment of the apostle to Timothy about the blamelessness [2] of the bishop's office, am beset with fear and trembling. And, when besides these things I contemplate also the turmoil which is increasing in the holy Churches and on the side of those who do not believe rightly, because they have reckoned religion as a means of profit for a time, and speak wickedness on high against their head, and divide God the Word, who became incarnate without variation and became perfectly man, I am beset with weeping and groans, and I mourn over myself, because I am unworthy. But trust [3] in God comforts me, as it is said, 'Look [4] at the generations of old and see; who hath trusted in the Lord and been confounded? or who hath abode in His fear and been forsaken? or hath called upon Him and He turned away from him? Because the Lord is compassionate and merciful, and forgiveth sins and saveth in time of affliction.'[5] Therefore all my hope and my thoughts [6] are set upon Him, that He will see our state and will hear,[7] He who made the eyes and planted the ears, and that He will reprove the turbulence of those who prevent right ways, and will call like the true shepherd who laid down his life for his sheep, because He said, 'No man shall snatch them out of mine hands':[8] for He foreordained your Holiness to stand at the head of the people of Alexandria the great, and established you as a tiller of the Church, not in calm, but in the turmoil of storms, that you might guide the ship above the waves into the peace of the harbour of Christ our God by the holy and adored Spirit.[9] For by the prayers of your holy fathers, the former rulers, you have, as it were, received the trust of standing at the head of a people which walks after the teaching of the fathers, and contends for its pastor unto death in word and deed.

---

[1] Ezek. iii. 17, 18.

[2] MS. ܟܟܡܟܬܐ, not ܟܟܝܟܐ, as L.   [3] Omit ܠ before ܣܒܪܐ.

[4] Read ܐܬܒܩܘ for ܐܬܒܪܩܘ.   [5] Sir. ii. 10, 11.

[6] The MS. has ܘܪܥܝܢܝ, not ܘܪܥܝܬܝ, as L. prints.

[7] The MS. has ܢܫܡܥ, not ܢܫܡܐ, as L. prints.

[8] John x. 29.   [9] Or, "wind."

" Embracing, therefore, union with you and brotherly unanimity in Christ and the laws [1] of the Church, we declare by this Synodical epistle that we cleave to the one definition of faith, that of our three hundred and eighteen holy fathers at Nicæa, which also the one hundred and fifty who assembled here against the fighters against the Spirit ratified, and to the holy Synod which met at Ephesus with the assent of Celestine and in the presence of Cyril, who in the twelve chapters demolished the doctrine of Nestorius. To these I assent, and I embrace the rest of his writings; and I receive the formula of Zeno uniting the Churches, which aimed at the annulling of the Synod of Chalcedon and of the Tome [2] of Leo. And I confess that God the Word, the only Son, who was begotten of the Father in eternity, through whom all things were made, Light of Light, living image of the Father and sharing His nature, in the last times became incarnate by the Holy Spirit and of Mary the Virgin, and became a man perfectly without variation and confusion, in everything like unto us except sin; and He remained God immutable, and, when He assumed our attributes, He was not diminished in His Godhead; and that which was derived from us He made His own by dispensation by a natural union. For He who was begotten without time and without a body of God the Father, the same underwent a second birth in flesh, inasmuch as in an ineffable manner He became incarnate of a virgin mother; and, after she had borne Him, she continued in her virginity; and we justly confess her to be the *Theotokos*, and that He who was born of her in the flesh is perfect God and perfect man, the same out of two natures one Son, one Lord, and one Christ, and one nature of God the Word who became incarnate; and each one of the natures which combined to form an indivisible unity remained without confusion. And so He is very rightly one of the holy and connatural Trinity, both before He took flesh and after He took flesh, and a fourth number was not added to the Trinity; and He is impassible in that He is of the nature of the Father, but passible

---

[1] Insert O before [Syriac].   [2] Read ? for [Syriac] before [Syriac].

19

in the flesh in that He is of our nature.   For God the Word did not suffer in His own nature, but in flesh of our nature; and He who personally united this to Himself suffered in our likeness.   And Gregory the Theologian defined the matter and called Him impassible in His Godhead, passible in the assumption of flesh.[1]   And He is one in the miracles, and also in the passions, and by dispensation[2] He made our passions His own, voluntary and innocent ones, in flesh which was passible and mortal after our[3] nature, endowed with a soul and an intellect, and passible and mortal all the time of the dispensation; for He suffered not in semblance but in reality, and in flesh that was capable of suffering He suffered and died on the cross; and by a Resurrection befitting God He made and rendered it impassible and immortal, and in every way incorruptible, since it came from the union of the womb, which[4] was holy and without sin.   While recognising, therefore, the distinction between the elements which have combined to form the unity of nature, I mean between the Godhead and the manhood, we yet do not separate them from one another; also we do not cut the One into or in two natures, nor yet do we confound Him by rejecting the distinction between the Godhead and the manhood, but we confess Him to be one out of two, Emmanuel.

" And, thus believing and taking my stand upon this belief, as upon a rock, I also anathematise the deviations from the truth of such and such men."

And the rest, consisting of the greeting in the epistle.

[1] Greg. Naz., *Or.* xl. 45.

[2] Read ܣܟܪܒܐ ܠܝ for ܣܟܪܒܐ, as in the parallel passage in ch. 21 (p. 274).

[3] Read ܕܠܢ for ܕܢ.

[4] Read ܗܘ for ܗܝ; or, perhaps, rather omit ܗܘܐ, and take ܦܪܘܩܘܬܐ as the antecedent, as in ch. 21 (p. 274, note 4).

CHAPTER XXVI

THE TWENTY-SIXTH CHAPTER OF THE NINTH BOOK, THE EPISTLE OF THEODOSIUS TO ANTHIMUS THE CHIEF PRIEST

" To [1] our all-pious and all-holy brother and fellow-minister, the archbishop and patriarch, my lord Anthimus, Theodosius greeting in our Lord.

" And how else could it have come about that you, a chief priest wise and watchful towards the Creator of all things and their Saviour and God, should in the midst of events openly show yourself crying out like Jeremiah the divine prophet, ' I have not wearied of going after thee, and the day of a man have I not desired,' [2] except that you despised such human honour, and placed the observance of religion before all things? The thing, therefore, which has been thus done by your Holiness is great without controversy, and all the believers who have heard of it are already wondering at it, while hereafter also all the bond-servants of the Lord who shall be, hereafter will wonder at it, when it is duly proclaimed in all the holy Churches. But it is no higher than the rest of your apostolic and truly sublime and holy life. For it was truly fitting for you, who by unceasing energy in ascetic exercise have mortified your earthly members, that you might speak [3] in the words of Scripture, and with Paul are able to say, ' I am crucified with Christ ; nevertheless I live, yet now not I, but Christ liveth in me,' [4] after the manner of Moses the great to esteem the reproach of Christ greater riches than the treasures of this world, and to choose rather to be afflicted with the people of God than to enjoy the temporal [5] pleasure of sin. [6]

" For I, who am feeble, judge that it is on account of my shortcomings that I endure all the troubles which befall me ;

---

[1] Mich. fol. 177 *v.*   [2] Jer. xvii. 16.

[3] The MS. has ܐܬܡܠܠ, not ܢܬܡܠܠ, as L. prints.

[4] Gal. ii. 20.

[5] Insert ܕ before ܚܛܝܬܐ.   [6] Heb. xi. 25, 26.

but, since I am bound to represent the Church which is under the evangelical throne, which [1] is now enduring many ills (and how many it is enduring is not easy to say), therefore in due season I say as the divine Paul said, 'As the sufferings of Christ abound in us, so also is our consolation great in Christ.' [2] For the fact that you, the pious chief priest and patriarch of the royal city, should use boldness on behalf of the right and apostolic faith, and should be eager to show that in respect of the strict observance of the divine doctrines you are of one mind and one accord with Severus, the holy patriarch of the Eastern Churches, has almost made me forget in the evangelical see and acceptation of the divine Mark the whole of the troubles which are upon us. For, 'what thanks can we render to God?' [3] For this apostolic saying also do I use on account of the help with which He has helped His holy Churches, who has now stablished you as a stablisher of these, and as a foremost fighter in the danger to religion. For you have shown, O pious man, that you have dwelling in you the holy utterance [4] of the Lord, which says, 'Fear not them which kill the body, but are not able to kill the soul; but rather fear Him which is able to destroy soul and body in hell,' [5] and that you 'reckon that the sufferings of this time are not worthy to be compared with the glory which shall be revealed in us.' [6] While, therefore, your spiritual light so shines before men, God is glorified in this great increase of those that are being saved, which His true Church receives.

"So it is with joyful exultation and delight that I have canonically [7] received your piety's letter of concord and union, which has just been brought to me, [8] because the holy patriarch Severus above mentioned told me beforehand that it was coming to me, who is the cause of all blessings and benefits to the Church of Christ and to me ; and he has also sent me, as befitted him, a copy of what you canonically wrote to one

---

[1] Read ‏ܘܗܝ‎ for ‏ܗܘ‎.

[2] 2 Cor. i. 5.

[3] 1 Thess. iii. 9.

[4] Insert ‏ܡܠܬܐ‎ after ‏ܕܒܟ‎.

[5] Matt. x. 28.

[6] Rom. viii. 18.

[7] Perhaps read ‏ܩܢܘܢܝܬܟܘܢ‎, "your canonical letter"; so Mich.

[8] What follows in our text is omitted by Mich.

another, which also made it clear that your communion was brought about with great caution and great benefit. And, while inditing this letter with my whole heart, I say the same things to your Holiness which also I wrote to him,[1] that I confess as the one definition of faith and accept that which was laid down by our three hundred and eighteen holy fathers at Nicæa through the Holy Spirit, and ratified by the Synod of one hundred and fifty and by that at Ephesus, which was assembled by our father Cyril, who in the twelve chapters rejected Nestorius; and I accept also the formula of Zeno uniting the Churches, which aimed at the annulling of the Synod of Chalcedon and of the Tome of Leo, while I confess that God the Word, of the nature of the eternal Father, Light of Light, Very God of Very God, became incarnate and also became man by the Holy Spirit and of Mary the ever-virgin, in flesh endowed with a soul and an intellect after our nature, and was made like unto us in everything except sin, for, 'sin He did not, neither was guile found in His mouth,'[2] as the Scripture said. For it was right and just that the nature which was vanquished in Adam should in Christ put on a crown of triumph over death. And so also the apostle said, 'Since the children partook of flesh and blood,[3] He also in like manner partook of the same, that through death He might bring to naught him that had the power of death, that is, Satan, and might deliver them who through fear of death were all their lifetime subject to sin.'[4] But, if we were vanquished in another nature, and the Word of God did not partake of it or make the same flesh which was assumed from us and personally united to Him impassible and immortal through the union[5] with Him, as some foolishly say, our faith is vain, because it is no great thing that Satan

---

[1] Not in the letter given above (ch. 24), but in the letter of Theodosius to Severus upon his election to the see (Brit. Mus. Add. MS. 14,602, fol. 2–4).

[2] 1 Pet. ii. 22.

[3] Insert ‏ܡܘܕ‎ after ‏ܒܣܪ‎, as necessitated by the plural following. So also in the letter to Severus (Add. MS. 14,602).

[4] Heb. ii. 14, 15.

[5] The MS. has ‏ܚܕܝܘܬܐ‎, not ‏ܚܢܝܘܬܐ‎, as L. prints.

should be vanquished by the Lord ; but in a body which was passible and of our nature He suffered innocent passions, and underwent death, and trampled on the sting of sin, and dissolved the power of death. Now, if He received the seed of Abraham, and in everything was made like unto us His brethren except sin, as the wise Paul said, and through death, which He underwent in His own flesh, vanquished Satan, who had the power of death, while He remained beyond the assault of passions in that He is recognised to be and is justly God, on account of His victory we glory, because we have been delivered from the yoke of bondage. Who is there, therefore, who will not marvel at the accuracy of the divine words, which everywhere supply due direction and in the same words refute the 'semblance' of Eutyches, and those who are like him, and the doctrine of Nestorius ? For he says that Christ partook of our likeness in flesh and blood ; and, that no one might think that He did so in phantasy, he went on to say that He partook of the same that through death He might bring to naught the power of death.

"Moreover they contend against those who divide the one Christ into two[1] natures by the example of children. For,[2] as the child and the man, who is made up of soul and body, is one out of two, and the two are called one nature, though the soul was not converted into flesh nor the body changed into the essence[3] of the soul ; so also Christ, who consists of the two elements, the Godhead and also the manhood, which have a perfect existence, each in its proper sphere, is one and is not divided ; and the union is not confused in Him in that [He united to Himself personally flesh of our nature and][4] allowed it in all the dispensation to be passible and mortal (but the same was holy without sin), and by the Resurrection made and rendered it impassible and immortal and in every

---

[1] The MS. has ܥܠ̈ܬܐ, not ܥܠ̈ܬܐ, as L. prints.

[2] Mich. fol. 177 *v*, 178 *r*.

[3] οὐσία.

[4] The sentence, as it stands in the text, is unintelligible, and from a comparison with the letter to Severus in Add. 14,602 it is clear that the bracketed words have fallen out.

way incorruptible. For our former[1] father Cyril said, 'He first raised His body in incorruption, and He first exalted it to heaven.'[2] So believing therefore, I anathematise such and such."

And the rest, consisting of the greeting in the epistle.

[1] ܩܘܡܬܐ has perhaps crept in from below (Hamilton).
[2] I do not know the source of this quotation.

BOOK X

In this tenth Book also and in the sixteen chapters contained in it, which are set forth below, are included the events which successively happened from the year fifteen, the year eight hundred and forty-eight according to the era of the Greeks,[1] down to the end of the year thirteen, the year eight hundred and fifty-nine of the Greeks,[2] still in the time which is concerned with this serene king of our day, Justinian.

The first chapter, concerning Ephraim, who went down to the East.

The second, concerning the doings of Bar Khili at Amida in the years fifteen and two.[3]

The third, concerning Cyrus, a presbyter of the town of L'gino,[4] who was burned in the *tetrapylon* of Amida.

The fourth, concerning the epistle of Rabbulo of Edessa to Gemellinus of Perrhe about those who eat the sacrament like ordinary bread.

The fifth, concerning the dedication of the church at Antioch, and also the Synod which was assembled by Ephraim.

The sixth, concerning Khosru, king of Persia, who went up and took Sura and Berrhœa and Antioch.

The seventh, concerning Belisarius, who went down and took Sisaurana, a fortress in Persian territory.

The eighth, concerning Khosru, who went up and took Callinicus and the other camps[5] on the frontier[6] of the Euphrates and the Chaboras.

---

[1] 537.

[2] One of these numbers must be erroneous, for the thirteenth year of the indiction ends with Aug. 31, 550, while the year 859 of the Seleucids ends with Sept. 30, 548. The latter is probably right, as the fall of Rome, with which the Book ends, was on Dec. 17, 546.

[3] 537 and 539. [4] Text "L'gin." [5] κάστρα. [6] λίμιτον.

The ninth, concerning the plague of tumours.

The tenth, concerning Martin and Justus, who entered Persian Armenia and returned.

The eleventh, concerning Khosru, who went up to Edessa and did not take it, and returned.

The twelfth, concerning James and Theodore, the pious believing bishops, who were consecrated and sent to the East and intrusted with the leadership.

The thirteenth, concerning the country of Lazica, which was conquered by Khosru.

The fourteenth, concerning the lack of corn and the scarcity of vegetables which occurred in the years nine and ten.[1]

The fifteenth, concerning Rome, which the barbarians took and sacked.

The sixteenth, concerning the decorations and buildings of Rome.

THE TENTH BOOK

CHAPTER I

THE FIRST CHAPTER[2]

When[3] Severus and Anthimus, the believing chief priests, had been driven out[4] by the king, as mentioned in the ninth Book above, and had withdrawn from the royal city on the arrival of Agapetus of Rome, who soon after died at the end of the month of March in the year fourteen,[5] as also did Sergius the *archiatros*, who brought him, then Ephraim, who held the see of Antioch in the East, was strengthened and invigorated, and upon his sending a message [to the king] (?)[6] there was sent

---

[1] 546 and 547.

[2] The words ܩܘܟܠܐ and ܩܦܠܐܘܢ seem to have been transposed, the text reading "book I, chapter 10."

[3] Mich. fol. 173 *v*.

[4] The MS. has ܐܬܛܪܝܘ, not ܐܬܛܪܕܘ, as L. prints.   [5] 536.

[6] In this chapter the MS. is very much torn and obliterated. The words in brackets are conjectural supplements.

[a force of Romans] (?)[1] and Clement[inus the tribune (?) : and] he received orders in the year fifteen[2] to traverse[3] the Eastern jurisdiction and to go all round it, and himself to give admonition in words, while Clementinus was to use force to make the inhabitants of the cities in the East accept the Synod, as had been done by the natives of Italy, the land of Rome.   And this same Ephraim, accompanied by Clementinus, went [to] Berrhœa and Chalcis and Hierapolis and Batnæ and Edessa, and to Sura and to Callinicus and the rest of the frontier,[4] and to Rhesaina and to Amida and to Constantia ; and he induced many persons to submit, some by words and by promising[5] them the friendship of the king, and some by fear of threats and also exile and spoliation of goods and degradation from their ranks[6] and exclusion from all trades ; and others they hunted and drove from country to country, among them the monks, who were found approved in the faith and true believers in time of trial.   And, as the winter was a severe one, so much so that from the large and unwonted quantity of snow the birds perished and . . . . , there was distress . . . among men . . . from the evil things. And[7] . . . in various countries . . . From the hill of Singara [in the land] of the Persians they took (?) . . . John, the

---

[1] This supplement is made probable by the account in Elijah's life of John of Constantia (ed. Kleyn, p. 47).

[2] 536-7.   [3] Read ܠܡܚܪ for ܠܡܚܪ.   [4] λίμιτον.

[5] The MS. has ܘܡܫܬܘܕܐ, not ܘܡܫܬܘܕܝ, as L. prints.

[6] ἀξίας.

[7] The MS. is here very indistinct, and, as Land's text is very incomplete, I give the text which I follow, conjectural supplements being enclosed in square brackets :

believing [bishop] of Constantia, [by means of] a man named Cons[tantius (?)], and he was imprisoned in A[n]t[i]o[ch] and afflicted and . . . he would not change but continued . . . until the beginning of the year one[1] [in] prison [and there] ended [his life] . . . and they were expelled . . . and lived in [various] countries . . . [until] the year three.[2] . . . Khos[r]u . . . and went up [to] S[ura] and Berrhœa and Anti[o]ch. Now Theodosius of Alexandria was summoned by the king to come to him, and went up with a few bishops from his jurisdiction; and he would in no wise accept the Synod of Chalcedon, until in the year one[3] Paul was appointed to the see. And, when Theodosius and the bishops who were with him came before the king, their [arrival] was announced by letter[4] to Ephraim . . . thence . . . But[5] The[odosius and those who were] with him [appeared] before the king and . . . , and without . . . , and they were removed . . . , and there they lived,[6] and the queen was studious in showing them honour, and[7] no one [of] their acquaintances or other discreet men was prevented from seeing them [or] ministering to them. . . . Now there went up . . . in [the year fif]teen,[8] and also (?) . . . the king . . . much[9] . . . he[10] told him about [a . . . man] named But[11] . . . , [who plotted] a rising[12] in Dara in the summer of the year, who was put to death. And he freed the king from distress of mind, but in what way I have not sure enough information to state, and therefore keep silence.

1 537-8. 2 540. 3 537-8.

4 ܐܬܟܬܒ[ܠ ܡܠܟܬ]ܐ ܗܘ[ܝ].

5 ܐ[ܬܚܙܝ]ܘ ܕܝܢ ܬ[ܐܕܘܣܝܣ ܘܕ]ܥܡܗ ܠܡܠܟܐ.

6 [ܥܡܪ]ܝܢ.

7 ܘܠܐ ܡܬܟܠܝܢ ܗܘܐ ܐܢܫ [ܡܢ ܝ]ܕ̈ܘܥܝܗܘܢ ܘܡܢ ܦܪ̈ܘܫ[ܐ ܐ]ܢ̈ܫܐ
ܕܢܚܙܐ ܐܢܘܢ [ܐܘ ܕܢܫ]ܡܫ ܐܢܘܢ.

8 537. A year ending with—*καιδέκατον* can hardly in this place be other than fifteen.

9 ܘܐܦ (?) . . . ܡܠܟܐ . . . ܣܓ[ܝ].

10 ܐܡܪ ܠܗ ܥܠ [ܐܢܫ . . . | . . . ܕ]ܫܡܗ ܒܘܛ . . . | [ܕܒܥ]ܐ ܕ
ܐܢܛܪܣܝܐ ܒܕܪܐ | ܒܩܝܛܐ ܕܠܗ ܕܫܢܬܐ | ܕܐܬܩ[ܛ]ܠ.

11 Or possibly Kut . . . 12 *ἀνταρσία*.

And, because Paul who succeeded[1] Th[eo]d[osius] (?) in the see . . . , he shut up . . . [2] on account of zeal for the faith [in] a bath and suffocated him ; and this man's son he arrested and put in the guard-house, that he might not make his father's death known.   But it so happened that he escaped and made his way to the queen, and through the believers who knew his father he told the news of his fearful death. And on this account Ephraim of Antioch was sent to Alexandria, and Abraham Bar Khili [accompanied him] ; and, as they passed[3] through Palestine, they took with them a monk named Zoilus.   And they went to Alex[andria and] investigated the action of Paul ; and they drove him from his see and enthroned Zoilus, a Synodite,[4] in the city : and in order to protect this man from the violence [of] the people of the city they appointed[5] Acacius Bar Eshkhofo[6] of Amida[7] tribune[8] of the Romans there.

CHAPTER II

THE SECOND CHAPTER OF THE TENTH BOOK, CONCERNING THE DOINGS OF ABRAHAM[9] [BAR KHILI AT AMIDA]

[Syriac text]

[2] Mich. : "he suffocated his archdeacon"; but I cannot get this from the letters remaining in our text.

[3] MS. *[Syriac]*, not *[Syriac]*, as L.

[4] συνοδικός.   [5] Only *[Syriac]* is visible.   Read *[Syriac]*.

[6] *I.e.* son of a cobbler.

[7] The MS. has *[Syriac]*, not *[Syriac]*, as L. prints.

[8] χιλίαρχος.

[9] Here the MS. breaks off.   The words in brackets I supply from the headings in the introduction to this Book.   The whole of this chapter and the following are missing.

CHAPTER IV

FROM THE EPISTLE WRITTEN BY RABBULO TO GEMELLINUS, BISHOP OF PERRHE, ABOUT THOSE WHO INSULT THE MYSTERIES AND SUPPORT THEMSELVES UPON THEM LIKE COMMON BREAD [1]

"I [2] have heard that in your country of Perrhe certain of the brethren, whose cloisters [3] are not known,[4] and others of the distinguished [5] archimandrites of the place, have falsely given out concerning themselves the vain report that they do not eat bread, and have lyingly uttered of themselves the empty boast that they do not drink water, and have asserted [6] of themselves that they abstain from wine. Accordingly I am afraid [7] to mention that I have heard that they insult the body and blood of Jesus, the Son of God; but, since necessity constrains me, I will, as is right, be bold to say things which are what these men are not afraid to do, who madly and without discrimination offer [8] the body and blood of Jesus Christ our Lord, that is, the holy and hallowing body which they have received and the living and life-giving blood which they have drunk. These men, whom I do not know how to name,[9] are said impiously to satisfy the constant wants of their natural hunger and thirst upon it, and it is impossible for them of their own will to go

---

[1] This letter is also published by Overbeck in his edition of Ephraim (p. 231 ff.) from our MS. The beginning of it is quoted by Assemani (*B. O.* vol. i. p. 409), as from John of Ephesus ap. "Dion." This extract bears no indication that it is part of a letter, and varies considerably from our author.

[2] Jo. Eph. ap. "Dion." (Assem., *B. O.* i. p. 409); Mich. fol. 179 ff.

[3] Read ⲟⲟⲗⲁⲫⲃⲟⲁⳙ for ⲟⲟⲣⳙⲃⲟⲁⳙ, with Jo. Eph.

[4] The MS. has ⲱⲗⲁⲣⲃ, not ⲱⲗⲣⲃ, as L. prints.

[5] For ⳃⲓⲁⳙⲟⲁⲫⳙⲟ read ⳃⲓⲟⲗⳙⲟⲁⲫⳙⲟ. Mich. ⲫⲟⳕⲁⳙⲟ.

[6] The MS. has ⲟⲟⳙⳙⲟⲁⲫ (so Overbeck), not ⲟⲟⳙⳙⲟⲁⳙ, as L. prints.

[7] Only ⳙ is visible. Read ⳙⲗⳙⲁⳙ. Mich. ⳃⲥⳗⲃⲟ.

[8] The MS. has ⲱⲃⳕⲓⳙⲃⲟ, not ⲱⲗⳕⲓⳙⲃⲟ, as L. prints.

[9] Read ⳃⲗⳕⲃⳙ for ⳃⲗⳕⲟⲁ. Mich. ⲫⳙⲟⲗⲁⳙⲟⲁⳙⳙ.

even one day without the oblation, which is their sustenance; but continually every day a large quantity of food is supplied by the sacrament. And for this reason also they richly [1] leaven the particle which they prepare, and diligently dress [2] it, and carefully seethe it, that it may serve them for food, and it is not treated as the mystery of the body of Christ, symbolised [3] in unleavened bread. And for the rest it is said that, whenever hard pressed, they even offer common unconsecrated bread over one another's hands and eat it. And it is said to be their practice, when walking from one place to another or going on a long journey, to satisfy their natural hunger and thirst on the same body of our Lord two or three times in one day, and, as soon as they have reached [4] their destination, in the evening they are said again to offer the oblation and partake of it as if fasting; nay, even in the holy days of the fast of Lent they presume to act in this manner without fear of God and without shame before men. And men who, as they say, refrain from [5] bread and water every day are found to eat the holy bread and drink the blessed wine on such glorious days, on which even the vile themselves abstain.

"Now the Spirit that is in me, holy brother ours, bears witness for me that I tremble to write to your reverence all that I have heard about them, because my heart could not really believe it: [6] and I would it had been possible for you to have known what I wish to learn [7] without an epistle or a word from me, and for these same men to have received correction from your uprightness, because neither did I wish that either you, my lord, or they should know what is rumoured about

---

[1] Instead of ܩܘܪܒܢܐ, Jo. Eph. has ܩܘܢܝܬܐ, "for a long time." Our text is supported by Mich. ܠܬܘܣܦܬܗ.

[2] Read ܡܨܠܠܝܢ for ܡܚܠܝܢ, with Jo. Eph.; so Mich. ܡܨܠܠܗܘ. If the MS. reading be retained, the meaning is "cleanse."

[3] Instead of ܡܬܠܝܠ, Jo. Eph. has ܡܬܐܟܠ, "eaten." Mich. omits the clause.

[4] Read ܡܛܝܢܘ for ܡܛܡܣܘ, with Jo. Eph.; so Mich. ܘܡܛܝܐ.

[5] Read ܡܬܟܠܝܢ for ܐܟܠܝܢ? (Hamilton). Mich. ܡܟܠܝܢܘܗܝ.

[6] Read ܐܠܝܢ for ܐܝܠܘ.

[7] We rather require "to state."

them.   Do not then think yourself or let them suppose that it is because I believe the evil report about them that I write these same things to you concerning them; but, being still in doubt, I say to others also that it is impossible that such a great sin should be committed by men who have ever been baptized in Christ.   For they say that, as soon as they have performed the sacrament in the paten, they lightly [1] (?) eat [2] as much as they want of it, while the cup of the blood each of them tempers with hot water, whenever they can, like mixed wine and drinks it, and again fills it and gives it to his neighbour; so that owing to the quantity of wine which they drink under the name of the sacrament they are often obliged actually to spit it out of their mouth.

"O what transcendent impiety, if it is the fact that these men, despising their life, have converted the revered vessels of the sacrament, which on account of the mysteries contained in them even for spiritual heavenly purposes men fear to approach boldly, into vessels of service for their belly, and did not even so much as remember the punishment which Belt'shatstsar, the heathen king, received and was reproved! For, because in the vessels of the service of God he purposed to insult God like a rebel by using them in a carnal fashion, the likeness of a palm of a hand that wrote was sent from on high to write on the wall of his house the righteous sentence of condemnation for his presumption: [3] though how indeed can the vessels of service of the temple in Jerusalem be compared to the glorious vessels of service of the body and blood of the Son of God?   For neither is the showbread of the priests of Israel in any way worthy to be compared to the glory of the transcendent mystery; and, if so be any man likens the bread of the table, which David ate when he was hungry, to the life-giving body of God the Word, we ought to look upon him as

---

[1] ܩܘ̈ܝܠܐ, "easily."   This word occurs three times in this chapter with reference to eating, and it is difficult to see the meaning of it.   Mich. has here ܟܠܒܩܗ, "sufficiently," and perhaps, therefore, read ܣܘܩܝ; in the other places he omits it.

[2] Read ܐܟܠܝ for ܐܟܠܘ.   So Mich.

[3] Read ܦܪܘܢܗ for ܦܪܘܣܝܘܢܗ.   Mich. ܗܣܪܗ.

a foolish man who does not distinguish the body and blood of the Lord from showbread: wherefore he is an offender against the body and blood of our Lord. For the showbread scarcely cleansed a bodily pollution, even when baptisms of various kinds were combined with it and observance of this and that: but this life-giving body and blood of our Lord Jesus not only purged and hallowed the sin of the soul and of the body in those who received it with faith, but also caused God to be in us, and that by His Spirit, as we are in Him by our body;[1] for, 'Whoso eateth My body and drinketh My blood,' says the Son of God, 'he is in Me and I in him, and I will raise him up at the last day.'[2] In another way again we may understand the greatness of this service, which is a new one, delivered to us by God the Word, from the hard and severe punishment which Paul pronounced against those who have enjoyed it, beyond that received[3] by those who offend against the old service introduced by Moses; for he said, 'If so be he who transgressed against Moses' law died without mercy at the mouth of two or three witnesses, of how much sorer punishment will he be worthy who hath trodden under foot the Son of God, and hath counted the blood of His covenant as that of an ordinary man, and hath done despite unto the Spirit of His grace, wherewith we were sanctified.'[4] Who is there, therefore, who is so mad as to compare this bread of life, which came down from heaven by virtue of its union with God the Word and gives life to the world, to the showbread with its earthly seasoning? But the opinion of anyone who thinks or acts in this manner[5] is manifest and is, moreover, clearly apparent, for he who thus madly receives it reckons it to be in fact common bread, as he sees it, and does not believe the Son who says, 'The bread which I will give is My body, which is given for the life of the world;'[6] for it follows that not only is the bread in the body of Christ, as is seen by them, but in the bread is the body of the invisible God,[7] as we believe and

---

[1] Mich. "his body."   [2] John vi. 54, 56.

[3] Omit ܐܬܬܒܝܢ; so Mich.   [4] Heb. x. 28, 29.

[5] Insert ؟ before ܗܢܐ.   [6] John vi. 52.

[7] Mich. "Son of God."

receive the body[1] not to satisfy our bellies but to heal our souls. For[2] those who eat the holy bread in faith do in it and with it eat the living body of God the Sanctifier, and those who eat it without faith receive sustenance, as with other things necessary for the body. For, if the bread is carried off and eaten by enemies by violence, they eat common bread, because those that eat it have not faith, which perceives its sweetness:[3] for the bread is tasted by the palate, but the virtue which is hidden in the bread is tasted by faith. For that which is eaten is not only the body of our Saviour, as we said a little before, but whatever is mingled with it, as we believe: for the virtue[4] which is not eaten is mingled with the edible bread, and to those that partake of it becomes one with it, even as the hidden heavens mingle with the visible water, and from them a new birth is born. For the Spirit secretly hovers over the visible water, so that from it a likeness of the heavenly Adam is born anew.[5] And, just as in the visible water, in order that it may impart to all who are outwardly baptized in it, there is invisible life, so also in the external bread food is hidden and concealed, of which everyone who rightly partakes obtains immortal life; and we believe the saying of Paul, that those who receive it slightingly obtain from it injury to soul and body and are not profited, even if they are reckoned among the believers. And would that they obeyed the saying of the apostle, who says, ' And let a man examine himself, and then let him eat of that bread and drink of that cup; and he that eateth of it when he is not fit for it eateth and drinketh condemnation to himself'![6] And the same proclaims by his words that it is on account of our enmity against the body and blood that the various infirmities

---

[1] A comparison with Mich. shows that at this point a leaf has been lost in our MS., which I supply from Mich. An extract from this portion is also contained in Add. MS. 14,532, fol. 67, from which it has been edited by Overbeck (*op. cit.* p. 230). The translation of the part which exists only in Arabic I submit with great diffidence, having but a very superficial knowledge of that language.

[2] Here the extract in 14,532 begins.

[3] Mich. has "its life," and therefore read ‫ܡܚܘܗܝ‬ for ‫ܚܝܠܘܬܗ‬.

[4] Mich. "the body."

[5] Here the extract in 14,532 ends.   [6] 1 Cor. xi. 28, 29.

20

and unexpectedly sudden death have befallen us by a righteous judgment. " By reason of this happen most of the diseases and sicknesses, and the fate of those who fall asleep suddenly. But, if we judged ourselves, we should not be judged. But, when our Lord judges us, He gives us a discipline, that we may not be condemned with the world."[1] And, if those who were in the fixed days of service were now to partake, they would receive one substance only of the body of life. If it be done without the sorrow of repentance, and men do not receive it in faith with reverent fear, even if they do not also commit a deed contrary to their faith, then they are guilty of the body and blood of the Lord, as Paul said, because they do not discern the Lord's body. What punishment can be too severe for this, too great even to be applied to the judgment of those who approach it without fear and do not receive an aliment of faith, but a thing necessitated by their hunger? O, what insolence is this, to which the divine retribution is not equal, if it slays the man! Who does not fear even heaven, when men satisfy the needs of their bodies on a coal of devouring fire, as if it were common bread? Who is not frightened at this statement, that of the coal on which our life depends, that which the seraph[2] revealed to us, grasping it with a fiery forceps in his hand, to signify the sublimity of our mystery, and, while meditating upon it with reverence, approached to take hold of it, of this these men eat to satiety and without fear? And before the body which is given for the life of the world their heart does not quake and they are not afraid, and their hands do not tremble or shake, and their knees do not slip that they should fall, when they eat it for the support of bodily life. And perhaps we ought to say that our Lord also in His full knowledge of all times knew the deed of these men; and for this reason, after they had eaten of the legal passover and were satisfied, then blessed the bread and gave it to His disciples, in order that these men might not say that, after He had blessed, they were satisfied (but, after they were satisfied, He blessed, when the Master and His disciples took a small particle of it); and over the cup He said,

---

[1] 1 Cor. i:. 30–32.   [2] MS. ܐܠܟܣܐ‎ ; cf. Isa. vi. 6.

'Take, drink ye all of it,' that they might understand by this that it was of this small cup of which twelve persons drank.

"And it must needs be said that they thought of themselves that they would attract the admiration of simple persons (?)[1] by their abstinence from bread and wine, and did not understand that the laughter of the intelligent would defeat and overcome them, and would fall upon their heads, prevailing over the praise of ignorant persons like them. Those who are like them have in all this unpardonable sin accepted for themselves glory from perishing men, even though it did not result to them. It is not fit that they should be named men, but, in justice, they should be named rabid dogs; for the sign of rabid dogs is this, that they suddenly attack the body of their master to eat it.

"And a man who has forbidden himself bread ought to be empty and not taste anything until the time appointed for him. And this is well known that, when Saul enacted that no one should taste anything on the day of battle until the evening, then Jonathan, because he tasted some honey on the end of his rod, incurred the penalty of death, if it had not been for the violence of the people until he was safe. For 'the foundation of the life of man is bread and water,'[2] says Jesus Bar Asira,[3] the son of Simeon. (Under the name of bread he extended his saying to all food.) And they say of these men that, after they have received the oblation in the morning, and partaken of it yet again in the evening, then they lightly (?)[4] eat other food and lightly (?) feed on dressed beet and pulse.[5] They are said to fill themselves[6] on cheese instead of bread; they are, moreover, in the habit of eating fish with all their pleasant taste; they sate themselves largely

---

[1] ‏ܐܠܩܘܣ‎ (‏ܐܠܩܘܣ‎ (?)).   Neither the reading nor the translation is clear.

[2] Sir. xxix. 21.

[3] Arabic ‏ܠܐܣܝܪܐ‎; but the Syriac must have been ‏ܒܪ ܐܣܝܪܐ‎.

[4] ‏ܩܘܠܛ‎. See p. 303, note 1. Here the Syriac text again begins.

[5] I insert "beet and" from Mich.

[6] Read ‏ܡܣܥܘܠܝܢ‎ for ‏ܡܣܥܘܠܝܢ‎, with Payne Smith. There seems to be some further error in this sentence, but the sense is clear.

on delicious fruit, and they delight in it particularly when dry, besides honey-combs and egg-cakes.[1] And, because the heat of the wine which they drink under the name of the Sacrament inflames them more with thirst, all through the summer season they are said regularly to drink the milk of sheep and goats ;[2] and this again they have done of set purpose, for they have also discovered that the moisture and coolness of milk[3] are found to temper the perpetual burning which results from the wine in their excess.   Now, because of these things, and by reason of them, there is in due season uttered, as it shall be spoken, against them also the righteous reproof of God which He pronounced to Eli because of his sons: 'Behold! I have given you all the good things of the earth, that ye might use them without sin; even as for them I set apart all the offerings of the children of Israel, that they might enjoy them without guilt.   Wherefore have ye also offended against My body and My blood, like those who wrought wickedness against My sacrifices and against My offerings?'   And, since the impiety of these men against God has far surpassed the impiety of those others, which was committed against the people, there has been fear and great trembling in case they should suffer, lest also a punishment like that which went forth against those should be pronounced against them. "'Wherefore,' thus said the Lord, the God of Israel, 'I said indeed that thy house and the house of thy father should minister before Me for ever'; but now the Lord saith, 'Be it far from Me! for them that honour Me I will honour, and they that despise Me shall be lightly esteemed.'"[4] You-see how He rejected them for ever from the priesthood, and made them outcasts and aliens from His house.

"Now, what shall I say[5] of men who are not in unison

---

[1] Or "round eggs": lit. "rounds ($\sigma\phi a\hat\iota\rho a\iota$) of eggs."

[2] Mich. omits "sheep," and adds "instead of water."

[3] The MS. has ܠܚܡܘܬܐ, "bread," which gives no intelligible sense. I read ܚܠܒܐ. So Mich., who, however, has "the moisture of the wine and the coolness of the milk."

[4] 1 Sam. ii. 30.

[5] Mich., apparently reading ܗܕܢܝ for ܘܡܢܐ, "thus he says."

with the prophets of the Old Testament, nor yet resemble [1] the apostles of the New? For they ought at least to have learned from the chief of the apostles, Peter, what his food was; since he has plainly stated in what his bodily life consisted. For, when his chosen disciple, Clement, asked him to allow him to be his only minister, he spoke thus to him, praising his zeal and jesting at his sustenance: 'Why! Who is strong enough for all this ministry? Are we not continually eating bread and olives? or perhaps it may be that sometimes there may also be a cabbage.' [2] Moreover, have they not also received a good tradition from Paul, the preacher of truth? For, behold! he also out of the greatness of his need sent and sold his tunic, and with the price of it it is written that they bought bread only and brought it to him with a cabbage,[3] that by his action he might lay down a law for us also, as in his saying, ' If we have food and raiment, that is enough for us.' [4] And, if it is a small thing for them to liken themselves to the apostles, the baptizers of the world, let them imitate even the Lord of the apostles, the Maker of the worlds, and of all that is in them; unless, perhaps, even the human dispensation of our God is contemptible and vile in their eyes. For, behold! as to our Lord, He has everywhere shown us that He ate bread; and the bread too was not of wheat, but it was of barley, and so were the seven other loaves, which were fruitful and multiplied at His word, and 4000 men ate of them and left seven baskets actually (?) [5] full of bread. And, when He ate the passover with His disciples, unleavened bread was set before Him. And also after His resurrection from the dead He ate bread with His disciples for forty days, that the dispensation of our Lord and His fleshly assumption of a body [6] might be believed by them, as they themselves wrote: [7] ' Jesus went in and out among them.' [8] And the house of Cleopas,

---

[1] Mich. "listen to."

[2] Clem. *Hom.* xii. 5, 6 ; id. *Recog.* vii. 5, 6.

[3] *Act. Paul. et Thecl.* xxiii. (Syriac, Wright, pp. 147, 148; translation, pp. 129, 130).

[4] I Tim. vi. 8.   [5] ‏ܘܐ ܕܝ ܣܗܘ‎ is probably corrupt.

[6] The MS. inserts ‏ܘ‎ before ‏ܩ ܡܪܝܬܗ‎ (so Overbeck), which L. does not print.

[7] MS. ‏ܐܒܒܩ‎, not ‏ܐܒܒܩ‎, as L.   [8] Acts i. 21.

because He did not wish them to recognise Him [1] while walking with them in the way, He blessed over bread and brake it for them within the house, and then they knew Him.

"But these men, as I hear, do not follow in their deeds those that err, nor yet are they in concord with the truth in their actions; for they are not circumcised like the Marcionists, neither are they ascetic after the manner of Christians. For, behold! they are not like those deniers of the truth who eat only pulse or bread, but do not presume to commit a lie at their oblations, neither yet do they resemble [2] us believers who eat common bread in moderation and receive the support [3] of our true life separately.

"Why have these gluttons not trained themselves, so that cheap things only might be enough for them? And why have these guzzlers not accustomed themselves [4] to repel the hunger of their belly with something mean and vile? And wherefore do they not eat ordinary, simple, common bread only? But it is plain that it is in order that they may not afflict themselves. But, if [5] they really wish to afflict their bodies, let them not sate themselves, but eat bread only. And, behold! they are wasted and shrunk and reduced to weakness. But it is plain and manifest that these men do not struggle with their bodies, nor yet do they wrestle [6] with Satan; but for the sake of vain glory they exercise themselves in the tricks of their evil devices, and not in the afflictions of asceticism."

And further the rest of the epistle with proofs from the Scriptures.

---

[1] Read ܢܗܝܘܕܥܘܢܝܗܝ for ܢܗܘܕܥܘܢܗܝ.

[2] Read ܡܟܣܒܘܗܝ for ܡܟܣ ܒܗ ܘܗܝ.

[3] The MS. has ܣܝܥܬܐ (so Overbeck), not ܣܥܬܐ, as L. prints.

[4] Read ܐܠܝܫܘ̈ܩ for ܐܠܝܫܘ̈ܩܗ, as Overbeck. The MS. has a dot both above and below the letter.

[5] The word ܐܢ is accidentally repeated in the MS.

[6] Read ܟܕ for ܟܕ.

CHAPTER V

THE FIFTH CHAPTER, CONCERNING THE DEDICATION OF THE CHURCH WHICH EPHRAIM OF ANTIOCH PERFORMED, AND THE SYNOD OF THE BISHOPS OF HIS JURISDICTION

Ephraim,[1] who was chief priest in Antioch, rebuilt from its foundations the round-shaped church in Antioch and the four *triklinia* adjoining it. And, when he performed the consecration of it, he assembled one hundred and thirty-two bishops from his jurisdiction in the year one;[2] and on the occasion of the dedication[3] of the church he received a contribution from each one of them, such as he pleased, on a lavish[4] scale. And he confirmed[5] the Synod of Chalcedon in a document which the bishops whom he had assembled were required to sign; and they anathematised the holy Severus, the believing patriarch, and everyone who agrees with him and does not accept the Synod.

But God, who makes judgment for the oppressed, after a short time roused up the Assyrian against him and against the city, according to the words of the prophet, who said, "The Assyrian is the rod of Mine anger and the whip wherewith I scourge: against a profane people will I send him, and against a peevish people will I give him a charge, to lead away captives and to take[6] the prey."[7] And two years afterwards, in the year three,[8] Khosru went up against Antioch, as described in the following chapter.[9]

The rest of the tenth Book is wanting in Add. 17,202. The sixteenth chapter and a fragment of the fifteenth are, however, contained in Cod. Rom., and the former exists also in a shortened form in Brit. Mus. Add. MS. 12,154 (fol. 158), from which it is published by Land. Part of the contents of

---

[1] Mich. fol. 173 *v.*   [2] 537-8.   [3] ἐγκαίνια.
[4] Read ‏‏ for ‏‏.   [5] Read ‏‏ for ‏‏.
[6] MS. ‏‏, not ‏‏, as L.   [7] Isa. x. 5, 6.   [8] 540.
[9] There follow in the MS. the words ‏‏ ‏‏, "the sixth chapter."

chapters 6–15 may also be recovered from the fragments of James of Edessa (Brit. Mus. Add. MS. 14,685, fol. 22), and from Michael and Gregory.

FRAGMENTS OF CHS. 6–8 FROM MICH. FOL. 173 *R*; GREG. P. 79, AND JAC. EDESS. *L.C.*[1]

In the eleventh year of Justinian, which is the year eight hundred and fifty of the Greeks,[2] in the month of December (?)[3] a great and terrible comet appeared in the sky[4] at evening-time for one hundred days.[5]   And that year the peace between the kingdoms was broken, and Khosru, king of the Persians, went up and carried off captives from the cities of Sura and Antioch and Berrhœa and Apamea and the districts belonging to them, a bitter captivity.   And the Romans also went down to Persia and carried off captives from the countries of Kurdistan and Arzanene and Arabia.

Then Khosru went up against Callinicus with a great army, and carried off captives from it and from the whole of the southern part[6] of the land between the Rivers.[7]

FRAGMENT OF CH. 9 FROM MICH. FOL. 184 *R*[8]

[Moreover Zachariah the Rhetor also writes concerning this scourge as follows.]

[1] The order and contents of these passages agree so well with the headings at the beginning of this Book, that I make no doubt that they are taken from our author. In general I follow Michael, whose account is the longest.

[2] 538–9.

[3] Or January, it not being stated whether it was the 1st or the 2nd *Khonun*. The month is only in Jac. Edess.

[4] " In the sky " is only in Jac. Edess.

[5] So Jac. Edess.   Mich. has " several days."

[6] " The southern part " is only in Jac. Edess.

[7] Mich. and Greg. afterwards relate the capture of Antioch and Callinicus over again.   As this second account occurs in similar words in " Dionysius " (Cod. Syr. Vat. 162, fol. 71), who writes out John of Ephesus, and is absent in Jac. Edess., it is almost certainly derived from John, a fact which strongly confirms the previous conclusion that the account in the text is derived from our author.

[8] Greg. (p. 80) also quotes a passage relating to the plague as from Zachariah ; but only the last sentence of this is identical with Mich.'s quotation, the rest being identical with a passage quoted by Mich. from Jo. Eph.   It is clear, therefore, that either Gregory has erred or his text is corrupted.

In the Greek version of the prophecy of Ezekiel is a passage referring to the plague of tumours ; and instead of what is stated in the Syriac language, " All knees shall flow with water," [1] he says, " All thighs shall be befouled with pus." [2]   And this plague, which is the rising of a swelling on the groins and in the arm-pits of men, began in Egypt and Ethiopia and Alexandria and Nubia [3] and Palestine and Phœnicia and Arabia and Byzantium (?) [4] and Italy and Africa and Sicily and Gaul, and it penetrated to Galatia and Cappadocia and Armenia and Antioch and Arzanene and Mesopotamia, and gradually to the land of the Persians and to the peoples of the North-East, and it slew.   And those who were afflicted (?) [5] with the scourge and happened to recover and not die trembled and shook : and it was known that it was a scourge from Satan, who was ordered by God to destroy men.

In the city of Emesa was the head of John the Baptist, and many sought refuge with it and escaped : and the demons were disturbed before men, being scattered (?) [6] by the saint.

FRAGMENTS OF CHS. 10, 11 FROM JAC. EDESS. *L.C.,* MICH. FOL. 173 *R*; GREG. P. 79 [7]

The Romans went down and did much destruction in the country of Armenia. [8]

---

[1] Ezek. vii. 17.

[2] This passage is written in the margin of 9. 13 in Cod. Rom., where it is printed by Mai (p. 358) as part of the text (see p. 242, note 1).

[3] Greg. " Libya."

[4] ܩܘܣܛܢܛܝܢܘܣ. If Byzantium is meant, the spelling is strange.   Moreover, the Syrians always call it " Constantinople," or " the royal city."   Greg. omits.

[5] MS. ܐܟܠܐ, " ate"; perhaps we should read ܐܚܕ, " took."

[6] I take ܡܬܒܕܪܝܢ to be an error for ܡܬܒܕܪܝܢ.

[7] The close correspondence of this account of the expedition against Edessa with the heading of ch. 9 seems to show that it is derived from our author.   Jac. Edess., indeed, inserts the capture of Petra between the Armenian campaign and the expedition to Edessa, but only by a slip, for the following sentence, " and from that time the Romans were attacking it " etc. (see ch. 13), must refer to Petra, not to Edessa, as is proved by the sense and by a comparison with Mich.

[8] In Jac. Edess. only.

And again Khosru went up and made an attack[1] upon Edessa, and, not being able to take it, he carried off captives from Batnæ and departed.

FRAGMENT OF CH. 12 FROM MICH. FOL. 186 *v*,[2] AND GREG. *HIST. ECCL.* PP. 215, 217.

And on account of the distress and scanty numbers of the pastors among the Persians there was a man named Cyrus, a believing bishop,[3] who consecrated and ordained priests, and that from the year one down to this year eight.[4]   And, lest the heads of the communities of believers should be blamed, or because the priests who were among the Persians belonged to the opposite party (?), and they were assailed by affliction and trouble, they procured provisions (?);[5] and then after due deliberation they consecrated and appointed chief priests in Arabia; and these were Theodore the monk, a strenuous man, and James, the laborious and industrious, the very strenuous,[6] who was then in the royal city.[7]   And he was to be found everywhere, visiting and exhorting with readiness. And he was a practiser of poverty and an ascetic, and swift on his feet, and travelled like 'Asahel.[8]   And he was a presbyter in the monastery of the Quarry in the village of Gamuwa, which is on the mountain of Izlo.[9]   And by the treaty which he concluded he rescued many from among the Persians.

[1] "And made an attack" is in Jac. Edess. only.

[2] That this passage is derived from our author is shown by the use of the indictional years, which is not found in Jo. Eph.   Moreover, according to our author's own peculiar fashion the numerals are given in Greek.

[3] "Of Singara" is added by Greg.   [4] 538–545.

[5] This sentence (not in Greg.) is extremely obscure and probably corrupt.   The real meaning seems to be that many Monophysites had been carried off by the Persians.

[6] Greg. adds "a simple man."

[7] In Mich. this clause is applied to Theodore, but is followed by the words "This is my lord James Burd"oyo," which seem to be a gloss intended to point out that they really belong to James.   After this Greg. inserts " and they ordained him œcumenical metropolitan."

[8] Mich.   "Active in his journeying, and travelled like a courier."

[9] Greg. adds, "and he began to go round the countries of the East and to give ordination to the orthodox, showing himself in the dress of a beggar, and chiefly on the roads from fear of the persecution."

FRAGMENTS OF CHS. 13, 14 FROM JAC. EDESS. *L.C.* ;
MICH. FOL. 185 *V*; GREG. P. 81 [1]

Khosru, king of the Persians, again went up and carried off captives from [2] Petra, a city in Lazica, and placed a garrison there.[3]   And from that time the Romans continued making attacks upon it for seven years, and then the Persians were defeated and the Romans took it from them.

And at that time there was a scarcity of produce and a lack of the fruit of trees, in the year nine,[4] and there was a famine which destroyed soul and body, and it was followed by emaciation such that a man ate 10 lbs. of bread at one time and whatever other kinds of food he could get with it through greediness and hunger.   And he became swollen and inflated from the food, but was not satisfied, but was hungry and greedy for food, and asked for bread to fill his belly, and so he died.

After this there was a plague among oxen in all countries, especially in the East, and it lasted two years, until the lands remained untilled for lack of oxen.

[1] That this passage comes from our author appears from the juxtaposition of these two events, the campaign in Lazica and the famine, as in the headings above, and from the use of the indictional reckoning with the numeral in Greek ; see note below.

[2] So Mich.   Jac. Edess. has " took."

[3] Here Jac. Edess. interpolates the attack on Edessa (see ch. 11, note).

[4] 546.   The translator of Mich., who alone records the date, has ‏ܩܘ ܒܩ‏ ‏ܗܢܬܐ‏, "in the district of Hanata" ; but no such place is known, and I have no doubt that it is a misunderstanding of ἔνατον, which our author transliterates as ‏ܗܢܬܐ‏ at p. 249, l. 7, 12 ; p. 258, l. 9, l..

CHAPTER XV

ABOUT THE SACK OF ROME, WHICH IN THE DAYS OF JUSTINIAN THE BARBARIANS TOOK AND SACKED [1]

[In the eighteenth year of Justinian, which is the year eight hundred and fifty-seven of the Greeks,[2] the barbarians[3] took Rome, the chief city of Italy; and since they could not guard it, they established themselves in the camp[4] by the side of it, while they left the city deserted and empty.[5]]

In[6] the third year after the sack of the city of Ilium, which was sacked in the days of Samson and Eli the priest in Jerusalem, kings began to be set up in the city of Rome, which was at first called Italy, and the kings who reigned in it were called[7] kings of the Latins. And in the days of Yotham and Ahaz, kings of Judah, Romulus became king there, and he built up the city with great and noble buildings, and it was called Rome after his name; and the kingdom of its inhabitants was called the kingdom of the Romans from the time of Hezekiah the king.

---

[1] The heading and the latter portion of the chapter are in Cod. Rom. The first paragraph, which seems to be derived from the same source, I supply from Mich. and Greg. (pp. 80, 81). A portion of the Syriac Michael containing this paragraph and the description of Rome in the next chapter has been edited by Prof. Guidi (*Bull. della Commiss. Arch. di Roma*, xix. p. 61 ff.).

[2] 546. This was the twentieth of Justinian, and the fact that the same misreckoning is found twice in 12. 4 and once in 12. 5 tends to show that this sentence is derived from our author.

[3] Mich. "the Romans."   [4] κάστρα.

[5] Mich. adds, "of its people. And that you may know what loss to the empire of the Romans was wrought at its capture, behold! I will write out an account, though only in a summary, composed by one that knew and saw its buildings."

[6] Mich. fol. 185 *r*.

[7] The MS. has ܟܠܘܪܬܐ, not ܟܠܘܪܬܐ, as Mai prints.

CHAPTER XVI

[FROM THE ECCLESIASTICAL HISTORY OF ZACHARIAH, FROM THE SIXTEENTH CHAPTER OF THE TENTH BOOK], ABOUT THE OBJECTS[1] AND BUILDINGS IN THE CITY OF ROME[2]

Now the description of the decorations of the city, given shortly, is as follows, with respect to the wealth of its inhabitants, and their great and pre-eminent prosperity, and their grand and glorious objects of luxury and pleasure, as in a great city of wonderful beauty.

Now its pre-eminent decorations are as follows, not to speak of the splendour inside the houses and the beautiful formation[3] of the columns in their halls and of their colonnades (?)[4] and of their staircases, and their lofty height,[5] as in the city of wonderful beauty.

It[6] contains 24 churches of the blessed apostles, Catholic churches. It contains 2 great *basilicæ*, where the king sits and the senators are assembled before him every day. It contains 324 great spacious streets. It contains 2 great capitols. It contains 80 golden gods.[7] It contains 64 ivory gods. It contains 46,603 dwelling-houses. It contains 1797 houses of magnates. It contains 1352 reservoirs[8] pouring

---

[1] ܠܩܘܬܐ is probably an error for ܠܩܒܐ, "decoration," as in Cod. Rom. and in the introduction to this book.

[2] This is the heading in 12,154 (see p. 311). Cod. Rom. has "a description of the decoration of Rome." The chapter has been edited with an introduction, notes, and translation by Prof. Guidi (*Bull. della Commiss. Arch. ai Roma*, xii. p. 218 ff. ; cf. xix. p. 61 ff.), from whose work I have derived much assistance.

[3] Read ܒܩܘܢܐ for ܒܩܘܢܐ.

[4] ܩܣܛܘܢܝܗܘܢ = περίστυλα (Guidi), or possibly προστάδες, vestibules.

[5] Omit ܕ before ܪܘܡܗܘܢ.

[6] Mich. (ed. Guidi); Notitia ap. Jordan *Top. der Stadt Rom*, 2. 571.

[7] The word ܪܘܪܒܐ, "great," has been corrected to ܕܕܗܒܐ in the margin of the MS., though Mai prints both (Guidi, p. 227).

[8] ܩܠܘܣ = κάναλος. *Notit.* "lacos."

forth water. It contains 274 bakers, who are constantly making and distributing *annonæ* to the inhabitants of the city, besides those who make and sell in the city. It contains 5000 cemeteries, where they lay out and bury. It contains 31 great marble pedestals.[1] It contains[2] 3785 bronze statues of kings and magistrates. It contains, moreover, 25 bronze statues of Abraham, Sarah, and Hagar, and of the kings of the house of David, which Vespasian the king brought up when he sacked Jerusalem, and the gates of Jerusalem and other bronze objects.[3] It contains 2 colossal[4] statues. It contains 2 columns of shells.[5] It contains 2 circuses. It contains 2 theatres and one.[6] It contains 2 amphitheatres.[7] It contains 4 *beth ulde*.[8] It contains 11 *imfiya*.[9] It contains 22 great and mighty bronze horses.[10] It contains[11] 926[12] baths. It contains 4 *orbilikon*.[13] It contains 14 *tinon enkofitoriyon*.[14] It contains

[1] *βάσεις*. *Notit.* "arci marmorei XXXVI."

[2] Before ܐܢܕܪ̈ܝܢܛܐ Cod. Rom. has ܐܝܬ ܒܗ, which Mai does not print. It is correctly given by Guidi.

[3] Mich. "and took the bronze gates and other objects."

[4] Read ܩܘܠܘܣ̈ܝܐ for ܩܘܠܘܣ̈ܝܗ.

[5] A misunderstanding of "columnæ coclides."

[6] MS. ܬܪܬܝܢ ܘܚܕܐ, not ܬܠܬܝܢ ܘܚܕܐ, as Mai prints. 12,154 has ܓ "3," and so Mich. *Notit.* "theatra III."

[7] 12,154, ܩܘܢ̈ܓܝܢ = *κυνήγια*. Cod. Rom. ܐܘܪ̈ܝܐ (Mich. ܐܘܪ̈ܝܐ), which Guidi takes to be a corruption of ܬܐܘܪ̈ܝܐ = *θεώρια*. *Notit.* "amphitheatra II."

[8] ܐܘ̈ܠܕܐ = λοῦδοι (Guidi). *Notit.* "ludi IIII." Mich. Arab. adds اهرا, "granaries."

[9] *νυμφεῖα* (Guidi). *Notit.* "nymfea XV" (MS. B "XI). Mich. Syr. ܐܘܠܘܡܦܝܐ ('Ολύμπια), Arab. ملاعب, "places of amusement."

[10] The MS. has ܢܚ̈ܫܐ, "feeble," not ܢܚܫܐ, "bronze," as Mai; but we must read ܢܚܫܐ, and so Mich.

[11] The words ܐܝܬ ܒܗ, omitted by Mai, are in the MS. So Guidi.

[12] Mich. Syr. 56, Arab. "956," and so MS. B of *Notitia*: *cet.* "856."

[13] ܐܘܪܒܝܠܝܩܘܢ = *κοόρτης βιγίλων* (Guidi). *Notit.* "Cohortes vigilum VII."

[14] ܛܝܢܘܢ ܐܢܩܘܦܝܛܘܪܝܘܢ (Mich. Syr. ܐܢܩܘܦܛܘܪ, Arab. انقوفطور) = *Notit.* "quorum excubitoria XIII," "quorum" having been translated *ὥντινων*, and *ὧν* omitted by the Syrian (Guidi).

2 *parenamabole* [1] of special bronze horses. [2]　It contains 45 *sistre*. [3]　It contains 2300 public oil-warehouses. [4]　It contains 291 prisons or *aspoke*. [5]　It contains in the regions 254 public places [6] or privies.　It contains 673 *emparkhe*, [7] who guard the city, and the men who command them all are 7.　The gates of the city are 37.　Now the circumference of the whole city is 216,036 feet, which is 40 miles; the diameter of the city from east to west is 12 miles, and from north to south 12 miles. [8]

But God is faithful, who will make its second prosperity greater than its first, because great is the glory of all the might of the dominion of the Romans.

The eleventh Book, the first three chapters of the twelfth Book, and the beginning of the fourth chapter are missing.

[1] [Syriac] (Mich. [Syriac]) = παρεμβολαί. *Notit.* "castra" (Guidi).

[2] A mistranslation of "equitum singularium" (Guidi).

[3] μαστρυλλεῖα (Guidi).　*Notit.* "lupanaria XLV."　MS. "46."　Read "45" with Mich.

[4] ἀποθηκάρια.

[5] *Notit.* "horrea CCXC" (MS. B "CCXCI"), so that [Syriac] is probably a corruption of [Syriac] (Duval in Guidi); but, as Mich. also has "prisons," the corruption may have existed in our author's original text, and I therefore do not emend.　[Syriac] Guidi takes to be a corruption of "ἀποθῆκαι."

[6] This word (δημόσια) generally means "public baths"; but the translation in the text accords with *Notit.* "latrinae publicae" (the *Curiosum* printed opposite adds "quod est sicessos") "CCXLIIII."

[7] ἔπαρχοι (Guidi).　Mich. Arab. [Arabic], "custodians"; *Notit.* "vicomagistri DCLXXII" (MS. B DCLXXIII).

[8] Here 12,154 adds, "These are exclusive of many things which we have not set down here.　And these things the author set down while weeping for the city, because in his time the barbarians entered it and sacked it."　This MS. omits the sentences containing corrupt or difficult words, as well as the introductory and concluding sentences.　Mich. (Arab. fol. 185 r) has, in place of the concluding sentence, "Verily for the sack of this great city, which was completely burnt at this time by a barbarian people, Justinian the king sorrowed exceedingly, and all the magnates of the kingdom clothed themselves in mourning.　And in those days the king's sorrow was increased by the death of the queen, the blessed Theodora, who departed in the twentieth year of the reign of Justinian, which is the year eight hundred and fifty-nine of the Greeks, and he gave a large quantity of gold on behalf of her soul."　Greg. (p. 81) has the same in a shorter form.

BOOK XII

CHAPTER IV

. . . earnestly [admonished] her not to do this in a vile manner [1] and injure her spirit on account of the future [2] righteous judgment. And she said to him, "How can I worship Him, when He is not visible and I do not know Him?" And after this one day, while she was in her park [3] (and these things were in her mind [4]), in a fountain of water which was in the park she saw a picture of Jesus our Lord, painted on a linen cloth, and it was in the water; and on taking it out she was surprised that it was not wet. And, to show her veneration for it, she concealed it in the head-dress [5] which she was wearing, and brought it and showed it to the man who was instructing her; and on the head-dress also was imprinted an exact copy of the picture which came out of the water. And one picture came to Cæsarea some time after our Lord's passion, and the other picture was kept in the village of Camulia, and a temple was built in honour of it by Hypatia, who became a Christian. But some time afterwards another woman from the village of Dibudin, mentioned above,[6] in the

---

[1] As there is room for another letter before ‏ܗܘܐ‎ and before ‏ܠܟ‎, I read ‏ܗܘܐ‎ and ‏ܠܟ‎. Land's text is unintelligible.

[2] There is room for another letter before ‏ܟܠ‎, and we should probably insert ‏ܕ‎.

[3] παράδεισος.

[4] Read ‏ܕܗ‎ for ‏ܕܠ‎.

[5] φακιόλιον (Brockelmann ποικίλη).

[6] In the lost beginning of the chapter (?).

jurisdiction [1] of Amasia, when she learned these things, was moved with enthusiasm, and somehow or other brought one copy of the picture from Camulia to her own village; and in that country men call it "ἀχειροποίητος," that is, "not made with hands"; and, moreover, she also built [2] a temple in honour of it. So much for these things.

In the twenty-seventh year of the reign of Justinian, the year three,[3] a marauding band of barbarians came to the village of Dibudin and burned it and the temple, and carried the people into captivity. And certain earnest men, natives of the country, informed the serene king of these things, and begged him to give a contribution [4] and to have the temple and the village restored (?)[5] and the people ransomed. And he gave what he pleased. But one of the men attached to the king's person in the palace advised him to have the picture of our Lord carried on a circular progress [6] through the cities by these priests, and a sum of money sufficient for the building of the temple and the village collected. And behold! from the year three until the year nine [7] they have been conveying it about.[8] And I believe that these things happened under the direction of Providence, because there are two comings of Christ according to the purport of the Scriptures, one in humility, which also took place five hundred and sixty-two years before this year nine, which is also the thirty-third of the reign of Justinian, and a future one in glory, which we are awaiting; and this same thing is a type of the progress [9] of the mystery and picture and wreathed image [10] of the King and Lord of those above and those below, which shall be quickly revealed. And, indeed, I admonish my own self and my brethren, since there is fear

---

[1] The word ‏ܡܛܪܦܘܠܝܣ‏ generally expresses metropolitan jurisdiction, so that the expression is equivalent to "in the province of Helenopontus."

[2] The MS. has ‏ܒܢܐ‏, not ‏ܒܢܐ‏, as L. prints.

[3] 554–5.   [4] φιλοτιμία.

[5] ‏ܢܬܩܢ‏. I can find no parallel for this use of the word in the lexicons, but it may perhaps be so rendered at p. 213, l. 10 (L.).

[6] ἐγκυκλία.   [7] 561.

[8] There is perhaps a gap here, as Land marks, though it is not certain that there ever was anything written there. So also in the next line.

[9] ἐγκυκλία.   [10] λαυρᾶτον.

21

of falling into the hands of God, that every man devote himself to affliction and penitence, for he shall be requited for his deeds; for the coming of our God, the righteous Judge, is already near; to whom with His Father and the Holy Spirit be glory.   Amen.

CHAPTER V

THE FIFTH CHAPTER TREATS OF THE POWDER, CONSISTING OF ASHES, WHICH FELL FROM HEAVEN

In addition to all the evil and fearful things described above and recorded below, the earthquakes and famines and wars in divers places, and the abundance of iniquity and the deficiency of love and faith, which have happened and are happening, there has also been fulfilled against us and against this last generation the curse of Moses in Deuteronomy, when he admonished the people who had come out of Egypt, when they were just about to enter the land of promise, and said to them, "If thou wilt not hearken unto the voice of the Lord thy God, and wilt nôt observe and do all His statutes and His commandments, which I command thee this day, all these curses shall come upon thee and overtake thee";[1] and a little further on he speaks thus: "The Lord shall give for the rain of thy land powder; and dust from heaven shall He send down upon thee, until He destroy thee.   And He shall smite thee before thine enemies; and thy carcase shall be meat unto the fowls of heaven and unto the beasts of the earth, and there shall be no man to fray them away."[2]

Such fearful things and more fearful things are coming; for in the year four,[3] on the first Sabbath, which is the Sabbath before [4] the feast of unleavened bread, the heavens above us

---

[1] Deut. xxviii. 15.   [2] Deut. xxviii. 24-26.   [3] 556.
[4] The MS. has ܣܘܒܬܐ, not ܩܘܒܬܐ, as L. prints.

were covered with stormy (?)[1] clouds, brought by the east winds, and instead of the usual rain and moistening water dropped upon the earth a powder composed of ashes and dust by the commandment of God. And it showed itself upon stones and fell upon walls; and discerning men were in fear and trepidation and anxiety, and instead of the joy of the Passover they were in sorrow, because all the things that are written had been fulfilled against us on account of our sins. Now it was the twenty-eighth year of this king.

Now, as regards the scope and sequence of the work, the book has brought us down in chronological order as far as the year four; but as to one chapter, concerning an event which happened here at the end of the year one,[2] which before this year four we omitted, we have retraced our steps like men on the sea through the violence of the waves and record it briefly, it being as follows:—

CHAPTER VI

THE SIXTH CHAPTER OF THE TWELFTH BOOK, CONCERNING BASILISCUS, A PRESBYTER OF ANTIOCH, WHO WENT TO AMIDA WITH AUDONO (?) THE DUKE

In the summer of the year one,[3] when the year was now just drawing to an end, and a council of bishops was being held in the royal city, certain men, their representatives[4] in the cities here, whose names I forbear to record, some of

---

[1] ‏ܣܥܘܦܗ‎. The adverb ‏ܣܥܘܦܗܐܝܬ‎ occurs in 1. 1 (p. 3, l. 22, L.), 7. 6 (p. 215, l. 2), and 7. 9 (p. 224, l. 13); see p. 13, note 6. Here, by a slight alteration of meaning, we may render it "violent" or "stormy," a meaning supported by the expression ‏ܡܝ̈ܐ ܣܥܘܦܐ‎ (stormy water?), which is quoted by Payne Smith from the Lexicon of Bar 'Ali. We might, however, read ‏ܣܥܘܦܐ‎, "thick," as proposed by Smith on 7. 9. The adjective also occurs in 1. 7 (p. 73, l. 5) as an epithet of words, where the meaning seems to be "heated," "violent."

[2] Summer 553.　　　[3] 553.

[4] Read ‏ܟܪܘܟܝ‎ for ‏ܟܪܘܟ‎.

them, as I think, acting out of jealousy (?)[1] or spite, wrote to
their bishops, who were sojourning in the West, in order to
please them and also to gratify their ears, saying, " There
are certain Schismatics,[2] that is, dividers, in the district, and
especially in the land between the Rivers, who are holding
councils and are, as it were,[3] attracting the whole people from
one end to the other to join them, and are in separation from
our Church."   And the bishops there brought the communication which they had received before the king, and he ordered
Audono (?)[4] the duke, who was at Hamimtho, to investigate
the matter in conjunction with Basiliscus, a presbyter of
Antioch ; and they were to reconcile them, if willing, to the
Church.   And, while the matter so stood, Bar Korgis,[5] a
presbyter of Amida, joined them at Hamimtho ; and he
assembled the priests and the inhabitants of the villages in
the district of the trench and put constraint on them, as [6]
well as from the property,[7] so to speak, of Dith, a believing
man, who had lately died,[8] and from Ingilene and Tzophanene.
And, when these men reached the city of Amida, then they
put pressure on the five chaste cloisters of monks [9] there with
the intention of ejecting them ; and they spoke with them and
listened to them.   And they readily met them, and especially
the gentle John the archimandrite, of whom we have mentioned [10]
that he was providentially [11] present, a Greek and a grammarian,
and the earnest Sergius, their visitor ; which men stood at their

---

[1] I read ‏ܢܝܘܐܪ̈ܐ‏ for ‏ܣܝܘܐܪ̈ܐ‏, as Dr. Hamilton suggests.

[2] ἀποσχίσται.   [3] Read ‏ܒܐܘܠܬܐ‏ for ‏ܒܐܘܠܬܐ‏.

[4] This perhaps represents the Teutonic Audwin or Aldwin ; or we might make the
easy correction ‏ܐܘܪ̈ܝܢ‏ for ‏ܐܘܪ̈ܝ‏, and translate "Evodian."

[5] The MS. has ‏ܩܘܪ̈ܓܝܣ‏, not ‏ܩܘܪ̈ܓܝܣ‏, as L. prints.

[6] It is probable that something has here dropped out.   [7] οὐσία.

[8] The MS. has ‏ܢܝܬ‏, not ‏ܢܝܬ‏, as L. prints.

[9] Insert ‏ܕ‏ before ‏ܕܝܪܐ‏.

[10] In the lost portion.   After this it is probable that something has been lost,
since the following statements can hardly apply to John.   In this case we may
render "of whom we have mentioned that [. . . , and X.,] who was providentially
present."

[11] By "πρόνοια."

head, supported by the learned and believing men, John and
Sobbo, and Stephen, an *archiatros* of the city.   And they did
not expel the cloister societies of monks, but they retired to
Izlo.[1]   And, since Peter, the master of the offices, arrived in
the year two,[2] and heard from the monks about the threats
made against them, he withdrew them.   The duke he restrained from again expelling the monks, and censured him.

CHAPTER VII

THE SEVENTH CHAPTER TREATS OF THE MAP[3] OF THE
WORLD WHICH WAS MADE BY THE DILIGENCE OF
PTOLEMY PHILOMETOR, KING OF EGYPT

Now Ptolemy Philadelphus, king of Egypt, as the Chronicle
of Eusebius of Cæsarea declares, two hundred and eighty years
and more before the birth of our Lord, at the beginning of
his reign, set the Jewish captives in Egypt free and sent
offerings to Jerusalem to Izra'el,[4] who was priest at that time;
and he assembled seventy men learned in the law and had
the Holy Scriptures translated from the Hebrew tongue into
Greek; and he stored them up and kept them with him; for
in this matter he was indeed moved by God, in order to
prepare for the calling of the nations who should attain to
knowledge, that they might be true worshippers of the glorious
Trinity through the ministration of the Spirit.
    Yet again about the space of one hundred and thirty years
after him Ptolemy Philometor also was honourably moved and
exerted himself, and by means of ambassadors and letters and
presents, which he sent and dispatched to the rulers of the
countries of the nations, he urged them to write down and
send to him the limits of the lands under their sway and
of the neighbouring peoples, and also a description of their
habitations and their customs.   And they wrote and sent
them to him except the northern region extending to the East

---

[1] The MS. has ܚܠܐ‍, not ܝܠܐ‍, as L.   [2] 553–4.
[3] σκάριφος.   [4] El'azar is meant.

and to the West.   And we have thought it necessary to write it out here at the end for the understanding of the discerning. And the account is as follows:—

[At this point follows an epitome of the geography of Claudius Ptolemæus, whom our author has taken for an Egyptian king.   As no good purpose would be served by publishing a translation of this section, I omit it.   A portion of it is also contained under Zachariah's name in Add. MS. 14,620, fol. 28, with considerable variations from our MS. After the description of the province of Africa this MS. has the curious addition, "and they speak Syriac and Latin." There is another addition to Ptolemy in the notice of the Scenitæ of Arabia Felix,[1] where our author adds, "who are called Sabæans," to which 17,202 further adds, "the same is Sh'ba," while in place of the Sabæans, whom Ptolemy mentions lower down,[2] our author has "the Ofirians, the same is Ofir."[3] These additions are of course due to our author himself or some earlier Christian translator; but there are others which point to a difference of reading.   Thus in place of "'Aθάκαι Aἰθίοπες"[4] he has "others who live in the water, who eat fruit," and to the notice of the Sachalites he adds, "from whence come pearls, and they sail on the water on bladders," an addition which in Nobbe's text of Ptolemy is printed as the note of a Scholiast.[5]   Again to the notice of the frankincense country in Ethiopia[6] he adds, "thence comes beet."   There are a few other places where our author throws some light on Ptolemy's text.   Thus in place of the $\Pi \epsilon \chi \hat{\imath} \nu o \iota$[7] of Ethiopia he has "cubit-men," and, therefore, perhaps read $\Pi \eta \chi \hat{\imath} \nu o \iota$, while among the tribes of Arabia Felix in the place where Nobbe's text has $\varDelta \omega \rho \eta \nu o \iota$[8] our author's reading ܕܘܣܪ̈ܢܝܐ (14,620, ܕܘܣܪ̈ܝܐ) shows that he read "$\varDelta \omega \sigma \alpha \rho \eta \nu o \iota$," as in the text of

---

[1] Ptol. *Geog.* vi. 7. 21.   [2] *Ibid.* vi. 7. 23.

[3] Similarly in place of "τῶν Ἀσαβῶν ὀρῶν" (vi. 7. 24) he has "the mountains of Ofir."

[4] Ptol. *Geog.* iv. 9. 3.

[5] *Ibid.* vi. 7. 11.   Montanus prints it as part of the text, and so it is in the Athos MS. reproduced by Langlois.   Wilberg brackets it.

[6] *Ibid.* iv. 7. 31.   [7] *Ibid.*

[8] *Ibid.* vi. 7. 23.   "Δωρηνοι" is the reading of nearly all the MSS.

Montanus.[1]   Other variations from Ptolemy's text are probably due to carelessness or misunderstanding.   There is, however, óne peculiar variation, of which it is hard to see the origin, in the account of Taprobane, where our author has "and their women are deaf," the corresponding statement in Ptolemy being "ἥ τις ἐκαλεῖτο πάλαι Σιμούνδου, νῦν δὲ Σαλίκη· καὶ οἱ κατέχοντες αὐτὴν κοινῶς Σάλαι, μαλλοῖς γυναικείοις εἰς ἅπαν ἀναδεδεμένοι."[2]   I continue the translation at p. 336, l. 13, of Land's text.]

This description of the peoples of the world was made, as recorded above, by the exertions of Ptolemy Philometor and in the thirtieth year of his reign, one hundred and fifty years before the birth of our Saviour, so that the space of time from that day to the present, which is the twenty-eighth year of the reign of Justinian, the serene king of our days, the eight hundred and sixty-sixth year of Alexander, and the three hundred and thirty-third Olympiad,[3] will be found to be a space of seven hundred and eleven years.   In such a space of time, therefore, how many cities have been built and added among all peoples in the world from the time of Ptolemy down to the present day, and especially since the birth of our Saviour!   And peace has reigned among nations and kindreds and tongues, and they have not observed their former custom, nor has nation stood up to make war or to use their swords against nation, nor have they contended in battle, in that the prophecy has been fulfilled in them which says, "They shall beat[4] their swords into plowshares and their spears into pruning-hooks."[5]

And besides these there are also in this northern region five believing peoples, and their bishops are twenty-four, and their Catholic lives at D'win, the chief city of Persian Armenia. The name of their Catholic[6] was Gregory, a righteous and a distinguished man.

---

[1] So in the case of the tribe who in Nobbe's text are called 'Ομαγκῖται, and in Montanus' 'Ομανῖται, our author's reading, ܩܘܠܣܛܢܝܘ (14,620, ܩܘܠܣܛܢܝܘ), though corrupt, is nearer to the latter than the former, and nearer still to 'Ομαμῖται, which is read by several MSS.

[2] *Ibid.* vii. 4. 1.   [3] 555.   [4] The MS. has ܢܪܕܘܢ, not ܢܪܕܘܢ, as L. prints.

[5] Isa. ii. 4.   [6] Probably the word "first" has dropped out.

Further Gurzan,[1] a country in Armenia, and its language is like Greek; and they have a Christian prince, who is subject to the king of Persia.

Further the country[2] of Arran in the country of Armenia, with a language of its own, a believing and baptized people; and it has a prince subject to the king of Persia.

Further the country of Sisagan, with a language of its own, a believing people, and there are also heathens living in it.

The country of Bazgun,[3] with a language of its own, which adjoins and extends to the Caspian Gates and sea, the Gates in the land of the Huns. And beyond the Gates are the Bulgarians with their own language, a heathen and barbarous people, and they have cities; and the Alans, and they have five cities; and the men of the race of Dadu (?), and they live on the mountains and have strongholds; the Unnogur, a people living in tents, the Ogor, the Sabir, the Bulgarian,[4] the Khorthrigor, the Avar, the Khasar, the Dirmar (?), the Sarurgur (?), the Bagarsik (?), the Khulas (?), the Abdel, the Ephthalite, these thirteen peoples dwelling in tents; and they live on the flesh of cattle and fish and wild beasts and by arms; and beyond them the tribe of the pigmies and of the dog-men, and north-west of them the Amazons,[5] women with one breast each, who live entirely by themselves and fight in arms and on horseback; and there is no male among them, but, when they wish to pair, they go [6] in peaceful fashion to a tribe near their country and hold intercourse with them for a month of days and return to their country; and, when they bear a child, if it is a male, they kill it, and, if it is a female, they preserve it alive; and in this way they keep up their ranks. And the tribe which lives near them is the Harus (?), tall, big-limbed (?) [7] men, who have no weapons of war, and

---

[1] *I.e.* Georgia or Iberia.   [2] Read ܐܪܙܢ for ܐܪܢ.

[3] *I.e.* Abasgia.

[4] This is probably a corruption or confusion, as the Bulgarians are said above to have had cities. The people here meant are perhaps the "Βουρούγουνδοι" of Agath. v. 11.

[5] Cf. Strabo, xi. 5. 1.

[6] The MS. has ܟܠܡܚܪܒ, not ܟܠܡܚܪܒ, as L. prints.

[7] ܟܠܡܦܪܕ. This should mean "cut limb from limb."

horses cannot carry them because of the bigness of their limbs (?).   And to the east again verging on the north are three other black tribes.

Now in the land of the Huns about twenty years and more ago some men translated some books into the native tongue ; and the origin of it, which the Lord brought about, I will relate as I heard it from certain truthful men, John of Rhesaina, who was in the monastery founded by Ishokuni close to Amida, and Thomas the tanner, who were carried into captivity when Kawad carried away captives fifty years and more ago.   And, when they reached the land of the Persians, they were again sold[1] to the Huns and went beyond the gates and were in their country more than thirty years ; and they took wives and begot children there.   But after about this space of time they returned and told us the story with their own mouths as follows :—

After the coming of the captives from the land of the Romans, whom the Huns had taken away with them, and after they had been in their country for thirty-four years, then an angel appeared to a man named Kardutsat, bishop of the country of Arran, as the bishop related, and said to him, "Take three pious priests and go out into the plain and receive from me a message sent to thee by the Lord of spirits, because I am guardian of the captives who have gone from the land of the Romans to the land of the nations and have offered up their prayer to God.   And he told me what to say to thee."   And, when this same Kardutsat, which, when translated into Greek, is *Theokletos*,[2] had gone zealously out into the plain and had . . .[3] called upon God, he and the three[4] presbyters, then the angel said to them, "Come, go into the land of the nations and warn the children of the dead, and ordain priests for them, and give them the mysteries, and strengthen them ; and behold ! I am with you and will deal graciously with you there, and signs shall ye do there among

---

[1] The MS. has O before ܩܘܒܪܐ, which L. does not print.

[2] From Armenian *kardal*, to call, and *Astuats*, God.

[3] MS. apparently ܚܝ ܒܬܘܪ, certainly not ܚܝ ܒܬܘܪܒ, as L.

[4] MS. ܝܐܬܠܘܘܗܝ, without division ; there is no O before it, as L.

the nations, and all that is needed for your service ye shall find." And four others went with them ; and in a country in which no peace is to be found these seven priests from evening to evening found a lodging and seven[1] loaves of bread and a jar of water. And they did not enter by way of the Gates, but were guided over the mountains. And, when they reached the place, they told these things to the captives, and many were baptized, and they made converts among the Huns also. They were there for a week of years,[2] and there they translated books into the Hunnic tongue.

Now at that time Probus happened to be sent on an embassy[3] to those parts by the king, in order to hire some of them to meet the nations in war. And, when he heard from the Huns about these holy men and understood their story also from the captives, he was very eager and desirous to see them. And he saw them, and received a blessing from them, and showed them much honour before the eyes of those nations.

And our king, when he heard from them[4] the facts recorded above, which the Lord so brought about, loaded thirty mules from the territories of the neighbouring Roman cities and sent them to them, and also flour and wine and oil and linen cloths and other commodities and sacramental vessels. And the animals he gave as a present to them, because Probus was a believing and a kindly man.

Now another Armenian bishop also, whose name was Maku (?),[5] was stirred to emulation by such noble deeds and went out after two more weeks of years ; and he was honourably moved and went to the country of his own accord and some of his priests with him. And he built a brick church and planted plants and sowed various kinds of seeds and did signs and baptized many. When the rulers of these nations saw something new happening, they admired the men and were greatly pleased with them and honoured them,[6] each

---

[1] Insert ⟨Syriac⟩ before ⟨Syriac⟩.   [2] Insert ⟨Syriac⟩ before ⟨Syriac⟩.   [3] πρεσβεία.

[4] Perhaps we should read ⟨Syriac⟩, " from him."

[5] The MS. has ⟨Syriac⟩, not ⟨Syriac⟩, as L. prints.

[6] The MS. has ⟨Syriac⟩, not ⟨Syriac⟩, as L. prints.

one[1] among them inviting them to his own district and his own people, and beseeching them to be his instructors : and behold ! they are there to this day. And this same thing is a token of the mercies of God, Who cares for everyone that is His in every place. And henceforth it is the time which is placed in His own power, that the fulness of the peoples may come in, as the apostle said.[2]

For for one week of years the king of Persia also, as those who know relate, has separated himself from the eating of things strangled and blood, and from [3] the flesh of unclean beasts and birds, from the time when Tribonian the *archiatros* came down to him, who was taken captive [4] at that time, and from our serene king came Birowi, a perfect [5] man, and after him Kashowi, and now [6] Gabriel, a Christian of Nisibis. From that time [7] he has understood his food, and his food is not polluted (?) [8] according to the former practice, but rather it is blessed, and then he eats. And Joseph also, the Catholic of the Christians, is high in his confidence, and is closely attached to him, because he is a physician, and he sits before him on the first seat after the chief of the Magians, and whatever he asks of him he receives.

Out of kindness towards the captives and the holy men he has now by the advice of the Christian physicians attached to him made a hospital,[9] a thing not previously known, and has given 100 mules and 50 camels laden with goods (?) [10] from

---

[1] Insert ܩ before ܠܗ.

[2] Rom. xi. 25.

[3] Omit ܕ before ܠܗ.

[4] The MS. reading seems to be ܐܬܠܩ, for which we must read ܐܬܠܩܒܝ, as L.

[5] Only ܩܠ is visible, but the word must be ܓܡܝܪܐ as no other word beginning with those letters suits the context.

[6] L. prints only ܗ ; the second letter seems to be ܒ : read ܗܒ.

[7] The MS. has ܗܝܡܢ, not ܗܪܝ, as L. prints.

[8] Only ܠ . . . ܠܘ is visible. I guess at the meaning. Perhaps ܠܬܝܠܘ.

[9] ξενοδοχεῖον (text ξενόδοχος).

[10] ܠܩ possibly, as Payne Smith suggests, = κλῆρος ; or perhaps κελλάριον, "store-room," might stand for "stores."

the royal stores, and 12 physicians, and whatever is required is given ; and [1] in the king's retinue (?) [2] . . .

[1] The MS. has ○ before ܦܠܓܘܬܐ, not ?, as L. prints.

[2] ܦܠܓܘܬܐ. At this point the MS. breaks off, which makes it hard to tell the meaning of this word. The ordinary meaning "division" or "half" seems impossible, and I therefore take it to be the other ܦܠܓܐ, which perhaps = φάλαγξ : cf. Bedjan, *Act. Mart. et Sanct.* vol. ii. p. 540, l. 10, where James, the Persian martyr, is said to have been in the ܦܠܓܐ at court. Across the last page of the MS. some illegible words are written in another hand.

INDEX OF NAMES AND THINGS

AARON, bp. of Arsamosata, 208.
Abasgia (Bazgun), 328.
Abbo, monastery of, 211.
Abdel, 328.
Abgersatum, 226.
Abraham, (1) (the humble) archimandrite (of Amida ?), 210.
    (2) (Bar Khili) bp. of Amida, 167, 296, 300.
    (3) (son of Euphrasius) presbyter, 193.
Acacius, (1) bp. of Constantinople, 80, 100, 104, 105, 112, 113, 117, 125, 127, 128, 129, 130, 133, 139, 144, 146.
    His letter cited, 128–130.
    (2) (Bar Eshkhofo) tribune, 300.
Ætheric, bp. of Smyrna, 177.
Aetius, deacon of Constantinople, 46.
'Afotho Ro'en (?), 162.
Africa, 38, 262–264, 313, 326.
Agapetus, Pope, 253, 264, 267, 268, 297.
Agathon, presbyter of Alexandria, 138.
Aglaophon, dialogue of Methodius addressed to, 14.
Ahlaf (?), 168 (note 3).
Akhore, 161.
Akhs'noyo, bp. of Hierapolis, 73, 176, 177, 179, 180, 183, 184, 207, 211, 243.
    His letters, 184, 207, 211.
'Akibo, monastery of, at Chalcis, 179, 210.
Akoimetoi, monastery of, 168.
Alans, 328.
Alexander, bp. of Hierapolis, 275.
Alexandria, 48, 57, 58, 59, 64–69, 75, 76, 78, 79, 81, 96, 110, 112, 113, 116–121, 124, 125, 133–136, 138, 140, 143, 207, 209, 243, 257, 258, 266, 286, 287, 288, 292, 300, 313.
    Synod at, 103.

Alexandrines, letter of the, 73.
Alimeric. See Theodoric.
Amantius, *præp. sacr. cubic.*, 189, 190.
Amasia, see of, 321.
Amazons, 328.
Ambrose, bp. of Milan, cited, 92.
Amida, 17, 151, 153–164, 187, 208, 209, 226, 227, 228, 296, 298, 300, 324, 325.
Ammodis, 165, 224.
Amon, monk of Alexandria, 103.
Amphilochius, bp. of Side, 43, 46, 74.
Amrin (?), 207.
Anachristo-Novatians, 111.
Anastasia, church at Berytus, 77.
Anastasia, town (?), 212, 228.
Anastasiopolis, 167.
Anastasius, (1) bp. of Jerusalem, 100, 107, 113, 146.
    (2) Emperor, 145, 148–151, 163–167, 169–185, 187, 189–191.
Anatolius, (1) bp. of Constantinople, 23, 24, 43, 44, 69, 74, 75, 79, 100.
    His letter cited, 75.
    (2) brother of Dioscorus, 111.
    (3) presbyter of Alexandria, 96.
Andrew, (1) archimandrite of Alexandria, 133, 135, 138.
    (2) bp. of Samosata, 177, 275.
    (3) brother of Asclepius, 203.
    (4) chamberlain, 189, 190.
    (5) deacon of Alexandria, 139, 144, 149.
Anthemius, Emperor, 59, 60, 61, 68.
Anthimus, bp. of Constantinople, 265, 268, 270–277, 279–282, 284–293, 297.
    Letters cited, 271–276, 287–290.
Anti-Cæsar, 145, 184, 221.
Antioch, 60, 126, 127, 168, 190, 205, 212, 213, 229, 296, 299, 311, 312, 313.
    See of, 180, 184, 209.
    Synods at, 126–128, 180, 311.

INDEX OF GREEK WORDS

ἀγωγός, 166.
ἀγωνιστής, 42, 49, 233.
ἀκκούβιτον, 153.
ἀνάγκη (pressure), 49 ; (stress), 287.
ἀνάλωμα, 55, 206.
ἀναφορά, 108, 151.
ἀννῶναι, 318.
ἀνταρσία, 299.
ἀντεγκύκλιον, 113.
ἀντίγραφον (answer), 235, 236, 237.
ἀξία, 228, 229.
ἀπὸ δικανικῶν, 180, 209.
ἀποθηκάριον, 319.
ἀποθήκη (!), 319.
ἀποσχίστης, 124, 133, 135, 138, 139, 324.
ἀρχιατρός, 266, 268, 297, 325, 331.
ἀσφάλεια (safe-conduct), 255.
ἀχειροποίητος, 321.

βαλανέα (?), 160, 168, 171.
βασιλική (*basilica*), 317.
βάσις (pedestal), 318.
βερηδάριος, 206, 208.
βῆμα (tribunal), 52, 258.
βιβλίον, 266.
βοήθεια (military force), 176.
βουλευτής, 155, 163.

γιστέρνα (= κιστέρνα), 166.
γνωστικός, 211.

δεκουρίων, 148.
δημόσιον (bath), 166, 167, 189 ; (*latrina*), 319.
δημοτικός, 78.
διαλαλιαί, 21.
διατάγματα, 55.
δίκαι (rights), 101.
διφυσίτης, 99, 120, 180, 184, 187, 205, 233, 252, 253, 264.
δογματικός, 22, 180.
δομέστικος, 190, 192.
δούξ, 119, 165, 222, 223, 227, 228, 229, 232, 248, 324, 325.
δωνατῖβον, 172.

ἐγκυκλία (circular progress), 321.
ἐγκύκλιος, 69, 74, 99, 100, 104, 105, 107, 109, 113.

ἐκβόησις, 151, 245.
ἔκδικος (*defensor civitatis*), 133.
ἐκκλησιαστική (ecclesiastical history), 15, 38.
ἔντευξις, 116.
ἐξέρκετον, 187.
ἐξκουβιτώρια, 318.
ἔπαρχος (officer), 319.
ἐπισκοπεῖον, 171.
εὐαγγέλιος (= εὐαγγελικός), 282, 285, 286, 292.
εὐταξία, 41.

θέατρον (theatre), 318.
θεωρητικός, 211.
θεωρία, 213, 243.
θεώριον (?), 318.

ἰδιώτης (foolish), 275.
ἰνδικτιών, 148.
ἱππικός (= ἱππικόν), 246, 263.
ἱππόδρομος, 66.

καλαμάριον, 178.
καναλος, 317.
καπιτώλιον, 317.
κάστρα, 187, 296, 316.
κάστρον, 189,
κατάστασις, 23.
κατήχησις (conversion), 15.
κεντηνάριον, 166, 206.
κίρκος, 318.
κλῆρος (?) (goods), 331.
κόδρα, 153.
κομβέντον, 174.
κόμης, 52, 160.
κόμης ἀνατολῆς, 205.
κοόρτης βιγίλων, 318.
κουροπαλάτης, 189, 190.
κυνήγιον, 318.

λαυρᾶτον, 321.
λίβελλος (λίβελλοι), 22, 23, 67, 113, 136, 171, 173.
λίμιτον, 296, 298.
λογοθέσία, 167.
λόγος (division of literary work), 126, 148, 168, 181, 203, 218, 219, 220, 224, 227, 232 ; (treatise), 233, 234, 266.

[1] The word is in the adjectival form, "the men of the *specula*," but this assumes the existence of the substantive.